"Yo

"Thanks for calling, Eric. I see what you mean. We've got a real rookie on our hands. White knuckles and all."

Emily whipped her head around. "Robbie called you?"

"I gave him my number when we were at Paisan's. Told him to keep in touch."

Robbie had had the man's phone number all this time and not said a word? Emily wanted to cry. She no longer knew her son at all.

Eric misunderstood her upset. "Hey, it's not so bad. Just give me your hands and—"

She yanked them out of his reach, not caring if she fell flat on her face. "No! Don't you understand? Either of you? I don't want to skate with you. I don't want to have anything to do with you."

The flash of hurt in his eyes made her look away, only to find a matching hurt in Robbie's face. What was it about this man that brought out the worst in her?

"Just once, Emily," Eric said quietly. "Just once around the rink. If you don't like it, we can stop. And if you do, as soon as you're able to skate alone, I'll leave you to it. It shouldn't take long. Fair enough?"

She lifted her head, and met his eyes beneath the brim of his black baseball cap. He hadn't shaved in at least a day or two, and looked a little scruffy, but she understood he was trying not to be recognized again.

Suddenly she appreciated his making the trip out here, risking the exposure, to help her out.

"All right. And I'm sorry for...for overreacting. I'm nervous about..." she nodded in the direction of the speeding skaters. "...all of this."

Eric's expression gentled in quiet understanding as he held out his hands. "Don't be. You can handle anything."

Thin Ice

by

Liana Laverentz

Thin Ice

Cover Art by *R.J.Morris*

The Wild Rose Press
PO Box 706
Adams Basin, NY 14410-0706
Visit us at www.thewildrosepress.com

Publishing History
First Champagne Rose Edition, January 2007
Print ISBN 1-60154-016-7

Published in the United States of America

Dedication

To Louis
Thank you for being my inspiration.

Chapter One

It was no way to spend a birthday, drinking alone in some hole-in-the wall dive, but it beat sitting home alone, staring at the rented contents of his apartment. Hunched over a beer in the smoky darkness of Harry's Place, Eric Cameron wondered where he'd gone wrong. By now he should have been a family man, with a wife and three or four kids to spoil—or at least someone to go home to who'd tell him he wasn't the major screw-up at least half the Twin Cities thought he was.

But all he had to show for his thirty years was a three-day-old black eye, two bruised ribs, knees that burned like hot coals, and the knowledge he'd only dug his NHL grave deeper tonight. Even the sassy little waitress who'd given him the eye when he'd walked in would probably change her mind when she recognized him. The Minneapolis Saints jersey she filled out so nicely might have made him smile back if the night had turned out differently.

But it hadn't, so instead he courted the shadows at the end of the bar, nursed his beer and wondered how many it would take to shut down his hearing. Judging by what he'd overheard since he'd wandered into the place, more than half of the maybe twenty men here had been at the game tonight and wished they'd spent their money drinking instead.

Eric didn't blame them. The Saints' first chance to beat the Wild all season, leading by two goals, and he'd blown it by mixing it up with the Merdham brothers. The Wild had scored four unanswered goals after his ejection from the game, proving once again the only thing Ronald Stump's Money-Is-No-Object team of All-Stars was capable of generating was hot air.

"You good?"

Eric looked up at the tall, skinny bartender wiping his hands almost compulsively on a dingy towel. He seemed a little edgy, but maybe he was always like that. Eric had no idea. He'd never been in Harry's Place before. But his liquor cabinet was as empty as his digs, by choice, so he'd opted for a late night walk to clear his head. Instead he'd found this dive within stumbling range of his apartment. Good selling point on an icy February night.

Still, he'd bet good money not many strangers wandered into Harry's Place, much less after eleven on a Sunday night. Especially not six-foot-four, two-hundred-thirty-pound bruisers wearing a fading black eye and freshly cut cheek.

"Gimme a shot. Bourbon." Time to switch poisons. The beer wasn't working fast enough.

The bartender picked up a bottle of the cheap stuff and poured. "You, uh, from around here?"

Was his face that messed up? Eric supposed he should consider it a blessing. "No."

"Been in town long?"

"No." He'd been let go without warning from the St. Louis Blues six weeks ago. It still burned him, how they'd traded him to Stump's farce of a team just before the playoffs. The Blues were sure to make the finals, at least. With or without him.

"Uh, go to the game tonight?"

Eric took a long look around the bar while he considered his answer. No one paid him any mind except the waitress, who winked at him from across the room. Go figure. His face had been all over the evening news, thanks to Stump. Maybe he needed some of whatever these guys were drinking. He'd love to forget who he was.

He looked back at the waitress. She smiled again. Not the hey-baby-let's-get-naked kind of smile he was used to. A more friendly kind of smile. Tentatively, he smiled back. He could use a friend.

"Yeah, I was there."

"The guys can't stop bitching about it. Some of them thought for sure with...with...with Cameron wearing the "C" the Saints'd win this time." He seemed to have trouble getting that last bit out. "'Specially McNally over there." The bartender nodded toward a group of five men playing

2

cards at a round table in the corner. "Swears he lost a bundle."

Eric eyed the group. Loggers on a bender by the looks of them. Four nearly empty plastic beer pitchers littered the table. The big one chomped on a cigar, an unpleasant reminder of Stump. As he raked in the pot, it looked like he was well on his way to recouping his game losses.

"Can't figure what got into the guy, myself," The bartender said beside him. Eric wondered how the hell this guy didn't recognize him if he followed hockey. "You'd a thought he'd a wanted to win this one, seein' as how it was against the Wild and all."

"You got any food around here?" Eric asked, not about to talk about himself like he wasn't even there. This was downright weird.

"Kitchen closed half an hour ago."

Okay. Eric knew how *this* game was played. He pulled out his wallet and slipped a twenty across the bar. The bartender eyed it, then Eric.

"I'll see what I can do." Darting a furtive look McNally's way, the bartender deftly pocketed the twenty, then disappeared.

Eric settled in while he waited. He took off his black leather jacket and set it on the empty barstool beside him, then downed his shot of bourbon. A slow heat seeped from the back of his neck into his aching shoulders. He lowered his head and moved it from side to side, cursing the Merdham brothers under his breath. Voices drifted across the smoke-filled bar as if filtered through fog. He tried to tune them out, but the booze hadn't fully kicked in yet. It had too much pain to wade through, first.

"Quitcher bitchin' Seamus, they still got a shot at the playoffs if they can get their shit together."

"Fat chance. Stump's Chumps ain't won a game in weeks."

"Thought that's why they traded for Cameron. To give the Saints the push they needed to make a run for the Cup."

"Friggin' waste of ten million. Stump shoulda left him and his bum knees to rot in St. Louis."

"Shit, man, give the guy a break. He's already got four Stanley Cup rings."

"Glory days. Dumb bastard oughtta know by now when to keep his eyes on the puck and his hands to himself."

"Try taking your own advice sometime," a woman snapped.

"What the hell's that supposed to mean?"

Eric heard hard plastic hit the wood table. "It means I'm tired of you trying to cop a feel every time I walk by."

"Izzat so?"

Eric didn't hear her reply, but several men hooted. He looked over and saw the waitress reach for the drained pitchers on McNally's table. Two in each hand, she turned to walk away from the men. Suddenly McNally reached out and hauled her onto his lap.

"Damn it, let go of me." She lunged forward, but didn't get anywhere. NcNally's buddies howled their approval as she tried to squirm out of his hold.

"That's it, Cass, move around some more. You're gettin' me all excited."

The waitress stilled, a strong look of fear entering her eyes.

"Aw come on, Cass. I was just startin' to have some fun."

"Let...me...go. Now."

McNally grinned at his buddies. "Think I can get her to wiggle again?" The waitress gritted her teeth and lunged again. Eric saw the man's hand sidle up her ribcage.

"Harry!" she shrieked.

McNally laughed and dropped his hand to her thigh. No one in the bar seemed to care that a woman was being molested right out in the open. "Harry's in the back, playin' with himself again. He knows better than to stick his nose where it don't belong. And you know better than to give me a hard time, don't you, Cass?" He paused. "Or maybe that's what you been looking for all along. A good, hard time." His beefy hand squeezed her thigh. "Been a while, ain't it, Cass?"

"You sorry son of a bitch." The woman's voice broke even as her body went rigid.

Every conversation in the place fell silent.

"What did you say?" McNally asked.

4

"She said it's time you let her get back to work."

All eyes turned toward the man seated at the end of the bar.

"Who the hell are you?" McNally demanded.

"A thirsty man, who'd like the lady to get him a drink since the bartender seems to have disappeared."

No one breathed. Obviously McNally was overlord of Harry's Place. Eric realized he should have picked up on that sooner, like when no one seemed to notice or care that the man and his friends were openly gambling. Must have been the beer dulling his brain. Or was it the bourbon? Either way, he was finally feeling no pain.

"Well you'll just have to wait, 'cause the *lady* ain't finished servin' me yet."

"Then I guess I'll have to serve myself."

Slowly, Eric slid to his feet. Calmly, he approached McNally's table. He met McNally's shrewd, flinty eyes, refilled his beer mug from a pitcher on the table, then held it up to McNally in salute. "Thanks. Appreciate it."

"Son of a bitch," a man in the far corner breathed into the stillness. "It's Cameron."

The waitress' eyes went wide with recognition, then flashed in pure fear. She dropped the empty pitchers, rammed her elbows into McNally's fat stomach and sprang to her feet. "I'm calling the cops," she said as she darted past Eric.

"The hell you are!" McNally snarled and lunged after her. He came nose to nose with Eric instead.

McNally hesitated, then smiled as if he'd just won the main event. It was all the warning Eric needed. No stranger to bar fights, Eric dropped his beer, ducked McNally's left hook and arrowed a fist into McNally's wide gut. The dough-like softness surrounding his hand startled Eric so much that McNally's bear hug caught him off-balance. Next thing he knew he'd crashed back-first onto McNally's table, sending cards, money and beer flying.

McNally erupted in a roar of something that sounded like a command, grabbed the man nearest him and shoved him at another man. One of the better-built card players launched himself at Eric. The table cracked beneath their weight and they rolled across the floor, grunting and swearing until Eric found his shot and knocked the guy out.

For the next several minutes Eric hit anything that came at him. Amid hoots, hollers, thuds and groans, fists, bottles, pitchers and chairs flew. The cigarette machine crashed to the floor just as Eric spotted the uniforms pouring through the front door.

Instinctively, he backed away from the fray. A fistfight was one thing, a crack on the head with a nightstick was another. He'd seen firsthand what those could do to a man's head.

Within minutes the cops had rounded up the rowdiest of the brawlers and were herding them out the door and into a paddy wagon. Eric flexed his bloody, aching hands, glad the worst of it was over. He needed to go home and get some sleep.

But McNally and his boys weren't through with him yet. Suddenly it was like watching a bad western—the kind where some big sleazebag owns the whole town. McNally's boys closed ranks, swearing up and down that Cameron alone was responsible for the brawl.

Yessir, Sheriff, we was just sittin' here mindin' our own sweet business when this here stranger walked in lookin' for trouble.

Someone wearing a badge and gun invited Eric to step outside. He ran through his options and agreed to go quietly. Something wasn't right here, but he didn't have time to figure out what it was. He wasn't innocent in this fiasco, but no way was he going to take the rap for all of it.

First he needed to get out of here. There would be plenty of time to straighten things out later. When his mind wasn't so damn fuzzy. When he wasn't feeling like he'd been run over by a locomotive. He was heading for the door, flanked by two uniforms, when he spotted McNally and the skinny bartender standing side by side, arms crossed over their chests, wearing almost identical pleased expressions.

Brothers, he realized.

Gotcha.

Eric stopped in his tracks. "Wait." Ignoring his police escort, he turned slowly, taking a long, bleary look around the destroyed bar. Hoping he was wrong. Knowing he wasn't.

The sassy little waitress in the Saints jersey was gone.

And so were his jacket and wallet.

Sonofabitch

He'd been set up.

Again.

Chapter Two

Midnight found Emily Jordan up to her elbows in split lips, broken noses, black eyes and bruised ribs. She patched, taped, splinted and stitched until her shoulders ached, her fingers cramped, and her feet felt cemented to the floor. Damn it. The world was too violent as it was. Didn't these imbeciles have anything better to do than get drunk and beat each other up?

"Hey there, Missy. Ease up a little. That hurt."

Emily looked up at her twelfth brawler in a row, her fourth with bruised ribs, and realized she'd jerked the adhesive tape holding the dressing over a gash on his chest a little harder than necessary. She started to apologize, then changed her mind. She had no sympathy for bear-size men who pummeled each other for kicks, then whined if she caught a few too many chest hairs under the tape. "More than it hurt when you were rolling on the floor with whoever cold-cocked you tonight?" she asked.

He glared and muttered something about uppity women doctors. Emily gritted her teeth and turned her attention to a blood-soaked swath of plaid flannel wrapped around his forearm. Finding an even nastier gash beneath his filthy makeshift bandage, she reeled off the items she'd need to Susan, the ER nurse assisting her. This one would need stitches. While Emily cleaned the wound, Susan gamely struck up a conversation with the man to distract him from Emily's stitching.

Apparently someone named Cameron had started the fight. It didn't explain why everyone *else* had felt compelled to get in on the act, but by the time Emily had patched up her fifteenth brawler, she'd gleaned this Cameron character had a reputation as a fighter, and the police had taken him into custody.

8

Good, she thought. May he stay there where he belongs. The man was clearly a menace to society.

She turned number fifteen over to Susan to dress his superficial wounds, and went to see who was next. The treatment rooms were empty, as was the waiting room, except for Augustus Caldwell, her boss and mentor, and a young woman who looked as frazzled as Emily felt. The woman held a sleeping infant in her arms and was apparently the mother of the toddler who sat behind her, his right arm in a sling.

Emily had to smile. She guessed they were waiting for a taxi. Augustus had a soft spot for single mothers with no sign of support.

The admissions clerk was busy flirting over the counter with two Minneapolis police officers, so Emily decided to prop up her feet until the next wave of activity hit, or until Augustus released her from duty. She headed for the staff lounge.

"Emily!" Her hand on the half-open door to the lounge, Emily turned to see Sarah Ferguson, head ER nurse, emerge from a nearby elevator, a mountain of starched and pressed linens in her arms. "How's it going with the Brady Bunch?"

The staff had already nicknamed the brawlers, who had come from some bar on Brady Street. Emily nodded wearily down the hall. "Susan's finishing up the last of them. I'm going to lie down for a while. Let Augustus know where I am if he needs me, okay?"

Sarah dropped the linens onto a cart for an orderly to collect later. "Sure. You look beat."

"I am. I swear, if I'd had to spend another five minutes breathing alcohol fumes and being insulted by some overgrown idiot who doesn't have the sense God gave a sheep, I would've—"

Just then one of the brawlers exited the men's room, withdrew a flask from inside his jacket and took a hefty swig. He spied Emily and Sarah and smirked, then belched before he tucked the bottle away and swaggered toward the main exit.

"I see what you mean," Sarah murmured, then strode after the man as it became clear he planned to leave without checking out.

9

Feeling drained, Emily entered the lounge. She crossed to the sink, turned on the faucet and splashed cool water on her face. Toweling her face dry, she caught her reflection in the mirror above the sink. First a twelve-hour shift, then being called back in to work barely four hours later...this had to stop. She was operating on two hours sleep and looked it. Her lab coat was covered with stains and smelled, her eyes bloodshot, her hair a disaster—

"Excuse me, Miss."

Emily stilled, wondering if she'd imagined the hoarse male voice. It almost sounded like...

But that was impossible. The owner of that raspy voice was seven hundred miles away and hadn't terrorized her for years. No. She was exhausted, her mind playing tricks on her. She turned, fully expecting to find herself alone.

Instead she found the most dangerous-looking man she'd seen in quite a while. He sat on the couch behind the door, his back propped against the wall, his long legs stretched out in front of him and crossed at the ankles. His blue oxford shirt was torn and bloodstained, his faded jeans filthy. His black eye was at least three days old, his dark hair a matted mess, his face and hands dirty, swollen and seriously scraped.

"Mind if I have a refill?"

Emily noticed the paper cup in his hand and smelled alcohol at the same time. She looked up and met eyes as bleary and bloodshot as her own.

Another drunk. For Pete's sake, hadn't she dealt with enough of them for one night?

"What do you think you're doing in here?"

His eyes not leaving hers, the man slowly, almost deliberately, set his paper cup aside. A long-suppressed memory flared in Emily and she felt a flash of remembered fear. She reminded herself those days were over. He was the fish out of water here, not she.

"Waiting for the doctor," he said. "Apparently someone forgot to tell him he has another overgrown idiot to examine."

So he'd overheard her conversation with Sarah. Too bad. "Her," she said.

"Her?"

"Her. Somebody apparently forgot to tell her."

Surprise skittered across his battered features. Awareness seeped into his dark brown eyes, as he slowly looked her up, then down, then lowered his head and shook it, chuckling softly.

Enough was enough. "Listen, if you have a problem with women doctors, I suggest you pick yourself up and stumble down to the waiting room, where you'll find—"

"Whoa. Whoa." He held up a puffy hand. "I didn't say I had anything against women doctors. I just wasn't expecting to meet one tonight, okay? I'm not exactly, uh, looking my best."

Emily crossed her arms and eyed him again. He had that right. He looked awful. He must have wandered in when no one was looking and decided to make himself at home instead of waiting in the lobby with the rest of the brawlers. Yet he acted as if he had every right to lounge on the sofa *she'd* intended to occupy.

"Why are you in here? This is the staff lounge."

"Guess they figured this was the best place to put me."

"They?"

"The man with the white hair and that chirpy nurse out front."

Emily relaxed a shade. Augustus had sent him here. Probably taken pity on him and—

"How long ago was that?"

"Couple of hours, maybe more. Hard to tell. I ah, fell asleep after we got here. Just woke up a few minutes ago."

A couple of hours, maybe more? Emily stared. Given the extent of his bruises, the man either had the patience of a saint or was in too much pain to move. The healer in her wanted to get right to work. The skeptic in her prevailed. "I assume our chief of staff had a reason for separating you from the others?"

"I think that was my escort's idea."

"Escort?"

"The boys in blue. They insisted we stop by on our way downtown. I told them not to bother, that I'd have my own doc—now what?"

11

"What's your name?" Emily asked, fearing she already knew. This had to be the infamous Cameron, whose thirst for a good fight had pulled her out of bed in the middle the night.

"Does it matter?" he asked.

"If I'm to examine you, I'll need to have someone bring me your chart. For that, I'll need your name. You did fill out an admissions form, didn't you? Or did your post-brawl nap take precedence?"

The man's dark eyes narrowed. Emily's irritation segued into dread. Damn it, what was she thinking? She knew better than to bait a sleeping bear. It had to be the lack of sleep.

"I filled it out. In triplicate."

"Then I'd appreciate it if you'd cooperate with me. Name?"

He hesitated. She wondered why. From what she'd heard, this Cameron fellow threw his name around as indiscriminately as his punches. Thought he was some kind of hot shot.

"Cameron. Eric Cameron," he said quietly.

She closed her eyes and prayed for patience.

"Something tells me you've heard the name before."

"Several times in the past few hours."

Oddly, he seemed to relax. "Ah, yes. From your patients. The ones who haven't got the sense God gave a sheep." He smiled grimly. "I couldn't agree with you more. So, where are they now?" he asked.

She pulled her focus away from his battered features. Nothing appeared to be broken, but Emily Jordan knew better than most how looks could be deceiving. "Who?"

"The lost sheep."

She thought of the belcher. "Who knows? The last of them left several minutes ago. You're the only one left."

"You mean *they walked? All* of them?"

"You didn't expect them to?" Was the man a lunatic?

"Hell no!" Eric erupted, losing his temper at last. "Not after I—" He swore and closed his eyes. How was he supposed to get to the bottom of what had happened in that bar without witnesses? After he'd explained his side of the story, he'd expected the police to hold at least a few of them for questioning. "Forget it," he muttered in disgust. It wasn't her problem. "Just do whatever you have to, to get me out of here."

The little redheaded doctor edged toward the door, her sudden nervousness surprising him. "Of course. If you'll excuse me, I'll check on your chart and be right back."

She was lying, her body language a dead give-away. After twenty-two years of playing hockey, Eric Cameron knew a deke when he saw one. "Yeah, right. Thanks."

Stepping into the corridor, Emily wasn't surprised to find her knees shaky. She hated the sound of voices raised in anger. Particularly when alcohol was involved. Usually she was able to deal with it, to move past her fear, but for some reason this time it wasn't happening.

"That was quick." Emily looked up to see Sarah coming out of the testing lab next door. "Your nap. Must have taken all of five minutes. What happened? Did we get a new hit?"

Emily shook her head. "Sarah, there's a man named Eric Cameron in there, who—"

"Really? Eric Cameron? In *our* lounge? What's he doing—"

"Shh...he's with the Brady Bun—" She noticed Sarah trying to peer past her into the lounge, her eyes bright with interest. Emily glanced over her shoulder, then pulled the door shut. "He's with the group of men who came in earlier."

"You're kidding! He was in the brawl?"

Emily didn't understand Sarah's excitement. In comparison, it made her fear and unease in his presence seem trite and unprofessional. "What difference does it make?" she snapped. "He's here and he's hurt. Augustus separated him from the others hours ago and no one's paid any attention to him since. If I hadn't wandered into the lounge he might have spent the night in there, untreated."

Sarah drew back in hurt surprise. Emily remembered Sarah was ultimately responsible for admissions. She opened her mouth to apologize, but Sarah spoke first. "I'm sorry, Doctor, I'll look into it and see that whoever's responsible is reprimanded."

Emily sighed and shook her head. She didn't have

the energy for this tonight. "Just get me his chart and I'll be happy. We'll be in room five."

"Of course, Doctor. Right away."

Knowing she'd handled *that* badly, Emily re-entered the lounge. She found her newest patient where she'd left him, propped up against the wall with his eyes closed. He didn't look so dangerous now, just resigned and battle weary.

His black eye drifted open. "Well, what do you know? The way you scooted out of here, I didn't expect to see you again."

The man was much too perceptive for a common drunk. "How do you feel?"

His second eye opened. He studied her for a long, unsmiling moment. "Like you'd expect any man in my situation to feel."

So his anger wasn't snuffed, just banked. Her heart thumped in dread. "I meant physically."

"So did I."

"Can you sit up by yourself?"

He offered her a dry look. "Of course."

"Then whenever you're ready, Mr. Cameron."

He closed his eyes and moved forward, moving much more slowly than she would have expected of a man his age, with his physique. She scanned his broad shoulders and lean hips, and suspected there wasn't an ounce of fat on him. She also suspected he'd taken quite a beating tonight, and wondered again why he hadn't demanded medical attention sooner. He had to be in pain. A lot of pain. What had really happened in that bar?

She looked into his battered face, found him watching her again, and decided she'd be better off not knowing.

"Do you feel up to taking a walk?"

"A walk?"

Emily almost smiled at his confusion. Almost. "I'm not a faith healer, Mr. Cameron. I can't help you without examining you. For that we need to move you into a treatment room."

Clearly he considered the prospect of moving unappealing. "It's only next door, but if you don't feel you can make it on your own, I can call an orderly—"

"I'll walk."

So he had an ego. No surprises there. "Fine. If you'll follow me..."

She heard him enter the room behind her as she snapped on her examination gloves. She turned and found him sitting on the gurney, legs spread, hands curled over the gurney's edge. Waiting. Watching. Watching her.

She decided not to wait for his chart. "I'll look at your hands first," she said as she moved forward.

"Not unless you tell me your name."

"My name?" She stopped and looked down to where her nametag should be. She must have left it at home. Beside the bed she'd had to vacate in such a hurry, thanks to this man.

"I told you mine, but we never got to yours."

"I'm Doctor Jordan."

"I want to know your first name."

"That's not necessary."

His dark, steady eyes captured hers. "I disagree."

Suddenly Emily understood how Eric Cameron had felt confident enough to take on fifteen men. The man had self-confidence to spare. She doubted there was any sort of confrontation he backed away from, and very few, if any, he lost.

But *she* was in charge here. "Which hand shall I check first, Mr. Cameron?"

He considered her for another long moment, then held up a swollen right hand. She took it in hers and ran her fingers over it, feeling for broken bones. Finding none, she checked his left hand. "You're lucky. They're only bruised."

"Tell me about it."

Emily wished she'd apologized to Sarah. She could do with some moral support right now. This Cameron character rattled her more than most. "You instigated the fight, didn't you, Mr. Cameron?"

"That's what they say."

She paused, waiting for more. He didn't oblige.

"I'll check your face now."

He nodded. Emily moved closer, her thigh brushing his as she stepped between his spread legs. Their eyes met, and in his she sensed a subtle change. Awareness of

her as a woman, for certain, but also a lessening of the
dark wariness in him. Acceptance of a sort, perhaps even
the beginnings of professional trust.

Encouraged by the thought, she did her best to
examine his face as carefully as she had his hands. He
didn't move so much as a muscle. In fact, he hardly
seemed to breathe.

"Your face looks good too," she said, and stepped
back. "It's a little swollen, but nothing that won't take
care of itself.

He exhaled and she caught a whiff of stale alcohol.
But not before she saw him flinch. Another case of bruised
ribs, she guessed. Possibly broken. She'd have to get his
shirt off to check. The thought had a thoroughly
*un*professional effect on her insides. She wondered where
the devil Sarah was with that chart. Or Susan. Or
anyone.

"What were you drinking?" she asked, as she
searched the cabinet beneath the sink for a cloth to clean
up his hands and face. The disposable wipes were more
likely to sting. Why that thought bothered her, she wasn't
sure. It didn't usually.

"What was I drinking? Beer, bourbon." He gave a
short, oddly deprecating laugh. "More beer."

Emily turned on the faucet a little harder than she'd
meant to. She really had a problem with men who drank
irresponsibly. "How much did you have?"

"What difference does it make?"

"None," she countered coolly. "As long as you don't
mind coming back later to have your stomach pumped
after taking the painkillers I plan to prescribe."

"Don't need any damn painkillers," he muttered.

Emily chose to ignore that as she focused on wiping
his hands free of dirt and dried blood. She'd dried his
hands and applied ointment to the cuts before asking,
"Can you take off your shirt?"

He looked startled. "What for?"

Emily frowned. Why the surprise? Surely he wasn't
shy about his body. He didn't seem to be shy about
anything else. "I suspect you may have a bruised or
broken rib...or two."

"Two's right," Eric informed her matter-of-factly.

"Bruised them last week. Had them looked at, too. You don't need to do it again."

His doctor's amazing green eyes narrowed sharply, and she started to say something, but apparently thought better of it. In that moment, Eric decided Emily Jordan had the prettiest red hair and clearest complexion he'd ever seen. She wasn't wearing any make-up, either. No way was he going to let anyone that perfect see the damage the Wild had done to him tonight.

Besides, gloves or no gloves, he wasn't sure he could trust his body not to respond if she put those incredibly gentle hands on his chest. Hell. She thought he'd been disappointed she was a woman. His only disappointment was they'd met under such humiliating circumstances.

"But thanks anyway. Emily," he added, trying out the name he'd overheard someone call her in the hall.

Her jaw tightened as she turned away to rinse out her washcloth. Eric smiled. The lady had a temper, but was doing her best to keep it under wraps. When she returned, fully composed again, to doctor his face, he closed his eyes and enjoyed himself. Beneath the scent of soap and antiseptic, she smelled faintly of peaches. Memories he'd shoved aside because they hurt too much filtered into his mind and, strangely enough, for the first time, they didn't seem so painful. More like nostalgic for a change.

"Was that when you got your black eye? Last week?"

He opened his eyes to see her studying his shiner. Emily. He liked the name. He liked her, temper and all.

"No, that was last Thursday night."

She dabbed at the souvenir Murder had left on his cheek. "How often do you get into fights, Mr. Cameron?"

"As often as I have to."

She studied him for a long moment, clearly debating whether to get personal with him. Eric suddenly hoped she would. Hoped hard.

"I would think," she said quietly, "That seeing you come home black and blue all the time would be hard on your family."

She couldn't have struck a more sensitive nerve if she'd tried. No one cared what he came home looking like, and hadn't for years. "No problem there, Doc. Don't have a family. So you can stop wondering if I'm beating anybody up at home, too."

Her eyes flashed, but she didn't take the bait. "How about your job? What does your boss say when you show up for work looking like this?"

Eric stared. She had to be kidding. But she wasn't. He knew that now. He'd been watching her all night, waiting for her to recognize him, but the woman had no clue what he did for a living. For a split second he considered telling her, then decided that once, just once, he wanted to be able to meet a woman as a man, not as Eric Cameron, seven-time-NHL-All-Star center and current involuntary captain of the fledgling Minneapolis Saints.

He offered his best smile. "Most of the time he probably figures he's getting his money's worth."

She frowned, looking adorable, then turned away and reached for the tube of ointment. Silently she applied the cool ointment to the cut on his cheek. Stump and the rest of the team would howl if they could see him now, being fussed over like this.

But Eric was enjoying every minute of it. The warmth of her fingers was an almost erotic contrast to the cool ointment.

He wished he had more cuts for her to doctor. He also wished she didn't have to wear those damned gloves.

"What were you fighting about tonight?"

His mind was still on how her bare hands would feel against his skin. "Hell if I know," he drawled contentedly.

She straightened abruptly, and recapped the tube of ointment with a snap. "Then you deserve what you got."

"Oh?" Her sudden shift in attitude soured his mellowing mood. "Tell me, *Doctor* Jordan, is that a medical opinion or a personal one?"

Emily gritted her teeth. She'd taken enough verbal abuse for one night, thank you. She started to tell him he was free to go when he suddenly shifted forward. Reflexively, Emily froze. He was still seated, but his body had become an unmistakable instrument of intimidation. Fear snaked down her spine as she forced herself to hold her ground, thinking she was a fool for it. He was easily a foot taller than she and at least a hundred pounds

18

heavier.

"You don't like me much, do you, Doctor?"

Her voice went tight. He was too close. Too big. "Don't worry about it." Damn it, where was Sarah?

"I won't. But only if you have dinner with me."

"What?" Emily stared, incredulous. "Have you lost your mind?"

Eric grinned. He could lose a lot more to this spunky lady if she'd give him half a chance. Brainy women fascinated him, but they didn't as a rule hang out in the sort of places hockey players frequented. This one intrigued the hell out of him with her big green eyes and oh-so-gentle hands.

"Possibly." He smiled his most disarming smile. "So how about it? Feel like sharing life stories over pasta and pesto sauce? Say Thursday night? Five o'clock?"

"No."

"No? Just like that? No 'I'll think about it—give me your number and I'll let you know?'"

"No."

He waited, watching her again, but she didn't back down. Didn't offer any excuses or apologies. Just held her ground. He liked that in her. Most women he met fawned all over him. "You're not big on compromise, are you Dr. Jordan?"

"I'm not big on men who enjoy violence, Mr. Cameron. Or men who drink. I find the fact that you clearly enjoy both appalling and repulsive. Now if you'll excuse me, I'm sure that by now I have other patients to see. Be sure to check with the front desk before you leave."

Eric felt as if she'd hooked his skates out from under him. Stunned, he watched her calmly turn her back on him, remove her gloves, and toss them into the trash.

Appalling and repulsive?

Okay, appalling he could deal with. But repulsive? The woman found him repulsive? He couldn't believe it. Not after that flicker of awareness that had passed between them when she'd first stepped up to examine his face. Not after the way she'd talked to him.

Not after the way she'd touched him. She'd been so gentle, so soothing, so unexpectedly—

He realized she was halfway out the door. "Emily. Wait."

She paused, her expression wary. He hesitated, and wondered if he was making a mistake. Maybe she really wasn't interested in him. But her opinion of him suddenly mattered. He needed to tell her who he was.

Great. You want to fall back on that one already? What happened to wanting to be accepted or rejected on your own merits? Coward.

"You, ah, never checked my ribs."

"I believe that was your decision, Mr. Cameron."

"I've changed my mind."

"Fine. I'll send in a nurse to help you undress."

The frost in her voice annoyed him. Especially since he had no idea where it came from. He pushed off the gurney. "Forget the nurse. We can manage without—"

Her eyes widened and she bolted. He went after her instinctively, catching her by the wrist as they entered the hallway. "Wait. What the hell's going on—?"

He froze. He'd never seen such contempt in a woman's eyes. Or was it fear? Eric stared in disbelief. It was. Pure, raw fear. Hiding behind her contempt.

Holy hell, the woman was afraid of him. Terrified of him.

"Let the doctor go, Cameron, before anyone gets hurt."

He looked up to see his police escort not ten feet away. Behind them stood the white-haired doctor and two blonde nurses close to his own age, looking both wary and angry. He looked back at Emily, glaring up at him, her cheeks a deep, fiery red.

She was so small. So delicate, her wrist so fragile beneath his hand. No wonder he'd scared her, coming after her like that. Especially after he'd come on to her so strong.

"I'm sorry," he said, releasing her gently. "I never meant to frighten you."

She backed away and turned to the white-haired guy. "If you don't need me any more..."

He nodded. "Go home, Emily. You deserve some rest."

She slipped past Eric and into the lounge.

"I'm sorry," he said to the assembled group of

20

onlookers, feeling a sudden need to explain. This whole evening wasn't like him at all. None of it. But they didn't know that. "I didn't mean to upset her."

Emily returned just then, bundled up in a dark hat and coat and carrying a big black purse. She didn't speak to or look at anyone as she blew past the entire group and out the front door.

Within seconds, she'd vanished into the frigid February night.

Chapter Three

"Got another one for you, Dr. Jordan."

Emily looked up from the safer sex lecture for the Women's Health Connection she was rehearsing in her office, and felt her stomach clench. The hospital florist stood in her doorway, grinning like a Cheshire cat. He carried an exquisite sea-green porcelain vase holding a dozen white roses.

Still grinning, he set them on her desk. He fussed with the blossoms and adjusted the forest green bow, then stepped back and eyed them critically. "Perfect."

Emily swallowed her rising nausea and forced a gracious smile. "Yes. They are. Thank you."

"Anytime, Doctor. Here's the card."

She waited until he left before she read it, then ripped it in half and threw the pieces in the trash. Then she cursed Eric Cameron again. Red. Yellow. Pink. White. Four colors in four days. What would he do when he ran out of colors? Start over again? Move on to a different variety of flora?

It was what Ryan had done. During the course of their marriage, he must have given her every type of flower known to man. But then Ryan had always been one for grand apologetic gestures after losing his temper. The more violent the episode, the more lavish the bouquet. It had become such a travesty between them that she never wanted to receive flowers again.

Especially not roses. They reminded her too much of the bruises and broken bones she'd suffered before their arrival. She'd always paid extra for the roses.

Closing her eyes, she saw Eric's message in her mind. It, too, was the same every day. *I'm sorry. Eric.* Underneath he'd written his telephone number.

She reached for the phone and dialed the nurse's

station. When the aide arrived minutes later, Emily asked her to take the roses to the children's ward and distribute them.

She wanted no part of Eric Cameron's apologies. She wanted no part of him at all.

****

"So you like hockey, do you?"

Hands stuffed in his pockets, Eric leaned against he concrete planter under the portico in front of St. Stephen's Elementary School and grinned at the animated third grader whose opinion of him was in direct opposition to Emily Jordan's.

"Yes sir, Mr. Cameron, I'm a real Saints fan. So's Nanna."

Eric smiled. "Why don't you call me Eric?"

The boy looked as if he'd just been handed the Stanley Cup. "Really? It's okay?"

"Really. It's okay. Now, who's Nanna?"

"Nanna? Oh she takes care of me while Mom's at work. Lets me watch the games on TV sometimes, until I have to go to bed. I been askin' Mom to let me sign up for the Mites League since my birthday last year. I'm eight, you know," he informed Eric importantly. "But she won't let me. She says it's too vi-lent. 'Specially hockey. She says nobody but dee...de...gen..." He trailed off, his earnest face twisted in concentration.

"Degenerates?" Eric supplied helpfully.

"Yeah! That's it!" The boy looked up, idolization shining in his hazel eyes. "Degenrits. Mom says nobody but degenrits plays hockey, and she won't have her son turning into one."

Eric had to laugh. Never had he been idolized and insulted at the same time. And with such enthusiasm. "I see. When did she say that?"

The boy offered a shy, sheepish smile. "She didn't say it to me. She told Nanna. I heard them talking when they thought I was asleep."

Eric decided he liked the little guy. He reminded him of himself—before he'd taken up hockey and become a degenerate, that was. He smiled again, but his new friend had gone back to admiring his Saints pennant, one of several hundred Eric had passed out after his anti-drug lecture that afternoon.

The boy traced a reverent finger across the purple and gold Saints insignia, then looked up at Eric, grinning from ear to ear. "This rocks. Soon as I get home I'm gonna hang this up over my bed, right next to my Saints team poster."

Eric appreciated his devotion to the team. He wished his teammates shared that devotion. Last night's win against Calgary had revived his hopes somewhat, but he knew he still had a long way to go. His teammates still didn't trust him, thanks to Stump.

"I'm glad you like it. I thought you and your friends might."

As usually happened after he gave one of his talks, he'd been swarmed by kids wanting souvenirs. He'd obliged cheerfully, feeling like Santa Claus, hoping the pennants would help to remind the kids of his visit and message.

The boy had waited on the fringes of the group with watchful eyes, until the rest of the miniature Saints fans had run off, shouting and pushing, honest-to-goodness team memorabilia clutched in their happy little fists. He had then accepted his own pennant, but instead of darting away like the others, had shyly lingered to talk. His shyness had evaporated once he knew his company was welcome, and for the past five minutes, the two of them had been discussing the boy's dream of one day playing pro hockey.

"Robbie? I didn't realize you were out here. You need to come inside and wait for your mom in the office."

Eric looked over to see the principal holding open the front door to the school.

"It's okay, Miranda. I don't mind."

"You're sure?"

"I'm sure." He smiled at Robbie. "We're just enjoying some of this surprising February sunshine." In one of those odd bursts of weather, the temperature had spiked to almost sixty that day.

"All right, but let me know if his mom's not here by the time you need to leave."

"Will do."

Apparently the boy was waiting for his mother to

pick him up and take him to dinner and an early movie. Since it was late Thursday afternoon and he hadn't heard from Emily—not that he expected to, but he'd hoped the roses would have at least softened her up some—Eric was happy to keep the kid company while he waited. It beat sitting in his apartment alone.

"...So, ya see, ya gotta talk to her, Eric. Tell her she's got it all wrong."

Eric pulled himself back to the present with an effort. "I'm sorry, Robert, I mean—"

"It's Robbie. Well, really it's Robin, but Mom only calls me that when she's mad."

"I see. All right, Robbie. Sorry, but my mind wandered while you were talking. Who do I have to talk to?"

"My mom. I bet if she met a real hockey player like you, she'd change her mind in a minute."

Eric chuckled. The optimism of youth. "Somehow I doubt that." Robbie looked disheartened. "I didn't mean it wouldn't happen," Eric gently amended. "I just don't think you should get your hopes up that my meeting your mother would change her mind about something she obviously feels strongly about."

Robbie scuffed the toes of his sneakers. "You mean things don't always work out the way you want them to."

Exactly. Take his four-day-old obsession with Dr. Emily Jordan, for instance. Eric hadn't been able to get her off his mind since the police had escorted him out the emergency room doors right behind her. He'd thought about her at the police station while he waited for his lawyer, in the training room while he waited for the team doctor to examine him to make sure none of his ribs had been broken, at home as he lay in bed and stared at the ceiling pretending he wasn't in pain...

"...always says."

Eric realized Robbie was speaking again. He had to get a grip. This Emily Jordan business was distracting him way too much. Maybe he'd stop by the hospital tonight and take his chances.

"I'm sorry. I wasn't listening again. What did you say?"

"I said that's what Mom always says. You know,

25

things don't always work out like you want them to."

Eric smiled. "She sounds like a wise woman." Except for her opinion of hockey, but he couldn't take offense at that. Maybe she'd met some of his teammates. No doubt their behavior could be brutal at times. Then again, he hadn't been a boy scout lately, either. Take Sunday night. The game, the brawl, the terrified woman.

"She's a doctor."

"She sure is," Eric murmured. *And light-years out of your league, Cameron. Forget about the emergency room.*

"That's why she's always late."

"Who's always late?"

"Mom. She's always late."

The boy's words held no resentment. Eric grinned, then recalled his own waiting. The only reason he'd waited so patiently in the emergency room the other night was to avoid media attention. He'd known he had this and several other school talks scheduled and the brawl would have been a perfect catalyst for the media to dredge up a past he considered nothing short of a nightmare.

He supposed he had the police to thank for keeping the incident quiet, but little else. Four hours he'd spent in that airless closet of a lounge, only to discover the city's finest had indeed chosen to let everyone else go home without formal questioning.

Since Harry hadn't pressed charges, they hadn't booked Eric, either, but he knew that could change at any time. Harry McNally and his brother wanted to see how much they could squeeze out of him, first. Their lawyer had contacted him the next day.

So now *his* lawyer was dragging out negotiations with the McNally brothers' lawyer, while discretely chasing down the brawlers treated at the hospital, hoping at least one in fifteen had a conscience. Otherwise, this episode was going to cost him a bundle. Eric couldn't afford any negative press right now and the McNally brothers knew it. Question was, how *much* did they know?

Eric realized he'd drifted off again, leaving the boy staring at him hopefully. "So...what does your dad think about all this?" he asked in an attempt to find his way back into their conversation.

Sadness entered the boy's eyes before he looked

26

away. "Don't have a dad."

Eric could have kicked himself. He should've known. Should've sensed the kid's interest in him stemmed from more than a love of hockey. The signs had been there all along, but he'd been too preoccupied to notice. Six years of public appearances had introduced him to countless kids like Robbie, youngsters in search of a role model to look up to.

"I'm sorry." He meant it. He knew what it was like to grow up without a father.

Robbie sent him another shy smile. "S'okay. I got Mom."

Eric knew it wasn't the same, but wasn't about to go there. "So, where are you and your mom going out to dinner?"

"Paisan's Pizza. At the mall. She hates to go there 'cause driving in traffic makes her all nervous and stuff, but it's my favorite place and—" Robbie brightened. "Wanna come with us?"

"To Paisan's?"

"Yeah! They make the best pizzas in the whole world. You can get anything you want on 'em and Mom always lets me pick what kind I want. But you could pick this time, if you come."

An iron fist squeezed Eric's heart at the naked hope in the boy's eyes. He should have disappeared right after his talk. He had no business using a fatherless kid to stave off his own case of the lonelies.

"Well, I'd like to, but..."

"Here she comes!" Robbie practically went airborne as an old white Chevy Suburban pulled into the circular drive. The redhead behind the wheel wore dark glasses, but Eric had the strangest feeling he'd seen her somewhere before. Recently. Suddenly she braked hard, whipped off her sunglasses, and stared at him in open disbelief.

Eric stared back, unable to believe what he was seeing, either. Robbie grabbed his arm. "C'mon. I'll interduce you."

"Er, Robbie, it might be better if we didn't..."

The boy tugged harder. "Don't worry. She's real nice. She'll like you, I promise. She likes all my friends."

But friendship wasn't on Emily Jordan's mind as she rounded the hood of her car. Finding out what Eric Cameron was doing at St. Stephen's Elementary School—talking alone with *her* son—was. And unless he had a very good, very *legal* reason for being there—

"Mom! Mom! Guess who this is?"

Emily faltered. She hadn't seen Robbie so fired up outside of Christmas morning. "It's Eric Cameron. You know, the Saints' new captain. Number sixteen."

Number sixteen? The Saints? She looked at Eric, who looked decidedly uncomfortable in his black leather jacket, and the puzzle pieces fell into place. "A hockey player," she said. "I should have guessed."

"Isn't it great? He came to school today to talk to us about drugs and alc'hol and how bad they are for you. Then he gave us these neat pennants." Robbie waved his pennant, almost poking Emily in the eye in his excitement. As she leaned back, Eric dropped a restraining hand on Robbie's shoulder.

"Careful, son. You don't want to hurt your mother."

"What? Oh, sorry, Mom."

Emily's protective instincts flared. She moved forward and speared Eric with a get-your-hands-off-my-son look before speaking to Robbie. "It's all right, sweetheart. Now why don't you thank Mr. Cameron for the pennant and say goodbye? We have to get going if we're going to make the early show."

"But he's coming with us. I invited him."

"You *what*?"

"I invited him. You said I could bring a friend."

Emily looked back at Eric in open dismay. "Honey, I don't think Mr. Cameron—"

"I would love to join you and your son for dinner, Doctor," Eric interrupted smoothly, "As long as you don't mind giving me a ride to the mall. My car's in the shop and I'm waiting for a ride, but my friend can meet me there. In fact, I think it might be more convenient for him."

"Great! You can sit up front!" Robbie took off for the car.

"That," Emily said slowly, "Was very uncool."

Eric grinned. "You told him he could bring a friend."

Emily said nothing, knowing she was bound to her word. One thing she and Robbie agreed on. A promise was a promise, an offer an offer. Once made, it was good for the duration. She turned on her heel and strode back to her car. She didn't speak at all, but it didn't matter, as Robbie was more than happy to keep up a running conversation with his new 'friend' all the way to the mall.

Emily found herself doubly grateful today that the Suburban was as large as it was. If she focused hard enough on her driving, she could pretend Eric Cameron and his new-smelling black leather jacket weren't anywhere near her.

She was unable to do the same, however, once they occupied Robbie's favorite window booth at Paisan's—the one that gave him a clear view of the video arcade across the hall. Seated opposite her, his back to the window, now wearing a black baseball cap he'd withdrawn from his jacket pocket, Eric and Robbie dickered over pizza toppings like a couple of kids who had the same friendly argument every week.

Covertly, Emily studied her unwanted dinner guest from behind her menu. He seemed to have recovered from Sunday night's escapades, and those that had preceded them. His bruised ribs didn't seem to bother him, his black eye was a mere crescent of brown beneath a thick fringe of equally brown eyelashes, and the cut she'd treated was healing well, although she now noticed his face bore testimony to several other small cuts received in the past, no doubt in the same manner.

It all made sense now, how he'd come to be in such bad shape that night. Running their conversation through her mind, she saw he hadn't lied to her about where he'd received his injuries; he'd been deliberately vague for some reason. Watching him now, it was hard to believe he was the same man who'd had her fleeing the ER. Tonight he seemed harmless, especially when he smiled the way he was now smiling at her son.

But Eric Cameron was far from harmless and Emily knew it.

Their waitress arrived and Eric coached Robbie in placing their order. Emily's heart twisted as her son lapped up the man's attention like a thirsty pup. She knew Robbie needed a male role model in his life, but Eric Cameron was not a viable candidate.

The waitress returned with their drinks, pop for Emily and Robbie, a large glass of water for their guest. She recalled Robbie mentioning a lecture on drug and alcohol abuse, and wondered why the man had chosen that as his topic. Several possibilities came to mind, none of which she found reassuring.

She watched him take a long swallow of water, his dark eyes scanning the restaurant from beneath the brim of his baseball cap while Robbie completed the crossword puzzle on his placemat. She'd noticed he did that every so often, and was careful to keep the brim tucked down low, no doubt so people wouldn't recognize him.

Eric set his glass aside and pointed to a clue Robbie had missed, drawing her attention to his hand. It looked as good as new. Larger than she would have thought, but long-fingered and oddly graceful. Skillful was the word that came to mind. Talented. She wondered if he painted, or played any musical instruments.

Hah. Not bloody likely. All hockey players cared about was ramming into each other like a bunch of overgrown adolescents with no sense and too much testosterone. She'd wasted several evenings watching hockey games. Made an effort for Robbie's sake. Tried to understand what the appeal was. And failed. Completely.

Robbie slid his crossword puzzle across the table. "Look, Mom, I filled in all the words by myself."

She smiled. "I noticed. I'd say that's worth a trip to Baskin-Robbins, wouldn't you?"

"Oh yeah. Oh yeah." Robbie made a circular motion with his fists, like he was celebrating. "Rocky Road!"

The pizza arrived and they ate, Emily keeping a polite distance while Eric kept everyone's plates filled. When Robbie nearly upset his drink in excitement, Eric was quick to catch it—great reflexes, she noted—and gloss over Robbie's embarrassment with an age-appropriate joke.

"You handled that well, Mr. Cameron," Emily offered grudgingly, while Robbie looked across at the video arcade and slurped his soda.

Eric paused, then smiled. "I appreciate your saying

so, Doctor. But please, call me Eric."

"Mom's name is Emily," Robbie piped up.

"Is it? It's a very pretty name. Just like your mom."

Robbie beamed. Emily wished she'd kept her mouth shut. She hadn't meant to encourage the man. In an effort to regain lost ground, she said, "I can't help but wonder why you agreed to join us tonight, Mr. Cameron."

"How's that?"

"I would have thought your preference would be more along the lines of Harry's Place, on Brady Street."

Wariness replaced the warmth in his eyes. "That was a temporary lapse in sanity. One I won't be repeating."

"I see."

"I doubt it."

"What's going on?" Robbie asked. "What are you guys talking about?"

Eric leaned back in his seat, a raised eyebrow asking Emily the same. She was scrambling to come up with an explanation Robbie would understand when someone rapped on the window beside their booth. She looked over to find Robbie's best friend Glen Simms mashing his nose and lips against the glass. He pulled back and grinned, held up a handful of quarters and jerked his thumb at the video arcade, inviting Robbie to join him.

"Can I go, Mom?" Robbie pleaded. "Just for a little bit? Glen said they got a new game in last week."

Her first impulse was to say no, to tell him to finish his dinner so they could leave, but the last two slices of pizza were on hers and Eric's plates. "All right, but come right back when you're done. We don't want to be late for the movie." She opened her wallet, fished out a few quarters, and handed them over.

Robbie bussed her on the cheek. "Thanks, Mom! You're the best. See ya later, Eric!" He started down the aisle, then bounced back and motioned for Eric to lean closer. "Don't forget what we talked about," he stage-whispered.

Eric nodded solemnly. "I'll do my best, Sport."

Robbie hooted and raced away. Emily waited until the boys disappeared in the cavernous darkness of the arcade before facing Eric head on. "What was that all about?"

Eric looked preoccupied, his gaze still on the arcade. "Is he always so energetic?"

"No more so than any other eight-year-old boy. I asked you a question. What were you talking to my son about?"

He studied her for a moment, then picked up his pizza. "Nothing that can't wait. First I want to know why you took those pot shots at me. I got the impression you didn't want Robbie to know we'd met before."

That he was right only increased her irritation. "I don't like lying to my son, Mr. Cameron. I like watching someone else lie to him even less."

Eric took a bite of his pizza. "Is that what you think I'm doing?"

"You seem to have a flair for it."

"I never lied to you, Emily."

"No. You just kept me in the dark. Deliberately."

"Are you saying that telling you what I do for a living would have made a difference?"

"I won't even bother to answer that."

Eric sighed and set his pizza aside. "All right. I'll try to explain. When I realized you didn't recognize my name, I opted for anonymity. Sometimes being Eric Cameron is more trouble than it's worth, and I wanted a chance at winning you over before dropping the bomb. I'm sorry if I hurt your feelings by not telling you I play pro hockey, but—"

"You were trying...to win me over?" Odd tactics he had.

"In an inept sort of way, yes. I wasn't thinking too clearly that night. But I knew right away I wanted to see you again."

Emily looked down at the napkin she'd been mangling beneath the table. He'd said as much in the ER, but tonight water was the only liquid loosening his tongue. The thought both flattered and frightened her. She didn't want this man to be interested in her.

"Did you get the roses?" he asked quietly.

"Yes."

"I sent them to apologize for my behavior Sunday night."

Emily flashed back to past hurts, past apologies.

Apologies that at the time had seemed just as romantic. Just as sincere. The memories stiffened her resolve.

"Can you forgive me?"

"You already know the answer to that."

Their gazes locked across the table.

"Why are you afraid of me, Emily?"

"I'm not afraid of you. I just don't trust you."

"Why not?"

"You have to ask? After you hunted down my son?"

"Hunted down your son?" He stared at her in disbelief, then shook his head. "I had no idea Robbie was your son. I didn't track him down because you didn't call me. Whatever else you may think of me, I don't use people. If you'd like, I can send you a copy of my speaking schedule. I've got six more talks lined up in the next two months, all of them at elementary schools."

"Six more? All at elementary schools?"

He smiled. "Yes ma'am. Call it preventive medicine. Catch them while they're young, before they get into junior high and some smooth eighth grader comes up with an offer they can't refuse."

"Is this something you have to do?"

"As in am I doing community service time instead of jail time?" Eric chuckled wryly. "You're determined to think the worst of me, aren't you?"

She would have expected him to be offended. Instead he was amused. Feeling off-kilter, she looked away, at the arcade.

Eric spoke again, his voice subdued. "I do the lectures for several reasons. For starters, I know something about the subject, I like kids, and it gives me a chance to be around them. I don't plan to stick around long enough to get invited to any backyard barbeques or pool parties. When the season ends, I'm out of here." He paused. "Have you ever tried it?"

Emily slid him a sideways glance. "Getting out of town, or volunteer work?"

He smiled, apparently finding something amusing in her answer. Inexplicably, she found herself wanting to smile back. She didn't.

"Volunteer work," he said.

Emily nodded, thinking of the battered women's

shelter she sat on the board of and donated her time to one night a week. "Now and then." She drank some pop and stared out the window again, uncomfortable with the intimate direction the conversation was taking. She didn't want Eric Cameron to know any more about her life than he already did. She noticed traffic in the hall picking up. The movie would start soon.

"It also helps to keep the lonelies at bay," Eric said.

Emily swung her head around. "Surely you don't expect me to believe you're lonely?"

"Why would you find that so hard to believe?"

"I thought all you sports heroes had your pick of...fans."

"You mean women?" He gave a nonchalant shrug, traced a long finger up, then down the side of his glass. Emily shivered in response, imagining those skillful fingers sliding across a woman's skin. "Sure, they're around," he said. "If that's what you're looking for."

"And you're not?"

He met her eyes, soul to soul. "I'm looking for one woman, Emily. That's all I need. All I want."

She swallowed, knowing she'd stepped into that one all by herself.

"How about you?" he asked. "What are you looking for?"

Certainly not you, she thought, even as heat rose in her at the idea. Unable to hold his gaze any longer, she tossed her destroyed napkin onto her plate. "I think I've made it clear I'm not looking for anyone. I mean anything."

"Maybe not, but your son is." Eric leaned forward. "As long as you've made your feelings clear, I might as well do the same. That boy of yours is starving for adult male companionship—oh, he loves you, no doubt about that—but you're stifling his natural male tendencies."

Emily bristled. "Meaning?"

"He wants to be one of the guys. He wants to play hockey."

"Never."

"It's your call. But one of these days his excess energy is going to need some sort of physical outlet and if it isn't sports...hockey, football, baseball, track, whatever...you could have a problem on your hands. With the stress you're already under, I don't think that's something you want to deal with."

"I resent that, Mr. Cameron. I'm not under any stress."

"Raising a child alone and working all hours of the day and night isn't stressful?"

"I've worked odd hours since before my son was born. He understands my job. Being on call is part of being a doctor. He knows that."

"Where's his father?"

"None of your business."

Eric said nothing, just stared at her with those dark, compelling eyes, willing her to tell him what he wanted to know. "Robbie's never given me a minute of trouble," she said instead, hating the defensive note in her voice.

"Not yet, maybe, but the time will come."

Emily glared at him. "What gives you the right to pass judgment on me? To tell me I'm raising my son wrong? What do you know about being a parent?"

Pain, deep and dark, flickered in his eyes. "About as much as you know about hockey. But that hasn't stopped you from passing judgment on me. Or condemning the entire sport."

"I have not—"

"Do the words 'No one but degenerates play hockey and I won't have my son turning into one' sound familiar?"

Emily flushed pink with embarrassment.

Eric leaned closer, resting his forearms on the table. "Come to think of it, you were pretty judgmental the other night, and you didn't even know I play hockey. You thought I was just a drunken troublemaker, didn't you? Whooping it up on a Sunday night for lack of anything better to do."

Emily's color went from pink to red.

"Tell me, Doctor, do you pigeonhole all your patients like that? Treat them with the same self-righteousness you showed me when they don't measure up to your standards?"

"Of course not!"

"Then as much as I hate to say this, you're a

hypocrite, Emily. You're supposed to treat your patients equally, but—"

Emily's palms hit the table. "*I'm* a hypocrite? Who got drunk and started a brawl, spent the night in jail and less than a week later preached about how bad drugs and alcohol are to a room full of impressionable little kids?"

"Hi, Mom. We're back."

Emily jerked her head around. Robbie and Glen stood beside the table. Robbie's confused gaze skipped back and forth between his mother and Eric, but Glen only had eyes for Eric.

"Wow," he said, awestruck. "It's really him. Can I have your autograph, Mr. Cameron?"

Emily wanted to scream in frustration. Instead she snatched up her coat and the check and stood. Daring Eric to move even an inch with her look, she addressed her son.

"Robin, when you're through making intro-ductions, I'd like you to meet me outside. Alone."

Chapter Four

"You didn't tell me you knew him, Mom."

Emily couldn't tell whether her son was more impressed or excited. She paid for their movie tickets and ushered him through the turnstile. "I don't *know* him. He came into the ER Sunday night—"

"Robbie's eyes widened. After the game?"

"No, after a—what game?"

"The Saints against the Wild. See, there was this big fight between Eric and the Wild's main goon, and—"

"Wait a minute. How do you know all this?" She didn't recall allowing him to watch any hockey game Sunday night.

"Mom. It was the Saints against the Wild," he said, as if that explained everything. "Everyone was talking about the game at school. Anyway, they said the Wild guy started the fight, then Eric got thrown out of the game and the Saints lost."

"Because of him? Because he got thrown out?"

Her son nodded vigorously. "Because he couldn't play no more."

"Any more," Emily corrected. "You mean he's that good?"

Robbie rolled his eyes in exasperation. "Mom, they traded four guys for him just so the Saints could get into the playoffs."

"And now they won't be going," she mused, and wondered if frustration was the reason he'd gotten involved in the brawl. That didn't make his actions right, but—

"Sure they will. The playoffs don't start until April."

Emily didn't ask him to explain. Hockey didn't interest her. All she needed to know about it was one of its more meddlesome proponents wouldn't be bothering

37

her or her son again.

She scanned the lobby, making sure their shadow hadn't followed them. To her relief, Robbie had emerged from Paisan's alone, and the last she'd seen of Eric Cameron was his well-formed backside as he headed into the video arcade with Glen Simms skipping along beside him.

Still, she couldn't shake the feeling he wasn't through with her yet.

She wasn't wrong. Five minutes into the film, she felt the hairs on the back of her neck prickle. Seconds later a large, hatless man smelling of pizza, peppermint and new leather eased into the seat to her left.

"Hi. Miss me?" he murmured into her ear.

She didn't miss the way Robbie wasn't surprised by the turn of events. She glared at him until he looked her way. Spotting Eric, Robbie smiled from his aisle seat and shrugged.

"Traitor," she muttered, then turned back to Eric. "What do you think you're doing in here?"

He grinned. "That seems to be your standard greeting." Ignoring her scowl, he removed his jacket and turned his attention to the screen. "I've never seen a Harry Potter movie. Glen recommended them highly, so I decided to join you once I made sure he hooked back up with his parents."

"I thought I—"

"Shh, Doctor. That's the problem. You think too much. Now why don't you relax and enjoy the movie. I hear the villainess in this is a real witch."

Emily snapped her mouth shut and sank into her seat. Eric settled deeper into his, clasped his hands over his waist and crossed his legs, bracing his right ankle on his left knee. The position brought his right thigh close enough for her to rest her hand on it...if she were so inclined.

She was *not*.

She tried her best to ignore him, but found it impossible. His occasional deep chuckles reminded her he was there. Clearly the two-hundred-plus pound hockey player was enjoying the film as much as her sneaky little son, if not more.

The two had more in common than conspiracy, she decided next. Like Robbie, Eric seemed to have trouble sitting still. Every few minutes he shifted restlessly, his arm or leg sometimes brushing hers as he tried to find a comfortable position in a seat that hadn't been designed for a man of his size. The contact was innocuous enough—his attention never strayed from the screen—but he must have bumped or brushed her at least a dozen times. Her awareness of him increased until it surrounded her like a cloud.

A thundercloud.

Through it all, he seemed oblivious to her darkening mood. As soon as the credits rolled, Emily sprang to her feet, collected her gloves and coat, then helped Robbie into his, despite his protests he could do it himself. She froze for a moment when Eric eased her coat out from under her arm and held it for her, but managed to slip into it more graciously than Robbie had his. Moving toward the exit, she heard someone behind her whisper Eric's name, then someone else. As they spilled into the lobby she noticed a group of twenty-something men in the ticket line nudging each other and grinning at them like crazy. She looked at the marquee to see what else was playing. No way that group was coming to see Harry Potter.

"Yo, Eric! Awesome fight last night, dude!"

"Put those Flames right out, man."

"Old Brodzac won't be able to skate for a week."

"About time somebody kicked his ass."

Emily would have sworn Eric looked embarrassed. "C'mon," he muttered, blocking her view of their rapidly growing audience as he ushered her and Robbie toward the exit. "Let's get going before the parking lot gets jammed."

Or before we get mobbed, she thought, reflexively catching Robbie's hand. But as soon as they stepped outside, the cold air cleared the fog in her brain. What was she thinking, allowing Eric Cameron to use her and Robbie as a smokescreen to avoid his fans?

"Wait."

She'd stopped so abruptly Eric nearly bumped into her. "What's the matter? Did you forget something?"

The genuine concern in his voice made her hesitate—

but only for a moment. Dinner was over. The movie was over. If Eric Cameron was looking for a family, he'd have to look somewhere else. Hers wasn't available. "No. I think it's time we said goodbye."

He took in her determined stance, shot her an annoyed look. "Fine. But I'm not leaving you two alone until I know you're safely on your way home. Is that a problem?"

Emily couldn't have felt more foolish. Robbie groaned in embarrassment. "Nice play, Mom."

She turned away and as the three of them—no longer moving as a single unit—crossed the parking lot, Emily knew she owed Eric an apology. But she couldn't come up with one that wouldn't compromise her need to keep him away from her and Robbie. Feeling trapped and angry she unlocked the driver's side door and wrenched it open, then turned back to see Eric offer Robbie his hand.

"I had a great time, Sport. Thanks for inviting me."

Robbie took his hand and offered a subdued, "Sure."

"Take good care of your mom, okay? You were right. She's something special."

Shame swamped Emily. She'd been a shrew most of the night and they all knew it. She couldn't miss Robbie's disappointment as he climbed into the seat behind hers. His hero hadn't said anything about seeing him again. She met Eric's guarded expression, and again felt the need to apologize, to make things right.

She couldn't. To encourage the man would be a mistake. A mistake she couldn't afford to repeat.

"Good night, Emily," he said quietly. "Thanks for the pizza, and the company. I enjoyed it."

He seemed so sincere, so kind. So...harmless. Their eyes locked and she inexplicably waited for him to say something more. Do something more. What, she had no idea. But now that their evening had finally come to an end, it somehow felt unfinished.

His cell phone rang and Eric checked it, but didn't answer it. Instead he stepped back and jammed his hands into his new-smelling leather jacket pockets. She wondered if he might have bought it that week, since she didn't remember him having a coat or jacket with him in the ER. Then again, he probably had a closet full of coats.

But the soft black leather suited him. She couldn't imagine him wearing anything else. She wondered again about that night, and what had caused the fight that had brought him into her ER.

"You'd better get going," he said, "That was my ride. I told him to meet me in front of the Road House at nine."

Emily recognized the name of the restaurant and bar. Of course. Disgusted with herself for even *considering* waffling, she said, "I see. Good bye, then."

She turned away and slid behind the wheel, then shut the door behind her with a firm bang. Still, she noticed he waited until she had the Suburban's engine smoothly running before turning away.

Feeling like she didn't know her own mind any more, Emily fiddled with the heat control and pulled herself together for the drive home. She told Robbie she was waiting for traffic to thin, let several cars pass behind her, then slowly backed out of her parking spot.

As she hit the brakes, she spotted Eric in her rearview mirror. He walked toward the mall, his hands still in his jacket pockets, his shoulders hunched, his breath creating cloud puffs as it hit the frigid night air. He looked tired and alone, and moved as if he were in pain. Remembering his bruised ribs, she wondered if that was why he'd been so restless during the movie. She wondered if he might have re-injured them during that "awesome" fight the night before.

And now he was going out to drink again?

Lord. Didn't the man have any sense?

You're determined to think the worst of me, aren't you?

She shifted into drive and tried not to think of him at all.

****

Monday afternoon Emily was at her desk auditing a stack of medical charts when Sarah Ferguson poked her head in the door.

"Hey, how's it going?"

"All right. I'm just trying to catch up on my paperwork."

"I see the flowers stopped coming."

"Yes, thank God. I was beginning to—"

41

The phone rang, interrupting her. She motioned for Sarah to stay and picked up the receiver. They'd long since ironed out the wrinkle in their friendship caused by Eric Cameron's visit. As for the man himself, Emily hadn't heard from him since she and Robbie had left him at the mall four nights ago.

"Dr. Jordan."

It was Robbie's principal, Dr. Manzelrod. "I'm sorry to disturb you at work, Dr. Jordan, but we need to talk. Your son's been in a fight with Glen Simms."

"Robbie? Fighting? With Glen?" Impossible. The boys were best friends. "Are you sure?"

She was. Both boys were sitting in her office, Glen nursing a split lip, Robbie sullen and refusing to speak to anyone. How soon could she get there?

"I'm on my way." Her mind spinning, Emily left the hospital. Robbie in a fight? She still couldn't believe it. He knew how she felt about fighting. About aggressive behavior. She'd made it clear to him the first time she'd caught him in a push and shove match on the playground. It had to be a mistake. An accident, at best.

Twenty minutes later Emily knew better. It hadn't been an accident at all. Her son had hauled off and hit his best friend when he'd refused to believe that Eric Cameron had said that Robbie had the makings of a born hockey player and promised to convince *her* to let him join the Mites Hockey League.

****

Robbie had to stay after school for three days as punishment. On the third day, running late as usual, Emily pulled out of the hospital parking lot in no mood for anything but a hot meal and a quiet evening at home. Within minutes she was caught in a snarl of rush-hour traffic. Rattled, she searched for a side street to exit onto. Usually she forced herself to face her fear of heavy traffic head on. She knew it was the only way she could hope to overcome her fears, but the stress of the past few days with Robbie was taking its toll.

The counselor at the women's shelter had told Emily her traffic anxieties stemmed from feelings of being trapped, of being unable to control her environment—of being unable to escape the danger that lurked outside her door. Traffic tended to bring out the worst in people and the impatient, angry looks on some drivers' faces reminded her of the look on her father's face—just before he would fly into one of his rages.

It had been thirty years, but Emily would never forget the hours she'd spent in her bedroom, afraid to move for fear of making noise, afraid to turn on the light when night fell for fear of attracting her father's attention. Feeling helpless and terrified, she'd huddled in a corner, hugging her Pooh bear to her chest as she listened to her father rant and rave, her mother plead and cry. She'd never known when the door might open, or what she might find on the other side of it when it did.

As she'd gotten older, the counselor had explained, her feelings of helplessness had transferred to other situations she couldn't control. Like the aggressive behavior of other drivers in heavy traffic. The Suburban provided some sense of security, being as big as it was, but the feeling that at any moment tempers could explode all around her never completely went away, even on the best of days, and today was far from that.

Odd, how she could deal with any crisis that came up in the ER, but outside of her professional setting...

It embarrassed her that the idea of someone losing his or her temper could still spook her. But that was the way it was.

She inched forward and nosed the Suburban into the right lane, then escaped the main road. But a few wrong turns on unfamiliar streets delayed her even more, and by the time she pulled into St. Stephens' circular drive she was distinctly edgy.

The sleek black Porsche parked in front of the school didn't help matters. For a split second she panicked, thinking it was Ryan's. He'd insisted Porsches were the only cars worth driving, and he'd favored black.

But then she remembered her ex-husband wouldn't be caught dead in a car that hadn't rolled off the assembly line within the past six months. This one was several years old, but well cared for from the looks of it.

As she entered the school's main office, a deep male voice drifted out from behind the principal's partially closed door. Not wanting to intrude on a private conversation—the woman was insisting that the man at least let her treat him to dinner—Emily waited impatiently at the front counter. A minute later, Dr. Manzelrod, a tall, striking blonde a few years Emily's junior emerged, laughing, in the company of Eric Cameron.

At Emily's strangled sound of disbelief, Dr. Manzelrod looked across the room in surprise, then smiled in welcome. "Dr. Jordan. I'm sorry. I didn't realize you were waiting."

"I...just got here."

Dr. Manzelrod's gaze went from Emily to Eric, then back again. "Have you two met?" When neither of them answered, she proceeded with introductions. "Dr. Jordan, I'd like you to meet Eric Cameron, one of Minnesota's premier hockey players and my—"

Eric's hand on her shoulder stopped her. "Thanks, Miranda, but Dr. Jordan already knows who I am."

Dr. Manzelrod looked startled, and Emily decided physical restraint seemed to be something Eric Cameron used instinctively. He and Dr. Manzelrod exchanged a long personal look before she offered a slow, "I see," then smiled and turned briskly back to Emily. "Then if you'll excuse me, I'll get Robbie."

"Robbie?" Eric's eyes narrowed on Emily as Dr. Manzelrod disappeared down the hall that led to the holding room at the rear of the office.

Emily lifted her chin. "He's serving detention. For fighting."

Instead of the I-told-you-so gleam she'd expected to see enter his dark brown eyes, she saw genuine concern. "Fighting? About what?"

Her first impulse was to tell him it was none of his business. Then again for the past three days, she'd burned with the need to confront Eric Cameron, the undisputed cause of her first major falling out with her son. For hours she'd fantasized about giving the man a piece of her mind. But now that he was here...

She hesitated, remembering the silent message she'd witnessed between him and 'Miranda.' Emily remembered all too well what a sudden hand on the shoulder had meant with Ryan. It meant she'd crossed some invisible line and would pay for it later. Still, it surprised her that Miranda Manzelrod had given in to him so easily. She'd always seemed so strong and independent to Emily.

Lifting her chin, she marshaled her outrage...and her courage. "He gave Glen a split lip because Glen refused to believe that *you* told Robbie he had the makings of an ace hockey player and you were going to get *me* to let him sign up for the Mites League."

Just then Robbie entered the room, his face filling with more animation than Emily had seen in a week. "Eric! You're back!" In elation he flung himself at his idol.

Eric caught the human missile and settled Robbie against his hip, something Emily hadn't been able to do for years because of Robbie's size. "Hi, Sport. I heard you spent some time in detention."

Robbie beamed. "Yeah. Just like you."

Eric winced and cast Emily an apologetic look. She ignored him, her focus on the easy rapport he shared with her son. *Her* son, who hadn't smiled at her in days. "Time to go, Robbie."

"Wait. I have something to ask Robbie, first." Eric wended his way to the front counter and set the boy atop it. Placing his hands on either side of Robbie, he commanded the eight-year-old's attention. "Did you tell Glen Simms I said you were an ace hockey player and I was going to convince your mother to let you play in the Mites League?"

Robbie dropped his head, his cheeks bright red.

"Why?" Eric asked quietly. He waited patiently, while Emily held her breath. She knew what was coming. Suddenly it explained everything that had happened between herself and Robbie that week.

"I'm sorry, Mom. I lied. Eric didn't really say that. I just wanted him to."

"Oh, Robbie."

"I'm sorry."

He wasn't the only one. Emily was sorry to the tips of her crepe-soled shoes. She looked at Eric. "I owe you an apology." Several, if she wanted to be honest about it.

"It's all right," Eric said with quiet smile. An inexplicable twinkle entered his dark brown eyes. "But if it's really bothering you, I'd settle for a home-cooked dinner."

The man was no slouch when it came to taking advantage of a sudden opening. Emily cast an embarrassed glance at Robbie's principal, who was tacking some notices on a bulletin board. Whatever her relationship to Eric, she seemed completely secure in it. Still, Emily wasn't about to disrespect herself or Dr. Manzelrod by accepting any dates with her...her *whatever*.

"I don't cook."

Eric smiled warmly, unfazed. "Then I guess I'll have to."

The accompanying warmth that entered his eyes almost made Emily relent, despite everything. The power of his gaze unsettled her so much she frost-coated her answer. "Guess again, Mr. Cameron."

"You want something more elaborate than steak and salad."

"No, I want you to drop the subject. I'm not interested." She collected her son and ushered him out the door.

Shot down again, Eric thought, watching her go. What was it about him the woman found so damned lacking?

Miranda's amused voice floated across to him. "Well, well, well, *Mr.* Cameron. What was that all about?" At his arched eyebrow, she said, "You know we educators are born eavesdroppers. Not to mention having eyes in the backs of our heads." She crossed her arms and studied him shrewdly. "I've never seen so many sparks fly between you and a woman, Eric. What's up with that?"

"She hates me," he said miserably.

"Wrong."

"What?" He looked at Miranda in confusion.

"In almost three years of Christmas pageants, bake sales, car washes, PTO meetings and open houses, not once have I seen Emily Jordan with a man. I've seen several men strike up conversations with her and while she's polite to them, it's obvious she forgets about them the minute they walk away. You, she remembers."

"That doesn't mean she likes me."

"No, but it means you've made an impression."

Eric thought of the terror in Emily's eyes when he'd

grabbed her wrist in the emergency room. The way her attention had shot to his hand when he'd cut in on Miranda's glowing introduction. "You can say that again."

"Listen, Eric, in the two years I've known you, I've never seen you look at a woman like that. Good choice, though. I don't think you could do any better. Emily Jordan's got brains, beauty, compassion and class. I also thought you were heading into the Vulcan death grip the way you squeezed my shoulder to shut me up. What gives?"

Eric winced. "I'm sorry if I hurt you, Miranda."

"I'm fine. You startled me, is all. Sometimes, you don't know your own strength. So, what's up with the good doctor?"

"I don't know. She...intrigues me. She seems so...self-contained."

"She has to be. She's a single mother. It's not only herself she has to look out for, but her child."

"I'm not after her money, Miranda."

Miranda laughed. "I meant emotionally, you dolt. Emily Jordan strikes me as the kind of woman who, if she were to get involved with a man, would carefully consider the effect the relationship would have on her son."

Eric recalled the misplaced pride with which Robbie had admitted to serving detention. "Which in my case is more negative than positive."

Miranda patted his cheek. "The woman's got a good head on her shoulders, *Mr.* Cameron. She knows trouble when she sees it."

Eric chuckled and headed for the door, already considering ways to change Emily's mind about him. "Catch you later, Miranda. I'll let you know when that equipment comes in."

"Thanks again, and Eric..."

He paused, the door halfway open.

She grinned. "Good luck."

47

Chapter Five

Outside, Eric was surprised to find Emily and Robbie hadn't left yet. Instead, Robbie was knee deep in admiring the Porsche while Emily tried in vain to peel him from the passenger window. "Look, Mom! A real Boxter! Man, it's got *everything!*"

At Eric's amused chuckle, Emily glanced over her shoulder. Before she could snatch up her son and disappear, Eric suggested, "Why don't you hop inside for a closer look, Sport?"

The boy didn't need a second invitation. When Emily didn't object, Eric's confidence rose. But as Robbie scrambled inside, Emily shut the passenger door behind him and whirled on Eric. "Why don't you just stay out of my life?"

Gone was the icy control with which she'd faced him in the office. In its place was raw fury. No...that wasn't it. She wasn't furious; the woman was frazzled. Right down to the bone. Dark shadows ringed her eyes, tiny stress lines creased her brow, her skirt and sweater were wrinkled and smudged beneath her open coat, a thick strand of deep auburn hair had escaped her drooping bun, and her hands and shoes were stained with a blue dye.

Never had a woman looked more appealing to him. And never in his adult life had Eric known one more in need of some serious TLC. Just the sight of her so close to coming undone made him want to wrap his arms around her, hold her close and tell her everything was going to be all right.

Miranda was right. He had it bad.

"I'm sorry, Emily. I can't do that."

She glared at him, looking ready to shatter.

"Listen, can we talk? Maybe grab a burger or something with Robbie? Get this...misunderstanding cleared up?"

She shook her head as if he somehow amazed her, and not in a positive way. "This misunderstanding," she said slowly, "is between my son and myself. I'll admit I may have judged you harshly, and that you may have been right about Robbie's excess energy, but he's *my* son, and whatever happens from here on out is *my* responsibility."

"Emily, I wasn't trying to interfere. I only want to help."

"Help?" she echoed, her voice cracking. "You've helped quite enough, thank you. Thanks to you, for the past three days my son has barely spoken to me. So please, do us all a favor and find someone else to *help*."

Eric felt terrible. He didn't know what to say. "Jeez, Emily, I'm sor—"

"Damn it, Eric. You're the last thing we need in our lives right now. How can I make that clear to you?"

He paused. She'd called him Eric. But this was no time to celebrate small victories. The woman was too close to her personal edge. Backing off, he knocked on the Boxter's passenger window. "Time's up, Robbie. I need to get going."

Robbie scrambled out of the car, disappointed, "Will you come back and take me for a ride sometime?"

Eric looked at Emily, whose body language screamed she was ready to explode, but her face showed no emotion at all. He really had to admire the way she held it all together.

"That's entirely up to your mother," he said, hoping she'd get the message that he'd never want to come between her and her son.

****

Thank you sooo much, Mr. Cameron, Emily seethed as the ride home with Robbie reverberated with strained silence. Why couldn't he have simply said no, he was sorry, he wouldn't be seeing them again? Robbie would have gotten over it in time, found a new hero to worship. Instead, she had somehow once again let the man maneuver her into the role of unfeeling, uncompromising witch.

Her attempts at dinner to mend her broken

relationship with Robbie failed. Her son again admitted he'd lied, apologized and promised not to do it again, but when she questioned him as to why he'd done it, he met her eyes and lifted his small, stubborn chin, so much like her own. "I want to be a hockey player, like Eric."

Forcing herself to stay calm when she wanted to weep in frustration, Emily repeated her objections. It wasn't safe. He didn't know how to skate. The season was almost over anyway.

Her son met her protests with uncharacteristic silence, his hazel eyes hurt and accusing. When she finished, he excused himself to go to his room, and when bedtime came he informed her she didn't need to tuck him in anymore because he wasn't a baby.

****

Emily didn't sleep at all that night. The next morning, she walked into the nearest ice rink and asked for the name of whoever ran the Mites Hockey League program. She was both surprised and grateful to learn that the man she sought coached a team based at that same rink, and would be there that evening. She'd had no idea where to begin, but knew this was something she had to do. She had to at least talk to someone about this before she saw Robbie again. She left her number, and Brian Parker called at lunchtime to set up an appointment after work, at the rink.

Emily liked Parker immediately. A friendly man, he was a computer salesman by day, fortyish and balding. He also knew hockey and kids, having been drafted into coaching five years earlier when his twin daughters were on the team. They'd since abandoned pads and helmets for lip gloss and perfume, but he'd stayed on because he enjoyed it so much. He also had a four-year-old son who would be coming through the program soon.

She watched the children exercise their "drills" as his two assistant coaches directed them on the ice. Not once did she see anyone maliciously trip or elbow another player as they scrambled after a dozen or more elusive pucks. "It doesn't look as dangerous as I thought," she said.

"They're not allowed to check for another two years," Coach Parker answered, smiling. "And they're well protected Ms. Jordan. I wouldn't let them on the ice otherwise. They all wear the same regulation equipment, and mouth and neck guards are required."

"Who provides this equipment?"

"The team's sponsor provides the game jerseys. The rest is up to the parents. You might want to check out the used sports equipment store, first. The cost of equipment is pretty steep."

"And it doesn't matter that the season's almost over?"

"It does to some, not to me. Fortunately, I'm in a position to be able to help you out. We lost a couple of players this year due to having to move. Personally, I'm always glad to take on kids with your son's determination and enthusiasm. This might be just what he—and you— need to get his feet wet. In a few weeks you'll both know whether you want to continue or not, and sign ups for spring hockey are just around the corner."

Later, in his office, the soft-spoken man summed it up. "We're here to have fun, Ms. Jordan, not win the Stanley Cup. I teach my kids the rules, a few plays, something about teamwork and fair play, and give them a chance to work off their excess energy. If we happen to win a few games along the way, so much the better."

Emily studied the shelf of trophies and wall of ribbons behind his desk. Obviously the Compucenter Red Wings, Compucenter for the computer store that sponsored the team, had won quite a few games.

"The kids get a real kick out of winning," he continued, following her gaze. "But that's not why they're here. They're here to learn and play. If you're looking for a more competitive league, you'll have to go over to—"

"Oh, no," Emily interrupted, smiling. "I think Robbie will be very happy playing for the Red Wings. How do I sign him up?"

Chapter Six

"Honey, I'm not sure this is a good idea."

"Sure it is, Mom," Robbie said from beside Emily as she wobbled around the edge of the crowded indoor ice rink. An unfamiliar rock tune blared from the overhead speakers, emphasizing the feeling she was hopelessly out of her element. "It's easy, see?" He sprinted away, into the path of oncoming skaters.

"Robbie! Get back over here!" Emily was positive she aged ten years as she slipped on the ice trying to reach him. He veered out of the way just in time, returning to her side with a triumphant grin. "How did you learn to do that?" she all but gasped as her heartbeat returned to normal. He couldn't possibly have learned how to skate in the past fifteen minutes.

"Melissa taught me."

"Melissa?" Melissa was Augustus' youngest daughter and Robbie's backup babysitter.

"She brings me on weekends sometimes when you're working."

Melissa was giving Robbie skating lessons? No one had mentioned it. Emily wondered what else she was missing out on in Robbie's life while she was working overtime to meet her financial commitments. Maybe it was time to re-think her priorities, cut back on her hours if she could swing it. She didn't like the idea that she might be losing touch with her son.

"She brings me when you're out with Dr. Caldwell sometimes, too."

Emily looked down at her hands, once again braced on the railing. "Out with Dr. Caldwell" was the euphemism they used for the one night a week she spent with Augustus at the women's shelter. She didn't want to explain to Robbie where she was going or why until he was old enough to understand. Her work at Harmony House was personal and she didn't need him casually spilling her secrets to everyone he met—like Eric Cameron. God only knew what her son had already told the man about her.

Not that it mattered anymore.

A shiver snaked its way down her spine. The temperature in the rink was frigid. If she didn't want to turn into an ice statue, she'd have to get moving. The song on the radio ended. A more familiar tune wafted on the air, making her feel less out of sorts. "I see. Well, maybe we should have invited Melissa along today. I could use a lesson or two."

"Then I'm the man you're looking for," an amused masculine voice said from behind her. "Skating lessons are my specialty."

Oh no. Not him again. Not now. *Am I being punished for something specific, Lord, or are you just playing with me for the fun of it?*

"Thanks for calling, Sport. I see what you mean. We've got a real rookie on our hands. White knuckles and all."

Emily whipped her head around. "Robbie called you?"

Eric studied her face before answering, as if gauging her mood. "I gave him my number when we were at Paisan's. Told him to keep in touch."

Robbie had had the man's phone number all this time and not said a word? Emily wanted to cry. She no longer knew her son at all.

Eric misunderstood her upset. "Hey, it's not so bad. Just give me your hands and—"

She yanked them out of his reach, not caring if she fell. "No! Don't you understand? Either of you? I don't want to skate with you. I don't want to have anything to do with you."

The flash of hurt in his eyes made her look away, only to find a matching hurt in Robbie's face. Emily felt ashamed of herself, and embarrassed for all of them. What was it about this man that brought out the worst in her?

"Just once, Emily," Eric said quietly. "Just once around the rink. If you don't like it, we can stop. And if you do, as soon as you're able to skate alone, I'll leave you to it. It shouldn't take long. Fair enough?"

Still too embarrassed to meet his eyes, she looked at his chest. He wore a black turtleneck beneath an open hip-length parka, and looked as big and tall as a mountain. Nobody, but nobody was going to skate over him. The thought was reassuring.

She lifted her head, and met his eyes beneath the brim of his black baseball cap. He hadn't shaved in at least a day or two, and looked a little scruffy, but she understood he was trying not to be recognized again. Suddenly she appreciated his making the trip out here, risking the exposure, to help her out.

"All right. And I'm sorry for...for overreacting. I'm nervous about..." she nodded in the direction of the speeding skaters. "...all of this."

Eric's expression gentled in understanding as he held out his hands. "Don't be. You can handle anything."

With a dry, disbelieving look, she laid her hands in his. He squeezed them reassuringly and a comforting warmth seeped into her limbs.

"That's it, Mom. You'll be all right now. Eric won't let you fall."

"He's got that right," Eric said, his dark brown eyes not leaving hers.

Emily suddenly wished she was tall, blonde, graceful and on the other side of thirty, like Miranda Manzelrod. Or at least that she'd put on makeup and worn something other than her oldest jeans and a washed out green sweater beneath an equally worn parka. But she'd planned on falling a lot, so...

Self-consciously she looked down at her scuffed rental skates. "What do I do first?"

Eric's hand slid up to encircle her wrists beneath her parka sleeves. "Just relax and let me lead the way, okay?"

She took a deep breath to calm her sudden attack of butterflies. His skin was so warm against hers, his touch so sure and self-confident. "I'll try."

Eric told Robbie to stay close to the edge of the rink, and started skating backward, gently pulling Emily with him. She let him tow her along, watching her feet slide rigidly across the ice, feeling like a barge behind a tugboat. Whenever she faltered, Eric's fingers tightened on her wrists, setting off little fires along her nerve endings. She didn't pull away, though. She couldn't afford to without falling flat on her face.

Instead she concentrated on his murmured instructions. With words alone he coaxed the stiffness from her muscles. She'd begun to think she had a handle on this skating business, when Eric eased them to a stop.

She looked up at him in surprise. "What?"

"We've finished our lap."

Already? She looked around and saw they were indeed at their point of departure. Robbie was practicing figure eights in the area at the end of the rink set aside for beginners and small children, safely out of the flow of traffic.

"Want to give it another shot?"

She met the hopeful look in his eyes and couldn't help but wonder if he was talking about more than skating. "If you don't mind moving at a snail's pace," she said quietly.

His eyes darkened, and then he smiled, a slow, soft smile that made her feel deliciously special. "For you, anything."

Before she knew it, they were moving again. Around and around they coasted, Eric skating backwards, Emily feeling more secure with each lap. It seemed her earlier assumption had been on target. Eric's size was a major deterrent to those who rode roughshod over the less skilled. Even when he eased her into the mainstream of traffic no one came near them. As skaters sped by on either side of them, she looked up at him and grinned.

"I think I've got it!" She hit a rut in the ice and stumbled. Without missing a beat, Eric caught her. Before she could blink, he'd flipped her around so that both of them were facing forward. "What are you—?"

"Relax. I won't hurt you. Now just follow my lead. One step at a time."

He nudged her forward, right arm around her waist, left hand holding hers. Emily had no choice but to relax or be run over. Forcing herself to ignore the feeling of being surrounded by him, she concentrated on his steady, "Left, right, left, right." Soon they were moving in tandem to the music of Faith Hill. Emily felt a chill on her back as Eric gently released her.

She started skating alone without realizing it.

"You're doing it, Mom! You're skating!" Robbie shouted in glee as she glided past the practice area.

She looked at him over her shoulder, and tripped. The next thing she knew, Eric and his magnificent reflexes had scooped her into his arms and was skating over to where Robbie waited, near to bursting with excitement. Wrapping an arm around Eric's parka-padded shoulders, Emily laughed in relief...and pure giddiness. Being swept off her feet by the man was heady stuff indeed.

"Not too shabby for a first-timer," Eric said with a grin, and set her down next to Robbie.

Damn, but she looked good, he thought, giving Emily's shoulders a light hug before he released her. Felt good, too. She smiled up at him, and the unexpected warmth of it nearly knocked him flat. With her dancing green eyes and silky auburn hair swept up in a loose topknot instead of her usual no-nonsense bun, she looked relaxed, approachable. Kissable.

He cleared his throat and tried to clear his mind. The idea of kissing Emily Jordan was a little too much to handle right now. "Now we need to work on a few technical points, and you'll be all set."

For the next ten minutes he drilled her on stops and starts. He loved how her little pink tongue curled out over her upper lip when she concentrated. He also couldn't decide which he enjoyed more, watching her skate away from him, catching tantalizing glimpses of the bottom half of her sweetly curved backside beneath her hip-length parka, or watching her return. Either way, her balance and coordination were exceptional.

Finally he pronounced her ready to skate solo, and with a determinedly casual arm around· her shoulders, turned her toward the flow of circling skaters. "Now get out there and show us your stuff," he ordered, and dropped his hand to the small of her back to nudge her forward.

"Oh, no. I couldn't." She looked up at him over her shoulder, her green eyes wide with trepidation. A boisterous group of skaters swept by and she backed up, her shoulders bumping his chest. A thrill shot straight to Eric's heart. Whether she realized it or not, Emily Jordan was warming up to him.

"You just did," he pointed out softly.

Her eyes darkened to jade, her tiny pink tongue darted out to wet her lips. Eric nearly groaned. Feeling his jeans grow tight, he moved back a few inches, putting some cool air between them. "Emily..."

"I don't think so, Eric," she said, turning to face him. "I couldn't keep up with all those people."

When she said his name like that, he wanted to tell her she could do anything she wanted to. Anytime. Anyplace.

Robbie was more objective. "Sure you can, Mom. It's easy. I'll even go with you."

A troubled look crossed her face, one Eric no longer had any problem recognizing. Emily Jordan had a hard time saying no to her son. "Tell you what, Sport. We'll all take a few turns around the rink. One of us on either side of your mom, okay?"

Emily vetoed that idea, reminding Eric she had no problem saying no to *him*, then nearly floored him with, "Would you mind skating in the middle instead? Robbie's been sticking pretty close to the edges and I'd feel better if I knew he was hanging on to you instead of me."

Eric smiled, feeling his whole being expand. "Not at all."

They skated for another half hour before Emily confessed her ankles felt rubbery and called for a time out. As Eric led them to the exit from the ice, she insisted he and Robbie continue skating. She stopped at a pop machine and bought herself a drink, then settled in the stands, unlaced her skates, and sat back with a satisfied sigh to enjoy her soda. The can halfway to her lips, she froze.

Hands in his parka pockets, Eric sped across the ice like a zephyr, weaving through the crowd in a flawless exhibition of masculine grace. With an ease that stole her breath he circled the rink three times in the amount of time it would have taken her to make half a lap. No flourishes, no figure skater's flamboyance, just a clean, fluid style that sent her pulse rate up a good ten points.

After his tenth lap he rejoined Robbie. The two of them made the next few laps together, Eric skating backward in front of Robbie, his expression serious. When she noticed him ticking off points on his fingers, she realized his impressive display of speed and skill hadn't been for her benefit, but her son's.

Within minutes she saw a marked improvement in Robbie's skating. No surprises there. His teacher earned his living on skates.

The thought brought Emily up short. How could she have forgotten who Eric was? What he did for a living?

A split second later, she had her answer. Eric noticed her watching him and flashed her a dazzling smile, pointed to Robbie and sent her an A-okay sign.

Emily smiled right back. Hockey player or no, Eric Cameron was one appealing man.

****

"So what do you say to a trip to Baskin-Robbins?" Eric asked, unlacing his huge black skates while Robbie returned his and Emily's skates to the rental booth.

"What size are those, anyway?"

Eric grinned. "Thirteen. Probably twice as big as yours."

Emily laughed. "They are. Exactly."

"So how about it? Up for some ice cream?"

Emily smiled. "Thank you. I appreciate your asking me while Robbie isn't around."

Eric chuckled. "I'm learning."

Emily looked out over the ice to break the intimacy of the moment. She wasn't sure how she felt about the idea of Eric Cameron starting to figure her out. "I don't know. We've got some shopping to do this afternoon. Robbie needs—" she looked back at Eric, "Did he tell you he's going to be playing hockey?"

Eric smiled and set his skates aside. "Of course. That's why he called. But before you get the wrong idea, I want you to know I made sure he understood it was your decision to sign him up and I had nothing to do with it."

"Wrong," she said dryly.

His smiled dimmed. "I never meant to come between you and your son, Emily. I'm sorry if that's the way it

58

seemed."

"I know," she said. "It's just that there's been only the two of us for so long that..."

"It hurts to think someone might be trying to horn in on your relationship."

"You sound as if you've been there."

A shadow crossed his face, the faint scars on his nose giving it added character. His stubbly beard hid the scars on his cheeks and chin, but she knew they were there. She felt oddly special, knowing something about him no one else around them did. He noticed her gaze had strayed to his stubble and said, "I'm sorry I didn't shave."

"I understand. You've managed to keep a low profile today."

"So far so good, anyway. It's mostly kids here today." He bent to tie his Reeboks.

"Do you have any children, Eric?" He paused in tying his shoes, his jaw tightening with suppressed emotion. Emily had seen patients do much the same when they denied their physical pain. "I'm sorry. I didn't mean to pry."

He finished with his shoes, looked her in the eye and smiled. "My ex-wife didn't want children."

He was so good at pretending it didn't matter that Emily's heart cracked. Suddenly her attempts to keep Eric and Robbie apart seemed cruelly selfish. The hockey season was almost over. When it ended Eric would leave. What could it hurt to let them enjoy a temporary friendship? Robbie adored the man, and she had to admit Eric had a lot to offer a boy Robbie's age. A boy or young man of any age. Patience, wisdom, understanding...the benefit of experience...

Suddenly she brightened. "Why don't you come shopping with us?"

Eric looked lost, as if she'd asked him to accompany her on an ambulance call. "Shopping?"

She laughed at his confusion. "I'm sorry. I just had a thought. Robbie needs some hockey equipment by Friday, and I have no idea where to begin."

Eric's grin dazzled her all over again. "I know right where to go."

Chapter Seven

Thirty minutes later, Emily turned the Suburban into a small industrial park tucked away in a part of town she suspected the city's road maintenance department had forgotten existed. Even with her tank of a car she was having trouble navigating all the potholes during the half-mile drive between the main road and the four long rows of squat, flat-topped buildings that made up the park.

She wended her way around as many potholes as she could, but wasn't able to avoid all of them. She wondered if Eric was at all worried about his Porsche dropping into one of them, never to be seen again, but somehow he managed to stay between the craters. Following his hand signals, she pulled up in front of a door with a sign on it proclaiming it Sam's Wholesale Sports Supply.

While Eric and Robbie—who'd leapt at the chance to ride with Eric—parked on the far side of the salt-coated pickup she'd pulled up next to, Emily took a moment to find some lipstick and freshen her perfume from a sampler bottle she carried in her purse. She capped her lipstick, then blindly dropped both lipstick and perfume back into her purse as she opened the driver's door...and slid out of the Suburban on legs that suddenly felt like lead weights.

"Whoa." She blinked in surprise. Apparently skating had awakened a few muscles she hadn't thought much about since med school.

"Emily? You all right?" Eric asked from where he stood near her front left fender.

"Sure." She smiled, hoping her smile wasn't as wobbly as she felt. She stepped back and shut the Suburban's door. "Just feeling a little...rubbery at the moment."

Eric smiled back. "That happens a lot, especially if

you're not used to skating."

Suddenly Emily appreciated the strength and stamina it took for him to take to the ice night after night. Her gaze dropped to his snug, well-worn jeans. The man was in fantastic shape, no doubt about it. Hubba hubba. She looked up to find Eric grinning at her like a cat with a mainline to the cream. Flushing at having been caught ogling him, Emily pointed to the *Sorry, We're Closed* sign in the lower left corner of the dusty picture window beside the door. "I think they're closed."

Eric just smiled and rapped on the door. The "I'm all yours" look in his eyes made her palms sweat. "Sam's here. I called him on the way over."

The door opened and a wiry black man in a blue plaid flannel shirt and jeans stepped back to admit them. "Eric, good to see you," he said. "Your stuff came in Friday afternoon."

"Glad to hear it, but that's not why I called. Sam, I'd like you to meet Emily Jordan and her son, Robbie."

Sam smiled in welcome. "Pleasure to meet you, Ms. Jordan. Robbie. I was just making some coffee." He turned and checked the pot. "It's almost done. Anyone care for a cup?"

Emily declined, but Eric accepted. After a brief pow-wow with Eric about the Saints' chances for making the playoffs while the coffee finished brewing, Sam turned to Emily with a warm smile. "What can we do for you today, Ms. Jordan, besides bore you with a lot of meaningless statistics?"

"Meaningless?" From the sound of it they'd been discussing the team's chances as intently as she'd consult with Augustus about a critically ill patient.

"Absolutely. Because no matter what the sports gurus say, the Saints are going all the way...and this guy right here is the one who's going to take them." He clapped Eric on the back, nearly sloshing the coffee Eric was staring into all over his front. "Yes ma'am, you've hooked up with a real champion here. Captain Cameron to the rescue."

The light in the storefront was dim, but Emily would have sworn she saw Eric's ears redden. "Emily doesn't really follow the sport, Sam," he said quietly.

Sam looked at her in startled surprise, then back at Eric. "She doesn't?" As if such a thing was inconceivable.

"No, but Robbie does, and he's joining the Mites League. I'd like you to set him up with the works."

"Sure. No problem. Got everything he needs right here. Top of the line."

Within minutes Robbie looked like a miniature gladiator. Emily felt a sharp pinch in her purse as the two men outfitted her son with layer upon layer of padding, the three of them conversing in a sports jargon she couldn't begin to comprehend. Secure in the knowledge her son was in the hands of experts, she changed her mind about Sam's offer of coffee and poured herself some.

She cradled the styrofoam cup in her hands and strolled over to the window. Peering through the dusty horizontal blinds, she studied the Suburban. Five years old already when she'd bought it last year, it desperately needed a tune-up and new tires. That might have to wait again, now with Robbie's newest expenses. Between paying off her school loans, Robbie's tuition and helping out her family, she was pushing her financial limits to the wall. And with the cost of gas these days...

She sighed. There were times when she wished she didn't have to drive such a big vehicle, but that was one phobia she couldn't seem to get rid of.

She turned away from the window and found Sam gone and Eric crouched before Robbie, testing the fit of his equipment. She sipped her coffee and felt the sting of tears as Robbie solemnly answered Eric's quiet questions. What she wouldn't give to have her family see Robbie right now. But home wasn't somewhere she could ever go again. Not as long as her father was alive. She wondered how her mother was doing, if her health was holding up. It was times like this, when she felt closest to Robbie, that she missed her own mother the most.

Sam reappeared with a fistful of hockey sticks, a pair of black leather skates and a huge white jersey. As her son stood there in a pair of black padded pants that looked five sizes too big but apparently fit perfectly, Eric slid the suspenders up over Robbie's shoulder pads, then dropped the huge jersey over his head. He asked Robbie to sit, then laced his skates. Only her son's face and hands resembled anything close to an eight year old's, and even that changed once Eric settled a hard red plastic helmet with a grid mask on Robbie's head.

Eric adjusted the chinstrap, while Sam handed Robbie a huge pair of padded black gloves to try on.

"So, what do you think, Ms. Jordan?" Sam asked, grinning.

Eric and Robbie looked her way, Robbie more still than Emily could remember him being while awake.

"I think you look wonderful," she told her son, her voice catching. "I can't wait to see you in action."

Robbie let out a whoop of joy. Emily lifted her eyes to Eric's, not caring that he saw the emotion in them. "Thank you," she mouthed, as Robbie waddled over to Sam to select a stick.

Eric's answering smile touched her mother's heart. "If that doesn't keep him safe, nothing will."

While Eric instructed Robbie on how to best extricate himself from his layers of armor, Emily approached Sam, checkbook in hand. "What do I owe you?"

"Not a thing," he answered easily. "I'll just put it on Eric's tab, like I do the others."

"Others?"

"Yeah, the man's always picking up strays and...begging your pardon, ma'am, I didn't mean to imply—"

"That's quite all right," Emily interrupted, cool but polite. "But we're not any of Mr. Cameron's strays. I asked him to help me shop for hockey gear since I'm unfamiliar with the sport, and he brought us to you."

"I see. Well, ma'am," he said, scratching the back of his neck, "I'm not licensed to sell to anyone but retailers and guys in the business, so...tell you what. I'll sell you the equipment, but you'll have to let Eric pay for it."

"Oh, no. I couldn't—"

"All you have to do is write him the check instead of me. I'll put the order in his name and..."

"Is there a problem?" Eric asked, coming up behind Emily.

"Lady wants to settle up."

"So what's the—oh, right. Sorry about that. I wasn't thinking."

"I told her she could write you a check to cover it."

"Sure."

Emily relaxed as she realized she wouldn't have to argue with Eric over the bill. Sam went behind the counter to prepare an invoice. "What about the rest of the stuff?" he asked. You ready to take delivery now?"

"No. I'll have to come back for it."

Sam sent him a strange look. "You been on my case for three weeks now, asking when it's coming in, and now you got time to spare?"

"Is there something I can help with?" Emily asked, handing Eric a check for nearly five hundred dollars.

He folded it in half and tucked it into his back pocket without even looking at it. Emily wished she could be so casual about money. She would miss that five hundred dollars.

"Not unless you've got a portable U-Haul in your purse," he said.

"I've got the Subway."

"The Subway?"

"My Suburban. Robbie and I named it the Subway one day because it seemed big enough to be a subway car and—oh, never mind. I guess you had to be there," she ended in embarrassment.

"At least take the balls off my hands. I've got another shipment coming in tomorrow. Don't know where I'm going to put it all."

Eric looked at Emily. "You sure you don't mind?"

Half an hour later, the Subway was packed with balls. Footballs, basketballs, volleyballs, baseballs. Some were deflated, which Sam explained was because the buyer often didn't know how long it would be before the balls were put into service.

"Jeez, Mom, there must be a million of them in there," Robbie said as Eric and Sam closed the door on her puzzling cargo.

"More like a hundred," Emily murmured.

"What's he gonna do with them all?"

"Good question." There wasn't a hockey puck in the bunch.

"That ought to make Miranda a happy woman," Sam said, bracing his hands on his hips as he studied the packed Suburban.

"Miranda?" Emily echoed in surprise.

Eric smiled at her across the roof of her vehicle. "I'm donating some stuff to the school. No big deal."

No big deal? Emily didn't think Miranda would agree. In fact, the woman would probably be downright ecstatic. What school administrator wouldn't be? "Does she know about this?"

"Been waiting with bated breath for the stuff for weeks," Sam said.

Emily recalled overhearing Robbie's principal saying "at least let me treat you to dinner" that day at the school. She must have been talking about this. About Eric's donation. And this would be her chance to repay him. Emily tried her best not to speculate on how grateful the woman might be for a boatload of free sports equipment. What was between Eric Cameron and Miranda Manzelrod was *their* business. Determinedly, she headed for the driver's seat.

Then let's not keep her waiting any longer, shall we?" Good grief. Was that *peevishness* in her voice?

"Uh, Emily, hold up a minute." Eric rounded the hood of her car, looking concerned. "We packed the balls pretty high."

She looked into the back of the Suburban and realized she wouldn't be able to see a thing in her rear view mirror. Great. Just what she needed to fuel her traffic anxieties.

"Why don't you let me drive? In fact, why don't you and Robbie take my car home? I'll call Miranda and deliver the goods, then swing by your place later to switch cars."

Emily stood there, not knowing what to say. If she declined driving his car, she'd be stuck delivering the balls with him. She didn't really care to witness the tall blonde's gratitude at receiving such a generous gift. But if she drove his car...

"You don't know where I live."

"Is your address on your check?"

"Sure, but—"

Eric smiled, and she lost her train of thought. "I'll just get the city map out of my glove compartment and we'll be all set."

Emily stood there, unable to think of any kind of reasonable argument. What she wouldn't give to have that kind of warm, easy smile and instant confidence. Looking up at him, she recalled the moment in the ice rink when he'd told her, "You can handle anything." No way was she going to let him in on her traffic anxieties after that. She'd bet Miranda Manzelrod wouldn't have any trouble driving his car.

She looked over at it. It was so dark, so sleek, so shiny, so...so small. She swallowed, hard. Maybe it wouldn't be so bad. It was Sunday afternoon. Traffic would be light.

Besides, it was only for a few minutes. Less than thirty.

She'd be all right. She had to be.

She took a deep breath, then exhaled slowly. "Sure," she said, her smile determined. "Give me the keys."

Chapter Eight

Feeling as if he'd just scored a particularly sweet goal, Eric watched his car glide out of sight, then pumped his arm in victory.

"*Yes!*"

He reached into his hip pocket, pulled out Emily's check, unfolded it and broke into a wide grin.

Hot damn. He had her address *and* her phone number.

Eric couldn't believe his luck. In less than two hours, he'd be knocking on Dr. Emily Jordan's front door. All he had to do was run by Bill and Miranda's, pick up a key to the school, unload the stuff, then motor on over to Emily's.

Still grinning, he climbed behind the wheel of her Suburban, slid the seat back and fired up the engine. Cautiously he clunked through the industrial park, trying to be as careful as he'd noticed Emily being—with both her car on the way in and his on the way out—to avoid as many potholes as he could. He had to admit it had been a heck of a lot easier to maneuver his Boxter through the sea of craters than he was managing to move Emily's tank through them. But he seemed to be doing all right.

Suddenly he picked up Emily's scent. He looked around and spied a small clear bottle of perfume wedged into the crease of the seat beside him. He fished it out and glanced at the label.

White Linen. He'd never heard of it, but it sounded like something Emily would wear. Clean and classy.

He smiled, remembering how she'd blushed bright red when he'd caught her checking him out. She'd touched him in so many ways that afternoon, each of them more precious than the next. Emily, looking to him for reassurance. Emily, her brow furrowed in concentration as she learned how to skate. Emily, her eyes full of excitement as she mastered her balance. Emily, on fire with the spark of an idea.

Emily, her big green eyes glistening with motherlove.

Emily, finally noticing him as a man.

The memory of it jolted him all over again. His smile broadened as he hit the gas. He couldn't wait to see her again.

Suddenly the Suburban dropped into a pothole the size of Canada. Swearing sharply, Eric unsuccessfully swerved to avoid a second huge hole, then a third, only to hear the gut-wrenching sound of tearing metal. Blindly he hit the brakes, but as the vehicle rocked to a lopsided halt he knew it was too late. He'd lost his focus, and now he'd messed up Emily's car.

With a sick, sinking feeling, he got out to assess the damage.

Sonofabitch. He'd ripped a big hole in the exhaust system.

****

By nine o'clock, Emily didn't know whether to call the police, the hospitals, Miranda Manzelrod or a therapist. For the dozenth time since Robbie had gone to bed, after stalling for all he was worth in the hopes of seeing Eric again, she peered past her living room drapes, hoping to see her Suburban pulling into her driveway. But all she saw was Eric Cameron's black Porsche, gleaming darkly in the glow of her gaslight.

Where was he? Why hadn't he called? Her mind was hip-deep in imagining increasingly catastrophic scenarios when the telephone startled her. She almost tripped in her hurry to answer it.

"Emily?"

Her heart took flight. "Eric? Are you all right?"

"Uh, yeah. But I'm afraid I have some bad news for you."

"Is my car all right?"

"Your car? Uh, sure...Nothing to worry about."

"And you're okay?"

"Yes. Yes, I'm fine, too."

Emily frowned. He didn't sound fine. He sounded uncomfortable. Exhausted. Almost...*guilty?* "Then what's wrong? Why aren't you here?"

68

"That's the problem. Believe me, I wish I *was* there, but...well, I ran into some trouble with...with delivering the equipment...and..."

"Eric?" Emily heard Miranda Manzelrod's voice in the background. "Oh, there you are. What are you doing hiding in the bedroom? Oh, I'm sorry. I didn't realize you were on the phone."

"It's all right," Eric said. "I'll only be a minute."

"Dinner's almost ready."

"Thanks. I'll be right down."

"You were saying?" Emily prompted—and quite politely, she thought, considering. No wonder he sounded so uncomfortable and exhausted. Poor things. They hadn't even had time for dinner.

"Right. Yeah." Eric seemed to have trouble coming up with complete sentences for her. He sighed wearily and she thought she heard the sound of a chair creaking, or maybe a bed. "I uh, hope you don't mind, but I won't be able to get over there tonight."

Emily's voice dropped several degrees. "I see."

"I'm sorry, Emily."

Trouble with the equipment indeed. "When are you bringing my car back?"

He hesitated, then exhaled sharply. "Tomorrow night, around six, if that's okay with you."

Emily said nothing, furious.

"You're welcome to drive my car to work."

"I need my car, Eric." Driving his hadn't been nearly as unpleasant an experience as she'd thought it would be, but that didn't mean she cared to repeat it.

"I know, but I can't bring it back tonight. Seriously. I'm really sorry to put you out like this, but—"

"You're kidding, right?"

"No, I'm not. I won't be able to get it back to you before tomorrow evening."

"And why not?"

"Because...because I have some things I need to take care of, first."

Like having dinner with Miranda Manzelrod? She wouldn't say it. She wouldn't humiliate herself that way. "Fine, then. I'll see you tomorrow."

"Wait. You might need my number if something

comes up."

"Doesn't Robbie have it?"

"Oh, right. I forgot about that. Um..." He paused, seemed to be considering something. Emily waited, letting him stew. "Well, I'd better get going," he finally said. "Miranda's got supper waiting."

Emily stared at the receiver, incredulous. Did the man *intend* to rub her nose in it, or was he simply clueless?

"I'll see you tomorrow, okay?"

Over my dead body, Emily wanted to say. "Fine."

"And Emily?"

What now? "What?" she snapped.

"I'm really sorry about this."

****

"She's pissed."

"Oh, so that was *Emily* you were talking to." Miranda smiled and pulled a pork roast out of the oven. She set it on the stove as her husband, Bill Saunders, emerged from the wine cellar, bottle in hand. Given the two men's erratic work schedule, late evening meals were nothing unusual in the Saunders household.

Miranda scooped mashed potatoes into a bowl. "Which is she more upset about—your waiting so long to call her, or her car?"

"I didn't tell her about the Suburban."

Miranda paused in mid-movement. "Why not?"

"I just couldn't, Miranda, okay? I mean, the woman was nice enough to loan me her car, and I tore it up."

"So what did you tell her?"

"That I got tied up here, and I'd bring it back tomorrow evening. By then I ought to have found someone who can replace the exhaust system for me."

Miranda set the bowl of potatoes down slowly. "Eric? Do you realize what she's probably thinking right now?"

"Yeah, that I'm a jerk."

"More than that, *Mr.* Cameron. She probably thinks you're sleeping with me."

****

Furious, Emily flipped off her front porch light. Eric Cameron wouldn't be stopping by tonight...or any other night if she could help it. Tomorrow she'd call the creep

70

and tell him to meet her in the hospital parking lot after work to exchange cars. She didn't want him anywhere near her home. Anywhere near her.

Better yet, maybe she'd just leave the keys for him to pick up at the front desk, and ask him to do the same.

"Jerk," she muttered, returning to the kitchen to collect the tax forms that littered the kitchen table and stuff them into an accordion file folder labeled "The Jordan Foundation." She'd have to get her tax information ready for her accountant some other night. Her concentration was shot for tonight.

The phone rang as she snapped the elastic band around the accordion folder. She checked her caller ID. She didn't recognize the number so she let the answering machine take it.

"Emily. It's Eric. I think we need to talk. We may have gotten our wires crossed and...oh, hell. I'll call back later."

It was all the notice she needed. Robbie was home and she wasn't on call. The answering machine could handle her calls for the night. She flipped the switch to silence the telephone's ringer. Upstairs, she silenced her bedroom extension. Her day was over. Emily Jordan was going to bed.

Half an hour later, she emerged from a hot shower feeling exhausted, but once again somewhat in control of her life. She hit the bed, and within minutes was sound asleep.

It was nearly noon before Emily worked up the nerve to call Eric and tell him she'd prefer that he drop her car off and pick his up at the hospital. She wasn't keen on getting an earful about not answering her phone, especially since Eric's third and last message had been quite blunt.

Damn it, Emily. Where the hell are you?

Rather than bother Robbie for the number, she'd taken it off of her caller ID. As she dialed it now, she reminded herself she didn't owe Eric Cameron any apologies or explanations. She wasn't the one who had disappeared with a car that wasn't hers.

She frowned as Miranda Manzelrod's voice told her they were sorry they couldn't come to the phone right now, but—

Emily slammed down the receiver, feeling as if she'd been slapped with a wet towel. He'd spent the night at another woman's house and had the nerve to ask her where *she'd* been?

Her day nose-dived after that. By the three o'clock staff meeting she could hardly move. Her skating muscles were letting her know how much they resented having been pressed into service. By the time she limped to Eric's Porsche at four-thirty, half an hour late, she had a throbbing headache and was ready to catch a plane to the nearest deserted island.

An hour later, Anna Hamilton Caldwell, Robbie's regular sitter and Emily's savior on earth, was still clucking about Emily's inability to do justice to her chicken cacciatore. Meanwhile Robbie was upstairs trashing his room, collecting materials for the science project he was doing with Glen Simms. Anna had volunteered to drop Robbie off at Glen's on her way to meet Augustus for dinner. Emily hoped they'd be gone by the time Eric arrived, so she could tell him what she thought of him without an audience.

"Mom, do you know where my scissors are?"

Emily sighed and went upstairs. She'd just bundled Robbie up against the February cold and kissed him goodbye when Eric pulled into the driveway, fifteen minutes early. So much for a private conversation. She snatched her parka from the hall closet and followed Robbie and Anna into the moonlit yard.

Eric grinned at the unexpected welcoming committee that tumbled out of the brightly lit two-story house, and rounded the hood of the Suburban to meet them on the sidewalk. "Going somewhere, Sport?"

Robbie held up a Dayton's shopping bag full of cardboard, string, construction paper and aluminum foil. "Me and Glen are going to work on our science project. We're making a rocket ship."

Eric pulled out an empty paper towel roll and examined it under the gaslight's glow. "These for the boosters?"

Robbie nodded vigorously. "And then we have to present it to the whole class."

72

Eric grinned and returned the cardboard roll to the bag. "Good for you. I can't wait to see it, myself." He offered a hand to Anna. "You must be Nanna."

She smiled. "It's Anna, unless you're eight years old and I've been taking care of you since before you were born."

Eric laughed, liking her immediately. "Robbie's spoken of you often. I'm pleased to meet you, Anna."

"The feeling's mutual, Mr. Cameron."

"Please, call me Eric." He turned to Emily, who stood apart from the group, hands deep in her parka pockets. She looked like she'd had another rough day at the hospital. He wished he had time to ask her about it. Instead he offered an empathetic smile. "Hi."

"Hi." Her voice held all the warmth of an outdoor ice rink at dawn. Eric braced himself. Miranda had most likely been right about Emily thinking he had something cooking with Miranda. Why else would Emily have chosen to ignore his calls last night?

Anna stepped into the chill between them. "We'd better get going, Robbie, or Glen will wonder if you're coming." She smiled at Eric again. "Good luck against Toronto tonight."

"Will you be at the game?"

"Wouldn't miss it. We've got season tickets in the lower gold section, right behind the penalty box."

"I'll look for you."

"Hopefully not from inside the box," she teased.

"I'll second that."

Acutely aware that Emily stood behind him in frozen silence, Eric watched Anna hustle Robbie across the street and into a late model Cadillac parked two doors down. He returned their waves as they drove by, and mulled over the irony of Emily's sitter driving a Caddy while Emily drove a clunker, and a behemoth at that. He turned and found her watching the Caddy's taillights disappear, a softness in her features that hadn't been there earlier.

"She seems like a very special woman."

"She is."

Craving her nearness, he stepped closer. "She's been taking care of Robbie since before he was born?"

"Yes."

The crisp night air sharpened his awareness of her subtle scent. White Linen. He smiled and thought of the tiny bottle on his nightstand. "It sounds like an interesting story."

She glanced at him, her expression flat. "Trust me. It isn't."

"I'd like to hear it sometime, anyway."

"I don't think so, Eric. Here." She held out his keys.

Here? That was it? She wasn't even going to *ask* him about Miranda, or why he'd taken so long to return her car? So she was back to condemning him out of hand. Great. He took the keys from her and inclined his head toward the Porsche. "Any problems with it?" She must have parked it on the street to keep the driveway open for the Suburban. When he'd cruised by in Bill's truck at midnight, his Boxter had been nestled close to the house.

Her smile was rueful. "No, it drove like a dream."

"It ought to, after what I just spent on repairs."

"Don't remind me. Most of my tax refund is going toward making sure that one lasts a little longer."

He looked at the Suburban, then at Emily. "Why do you need such a big car, Emily?"

She looked at him, not answering. Finally she said, "I just do."

Okay. So the subject was off limits. But since her finances were apparently on the tight side—she was probably still paying off her medical school loans—he decided not to mention the new exhaust system, or that he'd had the mechanic fix anything else on the Suburban that looked like it was about to break. Between that and the tune-up, Emily's Subway should last at least another six months before she'd need to dip into that tax refund.

He returned his gaze to the Suburban and congratulated himself on his restraint. He'd wanted to get her new tires, but knew that would be a dead giveaway. He hoped she wasn't the kind of woman who paid attention to what was under the hood of her car. Or the chassis. Good thing it was dark out or she might've spotted the new tailpipe. In a day or two the city's soot and slush would take care of that.

"Why wouldn't you answer the phone last night?" he

asked.

Again, she said nothing at first, then offered a deliberate, "I was sleeping."

He looked over at her, to find her eyes clear and steady. "Do you usually ignore the telephone when you're in bed?"

"When I'm sleeping, yes."

"What if the hospital calls?"

"I have a pager. If the hospital calls, I call them back."

Her deliberate coolness irritated him. That, and the fact that they were having this inane conversation in frigid darkness, when they could be inside, warm and cozy. Eric marshaled his patience and tried again. "Do they call often?"

"Often enough."

She'd closed up tighter than a manager negotiating a trade. He cut to the chase. "What happened last night, Emily?"

Her cool slipped into incredulity. "You're asking *me*?"

"Of course I'm asking you! You're the one who wouldn't answer the phone!"

Again she said nothing, and he realized she wouldn't. There were times when her stubbornness made him want to bang his head in frustration. "Emily?" he asked with quiet deliberation, "Is it possible you're jealous?"

"Of course not! What's between you and Dr. Manzelrod is your business."

Eric grinned. He was on to her now. "Then what's bothering you?"

Her mouth opened twice before she spoke. "I expected you to return my car sooner, that's all." She held out a palm, her emotions once again in check. "Now, may I have my keys?"

"I'll trade you. The keys for a cup of coffee. Inside."

"Forget it."

"Why? Are you afraid to be alone with me?"

"Don't you have a game to go to?"

He nodded and moved closer, watching her eyes darken as he did. "I have to be at the arena, suited up, in less than an hour. Which means I've got ten minutes, max, before I have to make tracks. Ten minutes, Emily.

What could happen in ten minutes?"

She met his gaze for the longest moment, her own quietly searching, then closed her eyes and sighed, as if exhausted. "Would you just leave, Eric? Take your car and go? Please?"

He saw what it cost her to say please, and didn't like the way it made him feel. But more was at stake here than transitory feelings. Something was happening between them. Something he wasn't about to ignore—and he wasn't about to let her ignore it either.

"After I kiss you."

She stepped back as if he were going to steal one right there in the driveway. "No."

"This isn't an impulse, Emily," he said, forcing himself to stay put when his instincts led him to follow her. It's something I've thought about almost constantly since we met. To be honest, I want to do a lot more than just kiss you, but—"

Shaking her head, she backed up another step and lifted a hand. "No."

Before she could turn away, Eric slowly, deliberately and carefully stepped forward. Just as carefully he reached up and gently wrapped his fingers around her upheld hand. He wanted her to see him coming. If she resisted at all, he'd release her and leave immediately.

His heart thudded hard as she went perfectly still.

Slowly, he drew her hand to his chest. "As I was saying, I'd like to do a whole lot more than kiss you, but it's kind of hard to make love to a woman who's always pushing you away."

She looked up at him, clearly confused. Eric took heart. Confusion beat rejection any day of the week. "Please don't push me away any more, Emily. I won't hurt you. I swear it." He splayed her palm across his heart, pounding inside his open jacket. "Can't you feel what you do to me?"

"Eric, no," she whispered, but this time it was almost a plea. "I can't."

"Of course you can. You can do anything you put your mind to."

"Not this time," she said.

He ventured a small smile. "Does that mean you're a

76

little bit interested?"

"Eric, you wouldn't understand."

"Try me."

"I can't." She stepped back and broke the connection.

"Okay," he said, mentally scrambling for the rebound. "No kiss, but how about a peek inside? I really don't have time for anything more, Emily."

She looked bewildered by his request. "Why?"

"I'm curious about you. Fascinated by you is more like it."

Slowly, she shook her head. His hopes sank. "There's not that much to see, Eric. We live a very ordinary life."

"That's part of the fascination."

Emily just looked at him. She didn't know what else to do. She'd never known a man like Eric Cameron. Her protests and rejections didn't seem to faze him at all. And when he pressed her, it was with the caution of one approaching a startled animal. He seemed to have some sort of instinct that told him what she needed from him. The idea fascinated her as much as he claimed to be fascinated by her. How did he get to be so sensitive to a woman's needs?

"All right then," she said slowly, not at all sure she was doing the right thing. "I'll give you the five-minute tour."

He smiled, and she could tell it was genuine. "Thank you."

They entered the house and she moved to the right. "The living room," she said, waving an arm to encompass her comfortable green couch, coffee table, pair of matching chairs, ancient console television and the piano on the far wall. Looking it over, she was grateful for Anna's penchant for good housekeeping. She took off her parka and hung it in the hall closet while Eric crossed the room to stand in front of the piano. His hands in his black leather jacket pockets, he studied the pewter-framed photos on top of the old upright. Lined up like trophies were pictures of Robbie in first, second and third grades.

"That's me, graduating from med school," she said, coming to stand beside him. "And that's two months later, when Robbie was born. That one was in front of Anna's house in St. Paul," she said of a shot of Robbie as a toddler playing with building blocks on the porch of a huge Victorian.

"You're very photogenic," Eric said quietly.

"Thank you."

"Do you play?"

"Anna does. The piano is hers."

"Why doesn't she keep it at her house?"

"She already has one there. This one was hers before she remarried. She enjoys playing while she waits for Robbie to come home from school."

Eric smiled and moved past her to her dark oak dining room, where he silently studied her floral watercolors, her Blue Willow china, and discovered she collected small silver crystal animals.

Running a lazy fingertip across her ivory lace tablecloth, he preceded her into the kitchen.

He smiled again. "Somehow I knew it would look like this—warm, cozy, cluttered in a really good way," he said, taking in her short trestle table and four chairs with hearts cut into the backs of them.

"You like clutter?"

Still smiling, he peered into a cow-shaped cookie jar. "I like feeling like I'm in a home where people who love each other live."

Emily went warm all over. She smiled, feeling more relaxed in his company than she would've thought possible. Amazingly, there was something about the sight of Eric Cameron poking around in her kitchen that felt right. Natural. Comfortable, even.

"Help yourself," she said, wishing she had that cup of coffee he'd wanted brewing, and a piece of her deep dish apple pie to offer him with it.

He withdrew two ginger snaps and munched on them as he studied Robbie's artwork on the refrigerator, her monthly calendar and the mishmash of photos, notes and lists tacked to the bulletin board by the phone. Coming to stand beside her, he looked out the multi-paned window over the sink. It was dark out now, but during the day she had a bird's eye view of her shed, and Robbie's swing set and sandbox, both long since outgrown. She supposed she should sell the swing set. It wasn't likely she'd be having any more children. The thought brought a stab of regret, but she dismissed it. She'd made her choices.

Besides, with the Foundation to support, she had enough on her plate as it was.

"Yeah, I like it," Eric said. "I like it a lot." He turned to her and smiled. "Robbie's very lucky."

The nostalgic note in his voice made her wonder where he'd grown up, what his life had been like before he'd become a star athlete. He'd denied it that night in the ER, but surely he had family *somewhere*.

The grandfather clock in the hall chimed six-fifteen. Emily looked at the kitchen clock in surprise. Eric had been in the house for over twenty minutes. "You're going to be late."

"I know." His eyes captured hers. "Walk me to the door?"

She swallowed, knowing what he was asking. "Sure."

But at the front door, she paused, suddenly unsure. What would happen now? Would he say goodbye and mean it this time? She doubted it. And how did she really feel about that?

"Thanks for letting me inside," Eric said quietly. "I know it wasn't easy for you."

"Easier than I expected it to be," she said wryly.

His eyes darkened to brown velvet. "I'm glad."

Their eyes locked and he slowly lowered his head. Heart hammering, Emily went perfectly still. But when his lips touched hers, everything faded away but the moment. And in that moment, Emily Jordan tasted heaven for the very first time.

Never had she been kissed with such quiet reverence or sensual finesse. Never. After a brief first kiss that barely brushed her lips, Eric kissed each corner of her mouth with whisper softness, then returned to press his lips to hers again in a kiss that made every part of her yearn for more.

He pulled away just as she swayed forward, catching her gently by the upper arms. He looked into her eyes for a long moment, then sent her a slow, sexy smile, a smile filled with a delicious sense of warmth and promise.

"See you soon," he said and released her.

Emily nodded, too dazed to speak. Her headache was gone. Her muscles no longer ached. Every ounce of her earlier tension had evaporated. She felt warm and fuzzy all over, as if she were floating. Eric opened the front door and loped across the lawn.

"Eric, wait!" she called when he was halfway to his car.

He turned, a distracted look on his moonlit face.

"My keys."

He pointed to the Suburban. "In the ignition."

Chapter Nine

Emily didn't see Eric again until Friday, but when she did, she spotted him right away. It didn't take much longer for the other parents in the rink to do the same. Within seconds of his arrival, she heard his name being tossed like a beach ball among the chilled spectators in the bleachers.

His hands tucked into the pockets of his black leather jacket, he stood near the rink's front entrance, a light dusting of snow on his shoulders. Seeming oblivious to the wave of excited whispers that rippled through the stands behind him, he studied the Mites game in progress, one Red Wings player in particular. It wasn't until Robbie returned to the bench after his shift on the ice that Eric turned to scan the stands.

Emily's pulse fluttered and she suddenly felt ten degrees warmer as he smiled and started toward her. A grinning elderly couple in matching Minneapolis Saints jerseys intercepted him. As the man pumped Eric's hand, Emily recovered from her surprise and smiled. In the last five days, Eric had played three games, two of them in Detroit and Toronto, and had gotten at least one goal or assist in each. Much to her son's delight, Emily had taken to reading the sports page. She'd even let him stay up to watch one of the games. They'd spilled popcorn all over her bed when Eric had scored the winning goal in overtime.

A young couple joined Eric, then a group of teenage boys, then a family of four. Emily divided the next fifteen minutes between corralling her own excitement at seeing Eric again, monitoring his snail-like progress toward her between handshakes and autographs, and watching Robbie's shifts on the ice. By the time Eric reached her, his smile looked a little thin.

81

"Sorry I'm late." He eased onto the bench beside her.

"Late? I didn't expect you at all."

He sent her a chiding look. "I couldn't miss Robbie's first game."

"How did you know—?"

He held up a hand and nodded at the rink, where Robbie had stepped onto the ice. Emily capped her curiosity, realizing he'd missed a good portion of the game while he catered to his fans. When Robbie's shift was over, she glanced back at Eric to find him still immersed in the game, his face impassive, his eyes not missing a trick. God help the fan who climbed into the bleachers to make his acquaintance now, she thought. Clearly no one, but no one, came between Eric Cameron and his sport.

During the next stoppage in play, he said, "I read the date on your calendar. The one from your insurance agent."

She smiled as she recalled the image of Eric poking around in her kitchen, studying the calendar next to the phone. The memory had kept her company as she'd muddled through the Foundation's finances at the kitchen table, all the while hoping he would call.

But he hadn't. Her smile faded. So why was he here?

"I've missed you," he said.

"I...imagine you've been busy."

"Not too busy to remember how wonderful you taste."

Emily flushed. A horn blared. One of the teams had scored. Unfortunately, it was the opposing team. For the rest of the game they focused on Robbie. Afterward, Eric joined Emily in the locker room with Robbie, much to the amazement of the other players and parents. As if he did it every day, Eric dropped to his haunches and began unlacing Robbie's skates.

"Great game, Sport," he said as Emily handed Robbie a bottle of water to drink.

Robbie's eyes, already bright with excitement, burned even brighter. "Did you really think so?"

"Especially the part where you almost got that goal. Not too shabby for your first game."

"Coach said I woulda had it, but I leaned back when I aimed."

"He's right, but even if you hadn't, you still might've

82

made it if you'd..." Eric described a move that locked in the attention of Robbie's closest teammates. As the room slowly fell silent, Emily couldn't tell who was more excited—the kids at listening to Eric Cameron speak up close and personal, or Eric at the opportunity to share his love of his sport with her son.

He finished unlacing Robbie's skates, pulled them off and stood—and noticed the silence in the room. "Oops."

"No, no, Mr. Cameron, please continue," Coach Parker said. "Please." The parents in the room heartily echoed the invitation.

"All right, then." Smiling, Eric slipped into the role of teacher, dispensing advice and encouragement to each player personally. His eye for detail and passion for the game shone through, and Emily thought it a shame he didn't have children of his own. Afterward, Coach Parker invited everyone to meet at Pizza King in half an hour to celebrate their victory. As the Red Wings bundled off with their families, all thanking Eric as they left, Emily helped Robbie reorganize his equipment, while Eric continued talking with the coach.

"Can we go to Pizza King, Mom? I'm starving."

She snapped his skate guards onto his blades and smiled. She suspected he'd say the same even if he wasn't. "I guess you are, with all that skating you did."

"I did good, didn't I?"

She zipped his hockey bag shut and set it aside, then bent to give him a big hug. "Sweetheart, you were wonderful."

"Aw, Mom."

"What?"

"People will see."

Sighing inwardly, Emily straightened. *And so it begins*, she thought with a maternal pang. Her little boy was growing up.

"Glen said I could ride with him and Marc and Joey."

"I think that's a great idea," Eric said from behind Emily. "That way your mom can ride with me."

Robbie's eyes went wide. "You're coming, too?"

"Yeah, but don't worry. We won't cramp your style. We'll sit in a corner and pretend we don't know you."

Robbie laughed in delight. "You guys."

****

The parking lot was deserted by the time they reached the Suburban. With mixed feelings at being alone with Eric, Emily opened the rear hatch door for him to load Robbie's equipment. They'd decided to take the Subway since they'd be bringing Robbie back with them. Rather, Eric had suggested it, making some cryptic remark about wanting to see how the car was running, anyhow.

Since it was only a five-minute drive, Emily had agreed. With her gloves, she dusted off the car's windows. A light snow had fallen, covering the cars, yet melting as it hit the ground.

Eric slammed the hatch door shut, jarring the night's stillness. "You want me to drive?"

"No, I'll be okay," Emily answered vaguely, and wondered not for the first time if Robbie had mentioned her driving phobia.

Eric draped an arm around her shoulders and nuzzled her neck. "Good. That way I won't have to keep my hands on the wheel."

She slipped away with a nervous laugh, not used to being cuddled by a man. Her father had never touched her, and Ryan had rarely been affectionate, touching her only when he wanted sex...or to inflict pain. She shuddered involuntarily, recalling how he'd used her need for simple human contact to his advantage.

"Emily?"

She looked over her shoulder as she unlocked the driver's door. "What?"

"Do I still frighten you?"

He did, but not in the way she suspected he meant. She was afraid of getting involved with him, of coming to care for him so much she forgot to keep her heart safe. "Of course not. I'm just anxious to get going before the others wonder what's keeping us."

He studied her for a long moment before apparently coming to a decision. Sighing, he leaned back against the side of the Suburban and held out an ungloved hand. "Come here." It wasn't an order. It wasn't even a request. It was more of a friendly, "C'mere, I want to show you something." When she hesitated, he wiggled his fingers.

84

"C'mon, Emily, I promise I won't bite."

She moved toward him uncertainly. He smiled his encouragement and drew her forward until she stood before him, their hands clasped, his back still against the side of the car. "I want you to kiss me, Emily."

The fire inside her rekindled.

He released her hands and held his up in surrender. "I'll even keep these behind my back if you want me to."

"Eric, this isn't necessary," she said in embarrassment.

"Oh, but it is. For whatever reason, it is, and tonight I'm playing by your rules. Now, where do you want my hands?"

Loaded, question, that. But she looked into his eyes and found them clear and direct. This wasn't a game to him. This wasn't teasing. This was real. "Behind *my* back," she whispered.

He opened his arms. She stepped forward and placed her hands on his chest. His cable knit sweater was soft beneath her palms, a sharp contrast to the hard strength it concealed. He spread his legs to accommodate her, then slid his hands around her down parka, linked them at the back of her waist and pulled her close.

"Perfect," he murmured.

"How so?" she asked uneasily, thankful the thickness of her coat prevented direct body contact.

He chuckled. "Because I've wanted to give you a hug for weeks, Emily Jordan. I don't think I've met anyone who deserved one more."

Wonder replaced wariness. She leaned back and looked into his dark eyes. "You're serious."

He tucked her head against his chest, settled his arms around her again and closed his eyes. "Dead serious."

For the longest time he simply held her. Security settled around Emily like a warm blanket. She could have stood there for hours, cocooned in his arms, listening to the steady beat of his heart beneath her ear, smelling the clean, musky scent of him mingled with the faint smell of leather and the crisp chill of winter. Only the idea of her son wondering aloud to a group of strangers what might've happened to them made her pull away.

Eric dropped his hands to his sides and smiled. "See? Told you I wouldn't bite." At her sheepish look, he grinned. "Now, how about that kiss?"

Emily smiled. "Something tells me your storehouse of slick moves isn't limited to those you use on the ice, *Mr.* Cameron."

He laughed, a deep, hearty, happy sound that made Emily want to join in. Instead she looped her arms around his neck and drew his head down to meet hers, taking him by surprise.

She kissed him six times, her hands moving to frame his face and brush back his chestnut brown hair after the second kiss. Each time, she studied his face first, fascinated by the restraint she saw in his features, his refusal to take control. Shamelessly she experimented, her last kiss a hedonistic freefall that left her breathless and weak-kneed.

"Enough," Eric moaned, sinking against the Suburban, keeping a steadying grip on Emily's elbows. For a long minute they stood there, heads bowed, breathing uneven. When she finally found the courage to look into his face, she found not the cool mockery she'd come to expect in the past...but tenderness and open delight.

And it terrified her.

She pulled away. Confusion flickered across Eric's features, but he let her go. In silence he opened the driver's door for her. She cast him a quick, embarrassed look as he as he shut the door behind her, then walked around the front of the car and climbed into the passenger seat. Once there, he smiled at her, but said nothing and waited patiently.

His message couldn't have been more clear. For the moment, Emily was in the driver's seat. He made no attempt to touch her once they were in the car and the disappointment of it rattled her so much she didn't say a word the whole two miles to Pizza King. *Good grief, woman. You push the man away, then feel hurt when he keeps his hands to himself. What is* wrong *with you?*

Eric made a point of it not to touch Emily again as she drove to Pizza King. But just before they reached the restaurant's door, he broke down and pulled Emily aside to kiss her again. She responded with an immediate, almost desperate sensuality that made his soul sing. The lady liked him, she just didn't know what to do about it.

A quick kiss to her temple, and he escorted her inside. Robbie spotted them and waved, then returned his attention to his friends. Since there were no unoccupied seats at the table, Eric ushered Emily to a booth in the far corner.

When the waitress arrived, he asked Emily if she wanted anything to eat or drink.

Emily asked for water, then turned to stare out the window. She looked a little dazed. Eric hid a smile. He felt much the same, but knew time would be his ally in winning over Emily Jordan. The woman kissed like an angel, but needed her space. The chatter of two dozen elementary schoolers filled the air as a minute passed, then two, before Emily dropped her gaze and made a show of rearranging the contents of the sugar bowl.

When it seemed to Eric the packets couldn't be lined up any straighter, he spoke up. "Can I ask you something?"

Emily looked over at her son and decided the odds of tearing him away from his teammates before the last slice of pizza was gone were slim to none. The chances that Eric would wait in silence until Robbie rejoined them were even slimmer.

She shrugged. "Shoot."

"Have you always wanted to be a doctor?"

Emily hid her surprise. She'd expected something more along the lines of, "So, what happens next?" Because something *had* happened between them in the parking lot, something that made her want to run as fast and as far away from Eric Cameron as possible. He was getting to her, sneaking past her defenses in a way no man had. She still couldn't believe how badly she wanted him to kiss her again, or how she'd thrown herself into his arms when he had.

Weakness, that's what it was. Pure weakness.

"Since I was seven or eight."

He smiled and she tried to relax. Robbie would ride back to the rink with them. She'd be all right as long as they weren't alone again. As long as he didn't touch her again.

"Somehow that doesn't surprise me," Eric said. "I'll bet you were a straight A student."

Considering the countless hours she'd spent at the library, hiding from her father's wrath, then Ryan's, it was no wonder. But she didn't care to go there. With anyone. "All the way through med school."

Eric's smile dimmed. He looked down at his plastic cup, twisted it idly, and studied its ripples and ridges before meeting her eyes again. "I never finished high school, myself."

At the unexpected note of insecurity in his voice, Emily forgot her own problems. Experience had taught her diplomas didn't confer intelligence on their owners. The thought that Eric might think less of himself because he didn't have one was too compelling to ignore.

She smiled. "I suspect it was because your priorities were elsewhere at the time."

His eyes registered surprise before he chuckled. "You're right. The only thing on my mind those days was playing hockey, morning, noon and night."

"I'd say your determination paid off."

He looked out the window, his expression suddenly oblique. "Maybe, maybe not."

Emily let the silence ride, keeping her distance.

"Do you ever wonder what your life might have been like if you hadn't made the choices you did?" Eric asked.

"No." She didn't have to wonder. She'd either be living under the thumb of her tyrannical father or in terror of her homicidal husband. School had been her avenue of escape in both cases. But she hadn't forgotten the loved ones she left behind. If it was the last thing she did, she'd see to it that her younger siblings found the same freedom and independence she had.

"No regrets? No second thoughts?"

"Not a one."

"Not even about Robbie's father?"

"Especially not about that."

His eyes held hers. "Were you married to him?"

"For three years."

He sat back, looking baffled. "What happened?"

"Excuse me?" Was he implying she was some sort of

failure?

"I'm just trying to understand. You're a beautiful, intelligent, caring, compassionate, and very passionate woman. One any man in his right mind would do his best to hold onto. Instead, you're raising his child alone." His eyes softened. "Did he hurt you, Emily? Did he decide one day fatherhood wasn't for him and disappear?"

She couldn't stand the thought of him pitying her. "He doesn't know about Robbie. I'm the one who disappeared."

Eric stared. "You left him? Knowing you were pregnant? Without telling him?"

Too late, she realized her mistake. "He...didn't want me to become a doctor." That much, at least, was true. Ryan had tried to sabotage her every chance he got, tried to force her to flunk out. But the truth was he would have tried to force her into getting an abortion if he'd known she was pregnant. Or worse, killed the baby inside her himself. Ryan Montgomery had no room in his life for anyone but Ryan Montgomery.

"So you deprived him of his child because he didn't want you to have a career?"

She knew how cold that sounded. Especially to a man who wanted children but didn't have any. But Emily wasn't prepared to unveil the horrors of her marriage. She doubted she ever would be.

"Yes," she answered quietly.

Eric's eyes darkened with disappointment...and anger. "I see. And since then you've decided not to let *any* man get close enough to interfere with your career."

If she wanted to drive him away, it was as good an opportunity as any. His quickness to judge cut deep, as deep as his quickness to believe she could be so self-centered as to consider her career more important than her marriage vows. Never mind that she'd been as quick to judge him in the beginning. This was different. They knew each other better, now. And that was the problem.

Catching the sound of a commotion across the room, she glanced at Robbie's table to see the group breaking up. She took a final drink of her soda, then met Eric's gaze.

"Exactly."

Chapter Ten

"Do you think he'll come tonight, Mom?"

"Who, sweetheart?" Emily asked absently as she dragged the hockey bag containing Robbie's uniform, pads, gloves, skates and helmet from the back of the Suburban. Her mind was still at the hospital, where she'd spent most of the past twenty-four hours. She'd barely made it home in time to collect her son and drive him to the rink for his game. As it was, they were running late.

"You know, Eric."

She paused, recalling the quiet finality of their parting in the Pizza King parking lot two weeks earlier. He'd chosen to walk back to the rink, leaving her feeling cold and empty.

"I doubt it, sweetheart." She handed Robbie his stick.

"I thought he liked us."

Emily slung the hockey bag over her shoulder and straightened, then bumped the door shut with her free hip. "I'm sure he does, honey," she prevaricated, "But that doesn't mean he doesn't have other plans."

"Like what? He doesn't have a game, like last week."

The strap dug into her shoulder and she shifted the bag, thankful Robbie wasn't playing goalie. Twenty-two pieces of equipment was enough, thank you. "He's still a very busy man."

"Like you?"

Emily went still and looked into her son's innocent eyes, and felt guilty for having spent the night at the hospital. But two of the other staff doctors were out with the flu, and Augustus had needed someone to pull a double. The good news was she'd have the rest of the weekend off to recuperate.

"Like me." She sent him a conspiratorial smile. "But not tomorrow. Tomorrow it's just you and me, kid. So

90

what do you say we—" Emily broke off as Eric strode out of the building, clearly scanning the parking lot for someone.

"There he is! Hi, Eric!"

"Hi, Sport. How come you're late?" Emily barely had time to recover from her surprise before Eric deftly slid the hockey bag from her shoulder and handed it to her son. "Did you have car trouble?"

"Nah. Mom had to work late."

Eric's gaze met Emily's. Clearly he hadn't forgotten their conversation at Pizza King. "I see. Well, I'm glad that's all it was." He ruffled Robbie's hair. "Better get inside, Sport, let Coach know you're here. I'll be in to help you in a minute."

Robbie didn't argue. The idea of Eric Cameron dressing him was way cooler than having Mom do it.

"You staying for the game?" Eric asked, as Robbie raced toward the rink, all but dragging his hockey bag behind him.

"Of course."

"I thought you might be headed back to work." His gaze swept over her, taking in the scrub pants peeking from beneath her winter coat and her splotched white shoes. She looked a mess and knew it, but hadn't been able to spare the time to change.

Piqued pride made her say, "I just might, now that you've obviously got things under control here."

He looked at her, sighed. "We need to talk."

"There's nothing to talk about."

"You're wrong. We—"

"There is no *we*, Eric, and I don't have the time or energy to argue with you today, so please, just let it go." Determinedly, she started for the rink.

"This conversation isn't over, Dr. Jordan."

The icy authority in his voice stopped her cold. Slowly, she turned. "Excuse me?"

"I don't appreciate your walking away from me like I'm invisible. It might work with your patients, but not me."

With an effort, Emily corralled her rising temper. "All right. Want do you want to talk about?"

"For starters, I'd like to know what you *do* have the

time and energy for. In case nothing comes to mind right away, I've come up with a list."

"I don't think I want to hear this."

"Tough. Because I find it hard to believe your life is so full that you can't take time out for (A) a casual dinner date, (B) a walk in the park, or (C) some quiet conversation with a man who finds you interesting and attractive." He paused and met her eyes, his voice silk over steel. "A man who might be able to take your mind off your troubles for a few hours."

It was tempting, oh so tempting. But try as she might, Emily couldn't get past the idea that the troubles Eric could take her mind off of would pale in comparison to the troubles he could cause her.

"I'm not asking you to marry me, Emily. Just for a date."

She wavered. The truth was she'd missed him, and had spent several restless nights trying to come to terms with the feelings he brought out in her. Her Ice Queen act at Pizza King had been a knee-jerk reaction to something she didn't understand. She still didn't understand it, but at least she now recognized it for what it was—a strong physical attraction to a man who, at best, would only bring her heartache.

"I'm not going to drop this, Emily." He stepped closer, touched her hair, her cheek. Her insides quickened, started to soften. Just like that. "We've got a chance of making something good happen between us. The chemistry is there. You know it is. The rest will take care of itself if you'll just..."

Emily didn't hear the rest of what he said. She'd heard it before. Ryan had played on her emotions in much the same way, using disarming smiles and soft, sweet words to gain concessions. First small ones, then increasingly bigger ones, until she'd all but lost herself completely.

The idea that Eric would try to lead her down the same destructive path snapped her from her silence.

"No."

He looked startled, then annoyed. "Emily—"

"My life is fine just the way it is, Eric. I don't need you mucking it up with your ideas about—"

"Mucking it up? Oh, for the love of—how can I muck up something that doesn't exist?"

She forgot what she'd been about to say. "What?"

"You don't have a life, Emily, you have a son and a job."

Stung, she lashed out. "Well, that's certainly more than you have."

He looked as if she'd stabbed him with a scalpel. Watching the heat rise in his face, Emily realized she'd made a mistake. A big one. She'd forgotten about Eric's explosive temper. A ripple of fear snaked down her spine as the memory returned full force.

Eric's jaw tightened. His fingers flexed at his sides. Another image of Ryan flashed across her mind—this one of him belting her for supposedly talking back to him. Warily, she stepped back. Eric's eyes jerked to hers. The emotion in them was so dark Emily couldn't suppress her shiver of dread.

"You're right," he said. "All I've got is a job."

With that, he brushed past her and strode into the rink, where he yanked open the door so hard Emily flinched, fully expecting it to hit the wall. But it didn't. He hadn't let himself go that far. Heart pounding, she watched it jerkily swing shut behind him, and—with no small amount of relief and surprise—realized she was safe. Unharmed. The fury had been there, in his hands and eyes and voice, but Eric hadn't made any attempt to vent it on *her*.

For a long moment she simply stood there, trying to assimilate what had just happened. When she finally entered the ice arena, still feeling disoriented, Eric was nowhere in sight.

Unsure whether to feel relieved or disappointed, Emily looked around again, trying to get her bearings. Everything was the same, yet suddenly it all felt different...as if she were seeing things in clear focus for the first time. The squeals and shouts that echoed across the rink, the scarred and pitted ice, the smell of grease from the snack bar, the dedicated parents huddled against the cold in the dimly lit stands.

Eric must have taken his first steps toward becoming a professional hockey player in some cold, dark and drafty place like this. She shivered at the thought and climbed into the stands. Hands jammed into her coat pockets for warmth, she stared at her still shaky knees and again tried to figure out what had just happened. If it hadn't been for Robbie—

Robbie. She hadn't gone into the locker room to help him dress. That must be where Eric was. Lord, how could she have let that totally slip her mind? Robbie couldn't get all his padding and equipment on by himself, and she'd forgotten all about him.

Damn it. She needed to think. Needed to go somewhere warm and quiet to sort things out in her mind—but she couldn't leave now. The game would start any second.

As if on cue, Robbie and his teammates spilled onto the ice in a blur of red and white. Emily spotted Eric standing by the locker room door, watching her, and knew she owed him yet another debt of gratitude. His impassive expression let her know the next move was up to her, but at the moment, she had no idea as to what that move should be. More confused than ever, she looked away, to where Robbie had skated into position for the opening face-off.

When she looked back at Eric, he was gone.

****

The following evening, as a blinding March snowstorm blanketed the Twin Cities, Emily puttered in her kitchen, making advance preparations for Sunday's dinner with Anna and Augustus and their four teenage daughters. She was mixing a salad for herself for tonight when the doorbell rang.

Her heart did a strange somersault as she recognized Eric standing on her porch, his parka collar turned up against the wind and hands in his pockets. His tall, bulky frame created an imposing silhouette against the curtain of white that billowed across her yard. He turned and stamped the snow off his boots as she opened the door. For several seconds they stared at each other, neither seeming to notice the frigid wind whipping around them.

"Got a few minutes?" he asked quietly.

She stepped back in silence. Folding her arms to fight the icy chill that entered the house with him, she wondered what he wanted this time. Instead of asking, though, she waited, wearing what she hoped was a neutral smile. In truth her heart was jackhammering against her ribs and she felt a nearly overwhelming urge to blurt out a litany of apologies for the things she'd said the night before.

He was staring at her again, her hair in particular. She stifled the urge to reach up and smooth what had to be a riot of curls. Wet curls. "You wanted to talk to me about something?"

"Your hair. What did you do to it?"

"Nothing. This is how it always looks after I wash it."

"You mean those curls are natural?" Emily stilled as he captured a long, curly auburn tendril between his fingers and studied it in the soft light that filtered down the hallway from the kitchen. "Why do you hide them?"

The sudden intimacy between them flooded her with heat. "I don't hide them, I manage them." Eric frowned, clearly confused. "My patients are nervous enough as it is. They don't need some wild-looking woman hovering over them when they're in pain. They need to know their doctor is someone they can trust. Someone who looks competent, in control and...and respectable." Even to her own ears, she sounded irrational.

"You're serious."

His amazement made her feel like an idiot. What had possessed her expose her deepest fear? The fear that Ryan Montgomery had been right. That no matter what she did, she'd never measure up. "Why else would I go to all the trouble of blow-drying the damned things straight?" she groused.

"I don't know. Why don't you tell me?"

His voice was soft and non-judgmental, more curious than anything else, but Emily felt cornered all the same. "Eric, if you've come to psychoanalyze me..."

"Where's Robbie?" he interrupted, looking up the stairs.

She was tempted to lie. But she was tired of lies. "On a sleepover at Glen's."

Eric resumed stroking the strand of her hair between his fingers, then smiled to himself as if he'd made some delicious discovery. As the light from the kitchen fell across his face, she noticed the lines of strain around his eyes and mouth.

"You look tired," she heard herself say, vaguely aware she sounded almost wifely, half-feeling the part dressed in her floor-length terrycloth robe and slippers. Strangely, she felt semi-comfortable with the role. Much more so than with the knowledge she was naked beneath her robe. She'd planned to eat dinner, then settle into bed with a smooth glass of White Zinfandel and a spicy novel.

"I didn't get much sleep last night."

"Neither did I," she admitted.

"I'm sorry for badgering you, Emily. I was out of line."

"So was I. I'm really sorry, Eric."

Hope etched his strong features. "Friends?"

She saw it as a start. Maybe even a whole new beginning. "Only if you stay for dinner."

He smiled. "I can deal with that."

Her insides turned to mush. Emily hoped she could deal with *that*. "Good. Think you can deal with turning off the oven for me? The chicken should be done by now."

"Sure, but—"

She shooed him into the kitchen. "Take off your coat and make yourself comfortable. I'll be back in five."

She returned in ten, using the extra minutes to brush out her rebellious fall of curls and add a touch of makeup to camouflage the circles under her eyes. Upon entering the kitchen she found Eric had done more than make himself comfortable, he'd taken off his boots and made himself at home. The five-minute wild rice she'd had sitting on the counter was done and he was adding the finishing touches to her salad.

The scene felt cozy and welcoming. His parka looked right at home hung over a kitchen chair. He'd set the table for two—facing each other. Emily relaxed, having battled a dozen second thoughts as she'd changed, then changed again, then changed a third time, finally settling on a comfortable dark green sweat suit that had seen better days. She wanted to be friends, not seduce the man.

Eric spied her reflection in the window over the sink, turned and smiled. "I hope you don't mind."

"Not at all." She crossed over to the refrigerator and withdrew the green bean casserole she'd made for Sunday night's dinner, suspecting Eric would appreciate something more elaborate than the spartan meal she'd planned for herself. Casserole in the microwave, she took the chicken from the oven. Indicating the unopened bottle of White Zinfandel on the counter, she asked Eric if he'd like some.

"No thanks, water's fine."

"I'm glad things are going so well for the Saints," she said as they sat down at the table. "You must be very happy."

Pleasant surprise lit his eyes. "I didn't realize you were following the games."

She'd surprised herself by continuing to watch his games. But oddly enough, she found them entertaining, now that she had an understanding of the rules. The Saints had lost the first game after that night at Pizza King, but had rallied on the road, winning four games straight. The newspaper accounts rightly gave Eric much of the credit.

She shrugged and reached for the salad. "Robbie keeps me posted. So do my patients. Apparently there's an epidemic of Saints fever sweeping the city."

"Oh, no. Is it fatal?"

She caught the twinkle in his eyes and grinned. "No, just highly contagious."

He grinned back and sliced into his chicken. "And how did you come to diagnose this startling condition, Doctor?"

Falling into the spirit of things, Emily pretended to consider the question. "Well, the symptoms are pretty clear cut. First, every third person seems to be wearing a Saints sweatshirt, button or hat. Then there are the bumper stickers, billboards and bus advertisements cheering the team on. And of course one can hardly turn on the television or open a newspaper without encountering a story about how the Saints are taking the NHL by storm."

"All thanks to Catherine Stump's carefully orchestrated marketing campaign."

"Hardly." Her eyes met his. "You're quite the star,

Eric. I had no idea."

He was silent for a moment. "Does it bother you?"

"The publicity? Why should it? It doesn't affect me."

Eric's hopes sank. She hadn't changed her mind about him after all. He'd spent most of last night mulling over reasons why she refused to date him. One possibility he'd come up with was his celebrity status. Emily Jordan had carved out a quiet, comfortable life for herself and her son. He could understand her reluctance to get involved with a man whose name and face drew national recognition. "Pass me those green beans, would you?"

She handed them over, smiling. "You like them?"

Odd question, he thought as he scooped a generous helping onto his plate and added seconds of chicken and rice as well. He hadn't eaten a meal this good since that night at Bill and Miranda's.

"The truth?" He grinned. "I like anything that isn't served off a menu."

With that, they segued into an easy conversation about life on the road. He told her about his upcoming trip to Montreal, Quebec, New York and New Jersey, and the team's need to win as many of those games as possible to earn a berth in the playoffs. When she commented on the strain the constant traveling and need to win must place him under, he was touched by her concern, but pointed out he wasn't the only player on the team. If he had an off night, there were nineteen others who could cover for him...

"As long as their egos don't get in the way," he finished dryly.

"Does that happen often?"

"Not as much as it used to, now that the guys have seen what a difference pulling together makes."

"They didn't before?"

He sent her a strange look, then remembered she was new to hockey. "No. Unfortunately, Stump went overboard when he first put the team together. He was so determined to give Minnesota a winning hockey club he refused to sign anybody but the best."

"Isn't that good?"

"In theory, yes, but Stump didn't take into account the personalities involved. When you get a room full of so-called stars, everyone thinking they're the best in the business, it gets tricky when you start dividing them into first, second, third and fourth lines. A player who's spent most of his career on the first line isn't going to like it when he gets assigned to the third or fourth line. Ice time is sacred to these guys. They don't want to give up a second of it."

"Where do you fit in?"

He grinned. "I'm the biggest ice hog of all."

Her elbows were on the table, her chin resting on her linked fingers. "Is that why they elected you captain?"

"Elected?" He snorted. "I wasn't elected. I was appointed by Stump for shooting off my big mouth."

She said nothing, simply smiled and nodded, as if confirming something she'd suspected all along. Eric smiled back, feeling utterly content. It didn't get any better than this. A quiet evening at home with a special woman. A bed waiting upstairs that—

Suddenly she stood, and crossed to the coffee pot. "Coffee? It's decaf."

Damn. She'd seen his thoughts in his eyes. "Sure. Black."

Silence fell between them as she poured. Eric waited it out, and wondered what was going through her mind. It was impossible to tell with a woman like Emily. She was so self-contained, so in control of herself. Hell, she even blow-dried her curly hair straight to keep it in line. Watching her calm, graceful movements as she poured her own cup of coffee, he wondered if she ever really let herself go.

"It sounds like an interesting conversation," she said.

Huh? What was she talking about? Oh, his run-in with Stump. "It wasn't a conversation. I ranted and raved, he listened—whether he wanted to or not."

She paused in clearing their plates, brow arched. "You lost your temper with Ronald Stump?"

She seemed more surprised than disapproving. Suddenly he needed to explain to someone what had happened that day—no one else had bothered to ask. "Only after six weeks of busting my butt and seeing my career sliding down the tubes for it. I stormed into Stump's office during one of his wheeler-dealer meetings

99

and told him if he didn't find a way to light a fire under those bas—men, he was going to be the laughingstock of the country. He was supposed to have created a Dream Team of All-Stars who'd show the league what the game is all about. Instead he ended up with a bunch of prima donnas who wouldn't stop infighting long enough to see they were headed straight for the golf course."

Emily glanced over her shoulder as she reached into a cupboard for some small plates. "And what was his response?"

Eric decided he liked watching her move around the kitchen while he talked. It made him feel more like family than a guest she felt obligated to give her undivided attention to.

"Then, he just nodded at me from behind his steepled fingers, thanked me and said he'd look into it. The next morning he visited practice—a payback, I suppose, for my barging in on his power lunch—personally stripped of his captaincy the man the team had elected, and named me as his replacement."

Emily winced. "I bet that went over real well."

"Especially when he fired the coach, too."

She paused, the refrigerator door half open. "He expected you to coach *and* play?"

"No, he named our general manager Bill Saunders the team's interim coach, but Bill and I go back a ways, so we're tight, and—is that a lemon meringue pie?"

"Homemade," she answered with a smug smile and placed a piece the size of Stump arena in front of him.

His mouth began to water. "Emily, you should've warned me."

"And ruined the surprise? Never."

"Good grief, I haven't had homemade lemon meringue pie since..." He closed his eyes against the sharp stab of pain at the memory of his mother surprising him after school, her face still young and pretty. Not ravaged by alcohol. "I'm sorry. I'm rambling again." He took a forkful of pie. He didn't want to talk about his mother. Not tonight.

"Well?" Emily asked, half a minute later, indicating the pie.

Eric grinned broadly, his taste buds rioting. "I think

I'm in love. What are the chances of Anna leaving her husband?"

"Anna!"

"Doesn't she do the cooking for you and Robbie?"

Emily turned an attractive shade of pink. "Well, yes, but only because I rarely have time to anymore."

"Are you telling me you made this fantastic pie?"

"And the green bean casserole."

Eric looked at the nearly empty casserole dish. "But you told me you don't cook."

"Just because I don't doesn't mean I can't."

He looked back to see her expression suspended between knowing she'd been caught in a fib and pleasure at having surprised him. Reaching across the table, he took her hand and slowly rubbed his thumb across her knuckles. "I'll keep that in mind."

She shivered, her eyes darkening to a deep sea green. "Behave yourself, Cameron, or I'll toss you out in the snow."

He laughed in delight. "Just make sure you toss the pie out behind me."

Chapter Eleven

Eric helped Emily with the dishes. Tomorrow the Saints would head out for their last road trip of the regular season and he wouldn't be back for ten days. The thought of leaving for so long with things so up in the air between himself and Emily didn't set well with Eric, but if he wanted to keep seeing her, he'd have to get used to it. His career didn't leave a lot of time for a steady relationship, and there was Emily's career to consider. She wasn't the kind of woman who could come running whenever he had a few hours to kill.

"Just slip the towel through the refrigerator door handle," she said from beside him as she reached into an overhead cupboard to put something away. Her loose hair brushed his arm, and sparked anew the idea of simply hauling her into his arms and taking his chances. She liked him, all right. The question was whether she liked him enough to—

"Yoo-hoo, Eric. You still with me?"

He blinked away an image of them getting naked on the kitchen table. "Sure. Sure. I was just...thinking."

She smiled. "Then I like how you look when you think. Would you like more coffee?"

He took a deep, shuddering breath. Pretty soon that smile would be his undoing. "I'd better not." He glanced out the window, where the snow had turned to sleet. "I should get going. It's getting bad out there."

"I'll wrap up the rest of the pie for you to take with you."

Trying not to feel put out by her easy willingness to let him go, he watched her smooth the lid of one of those plastic containers women stored leftovers in. Her corkscrew curls bounced gently as she forced air from the container. Eric found the picture of quiet domesticity she

102

presented impossible to resist. Gently he slipped his arms around her from behind.

She stilled, but didn't pull away. Taking it as a positive sign, he nuzzled her neck. "I'd rather take you with me."

She hesitated a beat, then laughed lightly. "Sorry. I don't have a Tupperware container big enough to fit me into. Besides, Robbie might notice I'm missing in the morning."

His eyes met hers in the kitchen window. "Then let me stay."

"The night?"

"At least." She felt too good in his arms, too right to let go when morning came.

She looked away first. "I can't."

"Why not? We're two unattached, consenting adults, who—"

She turned to face him and splayed her hands on his chest. "Who hardly know each other."

Her hair smelled of peaches. He smiled. "We could work on that."

"It would take a lot longer than one night, Eric."

Frustration nipped at him. "And you don't have time for that."

Gently, she shook her head. "Neither of us does right now."

"But if we did?"

Her eyes were clear and direct. "I'd very much like the chance to get to know you better."

"Then we'll *make* the time, Emily."

She smiled then, her smile so sweet it took his breath away. "Okay."

"Can I kiss you now?"

"Please do."

Carefully, he slid his fingers into her hair. Slowly, he explored her mouth and fed his curiosity the same way he'd let her feed hers that too-long-ago night in the ice rink parking lot. The scent of peaches and tang of lemon aroused him to an almost painful pitch, but didn't stop him from savoring her sweet softness melting against him. Her body responded to him so naturally, so honestly. He didn't doubt he could make her so hot they all but burned the house down around them.

But hot wasn't on the agenda tonight. Eric forced himself to pull back. She'd made herself clear on that point, and he wasn't about to cheat himself out of heaven by pushing for too much, too soon, no matter what his instincts told him.

"Oh, yeah, we'll make plenty of time for this," he breathed. "You taste so good, I don't think I'll ever get enough of you."

Her eyes sparkled like emeralds as she slipped her arms around his neck. "What are you doing tomorrow afternoon?"

"I leave at one for Montreal."

"But your game isn't until Monday night."

"We fly into town the day before a game if we can. Gives us time to get oriented. Besides, I have some business to take care of while I'm in town."

"On Sunday?"

"I own a restaurant there."

She leaned back. "You're kidding."

Eric chuckled. "Actually I own five. One in each city I've played pro for. They're called Amelia's. Named after my mother."

"How nice! Where does she live?"

"She's dead."

"Oh." Emily looked lost for a moment. "I'm sorry."

"It was a while ago. Before I made pro."

"Oh, Eric."

He wished he could shrug it off, but he couldn't quite manage it. His mother had always been a painful subject for him. Being with Emily made it not quite so painful, but he still didn't want to talk about it.

"So tell me about these Amelia's," Emily said, somehow sensing his thoughts. She spooked him when she did that, but this time he was grateful for it. "Are they...hockey hangouts?"

He laughed at the thought. "Hell, no. They've got more class than that. They're not really affiliated with my career. In fact, they're really good restaurants, but we do a hefty bar business in the evenings. They're decorated with plants and brass and antiques, the kind of stuff yuppies seem to appreciate."

"And you don't?"

He shrugged. "I'm more a hole-in-the-wall kind of guy. It's...what I grew up with."

"Then why invest in them and not some friendly neighborhood hole in the wall?"

Eric thought of the "friendly" neighborhood dive he'd visited the night he'd met Emily. His lawyer still wasn't able to prove he hadn't walked into Harry's Place looking for a fight. The regulars refused to change their story and Eric wasn't into forced confessions. If something didn't break soon, he was going to be out a lot of money. His insurance company had refused to cover the cost of the damages.

"Because, dives, my dear, don't make the money."

With that, he kissed her again. Time out was over.

Emily was more than happy to stop talking. In the past fifty minutes she'd learned more about Eric Cameron than she had in the past five weeks, and it was making her head spin. Or was it the way his tongue swept through her mouth like he was determined to capture every last trace of lemon meringue pie? Or the way his hands stole beneath her sweatshirt, his calluses sensitizing her skin until she fairly crackled with sexual energy?

It didn't matter. She was drowning in sweet sensation and loving every second of it. She tunneled her fingers through Eric's hair and reveled in its softness, so unlike the hard thigh that had slipped between her legs to tease the ache building at its apex. Soon she was pressed against him so fiercely they risked the need to be surgically separated. Leaning back to ride his thigh, she moaned, then arched her back when his hand slid up to capture a feverish breast that felt as if it had been custom made for his palm.

"Emily," he rasped as his talented fingers sent her into sensory overload. "We've got to stop. I don't think I can stand much more of this. I haven't been this hard since—"

"Oh no. Oh no." Her voice emerged high and breathless. "Eric...don't stop moving. Please. Not now." Her hands dug into his shoulders. Her teeth bit into her bottom lip. Eyes closed, she ground herself against his thigh.

With a startled oath, Eric realized what was happening. Gripping her hips, he lifted her higher against his thigh. "Hold on, Emily, it's going to be all right."

Emily could only wrap her arms around him and pant as he matched the rhythm of her grinding hips. She strained against him as he slid one of his oh-so-accurate hands inside her sweatpants. The instant he touched her she detonated. With a wild cry of release she felt the dam inside her burst and flood her with molten heat.

Slowly, ever so slowly, she drifted back to earth. Her nerve endings quivered as she slumped against Eric's chest, her forehead slick with sweat, her arms wrapped limply around his neck. The sound of sleet pelting the windows punctuated their ragged breathing. Gradually Emily became aware of Eric's hips braced against the kitchen counter, his hands on her bare bottom, and the soaking wetness between her legs.

She groaned in mortification.

"Emily? Are you all right?"

Stupid question, she thought. Stupid, stupid question. She'd never be all right again.

Torn between wanting to die on the spot and wanting to curl up in Eric's arms and drift off into the afterglow, she lifted her head and blinked at the kitchen light that suddenly seemed too bright. Eric eased his hands from her bottom to link them behind her back, providing her with much-needed support. Bonelessly she slid against him until her feet touched the floor, and remained that way as he straightened, her knees still too weak to hold her.

"I'm sorry. I...seem to be having trouble standing." Her body wouldn't stop tingling.

His smile was tenderness defined. "Then I guess I'll have to carry you to bed."

Emily was dead weight in his arms by the time he reached her bedroom. Gently he lowered her to the bed, amazed at how quickly she'd crashed after the most erotic sexual encounter he'd experienced. He still got mush-kneed thinking about it; the way her long auburn hair had flown wild around her flushed face as she tossed her head back and cried out her release. Caught in the grips of his fascination, he'd forgotten about his own need as he'd watched her control shatter right before his eyes.

Afterward, he'd held her. He'd cradled her close to his chest, closed his eyes and absorbed the rippling aftershocks of her release. He'd felt happier than he'd ever felt after making love to a woman, just knowing he'd brought her pleasure and she had let him. He looked down at her now, and decided Emily Jordan had to be every man's ideal of a fantasy lover.

Unfortunately, she was also asleep. He chuckled at the irony of it and pulled a neatly folded cream-colored afghan from the foot of the bed. He draped it over her, then smoothed her hair back and kissed her damp forehead. "G'night, love."

Wide awake himself, Eric straightened and looked around her room, illuminated only by the dim shaft of light from the hall. His first reaction was a long, approving smile. The room was peaches and cream, softness and light, efficiently organized...and undeniably feminine.

Just like Emily.

A note taped to the outdated VCR above the equally outdated television directly across from the bed caught his eye and he ambled over to check it out. He loved reading Emily's notes. She had some cute ones tacked onto the board by the downstairs phone.

In Emily's surprisingly neat printing—considering she was a doctor—was a list of the times and dates of the Saints' last ten televised games. Next to the television stood a stack of VCR tapes, some labeled, some not. Those that were, were labeled "Eric's games". Not Saints games, but "Eric's" games.

He looked back at Emily, and his heart swelled with a jumble of emotions he couldn't begin to sort out. Pride, pleasure, tenderness...and disappointment at having wasted so much time.

Oh, Emily. Why have you been fighting me so hard?

He wandered over to the window to look out at the night. Instead, he saw a film of ice. Tree branches snapped and crackled as they broke under the weight of the building ice.

Beside him stood a dainty oak desk, its roll top open,

the surface littered with papers. He picked up a brass paperweight shaped like a medical bag and noticed several bank statements beneath it. To the side lay an open business size checkbook, a stack of canceled checks, and a blank tax form. Knowing he shouldn't pry, but suddenly curious beyond scruples about anything that had to do with Emily, he flipped through the bank checks.

All were made out to people with the last name Jordan. There was a Mark, Mary Beth, Patrick and Tom. They covered the twelve months of the previous year and were arranged by month. Tom's went only through May.

Each check was written for several hundred dollars. All were dated the first of the month—and signed by Anna Louise Hamilton. Baffled, Eric looked in the upper left hand corner. The imprint read *The Jordan Foundation* and gave its address as a post office box in St. Paul.

He did some math and realized this Jordan Foundation had shelled out almost forty thousand dollars last year. For what?

What the hell? Was Emily supporting an entire family of Jordans somewhere?

He turned a few of the checks over. From what he could tell, they were drawn on four different banks, two in Michigan, one in Pennsylvania and the other he couldn't make out in the dim light.

Emily coughed. Eric started and glanced over his shoulder. She'd be furious if she caught him nosing through her stuff. He replaced the checks and the paperweight, then put a healthy distance between himself and Emily Jordan's financial affairs. She was still asleep when he went downstairs to turn off the lights.

On the way he peeked into Robbie's room, curious as to how an eight-year-old boy's room should look. A room of his own was a luxury Eric hadn't been able enjoy until he'd left home. He nodded in approval. Except for the single bed and Batman sheets, it looked pretty much like his apartment—as if a tornado had swept through it that afternoon.

Downstairs he turned on the news to catch the sports and weather and helped himself to some cold coffee and a few ginger snaps from the cow cookie jar. He knew he should get going, but he hated the thought of leaving Emily, and hated even more the thought that she might wake up and come looking for him, only to find him gone. If there was any chance she wanted to continue what they'd started in the kitchen, he didn't want to miss it.

At eleven-thirty he turned off the TV and went to get his parka. If he didn't leave now, the roads might be impassable, even in his Explorer. Because of the storm, he'd left the Boxter behind in Bill and Miranda's second garage. Good thing. A twenty-two-car pileup had stopped traffic in both directions on the city's main thoroughfare. The streets would be crawling with people taking alternate routes.

At the front door, he found he couldn't leave. Not until he checked on Emily one more time.

He hunkered down beside her bed and studied her face. She looked so soft and vulnerable in sleep, a different woman from the no-nonsense doctor he'd met in the ER five weeks ago. He had a hard time believing it was the same woman. Or that she was the same woman who'd gone up in flames in his arms tonight. Absently, he rubbed the dark spot on his jeans, high on his right thigh. Her scent wafted up to him, bringing his lower half to life.

"Down, boy," he murmured. "Can't you see the lady's not in the mood?"

Her eyes drifted open. "Eric?"

He stood. "I'm right here. Everything's fine."

She blinked at the parka in his hand. "You're not leaving, are you?"

He smiled. "I thought I might, since I've managed to put you to sleep."

She chuckled and rolled over. Her amusement faded as she gazed up at him with dark, steady eyes.

Eric's mouth went dry. It was all he could do not to dive into the bed beside her. He'd never met a sexier woman than Emily Jordan, covered from neck to ankle by an old sweat suit and an afghan that looked as if it had been made especially for her by someone who loved her very, very much.

Almost as much as he did.

He blinked. No. It's not possible. It can't be.

But it was. He could feel it in every thudding

heartbeat. He was in love with Emily Jordan.

He stepped backward, suddenly feeling more vulnerable and unsure of himself than he had since he'd left home for the juniors at sixteen. "I'll see you in a few days," he said abruptly, then realized how rough his voice sounded. He tried again. "I'll call you when I get to Montreal."

She looked so sexy. Too sexy to leave alone tonight. Any night. But he had to. She was all wrong for him. He was all wrong for her. Sex and companionship was fine, but love and marriage?

Marriage? Where the hell had that come from?

He backed away. He needed to bolt before he did something stupid. Like propose. It wouldn't be the first time he'd blurted out a proposal in the heat of the moment. But the last time he'd been nineteen and desperate for someone to call his own. His mother had just died and he hadn't known whether he was coming or going.

But Monica had. She'd known exactly what she was doing.

Emily rose onto her elbows and squinted at him as if he'd broken out in hives. "Eric? Are you all right?"

"I'm fine." His voice was no more than an embarrassing croak.

"Are you sure?"

"Positive. It's just late, and—"

"Have you changed your mind about wanting to spend more time with me in the last..." she glanced at the clock on her nightstand, "Good grief, have I been sleeping for two hours?"

He ignored that, choosing to answer her first question instead. "No," he breathed, hardly daring to hope. "I haven't changed my mind."

She smiled. "Then do you have any preference as to which side of the bed you like to sleep on?"

Chapter Twelve

Eric's stomach did a free-fall. The silence between them was so acute he could hear the branches breaking in the ice storm outside from clear across the room. He closed his eyes and took a deep, calming breath. "Emily, if I join you in that bed, it won't matter which side either of us prefers to sleep on."

She smiled softly. "That's what I was hoping."

He dropped his parka, along with his common sense. Emily threw off the afghan and opened her arms. With a groan of pure pleasure he pressed her deep into the bed's softness. He settled himself between her legs and rocked against her, kissing her with the heat of a man who'd just had the holy hell scared out of him.

He wanted her, but was terrified of losing his heart to her. Once she had it, Eric knew he would never get it back.

Never.

So he kissed her, and kissed her, and kissed her again, and tried to blot out everything but the hot, carnal pleasure of her body as it strained against his. His marriage had taught him if the sex was strong, the heart needn't be involved.

He might have been able to pull it off, if Emily hadn't giggled. He registered the sound slowly, lifted his head and looked down at her with eyes that felt slightly unfocused.

"What's so funny?" He'd never had a woman laugh at him in bed before.

She chuckled softly. "I know I'm a little rusty, but shouldn't we be doing this with our clothes off?"

He smiled, charmed, and kissed her again. "All in good time, Angel. Right now I just want to—rusty? How rusty?"

111

She looked up at him, her eyes wide and solemn. "Very rusty."

He saw it then, the hesitance he'd missed before. The apprehension that lurked behind the banter. And he died a little inside, knowing he'd planned to take her in lust, with no concession to love. "How long has it been?"

"Since before Robbie."

Guilt engulfed him. He groaned and rolled away from her.

"Eric?"

He reached for her hand and squeezed it. Give me a minute to change gear."

"Are you going to leave?"

He knew he should, if only to salve his conscience. "Do you want me to?"

"No."

Hope edged its way into his heart. Maybe they could find a way to make it work after all. He rose onto an elbow and met her eyes, to find them dark and deeply troubled. "Are you sure?"

"I want to try again." Her smile was fragile, her voice equally so. "Maybe this time I can get it right. You have to admit I, uh, sort of botched things earlier—in the kitchen."

Her insecurity melted him. If he awoke in the morning to find his heart missing, so be it. He refused to protect himself at her expense. He bent to her and kissed her far more gently than ever before. "You're wrong," he said, smiling. "What happened downstairs is was the best sexual experience I've ever had."

"But you didn't—"

He shushed her with his fingertips. I didn't have to. Watching you, knowing I was pleasing you, gave me more than enough satisfaction." Doubt lingered in her eyes. He traced his fingers along the curve of her jaw. She felt like peach silk. "You were beautiful, Emily."

Emily had never felt so cherished. Eric slid one hand into her hair and caressed her stomach with the other. Her butterflies stilled as he smiled into her eyes and promised her everything would be all right.

He didn't use words. He didn't have to. His eyes, his smile, his touch said it all. His hands trailed against her flushed skin, soothing her nerves like summer rain. As her body filled with renewed desire, he feathered her face with short, playful kisses between long, deep, soul kisses. Instinct and emotion took over as she lifted her arms to his neck. He pressed closer, glided his hands upward to soothe the aching fullness in her breasts. He enticed her upright until they sat facing each other, she on her knees before him, her hands on his shoulders. Gently he caught the hem of her sweatshirt. "I want to see you."

Anxiety arrowed straight into her womb as their eyes locked. She couldn't help but wonder if he'd be disappointed by what he saw. It had been so long, and Ryan had been so quick to criticize.

She nodded, and he lifted her sweatshirt over her head.

"You're more beautiful than I imagined," Eric whispered, his voice raw with restrained need.

She shuddered with an answering need. "Touch me, Eric. Please."

He did, and she nearly wept at the joy of it. She bit her lower lip to keep from moaning, and closed her eyes as his skilled hands skimmed her skin, his calluses offered sweet sensation. Her breathing soft and shallow, she leaned into his caresses, arched her neck, and let her hair fall to her hips.

"That's it sweetheart, don't hold back. Just let it go. There's nobody here but us and I love the sound of you aroused."

She exhaled on a ragged moan, then gasped as he replaced his hands with his mouth on her breasts. Blindly she reached for him as pleasure so intense it was almost painful shot through her.

"Easy, honey, easy."

He stilled and she relaxed, dropping her chin to her chest. Tentatively, she gathered him close. He smiled against her skin. "That's it, Emily. Just tell me what you want. Show me. I won't do anything you don't like."

His husky promise melted the last of her reservations. Wordlessly she guided him on a slow, sensual journey of discovery that brought her more pleasure than she had known was possible. He followed her lead until he had her nerve endings so sensitized the mere hint of his breath on her skin had her whimpering in response.

Eric eased her back onto the bed. He slipped his fingers inside the waistband of her sweatpants and gave a light tug. "Lift up, sweetheart. I need to find out if the rest of you tastes this good."

Within seconds her pants were a heap on the floor, Eric warm and naked beside her.

"Oh, Emily, you're so damn wet."

She smiled dreamily. "I can't imagine why."

Eric rumbled with low, satisfied laughter. Emily opened her eyes to find him propped on one elbow, shaking his head. "I had no idea you'd be this much fun in bed."

Emily grinned. "Neither did I."

He smoothed her hair away from her face. "We're going to be so good together."

She lifted a hand to his cheek. "We already are."

He kissed her palm, her wrist, her inner elbow. Then swore.

"Eric? What's wrong?"

Deep apology entered his eyes. "I'm sorry. I didn't mean to startle you. It's just that I, uh, didn't bring anything. As in I wasn't planning on this tonight?"

That he hadn't come to see her with sex in mind pleased Emily enormously. She raised her eyebrow and offered a sassy grin. "Then it's a good thing you're in bed with a doctor." She rolled across the bed and reached for her briefcase on the floor. "I just happen to have some samples you might like to try on for size."

Eric stared. "You carry condoms in your brief-case?"

Emily popped open the locks, pulled out a foil packet and wiggled it wickedly in front of him. "You're not the only one who gives lectures and passes out souvenirs afterward, Mr. Cameron."

His expression turned to one of delight. "You lecture about sex?"

"About safer sex," she corrected primly. "Once a month at the Women's Health Connection." She continued her spiel just as primly. "It's part of a program the hospital offers as a community service to women looking for advice on a variety of health-related topics. Diet, exercise, coping with stress..."

"And sex."

Emily broke into a wide grin, loving his delight. "And sex."

Eric shook his head in amazement. How...did I ever get so lucky?"

The catch in his voice told Emily the question had nothing to do with sex or condoms, and everything to do with the need that had drawn them toward this moment since the night they'd met. The need she had refused to examine, for fear of what she would find.

But the time for fear and mistrust was over. Emily closed the briefcase and set it back on the floor. Her heart in her eyes, she offered Eric her hand. "I'm the lucky one."

Chapter Thirteen

Eric wasn't sure if he'd found heaven or hell. On the one hand he'd just made the most amazing love with the one woman who had captured his mind, heart and soul from the moment he'd met her, and on the other he couldn't tell her how he felt about her.

He didn't dare. Not until she had a chance to experience what life as his lady would be like. No way he'd risk telling Emily he loved her until he was sure she knew what she was getting into and accepted it, warts and all. He didn't expect her to pack up her medical bag and follow him around the continent—but he did think she needed to take a fair shot at seeing what his life was like, both on and off the ice. It wasn't glamorous by any means; at times it was downright ugly.

Then again, maybe it would be better to keep her separate from his work. Keep her and Robbie protected from the fickleness of the media and fans, the volatility and crudity of his teammates, the explosive hostility of his opponents and their fans. The Saints were riding high, now, but a team was only as good as its last game and they couldn't keep winning forever.

But that would mean he'd hardly ever see her.

She stirred beside him. "You're awfully quiet."

He tightened his arm around her, kissed her hair. "Just thinking about the game."

Her fingers feathered playfully across his chest. "Sorry, Bud, you're not allowed to think about work when you're in bed."

He chuckled. "I like the way you think. Speaking of work, what happens to Robbie when you have to go in at night?"

"Anna stays with him."

"She comes over in the middle of the night?"

"She's been doing it for years."

Eric stared. "No wonder she's so special. That's one hell of a babysitter you've got. You don't happen to pay her in gold?"

Emily couldn't help but laugh. "I don't pay her at all. Unless you count outrageously lavish gifts at Christmas and for her birthday. She takes care of Robbie because she loves him."

"Would you mind if I asked what her husband thinks of all this?"

Emily smiled, enjoying herself. "Augustus? He's usually the one who calls her in the middle of the night and tells her I need her to come over. She's married to my boss."

"The white-haired guy?"

"They've been married for two years. Before that, she lived with me. And before that, I lived with her. She's a retired pediatric nurse and the closest thing to family I've got in this area. Any more questions?" she asked with another smile.

"Just one. Are you on call tonight?"

"Nope. Augustus gave me the weekend off." Her green eyes sparkled with mischief. "So we've got at least eleven more hours to get to know each other better."

"Eleven?"

"You're leaving at one, right? Well, it's two now, so..." She levered herself onto his chest. Her long hair formed a rippling veil of silk around them that blocked out the rest of the world. "Got any suggestions as to how we should spend the next eleven hours?"

Eric grinned in delight. "That, I do."

Fifteen minutes later the telephone rang.

With a scowl, Eric looked up from where he was nibbling on Emily's toes. Emily delighted in the view, even as her heart sank. Naked, with his hair mussed and jaw dark and shadowed, Eric reminded her of a pagan god. Maybe it was a wrong number. One could only hope. The phone rang again.

"Don't answer it," Eric whispered.

Emily grinned at the conspiracy in his voice, then wrinkled her nose. "Sorry. I have to."

He slid her arch along the stubble of his cheek,

sending spikes of sexual energy up her leg. "Why? You're not on call."

"Doesn't matter. I still have to answer it."

"Not even when I do...this?"

"Eric! Come on," She laughed and scooted upright, then squirmed away from his clever fingers as the phone rang a fourth time. "It might be Robbie."

"At this hour?"

"Accidents happen. Hello?"

A long silence echoed across the line, followed by someone clearing his throat. "Er...sorry to do this to you, Em."

Emily sagged against the pillows. "What is it this time, Augustus?"

"Twenty-two car pileup. They've been bringing them in for two hours. Hanson didn't show, and I had to send two residents home with the flu—"

"I'll be there as soon as I can."

He paused. "I owe you, Emily."

She looked at Eric, who sat cross-legged in the middle of her bed, her foot cradled in his hands. "That you do," she said, and hung up.

She met Eric's eyes and sighed, not for the first time in the past few months resenting the demands of her career. Maybe it was time for a change. But trauma medicine was all she'd ever wanted to practice, and she doubted an ER existed with enough doctors on staff to allow her the luxury of regular working hours. Turnover in the field was horrendous.

So was burnout.

She sighed again. "I have to go to work."

"I'll take you."

She smiled, touched. "Won't work. I could be there for hours."

"Or not get there at all."

"Excuse me?"

"I don't like the idea of you driving in this weather, Emily."

She lifted an eyebrow at that. "Oh?"

"Yeah, oh." He jerked a thumb at the window. "Take a look. You can't even see through the window. The roads are probably sheer ice by now."

"Eric, I've driven on ice before."

"Not when I was around."

So. A few hours in her bed and he was already trying to run things. "Listen, Eric, I appreciate your concern, but—"

"Concern? I make my living on ice, Emily. It's dangerous out there. I'm not just concerned, I'm *terrified* at the thought of you out there alone in a car with balding tires."

"And we're going to be safer in your little car?"

"I drove my Explorer tonight. I wouldn't take the Boxter out in this."

"Oh." She couldn't argue with that. "Okay, let's go."

The roads were a nightmare. They made the trip to the hospital in grim silence, Emily not wanting to distract Eric's driving, Eric too intent on getting them there in one piece to offer much in the way of conversation beyond an occasional curse.

He pulled up to the main ER entrance. "I'll let you off here and park the car."

"Eric, you can't stay. I could be all night. You need your rest. Augustus can take me home."

Eric's response was a kiss that made her body burn and a husky warning to "Get inside before I turn around and take you back to bed."

Breathless and flushed, she sailed through the ER doors just as Augustus was coming down the hall.

"Emily! Thank God you're safe."

She shrugged out of her coat and eyed the clipboard he carried. "Sorry it took so long. The roads were a mess. Where do you need me?"

He paused, and Emily looked up to find him staring at her hair. She'd pulled it back with barrettes instead of confining it in her usual smooth chignon. "Your hair. It's..."

She smiled. "Curly. I've heard. Now, where do you need me?"

"Nowhere, at the moment. We've stabilized everyone who's come in so far and either sent them upstairs or home, but another chopper's due any minute." After another glance at her hair, he filled her in on what to expect.

Satisfied she knew all she needed to know for the time being, she nodded. "Good. I've got time for coffee."

Augustus headed for the nurse's station while Emily headed for the coffee pot in the staff lounge. She poured two cups and returned to the deserted waiting area. Half a minute later, Eric strode through the door, his hair wet and windblown, his eyes scanning the corridor ahead of him.

"Over here."

He frowned and changed course. "Where is everyone? I thought the place would be jumping."

"A chopper's on its way. Coffee?"

He accepted his cup gratefully, took a long swallow and studied his surroundings. "It's so quiet. Almost eerie."

"The eye of the hurricane," she murmured, then sipped her coffee. On the heels of her remark came the approaching wail of a siren. They turned to watch as an ambulance, lights flashing surrealistically in the driving sleet, rolled past the front entrance and disappeared around the corner of the building.

Emily finished her coffee and mentally geared herself up for the long night ahead. "Time to roll."

Eric draped an arm across her shoulders and brushed her temple with a kiss. "I'll see you later."

She nodded, then leaned into him for a moment to draw on his strength. It wasn't until she turned away and faced Sarah Ferguson's slack-jawed stare that she realized what she'd done. By arriving with Eric in the dead of night and cozying up to him in the middle of the waiting room, she'd as good as announced on the PA system she was sleeping with the man.

Nothing she could do about it now. She sent Sarah a look that promised an explanation later—an explanation she planned to do everything in her power to *avoid*—and went to work.

Four grueling hours later, Emily wished she'd never become a doctor. It hurt too much. She'd done everything she could, but on nights like this it wasn't enough. God knew she wished she could numb herself to the pain when she lost a patient, but it never worked that way. She trudged out to the reception area to see if by some miracle Eric was still there. She'd caught a glimpse of him earlier in the hall, just as the last two accident victims had arrived by helicopter. Neither had survived, but even before the code blue team had ceased resuscitation efforts, two ambulances bearing victims of an apartment house fire had arrived to take their place. The team had succeeded in saving the fire victims, but the effort had sapped Emily of most of her strength. She needed an infusion of Eric's strength and didn't care if half the hospital witnessed it this time.

She found the waiting room filled with anxious relatives, but no Eric. Clamping down on her disappointment, she stopped in a treatment room to assure the terrified parents of her most recent patient that their daughter was receiving the best medical care possible, then shuffled back to Augustus' office to see if he was ready to leave. The morning shift had come on at seven and had the new arrivals well in hand.

Unable to find Augustus, she asked Sarah if she'd seen him, only to be told he'd left half an hour earlier. Emily accepted the news with weary resignation. She hadn't had a chance to ask him for a ride. She called a cab, but when the dispatcher told her it would be at least an hour before he could send anyone because, "It's crazy out there, lady," she decided to wait in the staff lounge, where she could at least prop up her aching feet.

The lounge was empty. Emily dropped onto the couch, stretched out and closed her eyes. A few minutes later she heard the door click open. She tried to open her eyes, but her eyelids refused to cooperate. "Let me know when it's a quarter to, she mumbled. "I'm expecting a cab."

The next thing she knew she was dreaming. A strong pair of arms lifted her against a warm, solid chest. She smelled cinnamon and musk and nestled closer, smiling. It was only when the unmistakable hum of a busy hospital intruded on her fantasy that her eyes fluttered open, then widened in horror.

"Eric! Put me down!"

He chuckled and did so as she started to squirm. "I had a feeling this wouldn't work."

Her cheeks felt on fire, but to her relief the corridor was empty. "Just what do you think you're doing?" she hissed as she shoved her arms into the coat he'd wrapped around her.

"Taking you home. I heard you needed a ride. Sarah called and told me you'd gone off duty. I'd slipped across the street for some donuts and coffee in case you had a break."

He smiled and held up a white bag redolent with the yeasty tang of fresh-baked cinnamon rolls. Her stomach gurgled as she reached for it.

Ten minutes later she was asleep in the Explorer, oblivious to the crystalline beauty of nature's treacherous handiwork the night before. The sun was warm on her face, the cello music floating through the sound system low and lulling. Only when she realized Eric intended to carry her into the house was she able to rally.

"I'd prefer not to be lugged around like a sack of potatoes, thank you," she said, placing her hand against his chest.

His good-natured laughter followed her up the stairs as she headed for her bathroom to shower the stench of death from her skin. She emerged marginally revived to find the house smelling of breakfast. The tantalizing aroma of ham, eggs, fried potatoes and coffee drew her toward the kitchen where Eric had, once again, wasted no time in making himself at home.

Emily leaned against the doorjamb and studied him as he turned the sizzling ham. He'd shaved, and looked better than a man had a right to puttering around in her kitchen. She'd never have guessed he'd spent a sleepless night in an ER doing Lord knew what while she worked herself to the bone.

"You're spoiling me," she accused contentedly as he removed the rest of the cinnamon rolls from the microwave. The one she'd wolfed down before dozing off had barely dented her hunger.

The warmth in his smile made her think of an entirely different hunger. "That's the general idea. Come, let's get a decent meal in you before you go back to sleep."

As ungrateful as it sounded, Emily would've preferred to skip breakfast and go straight to sleep—with Eric beside her. He had to be as exhausted as she. But Robbie needed to be picked up at nine and then...

She groaned as she remembered her Sunday dinner for Augustus and his family. She'd never have the time or energy to pull it off now.

"What? You don't like scrambled eggs?"

"Scrambled eggs are fine," she said, easing into her seat as he set a lumberjack-size plateful of food in front of her. "It's dinner I'm worried about." Briefly, she explained her plans.

"So you let me demolish half your menu last night?" he asked in chagrined disbelief. "Is there any way you can postpone it?"

Emily poured herself a cup of decaf and freshened his. "And disappoint Robbie?" she asked innocently, smiling. She suspected he'd asked the question partially in hopes of being invited to the rescheduled dinner. "Sorry. He loves these family dinners. Especially dessert."

"Which I also destroyed."

"Don't worry. I'll figure something out."

"Why don't you let me pick him up and take him skating this morning while you catch up on your sleep? Afterward, I'll take him out for a pizza, maybe to a movie, then bring him home too stuffed and exhausted to notice I ate his favorite pie."

"What about your trip?"

"I'll tell them I had an emergency. Catch a later flight."

She shook her head, touched beyond gratitude. "I can't let you do that. Robbie and I aren't your responsibility. Thank you very much for the offer, but we'll manage."

He took her hand across the table. "I want to help."

She looked into his compelling brown eyes, and realized he wanted to do much more than that. He wanted to be part of her life. She no longer had a problem with that, but she didn't want him to take it over.

And he would, if she let him. Not with the self-serving maliciousness that Ryan had, but with a simple generosity that would threaten her hard-won independence all the same. "There's a bakery down the street where I can get another pie. And the green bean casserole is a snap to put together."

"At least let me pick him up from Glen's for you."

When she opened her mouth to protest, he interrupted. "My bags are packed. I'll still have time to catch my flight."

She didn't want to press the point. Not after last night. She squeezed his hand. "All right. Thank you."

****

Superwoman, eat your heart out, Emily thought as she surveyed her dining room table set for eight. She'd pulled it off after all—with a little help from an absentee friend.

Refusing to let her spirits be dampened by Eric's absence, Emily walked back to the kitchen to toss the salad. The roast and sweet potatoes were done to perfection, the green bean casserole was back on the menu, her light and fluffy biscuits were in the bun warmer, and the wine was chilled and ready to pour.

All she needed now were her guests.

After breakfast, she'd slept until noon, and awoken to find the house uncommonly quiet. At first she'd thought Eric had sidestepped her refusal to let him abscond with Robbie, but a swift check of his room had yielded one angelic eight-year-old, exhausted from his night of deviltry. A post-it note on his door said, "Mum's the word, but check the fridge before you do anything else."

In the refrigerator she'd found a brand new lemon meringue pie.

The doorbell rang just as the grandfather clock in the hall chimed three. Emily wiped her hands on her apron and went to greet her surrogate family with a smile. Instead, she met a deliveryman bearing a long, rectangular box. Inside, she found a dozen long-stemmed peach roses.

For once the sight of flowers didn't make her stomach churn with revulsion. This time it filled her heart with a determination that matched her step as she returned to the dining room to ferret out her one and only vase, a never-used gift Anna had given her as a housewarming present.

As she knelt on the floor next to the china cabinet, dusting the exquisite crystal vase with her apron, her mind drifted back to a late summer afternoon three and a half years earlier. She and Anna had been sitting at a card table in the kitchen, watching Robbie play on the backyard swing set as they drank iced tea and waited for Emily's new furniture to arrive.

"I brought you a little something to brighten up your new home," Anna said, and beamed as she pulled an elegantly wrapped box from the shopping bag at her feet.

Emily accepted the rectangular package with both hands, her eyebrows lifting at its weight. "A little something?"

"Open it, open it."

Emily's stomach knotted when she turned back the tissue paper. It was a vase. A incredibly beautiful, incredibly expensive Baccarat vase. The kind that graced nearly every flat surface in Ryan's sprawling ancestral home. The kind she'd sworn never to own, because it would only remind her that hidden beneath the beauty of her former in-laws' exquisite estate lay an ugly, ugly secret.

"Oh, Anna. You shouldn't have." Her voice trembled with the power of the dark memories the vase evoked. "This...this must have cost you a fortune."

Anna's response was soft and tender. "It was worth every penny. When I saw it, it reminded me of you. Beautiful and delicate, yet strong enough to take whatever comes your way."

Shocking them both, Emily burst into tears. It was the only time Anna saw Emily cry. In the five years since Anna had opened her front door and unquestioningly agreed to rent her back bedroom to a pregnant and penniless Emily, Emily had made sure Anna never heard so much as a sniffle out of her. But that afternoon she more than made up for it. She cried in Anna's arms until Robbie skipped through the back door and demanded a snack.

Afterward, while Robbie napped for the first time in his new room, Emily told Anna about Ryan and his family's tradition of violence. The subject had never been mentioned since, and when the furniture had arrived that afternoon, the vase had been carefully tucked out of sight. Anna's doing, but Emily hadn't had the will or desire to pull it out again, even to please Anna.

Until tonight.

Chapter Fourteen

Gold, red, blue, orange. Upper, lower, even, odd. Emily felt as if she'd entered a foreign country and the road signs were in code. With a tight grip on Robbie's hand, she braved the throng of spectators that clogged Stump Arena's massive concrete corridors and wished she'd let Eric take her on a dry run that afternoon the way he'd wanted to.

But no, she'd had to insist she'd be fine. He had enough on his mind already. Tonight's game against the Wild was crucial in determining the Saints' chances of making the playoffs. Besides, the page in the telephone book describing the Arena's layout had seemed straightforward enough, and Anna had told Emily all she had to do was veer left beyond the turnstiles and keep walking until she hit section ten.

Instead she felt as if she'd circled the arena twice, all the while moving against traffic. She hadn't counted on the place being so huge. Or so crowded. People were everywhere, lining up in front of the concession stands until they were twelve deep or more, hovering around the booths selling T-shirts, hats, pennants and posters, loitering in front of the restrooms, holding up the walls as they waited for friends or family.

Fifteen. Fourteen. Thirteen. Doggedly she marched onward, determined not to miss their section. Robbie scampered beside her, too enraptured by the idea of attending his first NHL game to notice his mother was out of her element.

"There it is, Mom!" Robbie pointed to a large number ten painted in black on a Saints purple and gold background.

"Finally," she breathed, and cut across the flow of traffic. They approached a striking brunette wearing a

126

navy skirt and Saints purple blazer. Emily handed over their tickets, then pulled Robbie out of the path of a boisterous group of men carrying plastic cups of beer. The usherette escorted them to a lower-level section filled mostly with well-dressed women. Emily was wondering where the women's coats were when Robbie tugged at her arm.

"Can we go down and watch the team warm up, Mom?"

She looked over to where a small crowd stood next to the Plexiglas barrier that separated the seats from the rink, and mulled over the best way to get there without climbing over several rows of seated fans. "I suppose so, if—"

"Here they come!"

Emily blew out an exasperated sigh and tried to keep her sights on Robbie's red pullover as she followed him down the aisle. She reached the Plexiglas barrier as the last of the Saints emerged from the locker room to skate in circles around half of the rink. The Wild followed the Saints onto the ice, having to skate their way through the already circling Saints to get to their half of the rink. Murmuring, "Excuse me," left and right, Emily wedged her way closer to Robbie, pressed against the glass.

"There's Eric!" Robbie waved frantically, but Eric was skating with one of his alternate captains, their heads bent in conversation. They glided by, and entered the lineup of players practicing their shots.

Watching the players warm up, Emily couldn't get over how enormous they looked. How imposing. Their friendly expressions, however, softened the impression. As they laughed and joked with each other, they seemed more like a group of overgrown boys looking forward to a good time than a team of men determined to win a playoff berth.

"Here he comes again!" Robbie resumed his frantic waving. Eric looked Robbie dead in the eye and winked. A split second later he was gone again. "Did you see that, Mom? He winked! He knows we're here!"

Emily watched Eric return to the lineup for more practice shots and thought he was the sweetest man she'd met. Not to mention the most graceful. "I saw,

127

sweetheart. Now why don't we go back to our seats and let someone else watch for a while?"

The teams returned to the locker rooms. Emily settled in to peruse her program. Beside her, Robbie stood, a human lightning rod absorbing the electric current of excitement building in the air.

"Uh oh."

"What is it, sweetheart?" she asked absently as she studied the team's vital statistics. The chart listed Eric as 6'4" and 230 pounds, said he'd been born in Barton, Minnesota, he was thirty and his birthday was February 3...the night they'd met.

"It's *her*." Robbie made it sound as if the Wicked Witch of the West had appeared.

"Who?" Frowning, Emily looked up from her program.

Miranda Manzelrod, dressed in cowboy boots, designer jeans and a stunning powder blue Angora sweater, was making her way down the aisle. Emily watched as the beautiful blonde waved hello to three women seated two rows up and to the left of Emily, then tossed her luxurious mane over her shoulder and turned to scan the arena with a practiced eye.

Emily's stomach clenched as a primitive jealousy swept through her at the idea that the beautiful blonde had come to watch Eric play as well. Before she had time to absorb the idea and its implications, Miranda Manzelrod caught Emily's eye and smiled.

Completely unsettled, Emily smiled back.

"Oh, no, she's coming over!" Robbie said, horrified.

"Robbie, behave yourself," Emily said, but her dread echoed her son's.

"Hello, Robbie," Miranda said with a disarming smile. "Are you enjoying yourself?"

He suddenly became fascinated by his high tops. "Yes ma'am. We came to watch Eric play."

Emily tensed, but Miranda's cornflower blue eyes sparkled with welcome. "So I heard. I'm glad you could make it. I know he's happy you're here."

"That's nice of you to say," Emily replied cautiously.

"Is this your first game?"

"Other than Robbie's, yes."

"You're in for a treat. The guys are really revved up for the Wild, and it goes both ways." A blow horn blared overhead. Miranda looked up at the blower with indulgent amusement. "The fans are hyped, too. This is going to be a rough one, both on and off the ice."

"The atmosphere does seem a little...charged."

"Just watch out for flying objects. One of the disadvantages of sitting so close to the ice is you tend to get pelted with food and drink if things get crazy."

Emily smiled and relaxed. "Thanks for the warning."

"Anytime. Well, I'd better get going if I'm going to get dinner before the game starts. Would you or Robbie like something from the snack bar?"

Feeling oddly like a guest of honor, Emily decided it best to wait until both Robbie and her stomach settled down, and declined Miranda's offer. The woman's genuine warmth confused her. After Miranda left, Emily stared blankly at her program. Had she misinterpreted the relationship between Miranda Manzelrod and Eric? If so, why hadn't Eric said something?

Maybe because there was nothing to say.

Then why had he stayed at Miranda's the night he'd kept the Subway? It didn't make sense.

"Can I get a Coke, Mom?"

"Sure, sweetheart." A rousing roar swept through the stands. "But why don't we wait until that vendor comes over to this aisle? The teams are returning to the ice. It looks like the game's about to start."

The starting lineups were announced and the players removed their helmets for the opening ceremony. Emily zeroed in on Eric, standing tall and proud in the center of the rink. It felt good to know he wanted her here, watching him.

Thinking of their nightly telephone calls while he'd been on the road and the two quick lunches they'd shared in the hospital cafeteria since his return—their evening schedules hadn't meshed—she was only dimly aware of the local band singing the American and Canadian anthems in four-part harmony.

Miranda returned just as the game started. Emily's heart swelled with pride as she watched Eric speed across the ice. His energy and determination seemed boundless.

The game moved much faster than Robbie's games did, and as it progressed, Miranda treated Emily to a much-appreciated crash course in hockey techniques and terms. They shared a laugh when a flying puck smacked Eric in his well-padded rear, booed in tandem when he was illegally tripped, and exchanged dry looks when a Wild player 'accidentally' barreled into the net, knocking it off its moorings and preventing a Saints goal.

The stunt earned the Wild player a trip to the sin bin, which sent the Wild fans into a howling protest. Their howls became screams of denial when Eric suddenly scored on a breakaway in the last ten seconds of the period, tying the game at one all. Flushed and breathless from doing her own share of screaming, Emily thought it was adorable the way Eric's teammates crowded around him and patted him on the head with their thick gloves to congratulate him.

"I'm impressed," Emily said when the intermission began. You know so much about the game."

Miranda laughed. "I've been coming to these things since I was a kid. Of course, I was a die-hard North Stars fan back then. I was a Wild fan for a while, too, but now that Bill's signed on as general manager of the Saints, I've had to shift my loyalties."

"Bill?"

"My husband. He's the guy standing in the middle down there behind the player's bench—the one with his arms crossed and a perpetual frown on his face."

"The one wearing the really nice suit?"

"They've got him acting as interim coach until Stump decides on a replacement."

"I didn't know you were married."

Miranda smiled. "New Year's Eve. Eric was our best man."

"I see." Well, that explained a lot. For the first time, Emily noticed the sparkling wedding set on Miranda's left hand and wondered how she could have missed a rock like that before. Probably because it had never occurred to her to look for one, since Miranda had obviously kept her maiden name, at least professionally. "Congratulations."

"Thank you. I've been after Eric to bring you over for dinner but he keeps putting me off with vague murmurings about busy schedules and such." Miranda's eyes twinkled. "I bet it's really because he wants to keep you to himself. He thinks the world of you, you know. He wanted to die when he ripped that hole in your car's exhaust system."

"He what?"

"You didn't know? Lord. I'll kill him. He came back downstairs that night and told me everything was fine."

"Was this...the night he called me from your house?"

"After he delivered the PE equipment he donated to the school, he stayed for dinner, then crashed in the guest room—after staying up half the night talking shop with Bill. They used to play together for Montreal. Anyway, Eric said he hit a pothole or something and destroyed your exhaust system. He wasn't sure how to break the news to you. I guess he decided to get it fixed without telling you."

"I guess he did," Emily murmured, finally understanding Eric's preoccupation with the Subway...and why it hadn't done so much as hiccup since the day he'd borrowed it. He'd apparently gotten more then the exhaust system fixed.

"I'm sorry. I thought you knew. Tell you what. I'll help you give him hell for it after the game, when we go to Hooligans—to celebrate, I hope," Miranda added dryly. At Emily's blank look, she said, "What? He hasn't told you about Hooligans? We always go there after the games. Consider yourself invited."

Emily defended Eric, though why she couldn't say, considering not once had he mentioned anything Miranda had told her tonight. "He was probably thinking of Robbie. It's a school night and..." she sent a meaningful glance in her son's direction. He hung over the banister, watching the Zamboni machine resurface the ice, no doubt pretending he was half a mile away from his principal.

"You're right. I wasn't thinking. That's something else I'll have to adjust to. Having a child." Miranda sent Emily a radiant smile. "I'm expecting in October. A honeymoon baby."

Emily's insides curled in shame at how she'd jumped to the conclusions she had about Miranda and Eric. For the next few minutes she devoted herself to answering

Miranda's questions about what to expect in the coming months. By the time intermission was over, the two women were fast friends.

Meanwhile, tensions in the dressing rooms had escalated. As the teams returned to the ice, the air filled with an electric expectancy. The Wild came out fighting and the Saints were more than willing to oblige. As skirmish after skirmish erupted and the crowd grew more and more belligerent, Emily grew more and more anxious. Eric appeared to remain aloof from the tempers flaring all around him, but she feared for his safety nonetheless.

"Whoa. Things are getting pretty intense," Miranda commented mildly, while the grunts and curses that floated up from the rink had a much stronger effect on Emily. She looked around uneasily, disturbed that the fans so clearly enjoyed the game's escalating violence.

The game picked up speed. Penalties mounted. The Saints scored twice, but the Wild tied it up again. Amid the roar of the crowd, Eric seemed to become a different man. Where before he was determined, he now had an almost palpable aura of menace about him.

The Wild started hitting even harder. Eric was hit from behind as he raced along the edge of the rink with the puck. The two men slammed into the boards so hard the Plexiglas swayed dangerously. Emily's stomach churned as they tumbled over each other like clothes in a dryer, their razor sharp skates glinting as they caught the light.

The game came to a halt as the referee sorted out the tangle. The Wild player netted a penalty, giving the Saints a power play. Another face-off. Eric won the face-off and skated for the Wild's net, preparing to catch a pass. Suddenly a Wild player blindsided him.

"That's the one I told you about earlier," Miranda shouted to Emily over the crowd's angry protests. "He's the Wild's enforcer, you know, their designated fighter. He's trying to start something with—Look out, Eric!" Miranda screamed.

Emily surged to her feet with Miranda as the Wild player grabbed Eric and threw him to the ice. Eric didn't waste time looking surprised. Gloves flew as he pulled his attacker down with him, rolled on top of him, jumped to his feet and hauled the man up again by the jersey. One fist still clenching his opponent's jersey, Eric let fly with the other. The Wild player barreled into the boards with a crash that shattered the Plexiglas.

The crowd went wild. Emily went stock still. Two linesmen grabbed Eric from behind. He shook them off as if they were flies. He snarled something at his attacker, who sat stunned on the equipment-littered ice. His helmet spun like a top beside him. Eric's own helmet was off, his left shoulder pad poked out grotesquely from beneath his jersey, which had a fist-size rip in its back collar from where the Wild player had grabbed him. Eric's stick lay broken in two at his feet.

He turned away and skated to the penalty box. Then, to Emily's utter astonishment, he looked up at her...and smiled.

It wasn't a smug smile. Nor was it victorious, even though he'd clearly won the fight. It was more of a don't-worry-about-me-I'm-having-a-hell-of-a-good-time smile.

In that moment, Emily realized Eric *enjoyed* the violence in his work. For some reason, in the past few weeks, she'd convinced herself he opposed violence as much as she did. Not true. Not true at all. From the looks of him, he'd been waiting for the fight to happen, had been looking forward to it.

Just as Ryan had looked forward to their fights, secure in the knowledge he'd be the winner, while she lay hurt and helpless at his feet.

She had her coat on before she knew what she was doing. "Come on, Robbie. We're leaving."

Miranda turned in surprise. "Leaving? You can't leave."

"Watch me."

"Emily. You don't understand."

"I understand plenty. I understand I've made a big mistake. One I swore never to repeat."

"Listen, I don't know what you're talking about, but—"

"Let it go, Miranda. Robbie, get your coat."

Robbie obeyed, but Miranda followed them into the corridor. "Please don't walk out like this, Emily. Eric's going to be devastated when he—"

Emily whirled. "Devastated? That's his problem. He's the one who just knocked that man senseless."

"He didn't start the fight, Emily."

"No, but he enjoyed it."

By the time they reached the parking lot, Emily felt like she was going to hurl. Her hands shook so much she could hardly fit the key in the lock. Bile burned her throat. Tears blinded her. Dark images of the violence she'd just witnessed mingled with those of her past. Eric, smashing his fist into the other man's face. Ryan, smashing his fist into hers. Both of them smiling afterward, letting her know they'd enjoyed themselves thoroughly. It was a high with men like that, the adrenaline rush and the release that followed. And, Emily knew from experience, it was addictive.

She shuddered, her grip so tight on the steering wheel her hands cramped. Memories of her marriage flashed in her mind. Ryan standing over her as she cowered on the floor, Ryan spitting in her face. "Whore!" he'd shouted, then pulled her to her feet and backhanded her across the bed.

"Mom? Are you okay?"

Disoriented, she blinked and turned to her son. The raw fear in his eyes snapped Emily back to the present faster than anything else could have. "I'm fine, sweetheart. Just fine." With a shaky hand, she reached back and smoothed his hair, letting her love for him wash away her inner horrors. They were safe, now. Free from Ryan, and together. Just the two of them. "I got nervous in there, with all that shouting and noise. Like I do sometimes in traffic. I just needed to get out of there. But I'm fine now. Just fine."

He nodded, but looked far from convinced.

****

His hair still wet from his shower, Eric cut short his post-game radio interview and slipped away from the rowdy celebration in the dressing room to make a beeline for the wives' waiting room just down the hall. He'd asked Miranda to keep an eye out for Emily and Robbie, and bring them down after the game, win or lose. He spotted Miranda the minute he crossed the threshold.

"Where are they?" he asked, peering past her

shoulder into the room filled with card tables and couches. Many wives and girlfriends attended the games, some played cards while their partners were working, others read or napped while they waited to find out whether the night would end with a party or a silent ride home.

"They left. During the second period."

"Left?" Eric's stomach dropped. His gaze searched the room in disbelief. "But I saw her. After that mess with Murder..."

"That's when she left." Miranda scanned the clusters of people milling about and collecting their coats. She lowered her voice. "I don't know how to tell you this, but it did something to her, seeing you in that fight. She bundled Robbie up and took off like a shot."

"What?" Eric frowned. Maybe she'd thought he was hurt. But no, he'd done what he could to let her know he was all right. It was the only time during the game he'd allowed thoughts of Emily to take his mind off the game.

"She said something about having made a big mistake and..." With a helpless shrug, she reached for her own coat, draped across a nearby chair.

Eric's heart lurched. Emily thought she'd made a mistake? With him?

Miranda looked up at him, apology in her eyes. "Listen, I've got to go."

"Aren't you going to Hooligans?"

"Yes, but I have something special planned, and I need to get there before Bill does. He got waylaid by Stump, so I've got a window."

"I'll come with you." Eric helped her into her coat. "Tell me what she said," he insisted as they headed for the elevators to the parking garage.

"I don't know, Eric. I've probably said too much already. She was upset when she left and wasn't making much sense. Come to think of it," Miranda mused as they waited for an elevator, "she was more than upset. There was something in her eyes. I can't explain it, but she seemed...afraid." She looked at Eric in genuine confusion. "It was as if she pictured herself in Murder's shoes."

"Oh, for the love of—I'd never hurt Emily! She knows that."

Miranda peered past him at a group of players who'd

glanced their way at their captain's uncharacteristic outburst. She took his arm and pulled him into the elevator, then punched the number for the players parking level. "Does she? It was hard enough for me to watch you tear into him, and I'm used to seeing you play. Jesus, Eric, you broke the damn glass."

"It was an accident. Hell, I've shattered a few panels, myself. You know how it is."

"But Emily doesn't. Can you imagine what she must have felt, seeing the violence you're capable of?"

"She's a doctor, Miranda. She's seen blood before."

"Exactly. She probably sees more than enough at work. I doubt she wants to see it after hours, too."

"He railroaded me! I didn't stop to think, I just reacted."

"So did Emily. I've never seen anyone leave an arena so fast in my life."

"Murder had it coming. He'd been riding my ass all night."

"No argument there. But Emily doesn't know enough about the game to understand—"

"Then I'll explain it to her. I'll make her understand."

The elevator doors opened. He started forward, but Miranda pulled him back. Hard. He looked at her in surprise.

"I don't think so, Eric," she said. "Not tonight, anyway. You'll end up alienating her instead."

His surprise became a scowl. "Say what?"

"Look at you. You look like you're ready to tear apart anyone who dares to tell you you're wrong." She searched his eyes, her own softening in compassion. "I know this is the last thing you want to hear, but give it some time, okay? Give *her* some time. Wait a day or two for her to put what she's seen, what she's feeling, into perspective. Maybe she'll come around on her own."

"I can't even call her?"

Miranda touched his arm. "She cares for you, Eric. Deeply. She didn't take her eyes off of you from the minute you stepped onto the ice. Whatever happened to her when you mixed it up with Murder is something my gut tells me she'll have to sort out in her own mind before she can discuss it with anyone else. It won't do either of you any good if you go charging after her to demand answers she doesn't have. And I *know* she won't appreciate you trying to force feed her your version of what she saw."

"I wouldn't—"

"You just said you would. Trust me on this one. Please?"

Eric faltered, torn between the need to see Emily and a bone-deep fear of losing her. Swearing sharply, he ran a hand through his still-damp hair. "All right." He jabbed the button to re-open the elevator door. "Let's get the hell out of here."

Chapter Fifteen

A tall beer and a Hooligan's steak dinner later, Eric left Bill and Miranda at a table in the restaurant section of the Irish pub that had become a second home to the Saints and their followers after the games. For dessert Miranda had ordered Bill's favorite cake to celebrate his impending fatherhood. Fortunately, Bill already knew the happy news, or Eric would've felt like a complete dolt for intruding on their evening. But as soon as dinner was over, Eric knew he was on his own for the rest of the night.

Pushing aside the emptiness that came on the heels of his heartfelt congratulations to the glowing couple, he wandered downstairs to the bar where the rest of the team celebrated. He joined his teammates at a group of tables in the back of the bar and accepted the foaming mug of beer pressed into his hand. Soon the hearty camaraderie of a group of men who'd done a hell of a good job that night and knew it surrounded him. Even the women—the wives, girlfriends and wannabes—who were out in full force tonight—didn't seem to mind as the men launched into a play-by-play recounting of the game.

The guys were entitled to crow a bit. Against incredible odds, they'd made good Ronald Stump's promise to deliver a championship caliber team in a town everyone had said couldn't support another NHL team. Now, with their hometown arch-rivals knocked out of the running, for the first time Eric thought they might have a solid chance to take the Cup. From the sounds of it, his teammates agreed.

"What'll it be, everyone? Ready for another round?"

Feeling generous, Eric looked up with smile to tell the waitress yes, and to put it on his tab.

Instead he knocked over his beer. The curvy brunette

in the red leather miniskirt who'd maneuvered her way into the seat beside him squealed in surprise as ice-cold beer flooded her barely covered lap. Eric ignored the brunette's squeal and stared at the waitress as she righted his mug and mopped up the mess.

It was she. The woman from Harry's Place. The sassy little waitress who'd high-tailed it out of there and left him with a hefty bill to pay if he didn't want his name dragged through the mud all over again by a trumped-up lawsuit.

Her eyes met his, widened in recognition. She straightened and backed up a step, but Eric caught her by the wrist. "Oh, no you don't. You're not running out on me again."

The hush that fell over the table warned him he was dangerously close to making a fool out of himself. Rather than let his teammates know he'd been suckered big time by this woman, he released her slowly. His eyes locked on hers, he said, "I'm sorry. I thought you were someone else."

The woman was quick. She smiled dismissively. "No problem. Happens all the time. I usually tend bar, but your waitress went on break. Would you care for another beer?"

"Make it a round. Put it on my tab and I'll catch up with you later."

His teammates chorused their approval. The woman nodded, her eyes still locked with his. "I'll be right back."

Strangely enough, Eric believed her.

The curvy brunette sidled off to the ladies room. Eric curbed his impatience as the bartender-turned-waitress in black satin hot pants returned with more beer and fresh napkins. He waited until the conversation had returned to a dull roar then excused himself to the leggy blonde in black stretch lace who'd commandeered the curvy brunette's seat. He found his target at the bar, filling another drink order.

"About time you showed up," she said, her eyes on the blender as she mixed some frothy green concoction.

"Excuse me?"

"I've been looking for you for weeks. We need to talk."

"When?"

"I get off at two."

"I'll be waiting."

She pulled a napkin out of her pocket and stuffed it into his hand. "Just in case you get sidetracked between now and then."

He frowned and glanced at the napkin. On it, she'd written her name and address. When he looked up again, Cassandra Miller was at the other end of the bar, taking drink orders.

****

"Where do you want to talk?"

Eric looked at the icy drizzle that had begun to fall, eyed the dark, silent arena across the street, and considered his options. "Is there an all-night coffee shop nearby?"

"No, but my apartment's just a few blocks over."

Great. He'd heard variations on that tired theme for the past few hours and it was wearing thin. But unlike the string of women who'd offered to keep him company tonight, Cassandra Miller had something he wanted. He mustered a bland smile. The least he could do was walk her home. "Let's go."

She led him to a fifth-floor walk-up in a building that seemed as old as the city. "Nice place," he managed when she turned on the light to reveal a three-room efficiency even more barren than his own.

"Nice try." She shrugged out of her coat, hung it in the closet, and held out a hand for his. Reluctantly he handed it over. He didn't want to stay any longer than he had to.

"Coffee?" As she walked to the kitchenette, her black satin hot pants rustled in the silence. Eric stayed put and scoped out his surroundings. The room was impeccably clean, but reeked of loneliness. The walls were bare except for several holes and faded squares where pictures had once hung. Cheap polyester curtains sagged from the apartment's only window. Dollars to donuts the only view she had was of the bricks of the building next door.

Against the far wall was a queen-size sleeper sofa, pulled out to reveal a neatly made bed. Beside the bed stood a battered nightstand with a radio alarm clock and a stack of fat library books. Biographies. Iacocca,

Churchill, Gandhi. Between the window and bed, a television set even older than Emily's sat on a metal cart that looked as if it had gone a few rounds with the Merdham brothers. On top of the TV, two photographs in flimsy frames faced the bed. Beyond that, the room held no personal touches. It also had no other furniture.

"Have a seat. I'll be right out."

She disappeared behind a door that had to lead to the bathroom. Eric looked at the bed, back at the bathroom door. He hoped she wasn't changing into something slinky. Sex wasn't what he'd had in mind when he'd agreed to come here, information was. If she planned to trade one for the other they'd both be SOL.

He checked the coffee, filled the mismatched mugs she'd set out. She came out of the bathroom in a pair of faded jeans and a man's Iowa State University sweatshirt. He relaxed a shade. Seduction apparently wasn't on the agenda.

What then? Blackmail? She had to know the brawl had never made the papers. Or maybe her game plan was simpler than that. Maybe she hoped to sell him the information he needed to prove his innocence. It was obvious she was hurting for money.

"There's milk in the refrigerator," she said, joining him.

"Black's fine."

She accepted her cup and studied him over the rim. "You must have a hundred questions. Where do you want to start?"

"How about with you? What's the story here?" His gaze encompassed the all-but-empty apartment.

She smiled, surprising him. "As in do I often invite strange men into my even stranger apartment? The answer is no. I watched you tonight with those women. You're a man with a lot on his mind, but getting lucky isn't on the list. At least not with some fly-by-night floozy who sees you as her ticket to the big time."

"Is that how you see me? As a ticket to the big time?"

"No." She sipped her coffee.

He waited, but she didn't elaborate. "You said you'd been looking for me for weeks. Why?"

"Mind if we sit down? I've been on my feet for ten

hours."

He followed her into the living room. She dropped onto the bed, braced her back against the couch, crossed her legs beneath her. He sat near the foot of the bed, both feet on the floor, and cradled his mug between his hands.

She stared into her coffee. "Harry and his brother set you up that night. They'd done it before, to other first-timers. Not on so broad a scale, but fleeced them just the same. They must've recognized you when you came in. Must've pulled something together quick. McNally can be a quick one when he chooses to be."

"Were you in on the scam?"

Her head came up, her eyes direct. "No, I was the one who called the cops, remember? As soon as I realized who you were and what was happening, I ran for the nearest phone booth."

"Why didn't you come back?"

"I knew I was done there. McNally's half-owner of Harry's Place, and, as you might have noticed, twists the law to suit himself. In the end, I did manage to scrape up the nerve to go back and ask for my last paycheck. For all the good it did me."

"They stiffed you?"

She shrugged, which only increased Eric's anger at the McNally brothers. "It was worth a try, but I hated working for that slime ball and he knew it. He knew I couldn't afford to lose my job, and I knew it was only a matter of time before I'd have to make a decision—of one kind or another. When I saw the damage they'd done to the bar and realized they planned to nail *you* for it, I knew I had to find you. I called the arena and asked for your number, but they wouldn't give it to me. I left a couple of messages, but I guess they never got to you."

"What did you say?"

"Cass from Harry's Place called. Call back. I didn't figure you'd want your business spread all over town. I hoped you'd put two and two together."

"I would have if I'd gotten the messages. Unfortunately, I get calls from women there all the time. The front office just ignores them. They know if I want to be found, I'll give out my number."

"I guessed as much, so I applied for the bartending

job at Hooligans when I heard the team hung out there. I've been hoping to run into you ever since. You don't socialize much with the team, do you?"

"I've been...busy. How long have you been working there, waiting for me to show up?"

"About five weeks. I went home between jobs." She nodded at the television. To see my kids."

For the first time, Eric looked at the framed photographs. Cassandra, with her arms around a pair of freckled boys with missing front teeth and carrot-red hair grinned back at him. In the second picture she wore a soft, filmy-looking dress with flowers on it and sat on a tree swing. A tall, ruddy-complexioned man in a dark suit stood behind her, his hand on her shoulder, her hand covering his. They looked as happy as he felt when he was with Emily. Sadness stabbed him again.

"Twins?" he asked.

"Five years old next month. They're staying with my mother in Hayfield until I can save enough money to send for them. Their father...Luke..." she smiled softly at the second picture "...died unexpectedly and didn't leave any insurance."

With that, everything clicked into place. Cassandra Miller wasn't interested in him sexually. She never had been. Her sassy smile was for show, part of her waitress persona. Her apartment was bare because she saved every penny she made so she could be reunited with her children. It reeked of loneliness because she missed them—and her husband—so much.

Eric thought of Emily, the sacrifices she made for Robbie, and, fleetingly, of his own mother.

Pushing the past aside, he asked Cassandra about the rest of her family. For the next several hours they drank coffee and talked, two wide-awake, lonely people sharing the night. He learned she'd gone to college to study business, but dropped out in her sophomore year to get married. Her husband had died in a tractor accident shortly after their fifth anniversary. Unable to find work in Hayfield, Iowa, she'd set off for the city.

"I'd been working at Harry's Place for three months—trying to avoid McNally's groping hands until I could afford to tell him to take his miserable job and shove it—

when you wandered in."

"Have you ever considered relocating?" Eric asked.

"Right. To where?"

"East Rutherford, New Jersey, Denver, Tampa Bay, maybe St. Louis?" Montreal was out. She didn't speak French.

She laughed. "You've got to be kidding. I can barely spare bus fare to Hayfield."

"Well that, Cassandra Miller, is about to change."

He told her about his restaurants, offered her a job in whichever Amelia's she chose, told her he'd pick up her moving expenses.

"No, I couldn't. No. It's too much."

"It's the least I can do since your statement to the police will save me a hell of a lot of money."

"What about the McNally brothers?"

"We'll let the police take care of them. No sense leaving any loose ends lying around."

"They'll drag you into it somehow."

"Yeah, but if I'm going down, I'm not going alone."

Cassandra agreed to let him know what she'd decided after she talked with her children that weekend by telephone. Pay phone. Eric pressed the bus fare into her hand and told her to go and see them in person first chance she got.

At dawn, she walked him to the door. "You're a good man, Eric Cameron," she said, smiling.

Eric hoped Emily would come to the same conclusion. He couldn't believe how much he missed her. He'd thought about her over and over again as he'd talked with Cassie. The two women were alike in many ways. Strong, independent, full of spunk. After hearing Cassie's story, he ached to hear Emily's. Maybe it would explain why she'd run out on him.

"What's her name?" Cassandra asked softly.

Startled, he met her eyes. "Emily."

"And I'd bet a month's pay you didn't know her the night you came into Harry's Place."

He chuckled. "How did you know?"

"You had a wild, restless look about you that night. You flirted back, if I recall. And to tell the truth, I was tempted to take you home with me."

"You brought me home last night."

"And you sat as far away from me as you politely could." She grinned. "No wonder those groupies were getting nowhere with you last night. You're not available." She opened the closet, handed him his coat—then handed him the black leather jacket he'd lost in Harry's Place.

He looked down at her in surprise.

Her smile broadened. "I wasn't about to let them take *anything* off of you if I could help it. Not after the way you came to my rescue. I grabbed it on my way out the door."

He smiled, touched by her kindness. "Thank you."

She nodded, still smiling. "You're welcome. Your wallet's in there, too, untouched. Although I did look for your address. Seems you haven't gotten around to changing it from St. Louis." She unlocked and opened the apartment door. "Now go home and get some sleep. I'll see you Monday morning at the police station."

"No."

"No?"

"Let's forget about the police for now. Let's try a meeting of the minds instead. If that doesn't work, we can go to the cops. How about I pick you up at nine, and we meet with my lawyer, then give the McNally brothers a call and see what happens?"

Cassandra broke into a slow smile. "I like it. I like it a lot."

****

On Monday at noon Eric called the ER from the empty conference room in his lawyer's office. Cassie had slipped off to the ladies room so he had a few minutes to kill. Her deposition had exonerated him of all blame in the incident at Harry's Place—and let him and his attorney in on a few other things the McNally brothers were up to that they shouldn't be. Once they and their lawyer had heard Eric had Cassandra Miller on board, they'd dropped all claims against him.

Eric felt pretty good for a change. He'd gotten Cassie her back pay and two weeks severance pay, too, kept the police and the media out of his business and avoided digging up a past that was nothing short of a personal nightmare. The Saints had won in Toronto Saturday night, and he was in a mood to celebrate.

With Emily.

Someone answered, and he asked for Dr. Jordan. Forget giving the woman more "time to think." Every time he did that, he ended up moving ten steps backward. Probably twenty or more this time. She hadn't called him once all weekend.

"Dr. Jordan speaking."

"Emily. Hi." His heart zipped into his throat and he had to swallow hard before he could speak again. "Uh, sorry to bother you at work, but I'm just a couple of blocks away. Can you get away for lunch?" Casual, he thought, keep it casual. Don't let her know you're practically foaming at the mouth to see her.

"I'm sorry, Eric. I'm busy."

"I see." Disappointment and frustration nipped him, hard. "Then how about a bite in the cafeteria?"

"I'd rather not."

He couldn't take her freezing him out again. Not this time. "Damn it, Emily," he said soft and low, turning toward the window, even though no one else was in the room. "I need to see you."

The silence on her end was deafening. Then, "I have to go now. Please don't call here again. We need to keep the lines open for emergencies."

"Emily, wait!" But it was too late. She'd hung up. Eric stared at the receiver. Something was wrong. Very wrong. She'd sounded as if she was near tears.

"Trouble in paradise?" Cassie asked cautiously behind him.

Eric grimaced and passed a hand over his face. "Don't even ask."

****

Emily's hands shook as she cradled the receiver. She'd expected Eric to call, but not here. She'd lain awake all night Thursday, waited for the phone to ring, listened for his knock on her door. She'd changed her sheets in a futile attempt to rid her bed of his scent—the same scent that had brought her quiet comfort on previous nights— then, finally, fallen asleep at dawn.

Closing her eyes now, she realized she didn't have to be in bed to pretend he was next to her. He was with her always, embedded in her heart, her mind, her soul. Not

146

an hour went by that she didn't think of him, miss him, ache for him.

But she couldn't condone the fact that Eric had enjoyed himself during his fight on Thursday night. Or that in Saturday night's game, which she'd secretly—masochistically—taped and watched after Robbie had gone to bed, he'd done it again.

Twice.

"Emily."

Her heart stopped. Eric stood in the doorway to her office, looking sexy as hell in a charcoal gray pinstripe suit.

He smiled tentatively, stepped inside. "I told you I was just a couple of blocks away."

"Were you?" she asked, mentally scrambling for the quickest way to get him out of her office without touching him. If she did, she'd be lost. She began to rearrange the files on her desk.

"I was at my lawyer's, taking care of some leftover business from the night we met."

Her head came up at that. "I...see." An image of him that night popped into her mind—bruised and cut face, swollen hands, tender ribs. Looking at him now, in his conservative silk business suit and tie, it was hard to believe he'd ever been anywhere *near* a bar.

"I'd like to tell you about that night. There's more to the story than what you were exposed to."

"I'm sure there is. But it's over now, so we really don't need to rehash it, do we?"

He studied her, his dark, hungry eyes taking in every sleep-deprived detail. "If I've done something wrong, Emily, I need to know what it is. I've wracked my brain, but I can't come up with one good reason why you left the arena Thursday night."

"Maybe I decided I don't like hockey after all."

He looked as if she'd sliced open his chest. "I can't believe that. Miranda told me about the questions you asked. How you cheered in the first period."

"I was being polite."

"Then be polite now and tell the truth."

Feeling cornered, she attacked. "The truth? You want to talk about the truth? Who had my exhaust system

147

replaced and my engine overhauled without telling me?"

Eric blinked, but recovered quickly. "It was just a couple of parts you needed to have replaced. Hardly worth mentioning."

"Bull. I took it to my regular mechanic. He said I might as well have dropped a brand new engine in there."

The look on his face told her he knew he'd been busted. It also told her he'd do the same again in a minute.

"What were you thinking? Did you think I wouldn't mind?"

He snorted. "Hell, if I'd thought that, I'd have told you about it. Truth was, I knew you'd raise such a stink, I—"

"I pay my own bills, Eric."

"Oh, for Pete's sake. A few hundred dollars isn't going to break me."

"That's not the point! Just because you have more money than you know what to do with doesn't give you the right to run around granting wishes left and right!"

"And you don't? Tell me, Dr. Jordan, how many wishes have *you* granted lately, the operative word being *grant*?"

Emily swallowed. He couldn't know about the foundation. No one knew about it except Anna. "What are you talking about?"

"The Jordan Foundation. The fact that you gave away almost forty thousand dollars last year to—"

"You went through my desk!"

"Damn right I did. You won't tell me anything about what's going on inside your head, or what your life is like beyond the confines of this hospital. If I didn't know better, I'd say you were born the day I met you for all I know about your past."

"Could you two keep it down? I can hear you halfway down the hall."

Emily and Eric whipped their heads around, but Sarah was already gone. Silence reigned as their tempers chilled.

"We need to talk," Eric said.

"There's nothing to talk about."

"Then you need to listen. I want an hour of your time,

Emily. Alone. Away from Robbie. Away from the hospital. Just you and me, one on one, across a table, on a park bench, in your car or mine, wherever. We've got some issues to deal with and I'm tired of having to second guess your feelings across a phone line."

"Forget it. I'm not about to dump my child with a sitter just so you can lecture me about how I choose to run my life."

"I think you owe it to me to hear me out, Emily."

It was the wrong thing to say. Emily had spent the last ten years making sure she didn't owe anybody *anything*. "Owe you? You think I *owe* you something? Just because you got my car fixed?"

"Of course not!"

"Or is it because you still haven't cashed my check for Robbie's hockey equipment? Or maybe because you spent half the night in the ER when I asked you to go home? Or, I know, how about because we slept together and—"

"How about because I love you?"

Chapter Sixteen

"I told her I love her."

"That's wonderful! When did she call?"

"She didn't. I went to see her at work. I couldn't wait."

"Oh, Eric. You didn't."

"I couldn't help it, Miranda. I hadn't seen her in almost a week. We were talking every night on the phone. I miss her."

"How did it go?"

"We fought. Why did you have to tell her about the car?"

"I thought she knew. You let me think she knew."

"Oh. Sorry."

A pause.

"So...what did she say?"

"About what? She had plenty to say about a lot of things."

"Oh, no, Eric. You didn't tell her you loved her just to shut her up, did you?"

Silence.

"Eric?"

"I'm here."

"What happened when you told her?"

"All hell broke loose."

"I can imagine."

"No, it really did. They called a code blue and she went racing down the hall. I didn't stick around."

"Speaking of sticking around, I heard you closed Hooligans Thursday night. That's not like you, Eric."

"I met someone I wanted to talk to."

"Kim told me she saw you leave with a woman."

"Kim needs to mind her own business."

"We wives have to stick together, you know that. Who was she?"

"A friend."

"Did you spend the night?"

"You're not my keeper, Miranda."

"Then why did you call me? I could have happily lived the rest of my life without this conversation."

Eric sighed. Women. Sometimes he didn't understand them at all. "I called because...oh, hell, I called because I want to know what I should do now."

"Same thing as before. Give her time."

"I'm going crazy, giving her time."

****

Emily sat in the middle of her bed, glued to the game, and strained for a glimpse of Eric. Vancouver was winning, 5-3. Eric had been helped off the ice after someone had high-sticked him in the face, and it had taken considerable willpower not to get in her car and rush to the arena.

But then the screen flashed a close-up of him seated on the bench with a towel pressed against his cheek. Shortly thereafter he returned to the game. Miranda had told her the more determined players often played while injured. Eric definitely fell into the "more determined" category. Not only when it came to hockey, but when it came to causing havoc in her heart.

How about because I love you?

Damn him. How could he have done that to her? Flayed her heart wide open like that with six simple words?

She wanted to strangle him.

She wanted to believe him.

And that scared her like nothing else could.

****

Eric looked in his rearview mirror, eyed the two-inch dogleg shaped cut on his right cheekbone, and wondered what Emily would have to say about it. Probably nothing good.

It had been an endless two days and nights since he'd told her he loved her. Admittedly his timing had been off, but he knew she'd heard him. Her face had gone soft, and for a heart-stopping moment he'd thought she might open her arms to him.

But then the world had come crashing in on them.

151

The next thing he knew, she'd flown past him and down the hall without a backward glance. He didn't object to that, but it bothered him to no end that he hadn't heard from her since. What kind of woman let a man hang like that, twisting in the wind, after he'd told her he loved her?

Miranda didn't have a clue as to what was going on with Emily. To hell with biding his time. Tomorrow night the Saints played again, then on Saturday he left for Chicago for the first round of the playoffs. Tonight was the only chance he'd have to see Emily before another week went by and he'd be damned if he'd spend it going crazy with wondering what went wrong.

"Eric!" Robbie grinned up at him, a bundle of excitement in his Batman pajamas.

"Hi, Sport. Thought I'd drop by and see what you and your Mom thought of the game the other night."

"Robbie? Who is it?" A young female voice called out.

"It's Eric, Melissa."

"What's he doing out at this...oh, hello." Clearly she'd expected to find another eight-year-old standing on the doorstep.

Eric smiled, reigning in his surprise at finding Robbie with a sitter while Emily's Suburban sat in the driveway. "Hello. I'm Eric Cameron. Is Dr. Jordan in?"

"I'm sorry. She's not here right now."

"She's out with Dr. Caldwell," Robbie piped up.

Emily was out on a date? "Will she be back soon?"

Uncertainty flashed across the teenager's face. "It's hard to say."

Eric bit back the impulse to ask where they'd gone. He could see himself bearing down on their table in some elegant, dimly lit restaurant. He wouldn't be responsible for his actions after that.

"Wanna come in and wait for her?" Robbie asked.

"Robbie..."

"It's okay, Melissa. Eric's our friend. Mom won't mind, honest."

Eric wished he could be so sure. But he wasn't about to pass up a chance to spend some time with Robbie. He'd missed the boy.

After a moment, Melissa stepped back. "Okay. You

152

can come in. But you're not staying up past nine," she warned Robbie.

It was after eight. If Emily wasn't back in forty minutes, he'd leave. "Thank you," Eric said, and stepped inside.

"All right!" Robbie grabbed Eric's hand. "C'mon. I gotta show you something. Mom bought me a new computer."

"Robbie, wait. Did you dry your ears out after your bath?"

Still holding Eric's hand, he rolled his eyes. "Yes, Melissa."

"You know I have to ask."

"What was that all about?" Eric asked when they were in Robbie's room.

"I get infections if I don't dry my ears. Wanna see some really cool dinosaurs? Mom got me this great new game."

"I thought your birthday was in September."

"It is. She said she wanted to give me the computer early, though, so's I can use it for school now."

The last Eric had heard, Emily had planned to wait until Robbie's ninth birthday to give him the computer. Why the sudden change in plans? Was she feeling guilty about dragging him away from the game? Or had she decided since his Mites League season was over, she'd channel his energy into something more educational?

Eric had regretted having to miss Robbie's last game. Disappointment sliced through him now at the thought of Emily moving forward without him. They'd talked of Robbie's future often those nights he was on the road. He'd come to enjoy being her sounding board.

For the next hour or more they played computer games. The telephone rang, but Melissa answered it. At nine-thirty, she came upstairs, looking agitated. "Bedtime, Robbie. Lights out in ten minutes. Go brush your teeth."

"Aw, we were just gettin' started."

"Wrong, kiddo. You're just finishing up. You should have been in bed half an hour ago."

Eric smiled, grateful for Melissa's interruption. An hour of hunting for dinosaurs was enough for one night.

He wondered if Melissa would ask him to leave now that Robbie was going to bed. He wouldn't blame her if she did, but he didn't enjoy the idea of lurking outside in his car like some jilted, jealous lover.

"Mr. Cameron? Could I ask you a favor? I called my mom and she said it was okay to leave Robbie with you if you wanted to stay and wait for Dr. Jordan."

"Your mom?"

"She takes care of Robbie during the day."

"Oh, Anna." So this was one of Augustus' four daughters. "Sure. So you're leaving?"

"My ex-boyfriend called...that was him on the phone...and uh..." her cheeks pinkened "...well, we broke up three weeks ago, but he asked if he could come over tonight, so I wondered if it would be all right to leave Robbie with you so I can see him. Otherwise I'll have to wait until tomorrow. He's not allowed over when I'm babysitting."

Eric smiled. She'd made it sound like she'd have to wait an eternity. He sympathized completely. "I'd be happy to stay."

She beamed. "Thanks."

****

Emily sank deeper into the plush leather of the Lincoln Town Car, stretched her legs, and leaned back against the headrest as she fought the urge to fall asleep for three straight days. It had been a hellish night, one she wouldn't have wished on anyone.

"Thank you for waiting, Augustus. I know how you hate to miss Letterman."

"No problem, my dear. I had some reading to catch up on. Besides, Anna would boil me alive if I left you alone downtown at this time of night."

Emily squinted at the clock on the console. Two-ten. She'd been on the go since five-thirty the previous morning. After putting in a full day's work, she'd spent two hours with Robbie trying to figure out the new computer Brian Parker had sold her, then joined Augustus for their weekly visit to Harmony House.

Normally they were there from eight to eleven, holding a free clinic for the ever-changing residents of the shelter. But tonight as they were leaving a woman had

154

come in, clearly in need of more than routine medical care.

Earlier that evening she'd attended a dinner party with her attorney husband. In the car afterward, he'd attacked her, accusing her of smiling too much at his colleagues.

Calling her vile names, he'd beaten her savagely, then ripped open the low-cut cocktail dress he'd insisted she wear that night. When he'd paused to fumble with his pants before "giving her what she'd been asking for all night," she'd hit him over the head with an ice scraper and scrambled out of the car.

The police had found her stumbling barefoot along the side of the road. They'd brought her to Harmony House when she'd refused to give her name or press charges against her husband, but insisted she couldn't go home or to a hospital. Her husband was too well-known.

"I couldn't leave her."

"I know you couldn't, dear. That's why you're so well liked at the shelter. The women know you care."

"It's more than that." Emily wouldn't have admitted even that much had she been in a stronger frame of mind. But this was Augustus. Her friend, her mentor, the man who joined her in the work that gave her a good part of her own peace and strength. Working with the women at the shelter reminded Emily weekly of how far she'd come; how very much she had to be grateful for.

"Her situation was too much like my own," she whispered, remembering her instant recognition of the fear and desperation in the woman's eyes.

Augustus was silent for a moment. "I've wondered about that." When he continued, Emily realized Anna hadn't betrayed her secrets. "I noticed right away you had a special empathy for your patients at the shelter."

Augustus had been volunteering at the shelter for years before Emily had come along. From what she understood, he'd started the practice as a favor to a friend, long since repaid. Six months after joining his staff, Emily had asked if she might occasionally accompany him. Since then it had evolved into their Wednesday night "date," but she'd never discussed her reasons for wanting to help him.

"It happened a long time ago, Augustus."

"That may be, but I sense it's not over yet."

"Excuse me?"

"May I speak bluntly?"

"Of course."

"I'm sure it comes as no surprise to you that Anna and I share confidences. We care for you as if you were our own daughter, and Robbie our grandson. When you're troubled, we're troubled. That's why this recent...difficulty you're having concerns us."

Emily wasn't sure what to say. "It hasn't affected my work..." she began, but Augustus was quick to reassure her.

"Of course not, but it's affected you. Anna says you're not eating well, and we see your light on at night long after you should be asleep." Gently, he asked, "Might it have something to do with a certain hockey player I've seen you sharing lunch with in the hospital cafeteria?"

Augustus was much too discreet to mention Emily's arrival at the ER with Eric in the middle of the night. She sighed. "It might."

"Do you love him?"

Did she? Was that why she felt so listless, so steeped in dull, unrelenting pain? Was that why the sight of roses, or the smell of fresh-baked cinnamon rolls made her eyes mist without warning? Was love the reason she ached for Eric at night? The reason she tossed and turned for hours before falling asleep?

It couldn't be love. Love was supposed to be sunshine and flowers, favorite songs on the radio, whispered secrets in the night. Love was a gentle touch, a look that caressed, two hearts beating in tandem...wishing the moment would never end.

"I don't know."

"Ah. Then that explains the sleepless nights."

"I'm afraid, Augustus."

"Of love?"

"Of repeating past mistakes. My ex-husband beat me."

"Has Eric given you any indication he would ever harm you?"

"No."

"Has he ever been angry enough at you that you felt he might consider it?"

Her laugh was mirthless. "Several times."

"And yet he didn't."

"No," she said, thinking of that day at Robbie's game. "He didn't. He didn't even come close to it."

"Then why the doubts? Is it his profession?"

She shifted to face his profile. "I thought so at first, but...the more I learn about hockey, the more I understand he's simply doing his job. Granted, it's a job he enjoys, but it's his enjoyment of his work that makes him so...effective."

Augustus remained silent, clearly giving her time to compose her thoughts.

"Do you suppose that for Eric it's the same as when you or I go to work? As in who we are on the job isn't necessarily who we are away from the hospital?"

His smile was droll. "You mean you're not always completely cool, competent and professional?"

Emily laughed. It felt good to laugh for a change.

Augustus pulled into the passing lane to overtake a salt truck chugging up the incline. "I'm afraid I can't answer your questions. I don't know Eric. From what Anna's told me, he seems to care for you, but whether his professional demeanor is something he employs only on the ice is something only you can decide."

Emily plucked idly at a crease in the leather seat. "There's a look he gets in his eyes sometimes. It's so intense, it...frightens me."

"Intense, you say?" Augustus considered that for a moment. "May I play devil's advocate?"

Emily smiled. He always asked permission. And he was usually right. "By all means."

"Have you considered the possibility that this look you see in Eric's eyes might be one of passion?"

"Passion?" Emily's cheeks warmed. "As in lust?"

"Passion comes in many forms, my dear, not all of them sexual."

The heat in her cheeks became a full-fledged blush. Emily was glad Augustus kept his eyes on the road.

"At the risk of sounding pompous, passion is a sign of strong feelings, a state of intense emotional excitement, or, in your case, perhaps even upheaval. From a man's perspective, if Eric cares for you, I'd wager that what he feels in those moments when you think you see anger in his eyes is probably more along the lines of frustration...or despair."

"Despair?"

Augustus nodded. "Because I'd also wager that what he sees in *your* eyes causes him to fear losing the one thing he desires the most. Your trust. Possibly your love." Augustus glided the car onto the exit ramp. "A smile or a soft word in those moments would no doubt contribute a great deal toward easing the anxiety felt on both sides," he added quietly.

They rode the rest of the way in silence until Augustus broke it with, "You have company."

Spotting Eric's Explorer in her driveway, Emily straightened.

Augustus chuckled and eased to a stop in front of the house. "It seems your young man suffers from sleepless nights as well."

Emily smiled, unable to contain her sudden hope at the thought of seeing Eric again. Maybe they *could* work things out.

Augustus reached out and covered her hand. "Talk to him, Emily. Tell him what you've told me. If not tonight, then soon. Don't let the pain of your past mar your present. Above all, don't let memories that should have been laid to rest long ago cheat you out of a promising future."

Touched, Emily wrapped her fingers around Augustus' hand and squeezed. "Thank you."

"Thank *you*. It's good to know not all of the young females of my acquaintance consider me too ancient to understand what it feels like to be in love."

Emily grinned. "Your daughters?"

"Thank God Anna has them in hand. I suspect they would have packed up and moved out on me if not for her."

Emily laughed and pulled Augustus to her for a long, genuine father-daughter hug, the first they'd shared. "Well, I won't leave you."

"Don't be so sure of that, my dear. A hockey player's

life is transient at best. If you decide you love Eric, you may find yourself seeing more of the world than you expected."

Chapter Seventeen

Silently, Emily let herself into the house. She didn't want to wake Robbie. Still mulling over Augustus' parting words, she gently closed the door and slipped off her coat and shoes. She was halfway to the hall closet when she noticed Eric, standing in the kitchen doorway, watching her.

He was so still. She couldn't see his expression, his back was to the low light coming from the kitchen, but he was probably wondering what she had to say about finding him in her house at two thirty in the morning.

She offered a pleasant smile. "Eric. This is a surprise."

"I'll just bet it is. Where have you been?"

Her smile faded. Anxiety snaked down her spine as she recalled other nights, nights when Ryan had asked her that same question in an eerily similar tone of voice. She flashed back to the lawyer's wife she'd just comforted. To stall for time, she reached into the closet for a hanger and hung up her coat, then reminded herself Eric wasn't Ryan. "Is Melissa upstairs?"

"She went home at nine-thirty."

Nine-thirty? He'd been waiting for her for over five hours? No wonder he was upset.

"Would you like some tea?" The first thing they needed to clear up was the reason she'd left his game. She wasn't ready to tell him about Ryan just yet, but an explanation of her work at the shelter might help Eric understand her reaction on Thursday night better.

"I'd like an answer."

Hello? Another uneasy tremor rippled through her. She let it pass. This was no doubt one of those moments Augustus had mentioned, when a soft word or smile might go a long way toward putting her anxieties to rest.

160

She smiled. "I was out with—"

"Dr. Caldwell, I know. Robbie told me."

"I see," she said, not seeing at all. Then what was the problem?

"Do you go out with him often?"

"Every Wednesday night."

His dark eyes bored into hers as he stepped toward her. Emily could now see he was furious. Feel the anger radiating from him in hot waves. She fought the urge to step back. This was Eric, but something was wrong. Very, very wrong.

"Why did you lie to me?"

Her throat went dry. Nervously, she wet her lips. "Lie to you? What did I lie to you about?"

"You told me you couldn't get a sitter for Robbie when I asked you to, but you found one so you could go out with another man until all hours of the night."

"Another man?" She exhaled in relief and started to walk past him into the kitchen. "Oh, for heaven's sake, that was Augustus."

He caught her arm and stopped her. "That was *Augustus* you were locked in a clinch with?"

She looked at his hand on her arm, then up at him. "That was no *clinch*, that was a hug, and why I am standing here in the middle of the night explaining myself to you, I have no idea."

Eric seemed to realize what he'd done. "I'm sorry," he said, and let go of her arm. "I didn't mean to do that."

Emily continued into the kitchen and turned when she reached the sink. She folded her arms across her chest to contain her building anger and said, "You know, I thought maybe we could get a few things worked out tonight, but I've changed my mind. I think you should leave."

"No. Not until I get some answers."

Emily's patience snapped. "No? Eric, this is *my* home," she said, pointing to herself. "It is not for *you* to decide when you leave. In fact, you shouldn't be here at all. I didn't invite you. And if I *had* been out on a date tonight, that would have been my choice as well. Whom I choose to see, when or where or why, is none of your business. It never was."

"You didn't feel that way before last Thursday night, before you saw me mix it up with Murder."

Her hands moved to her hips. "Mix it up? Is that what you call it? If you'd done what you did to that man anywhere else, you could have been prosecuted for assault."

"Emily, you don't understand. It's part of the game."

"I understand plenty. And you know what? I was right that night. This is a game I want no part of."

"You can't mean that."

"I can, and I do. Since I walked in the door, you have practically accused me of being with another man, attempted to physically intimidate me, informed me you are not leaving until you get some answers, told me I don't understand hockey, and now you're telling me I can't mean what I'm saying."

"Emily, I—"

"I understand plenty, Eric, and I mean it when I say I want no part of this."

She watched as Eric took a deep, calming breath. "Emily," he said with surprising patience, "What happens on the ice has nothing to do with what happens between you and me."

"I disagree."

"Are you saying you think I would *hit* you?"

"You enjoy physical confrontations too much, Eric. Don't tell me you don't. I don't want to have to deal with that, and I shouldn't have to. I deserve better."

He looked as if she'd just stabbed him in the heart all over again. "Emily, I swear to you, I'd never—"

"Mommy?"

Both heads turned toward the sleepy, plaintive voice. Robbie stood in the kitchen doorway, rubbing his eyes. Emily stepped past Eric to face her son. What had he seen? What had he heard? "What do you need, honey?"

"Why are you and Eric fighting?"

Emily shot Eric a look over her shoulder. "We're not fighting, sweetheart, we're just talking too loud. I'm sorry we woke you. Go back to sleep, now. I'll be up soon."

"Can I have a glass of water?"

For once, she was grateful for the request. "All right, but wait for me in your room."

"Can Eric bring it up?"

Emily straightened and looked at Eric, who looked determined enough to wear her down completely before he left. Sheer exhaustion made her decision easy. She wasn't up to any more talking tonight. Any more disagreements. This was her home and she made the rules here.

"No. He's leaving."

****

Seated at a table in the far corner of Hooligans, Miranda ground an ice cube between her teeth, her eyes narrowed against the smoke as she kept a vigilant watch on the couple at the bar. She didn't like what she saw.

Earlier that evening, Kim had confirmed that the vivacious bartender Eric had abandoned his teammates in favor of was the same woman he'd left Hooligans with that night almost three weeks ago. She'd also learned he'd been occupying that particular bar stool until closing every night the Saints were in town, since. What happened afterward was anyone's guess, but watching them now, with their heads bent together, Miranda had a pretty good idea of where they were headed. Maybe she needed to go over there and remind Eric just who he was supposed to be in love with.

"Ooo-ee, would you take a look at that?"

Miranda dragged her attention from the tête-à-tête at the bar, and turned to see what hapless victim Peter Cordell, the Saints' deposed captain, was setting his sights on this time.

She nearly choked on her ice cube.

Emily Jordan stood at the foot of the stairs looking uncertain and uneasy. Miranda suspected she didn't spend much time in bars, had never entered one alone. She had that vulnerable look vultures like Cordell could spot a mile away.

"Now that's one classy piece. I wonder what she'd say if I invited her to my place to practice my quickshot?"

"Try it and you'll be lucky if your captain lets you live," Bill said from behind Miranda.

Miranda and Cordell shot Bill a surprised look, Miranda grateful for his show of support. She didn't want Emily anywhere near Cordell.

"No shit? She's Cameron's squeeze?" Cordell's gaze

sidled over to Eric and Cassandra at the bar, a smarmy smirk curling his lips. "This ought to be interesting."

Emily stood at the entrance to the bar, her heart thudding in her throat as her eyes adjusted to the dimness beyond. It had been exactly two weeks since she'd seen Eric, and she wasn't sure what her reception would be.

The only thing she knew was she owed him an apology. He wasn't a monster like Ryan or the lawyer who had beaten his wife. It had been rude, if not cruel to throw him out the way she had, after he'd spent five hours waiting for her and watching over her son. The look in his eyes when she'd said he was leaving had been desolate. She might as well have branded him a child abuser while she was at it.

"That's right," he'd told Robbie quietly, after a long, tense silence. "I'm on my way out. Good night again, Sport. Happy dinosaur hunting." With a last look at Emily, he'd let himself out the front door, and left her to put Robbie back to bed alone.

She knew the team came here after the games to celebrate, and as soon as the final siren had sounded after tonight's game she'd made up her mind. She'd find Eric, congratulate him, and apologize. She supposed she could have called him, but she wanted to do it face to face. She owed him that much.

From the sound of it, tonight's celebration was in full swing. A sizeable crowd in the back of the room seemed to be where the team had gathered. Emily just hoped Eric was among them. As she mustered her courage to approach the group, she heard a burst of familiar laughter coming from the bar.

Eric sat at the end, clearly enjoying the company of a petite brunette in black satin hot pants. Emily watched as he motioned for the woman to come closer, whispered something in her ear. The woman put her hand on his arm and whispered something back. They shared a smile that split Emily's heart in two.

It also made her mad. The man claimed to love her, yet here he was, less than three weeks later, making passes at his bartender? Was this how he entertained himself when he was on the road? If so, he had a lot of nerve questioning *her* fidelity.

She started for the bar.

Still chuckling at Cassie's latest off-color joke, Eric made water designs on the bar with his beer bottle. The woman would go far. America's Gateway to the West would never be the same. She'd given her notice at Hooligans, and in less than a week, she'd be back together with her kids. His St. Louis manager had already found her a nice place to live near the Amelia's there. Eric was glad to have helped her out.

She'd been good about helping him out, too. If it hadn't been for Cassie, he'd be staring at his apartment walls night after night with nothing but the hole in his heart to keep him company.

God, how he missed Emily. Cassie made him laugh, but Emily made him happy. When she wasn't slicing him to the bone, that was. Did she really believe he could hurt her or Robbie?

"You're wearing your lost puppy look again, Cameron." He met Cassie's smile as she toweled away his crooked Olympics logo. "I wish there was something I could do."

"You got any miracles in your pocket?"

"No, but I've got coffee. Looks like you've reached the bottom of your two-beer limit, my friend. How about it?"

"Sounds good. I'll take it over to the table. Miranda's been giving me the evil eye again. Between the two of you, I swear—" He froze, spotting Emily's reflection in the backbar mirror. She looked so real he almost leapt across the bar to touch the smoky glass. He shook his head and pushed his beer aside. "Make it strong, Cassie, I'm starting to hallucinate."

"Maybe not," she murmured, and nodded at someone behind him.

Slowly, Eric turned around. "Emily?"

"I thought I'd drop by and congratulate you on winning the first round of the playoffs."

For the longest moment, all he could do was stare.

Cassie cleared her throat. "Eric, why don't you offer the lady a seat?"

Blindly he removed the leather jacket Cassie had returned to him from the bar stool beside him. Anytime

165

someone had asked, he'd all but snarled that the seat was taken. "Would you like something to drink?"

Emily sent Cassie a cool smile. "A glass of white Zinfandel would be nice, thank you."

"I'll open a fresh bottle. Be back in a jif." She scooted away, humming what suspiciously sounded like Happy Days are Here Again.

"She's very attractive."

"She reminds me of you. I can't believe you're here."

Emily looked around the bar, took a deep breath. "You were right. We need to talk."

"I'm all yours. Where do you want to go?"

She smiled, looking relieved. "Here's fine for now. I could use that glass of wine."

Cassie returned with Emily's wine and a friendly smile. "On me. It's not every day my new boss's lady stops by for a visit."

Emily looked at Eric. "You've bought Hooligans?"

He laughed and shook his head. "Not quite. Emily, meet Cassandra Miller, who's soon to be the most popular bartender in St. Louis. Cassandra, Emily Jordan."

Cassie held out her hand. "Eric's hired me to work at his restaurant in St. Louis. I leave next week."

"I'm pleased to meet you."

Cassie smiled and poured Eric's coffee. "Not half as pleased as I am to meet you. I've been hoping for a chance to tell you how wonderful I think this man of yours is."

"Cassie—"

"Hush, Eric. It's true. If it weren't for you, I'd still be serving swill at Harry's Place."

"You worked at Harry's Place...on Brady Street?" Emily asked.

"I'm half ashamed to admit it, but yes. That's where I met this character. I was working the night those crooks tried to..."

While Cassie talked, Eric sank back, drank his coffee, and absorbed the sight of Emily, sitting close enough for him to touch. Her elbows on the bar, her eyes wide with fascination as Cassie relayed her story, she sipped her wine and looked as lovely—and as fragile—as an angel.

Suddenly he began to understand how she might fear his strength. He'd always been a physical man, using his body as much as his words to communicate, both on and off the ice, but if it meant losing Emily, he'd curb his style around her or die trying.

Her hair fell down her back like flame-colored silk, and enchanted him as it caught the low light in the bar. He reached out to capture a tendril, smiled when she glanced over at him to see what he was up to.

He stroked her hair between his fingers and remembered the first time he'd seen it in its natural state, the night they'd made love, five brutally long weeks ago. His thoughts drifted back to that night, to the gentle love they'd shared, the whispered secrets, the passion that had exploded between them.

Just then Emily turned to look at him. For a sizzling moment time stood still. Everything he felt for her was reflected in her sea green eyes—the passion, the need, the regret for the time wasted.

Desire washed him from his seat. "Finished your wine yet?"

Emily's eyes never left his. "I think so."

Her hand slid into his as they climbed the steps to the front door. By the time they reached the parking lot, Eric couldn't wait any longer. He stopped and hauled Emily into his arms. She met him more than half way. What started out as one soul-searing kiss soon became half a dozen or more, until a wisecracking by-passer suggested they "Get a room."

Breathing hard, Eric pulled away. He looked down to find Emily grinning up at him, clearly not caring who saw them making out in the parking lot. He kissed her nose. "Come home with me. My apartment's only a few miles—"

She shook her head, her smile regretful. "I can't. I promised Melissa I'd be back in an hour."

"An hour?" That hardly gave them enough time to say hello. "Tell me you didn't drive all this way just to congratulate me on the game."

"I came to apologize. I was wrong the other night. I know you weren't trying to intimidate me, and that you'd never hurt me—or Robbie—in that way."

"Emily, I am so sorry—"

"In fact," she continued, "I was telling Augustus that not two minutes before I walked through the door that night."

"You were?" Eric suddenly noticed a group of catcalling teammates headed their way. "C'mon. We need to get out of the flow of traffic here."

"Good idea." When they were settled in the front seat of the Suburban, Emily backtracked to her reason for coming to Hooligans. "Augustus and I were at Harmony House that night."

"Harmony House? Isn't that a women's shelter?" At Emily's look of surprise, Eric said, "The wives were talking about doing a fundraiser for the shelter before things got so crazy with the playoffs. They were going to sponsor a dinner at *Maison Rouge* and have the guys serve as waiters. They still might, depending on how things go." He smiled. "If not, they'll do it next year. The guys are all for it."

For the longest moment Emily couldn't speak. *Maison Rouge* was one of the most exclusive restaurants in town. The money such a fundraiser would bring in would be phenomenal. And Eric made it sound as if it were the most natural thing in the world to want to take part in it.

"What's the matter? Can't you picture me in a tux with a towel over my arm?"

Emily swallowed the lump in her throat and shook her head. Tears threatened to spill past her lashes.

Eric sobered. "I'm sorry. I shouldn't have interrupted. So you and Augustus were at Harmony House?"

Emily regrouped. She didn't have time for tears. "We donate our time on Wednesday evenings. Usually we're home in time for Augustus to watch Letterman, but last week the police brought in a woman who'd been assaulted by her husband, and..." She told him as much of the story as she could without compromising the woman's confidences. "So I was a little on edge that night...prone to jumping to conclusions and making connections I had no business making. I'm sorry if I hurt you."

"It doesn't matter," he said, stroking her hair. "What matters is you're here now. You needed time to sort things out, and I was too busy pushing you and jumping to my own conclusions to see that." He chuckled softly. "So Miranda was right after all."

"Miranda?"

Somewhat sheepishly, Eric confessed to having gone to Miranda for advice.

"You seem to have a lot of female friends."

"They're just friends, Emily. I know for a while you thought there was something up with Miranda. I'm sorry I didn't tell you sooner. I was just so...frustrated with you that night. I wanted to shake you up."

"Well, it worked...until Miranda set me straight. Speaking of which..."

The conversation segued into a lively discussion over her car and exactly what he'd had done to it. She insisted on reimbursing him for the repairs, he refused to consider it.

"Unless," he said, leering suggestively, "You could be persuaded to make me another lemon meringue pie."

Emily burst into laughter. "I'll see what I can do."

But when the laughter died, Eric's intensity returned. Reaching over, he took her hand and kissed it. "There's a banquet at the Heritage Arms on Saturday night," he said quietly. "I want you to come with me—and plan on staying the night at my place."

Chapter Eighteen

Emily awoke to a storm of doubts about attending Eric's banquet. Her former mother-in-law, Patricia Montgomery, was prominently active in community affairs. And Ryan—who early in their relationship had claimed charity events bored him senseless—had by the end of their marriage taken perverse delight in dragging her away from her studies to those same events. The United Hope banquet would be precisely Patricia Montgomery's cup of tea.

Emily had avoided contact with the Montgomery's these past years by steering clear of events favored by the country club and charity ball set. But now Eric had asked her to re-enter the world that had been one of Ryan's most powerful weapons against her. Over and over again he'd told her she didn't have what it took to compete with his friends. She had no class. She had no style. She danced like an elephant. She couldn't carry a conversation in a box. She didn't even know which spoon to use for her fruit salad.

In short, she wasn't good enough, and never would be.

In her saner moments, Emily knew it wasn't true. But after Ryan, it had taken years to recover her self-confidence enough to attend even the hospital Christmas party.

Still, shoptalk over cookies and punch was a far cry from a seven-course meal and champagne in the glittering company of the Twin Cities' upper echelon at the Heritage Arms. Just the *thought* of going dredged up her deepest insecurities.

Logic told her it was only one night, but she couldn't shake the feeling she was tempting fate. Her doubts snowballed as the day wore on. When Eric called that night, she asked if he really *had* to be there. The pause that followed gave her the sinking feeling she'd disappointed him.

"Sorry," he finally said. "Stump's put out the word he wants the team to make a good showing. Are you having problems getting a sitter?"

"No, Robbie's spending the night at Glen's."

She felt Eric's smile across the line. They talked for another hour, and by the time she hung up, Emily was more worried about what she would wear to the banquet than the prospect of running into her former in-laws. Eric had planted the seed in her mind that the evening might be a good opportunity to talk up her own charitable cause, Harmony House.

Given that perspective, Emily couldn't help but push her personal fears aside. The women and children at Harmony House needed all the help they could get. As one of their board of directors, she knew exactly how tight things were at the shelter.

But by five o'clock Saturday night, Emily was spooked all over again. Pacing the bedroom, she waved her hands to dry her nails and tried to walk off her nervous energy. The morning paper had featured a story on the banquet, mentioning several notables expected to attend. She hadn't recognized any of the names, but that didn't mean she was in the clear.

"Think safety in numbers," she muttered, as she re-checked her makeup in the mirror and touched up the spot where she'd chewed off her lipstick. "With five hundred people there, the odds of running into anyone you know are..." She sighed resignedly. Math wasn't her strong suit. Not when her stomach was tied in knots.

She checked her stockings for runs. Again. Her hands had shaken so badly when she'd put them on she could've sworn she punctured the sheer black silk with her nails. No runs. No last-minute trip to the store to delay the inevitable.

She looked into the mirror one last time. The woman who stared back at her was someone she hardly recognized. Sleek and sophisticated. Not words she would usually reach for when asked to describe herself, but tonight they seemed to fit.

She felt like an imposter. Her elegantly simple forest green (should she have bought it in black?) cocktail dress had cost more than she'd spent on clothes in the last six months—Robbie's included.

She snorted. Nobody said it was cheap to slay dragons.

Then again, she mused, as she eyed her smooth French twist and re-adjusted the black satin bow that held it in place, if she could hardly recognize herself, people she hadn't seen in ten years would probably look past her without a second glance.

The doorbell rang. Her stomach dipped. As she went downstairs to answer the door, her nerves twisted into knots all over again.

But one look at Eric and her doubts disappeared. Nobody, but nobody was going to look at her twice with him standing beside her.

Her heart swelled with pure female pride. "Hi," she breathed, staring at him in his custom-tailored black tuxedo. "You look...incredible."

His smile as he stepped inside made her tingle all over. "That's supposed to be my line."

No man had the right to look so sexy. Or so confident. "I'll...get my bag."

"First things first." He pulled her into his arms and kissed her, long and hard. By the time they were done, she'd lost her black satin shoes, three hairpins, and forgotten every last one of her reservations about attending the banquet.

"Sorry about that," he murmured. He handed over the pins he'd collected from the floor. "I had to make sure you weren't a figment of my imagination." His eyes were a study in masculine appreciation as he slowly shook his head. "I knew you were beautiful, Emily, but you're a total knock-out tonight."

She flushed with pleasure, then reached past him and opened the closet door to pull a tissue from a pack she'd tucked into the pocket of her new black cashmere coat.

"Lipstick," she explained, and carefully offered him the tissue. If she touched him again, they might never leave the house.

His wicked grin told her he knew what she was thinking, and agreed. He nodded toward the stairs. "Make it quick, or I won't be held accountable for my actions."

Back at her mirror, she noted her cheeks held a rosy glow that had been missing before. Tilting her head to one side, she decided the changes Eric had made in her appearance were for the better. The French twist she'd struggled to get just right was looser now, more feminine. With one supercharged kiss, he'd changed sophisticated and sleek into sophisticated and sexy.

She grinned, snatched up her overnight bag and breezed back downstairs. Her spirits stayed high until she spotted the hotel, with its gleaming mahogany doors and imposing Doric columns. She swallowed, suddenly thinking of a carnival fun house, with jack-in-the-boxes wearing huge false smiles hiding inside, preparing to pop out at her when she least expected it.

Nervously she smoothed her skirt as Eric pulled the Boxter into the curving drive behind four other cars. Would she be able to pull it off? Would she make it through the evening without someone recognizing her and spilling some of her past to Eric?

Why hadn't she told him about her marriage?

"Second thoughts?"

Startled, she looked up at him. In that moment she knew she was falling in love with him. The knowledge made her want to dive into the driver's seat and whisk him away to somewhere where they could be alone and she could tell him everything.

Instead she shook her head, and cursed the stubborn pride that had brought her to this. Ryan had been right. She wasn't cut out for this sort of thing.

"Then what's up?"

"I was just wondering what's in store for us tonight."

He flashed her a devilish grin. "During the banquet, or after?"

Her answering smile faltered. "During."

He looked surprised, then at her hands, fisted in her lap. "You've never been to one of these things before?"

"It's...been a few years."

"Doesn't matter. They're all pretty much the same. Cocktails at six, dinner at seven, the awards program at eight and—"

"Dancing at nine," she finished with him.

He smiled and reached out to cover her hands. "See? Piece of cake."

Grateful for the contact, she linked her fingers with his. "Do you dance?"

He warmed her with a leisurely head-to-toe and back look. "Ordinarily, no, but with you I'll have to make an exception. I don't think I can wait until ten to hold you against me again."

"Ten?" They were going to be here for *four hours*? She'd thought they were just putting in an appearance for Stump's sake.

Eric glided the Porsche under the portico, toward a waiting valet. "I figure by then we'll be able to sneak out without anyone noticing." His free hand slipped from hers to stroke her thigh. Heat ribboned its way into her womb. "In the meantime, I'll be going crazy wondering what you're wearing under that incredible dress."

"Try nothing." Not quite true, but if it got them out of there even five minutes sooner it was worth it.

His hand froze. "You're kidding."

She met his eyes, her confidence rising. He looked half shocked, half thrilled, and ready to pounce. Emily smiled. They'd be out of there by nine, if not sooner. She lifted a that's-for-me-to-know-and-you-to-find-out eyebrow at Eric, then allowed the valet to help her out of the Boxter.

Eric was enchanted. "You're incredible," he murmured, offering his arm as they crossed the threshold.

"Eric! Over here!"

Miranda waved at them from the registration table. Bill stood beside her, an indulgent look on his face. Eric smiled. His friend had been wearing that same sappy expression around Miranda ever since he'd found out he was going to be a father.

Eric didn't blame him. He slid Emily a sidelong glance. If she'd told him she was going to have his baby he'd probably break the world record for sappiness. God knew he'd come close enough the last time he'd been told he was about to become a father. And even then, Monica had been lying.

"We saw you pull in as we got out of our car," Miranda said, mercifully dragging him back to the present. She handed him a program. "I already checked us all in. Emily, you look fantastic."

"So do you, little mama," Eric offered with a grin.

Bill beamed. "I'll second that." He offered Emily his hand. "It's a pleasure to finally meet you. Eric, ah, forgot to introduce us the other night at Hooligans."

Emily laughed, her cheeks turning a shade pinker at the reminder of how she and Eric had been kissing outside the restaurant. "How do you feel?" she asked Miranda.

"Fine. I'm not getting sick any more, but I am having trouble staying awake past nine. So if I flop face down in my plate, give me a nudge, okay?"

After a visit to the bar, Bill suggested to Miranda that they mingle now, since they wouldn't be staying past dinner. Eric half-heartedly suggested he and Emily do the same, and was mildly surprised when she smiled broadly and told him to lead the way. Apparently she'd decided to throw herself into the evening heart and soul once he'd made it clear he had to be there.

From across a circle of people who'd somehow gotten between them, he feasted his eyes on the sight of her, dressed like no doctor he'd met. Lord, he'd never seen her look so stunning.

Or so sexy. Her dark green dress matched the color of her eyes when he kissed her. The watered silk caressed her curves so softly it made him jealous. It also made the most delicious rustling sounds when she moved. He ached to buy her a dozen dresses just like it, so he could enjoy peeling them off of her.

Or ripping them off, depending.

He wondered if he should have warned her he was going to be spotlighted tonight. But she'd seemed so skittish about coming he hadn't wanted to make a big deal of it. Studying her face, he realized he'd never seen her so bright-eyed and bubbly before. Remembering the way she'd chattered non-stop in the car, he decided he couldn't have gotten a word in edgewise if he'd tried.

As she engaged some investment banker in a conversation about market interest rates, it occurred to him she wasn't usually so talkative. Could she still be nervous? Why? There wasn't anyone here she had to impress.

Or was there? He frowned as the banker's dragon lady of a wife descended on the group and—after a curious stare at Emily—herded her husband toward their table. The rest of the group drifted apart as the announcement came to be seated for dinner. Emily sipped her mineral water, her gaze following the banker and his wife, her expression oddly strained.

"Ready to sit down?" he asked, coming up behind her.

She looked up at him, wearing the same smile he'd seen her offer everyone she'd met since leaving Miranda and Bill. Perfect in its execution, but with no genuine emotion behind it.

"Thank you, I'd love to."

Eric suddenly realized she was terrified.

Guided by Eric's hand on her lower back, Emily crossed the ballroom to their table, and wished she'd ordered something alcoholic. But this was one night she needed to keep her mind sharp.

So far her luck was holding out. With the exception of that brief, haven't-I-seen-you-somewhere-before look she'd gotten from Amanda Cathcart, she hadn't encountered anyone who might give her away. She glanced at her watch, and saw it was only seven o'clock.

They reached their table, three of the ten seats still available. Miranda looked up from her conversation and smiled encouragingly across a sea of crystal and mauve linen, and Emily realized she and Miranda would be the only women at the table. The rest were apparently Eric's teammates. She also noted uneasily that he suddenly treated her as if she were made of spun glass.

Never mind it was how she felt. What bothered her was he'd somehow figured out she was putting up a major front. She tried to catch his eye as he seated her. He smiled reassuringly and introduced her to one of his alternate captains.

Soon the men were hip deep in discussing the strengths and weaknesses of the St. Louis Blues, Eric's previous team and the Saints' opponents in the next round of playoff games. Miranda sent her a dry look of commiseration, but Emily waved it off, grateful for the opportunity to regroup. With Eric immersed in hockey talk, she was free to scan the room.

Seconds later, she wished she hadn't.

John and Patricia Montgomery sat two tables away.

Chapter Nineteen

"You've hardly touched a bite."

"I'm not much on chicken," Emily replied, knowing it was a mistake the minute the words were out. Eric knew better.

"Or green beans or salad?"

Emily speared two beans, and willed herself to eat them without gagging. Eric's frown deepened as he watched. "What's wrong? Do you feel all right?"

She felt like leaving, but wasn't about to admit it. She reached for her water goblet. The slice of lemon inside bumped her upper lip as she sipped her water. "I think the heat may be getting to me." It was a safe enough answer. Several players at the table had already commented on how hot the room seemed.

"I don't think they were expecting all five hundred guests to show up." Eric's hand covered hers, squeezed reassuringly. "It'll be over soon. We'll leave right after dinner if you want to."

"No. I saw Ronald Stump counting heads. Probably checking to see if all the players were here. I wouldn't want to get you in trouble with him again."

"To hell with that, Emily. You're more important."

Emily looked past Eric to find Peter Cordell watching them. He'd joined them after the fresh fruit salad had been served, taking the last seat at the table. From the moment he'd arrived, he'd made Emily uneasy. On the surface his polite questions had seemed innocuous enough, but there was something about the way he looked at her, as if he knew something about her no one else did.

Paranoia. It was invading her pores.

She forced a smile. "I'm fine. Really."

The waiter arrived to clear their plates. Emily indicated she was finished with hers. While Eric brooded,

178

she determinedly dug into her apple strudel. The awards program began halfway through dessert. The lights dimmed and Emily felt better. Safer. Eric reached for her hand. She caught Cordell watching her again and stifled the urge to shift in her seat.

Keeping his eyes on the speaker, Eric slowly, erotically rubbed his thumb across the palm of her hand. Within minutes all Emily could think about was the sweet heat unfolding inside her and the knowledge that soon they'd be alone and she'd explain everything.

"This is the last one," Eric whispered half an hour later. After this, we're home free."

Emily smiled and turned her attention to the dais as the speaker waxed eloquent on the virtues of the recipient of the organization's annual Community Service award. Whoever he was, the man was well-traveled, involved in sports and a regular paragon. Selfless, dedicated, generous, humble, kind.

Apparently he'd donated blocks of seats for local sports events to senior citizen's groups, outfitted needy youngsters who had exceptional athletic ability (and some with simply a strong desire to play) with the proper equipment, was a major contributor to the Special Olympics, and lectured elementary school children on the virtues of sportsmanlike conduct both on and off the...

Lectured elementary school children?

Emily barely had time to realize what was happening before Eric squeezed her hand and a huge white spotlight caught them in its blinding glare. Applause roared in her ears as Eric stood and met her horrified stare. Heat swamped her as her heart jackhammered in her chest. Her hands shook, her forehead broke out in a cold sweat. Everyone was looking at them and she suddenly felt as if she were suffocating.

"Emily?"

Eric's voice sounded as if it were coming to her through a long, dark tunnel. She fought the encroaching blackness, and wished she'd eaten more. She would not faint. She would not make a scene. She would not attract any more attention to herself than she already had.

"Emily?" Eric stepped toward her, his face creased with concern.

179

"Please...just go up there...just go...*now*."

He did, but not before she saw the disappointment in his eyes. He turned and strode to the podium, the spotlight marking his progress amid resounding applause. Emily sank back in her seat, weak with relief at being left behind in the embalming darkness. She would have fled the room if she thought her legs would carry her.

"Not used to being in the spotlight, are you?"

Peter Cordell had slipped into Eric's empty seat. Emily closed her eyes and composed herself, then met his superior smirk head on. "I guess not," she said coolly.

He chuckled, and the sound grated on her already frayed nerves. "You've changed. You used to be such a mousy little thing."

"You have me confused with someone else. We've never met."

"Not officially, no. But there was a garden party at Amanda Cathcart's several years ago where your husband...accidentally spilled his drink on your dress."

Emily paled. Ryan had in fact tossed his scotch and soda in her face. Several people had witnessed the humiliating incident.

Cordell smiled. "I wondered what happened to you. Now I know."

With as much grace as she could muster, Emily slid her chair back and stood. She was *not* about to discuss her past with Peter Cordell. "If you'll excuse me," she said icily, then sailed from the room, grateful that Miranda and Bill were already gone. Miranda would have followed her if she'd been there, and Emily needed to be alone. In the powder room she flattened her palms on the cool marble vanity and stared at her reflection. Her color was high, her eyes unnaturally bright. She had to get a grip. Eric would take one look at her and—

Eric. She'd walked out on his acceptance speech. Oh, no. What had she done? Obviously he'd wanted to surprise her. Remembering the expectant look in his eyes, she realized he'd thought she'd be pleased, maybe even hoped she'd be proud of him.

Instead she'd recoiled in horror, then walked out on him.

She had to find him, apologize, try to explain. With

Peter Cordell sniffing around, clearly in a mood to cause trouble, she'd have to do it fast. Quickly she touched up her hair and lipstick. She heard voices approach the door, turned to make her exit...

And came face to face with Patricia Montgomery.

Patricia recovered first, as cool and gracious as ever. "Emily. I thought that was you I saw standing near the bar when we came in." She turned to the young woman beside her, a stunning brunette in gold lamé Emily recognized from the newspaper as Ronald Stump's daughter, Catherine, and the Saints' highly touted marketing manager. "Catherine, I'd like you to meet...an old friend, Emily Jordan. Emily, Catherine Stump."

Catherine's shrewd smile unsettled Emily even more. "Emily. Would you by any chance be Ryan's ex-wife?"

Patricia winced. Emily felt the ground shift beneath her. "Do you know him?"

Catherine laughed. "Ryan's my fiancé."

Emily stared, dumbfounded.

"Small world, isn't it?" Patricia offered somewhat lamely. She looked almost flustered—a first in Emily's experience. Nothing ruffled her ex-mother-in-law. Nothing. Only Emily knew how hard she worked to maintain that cool, controlled image. Battered wives had more to hide than most.

"Congratulations," Emily responded slowly. "I hope you'll be...very happy."

Catherine's smile was surprisingly warm and open. "I intend to be."

"Is he here with you tonight?" Emily heard herself ask.

"Lord, no. He hates these things. I'm here with my father. Patricia and I decided to slip out early to enjoy a cigarette before the crowd breaks up." She reached into her purse and withdrew a gold lighter and a pack of Virginia Slims, offered one to Patricia—who to Emily's surprise accepted it—then Emily.

Emily declined, and wondered if Catherine had any idea what she was getting into, marrying into the Montgomery family. One glance at Patricia told her she didn't. Her ex-mother-in-law had retreated from the conversation and watched her with a look that seemed part wariness, part admiration.

Admiration? Impossible. She'd been the one to tell Emily her only option was to accept her lot in life...as she had. As she was apparently still doing. Emily had spotted three finger bruises on Patricia's inner wrist when she'd held her cigarette away from her face to blow out her first stream of smoke.

Speaking of which, Emily didn't think smoking was allowed in the ladies room. Apparently things like that didn't concern Catherine Stump. She seemed to be a woman who made her own rules to live by. An odd partner for Ryan, if there ever was one. From what she remembered, Ryan liked his women docile and obedient.

The sound of applause filtered into the room and jarred Emily back to the present. "Well, I'd better get back to my table."

"You're here with Eric aren't you?" Catherine smiled as she exhaled, her eyes meeting Emily's, woman to woman. "Lucky you. He's gorgeous. Daddy thinks he's made of stone and as hard to tame as a hungry lion, but I had a feeling there was more to him than meets the eye. You must be so proud of him tonight."

****

Eric stood on the dais and surveyed the crowd rising from their seats. As refracted light from the overhead chandeliers sparkled across the room, he felt the band of iron holding his heart together squeeze tighter. Emily was gone again.

Damn it. He should have warned her. Should have taken her home as soon as he'd realized how nervous she was. He scanned the Twin Cities' glitterati, hoping she'd only stepped out for some fresh air, or made a trip to the ladies room.

The hair on the back of his neck prickled as he realized Cordell was missing, too. Cordell, always on the lookout for an opportunity to mix things up—as long as it wasn't on the ice. There, the flashy center could carry eggs in his pockets and not have them broken by the end of the game.

Eric had never understood why the guys had elected Cordell captain, unless it was because he was distantly related to the club's real estate mogul owner and continually reminded everyone of it. Usually Eric ignored Cordell, but not tonight. He'd seen the way the man looked at Emily, sensed the tension between her and Cordell as if it had been served right along with the entrée.

He scanned the room again, searching for the man who had smoothly quizzed Emily about where she lived and worked, how long she'd been living in the area. Innocent enough questions, but coming from Cordell they'd sounded like he was compiling a private dossier. Or trying to move in on her.

He'd kill the bastard. If Cordell was responsible for Emily's disappearance—

"Cameron! Hold up a minute. I want to talk to you."

Eric swung around to see Ronald Stump lumber across the dais. Clearly, his silver-haired owner had had one too many. He endured the man's over-the-top congratulations before being dragged into the crowd to meet a group of the team's foremost fans. A hundred smiles and an agonizing ten minutes later he escaped the ballroom, only to have his arm snared by the reigning queen of the senior citizen set.

The next thing Eric new she was herding him toward a group of blue-haired grandmas who had their hearts set on meeting him. Gently he tried to extricate himself, but the woman's bony grip was as strong as a python's. He suspected she'd been a grade school teacher at some point in her life, maybe even a principal.

Curbing his frustration, Eric smiled and allowed himself to be presented to the ladies of the Twin Cities Garden Club.

Emily emerged from the powder room feeling more confident than she had all night. She had nothing to fear from Patricia Montgomery or Catherine Stump. They'd talked until the first wave of women had burst through the door, making a beeline for the half-dozen stalls in the next room, then parted amicably.

Now all she had to do was find Eric and explain.

She looked toward the ballroom and spotted him being towed toward a group of sweet-looking little old ladies. She smiled in wry amusement. He'd be occupied for a while. Sweet-looking little old ladies could be harder to shake than the flu.

"Cameron doesn't know who you are, does he?"

Her smile fell. Turning slowly, she faced Peter Cordell. "Excuse me?"

"Your date doesn't know you're Ryan Montgomery's ex-wife."

"I fail to see how any of this concerns you, Mr. Cordell."

"Please. Call me Peter. After all, we're old friends."

"Hardly."

He ignored her insult. "So, why don't you want Cameron to know?"

She looked at him as if he'd said something that made no sense. "Don't you have anything better to do than bother me?"

"Not tonight." Cordell smiled, shaking his head. "Montgomery didn't deserve you, Emily. Neither does Cameron. In fact, I'm surprised you're with him. I'd think you would have learned from your mistakes."

Mistakes? The word jarred her, even considering the source.

"They're two of a kind, you know. Only Cameron got caught." Cordell broke into an almost gleeful smirk. "You really don't know, do you?" He scanned the room behind her, then moved closer and took her elbow. "Tell you what? Why don't we get out of here and I'll tell you all about it. Cameron won't care. He's too busy playing hotshot."

His suggestion completed her confusion. Frowning, Emily looked over to where Eric was signing autographs for the little old ladies. He smiled and talked as if he couldn't care less where she'd disappeared to.

"Face it, Emily," Cordell said close to her ear. Your date's deserted you." His grip on her arm tightened. "Come on, my car's right outside."

Suddenly it hit her. Cordell didn't have any stories to tell. He was playing mind games. Preying on her in some sort of attempt to get revenge on Eric. Hadn't Miranda told her that Peter Cordell had been the team's captain before Eric? And of the two centers, Eric was getting the bulk of the ice time. Cordell had to be sick with envy. He'd love to steal Eric's date tonight.

He nudged her toward the door. "He'll never even notice you're gone."

She rounded on him, her mood dark and stormy. "Get your hands off of me. Now."

His eyes flashed, but he let go of her arm. "Fine. If you'd rather be ignored for the rest of the night, it's your choice. But I'll warn you. Ignoring people who don't pander to his ego is what our good captain does best. He thinks it will bring them to heel."

"Is that so?" a deep male voice asked from behind her.

Cordell looked up, his eyes narrowing. "Cameron."

Emily turned to see Eric standing behind her, murder in his eye. Without thinking twice she moved so that she stood dead center between the two men. Eric noticed, and his eyes hardened to stone. Emily didn't see the smugly superior smile Cordell offered from behind her, but she saw Eric's mouth tighten and knew that somehow Cordell had drawn first blood.

"Move out of the way, Emily," Eric said so coldly and quietly she couldn't mistake his intent.

"Eric, there's no need for—"

"There's every need," Eric interrupted, his eyes never leaving Cordell. "And Cordell understands that. Now move."

He was going to fight. She couldn't believe it. Here. Over her. Over nothing. "Eric. Please. We were just talking."

He looked at her then, looked through her, it seemed. Eventually his focus returned and the dark fury in his eyes died down. "I see," he said stiffly, almost formally. "Well, when you're finished, I'll be in the ballroom."

"Eric—"

She started after him, but Cordell caught her arm again. "Let him go, Emily, he's only trying to make you feel—"

She shook him off, hard. "Oh, grow up and get a life, will you?"

Cordell flushed deeply, but Emily didn't care. She left him alone in the hallway and went after Eric.

His fury barely contained, Cordell watched her follow Cameron into the ballroom. A long minute later, he smiled. Peter Cordell's day wasn't complete unless he'd caused Eric Cameron some kind of trouble. Tonight, with Emily, he realized he'd hit the jackpot. The bitch had to have her hooks in Cameron, deep, to get him to back off like that. Cordell's smile widened as he realized the power that gave him. Over them both.

The former Mrs. Ryan Montgomery wasn't the only one with interesting skeletons rattling around in her closet. Cameron had a few that, when his precious Emily found out about them, would blow their touching little romance to bits.

Cordell knew exactly how to light the fuse.

Whistling, he followed his latest quarry into the ballroom.

****

Eric's emotions churned as he watched the band warm up. Seeing Emily with Cordell had snapped something inside him. Without warning, he'd flashed back to another banquet, where he'd spotted his wife in deep conversation with a man she'd claimed to hate. Then Cordell had touched Emily, and the memory of Monica's betrayal had washed over Eric like acid. Before he'd known it, he'd been halfway across the room, primed to tear Cordell to pieces. Only the fact that he refused to mow Emily down to get to the bastard had kept him from making a complete fool of himself.

Damn it. He had to pull himself together. Emily wasn't Monica. Cordell wasn't Granger.

"Are we still going to dance?"

Eric looked down to see Emily standing beside him. What the hell had she been talking to Cordell so intently about? He'd quit hockey before he asked. He looked back at the band. "Probably not."

"Listen, Eric. About what happened earlier. I'm sorry I walked out on—"

"Forget it. It's over."

She touched his sleeve. "Please, I'd like to explain."

"Not now, Emily. I'm feeling a little too raw for explanations right now." He needed to get his emotions back in harness. Maybe he'd only imagined the tension between Cordell and Emily at dinner. Maybe he'd allowed his own dislike for the man to skew his perceptions.

186

Yeah, and maybe pigs flew.

"I didn't leave the ballroom with him, Eric. He followed me. He was waiting for me when I came out of the ladies room."

He looked down at her, and wondered how she could be so calm when he was falling apart inside. "Why?"

"To spite you. He told me you were too busy to bother with me after winning your award and tried to convince me to leave with him."

"Would you have?"

Her eyes flashed fire. "That doesn't even deserve an answer."

"Then why did you protect him?"

Emily stared. "Protect him? I wasn't protecting him. If anyone, I was protecting *you*."

Eric snorted. "I can take care of myself, Emily."

"No kidding," she snapped. "The point is, Cordell was using me to provoke you into losing your temper. To embarrass you in front of the same people who applauded you as you accepted an award he'll never come within ten miles of receiving and he knows it. I wasn't about to let that happen."

Eric stared at her, stunned. But as he looked into her eyes and saw she meant every furious word, his pain receded. His ghosts faded. Emily wasn't Monica, not by a long shot. Monica would have leapt at the chance to have two men fighting over her in public.

The band struck up a romantic ballad. Shaking his head at his own stupidity, Eric held out his hand. "Dance with me?"

"Why didn't you tell me you were getting an award tonight?" Emily asked during their third dance.

Eric smiled against her temple. She felt so good nestled against him. So warm and soft and incredibly sexy. He wished they were alone. He was having trouble keeping his hands from roaming. "I wasn't supposed to know. I got the word last week when I sent my regrets. The committee apparently decided it wasn't kosher to have me not show up."

"You weren't planning to be here tonight?"

"I didn't have a date."

She looked up at him. "But you told me Stump..."

"I stretched the truth. He wanted the team here, but I wanted you here with me more." He smiled softly. "I wanted to see your face when you found out I wasn't exactly the poor excuse for a human being you thought I was when we met."

Embarrassed, Emily pressed her cheek against his chest. "I'm sorry I freaked out when they announced your name."

He tightened his arms around her. "I should have warned you."

"I think that would have made it worse."

The music started again, another slow number. Eric let the conversation go, needing to hold Emily more than he needed to talk. She was with him now, and that was all that mattered.

"I meant what I said the other night about finding you some contacts to help out with the shelter," Eric said as they relaxed at their table during the band's second break.

Emily felt a twinge of guilt. She'd been having so much fun dancing with Eric she'd forgotten her plans to solicit support for Harmony House. "I'd like that," she said, and smiled as he traced a long finger up and down her forearm. The tingles reached all the way to her toes. "But how many people here do you know well enough to approach?"

He looked up at her, his eyes gleaming mischief. "Doesn't matter. As of tonight, they know me." He stood and reached for her hand. "C'mon. Let's get some mileage out of this award."

They mingled, Eric introducing Emily to people he'd scoped out earlier as likely candidates for financial contributors to Harmony House. He soon discovered that Dr. Emily Jordan was no rookie when it came to the fine art of fundraising. When invited to, she stated her case with a minimum of fuss, and seemed to know exactly what to say to whom and when to back off.

The only awkward moment he sensed was when he introduced her to Ronald Stump—who appeared to have eased up on his trips to the bar—and his daughter, Catherine. Emily seemed to falter as Stump in turn introduced her to the couple standing beside him, Dr. and

Mrs. John Montgomery.

It was Catherine who gracefully stepped into the weird silence that followed, with a compliment on Emily's dress. As the two women talked, Catherine's charisma once again impressed Eric. They'd met several times, and each time he'd come away with the feeling that behind her warm smile and intelligent eyes lived a woman who knew what she wanted out of life and how to get it.

What baffled him was why she'd want Ryan Montgomery. He'd only met Catherine's fiancé twice, but disliked the man intensely. For one, Eric didn't trust him. Or his obvious disdain for the sport Catherine devoted herself to promoting—and the way he kept his disdain hidden from her. Montgomery waited until she was out of earshot to take pot shots at the players.

But Eric didn't care what Catherine's fiancé thought of him or his sport. It was Catherine's opinion that counted, and it was Catherine who had kept the Saints in the running when not even the team had cared enough to show up for the games. Oh, they were there physically, but mentally—totally out of the arena. Catherine's promotional campaign had drawn the crowds to Stump Arena long before the team had finally gotten its act together, and now she had their fan base practically bursting at the seams with support for a team that nobody but Stump had thought could make it in a town that already had a decent team. After all, the Wild had made it as far as the Western Finals before the Saints came along.

For her sheer determination alone Catherine had Eric's undying admiration, no matter what kind of slime she wanted to marry.

"Dr. Jordan and I met earlier, in the powder room," Catherine told her father. But I didn't realize she was here on behalf of Harmony House. Please, tell us more. I might know of some people who could help."

Stump echoed his daughter's invitation, but the woman who stood beside Catherine—Montgomery's mother, Eric gathered—seemed to retreat into a world of her own. The lights were on, but nobody was home. Montgomery's father, on the other hand, sipped his Manhattan and rudely scanned the room while Emily spoke.

When Catherine promised to pass the information on to her contacts, Emily smoothly offered her several of the shelter's business cards, "In case your contacts need more information."

Eric smiled. She'd been slipping those little cards into people's hands for the past hour.

The group disbanded as their hostess breezed by with the news the late night snack was ready to be served.

"That was some pitch you gave Stump and company, Dr. Jordan. I'm impressed," Eric said after he and Emily had left the buffet line and found a quiet corner table.

"I just hope they got the message." She bit into her ham and cheese croissant. "Mmmmm, this is great. I was starving."

"I'm glad to see your appetite's returned."

She smiled wryly. "It seems I spent the first half of the evening worried about nothing."

It was true. Her bizarre encounter with her former in-laws had made it clear to Emily that Robbie was safe. John and Patricia Montgomery had no desire to associate with her on any level again. The tip-off had been John. Other than a barely civil nod when Stump had introduced them, he'd pretended she didn't exist.

In turn, she'd made sure Patricia knew help was available should she ever decide to break free of her husband. Catherine Stump's support had been an unexpected bonus. Not to mention her silence on the delicate matter of Emily's former relationship to Ryan. Clearly, the woman wasn't one to dwell on the past.

All in all, Emily was more than pleased with the evening's outcome. She was also relieved to find she no longer felt the gut-clenching fear of Ryan's parents that she once had. Only pity.

"Thank you," she said.

Eric looked up from his plate. "For what?"

Taking his hand, she brought it to her lips. "For not letting me weasel out of coming here tonight. I needed this."

His eyes darkened to brown velvet. "And I need you."

Chapter Twenty

As soon as the door snicked shut behind them they were in each other's arms. Hunger fueled hunger as their mouths met and mated, their hands raced to remove the clothing between them. Not once did it occur to them to slow down; they'd wasted too much time already. Their need to become one again was paramount, the fire between them too hot to extinguish any other way.

Naked, Emily felt Eric's mattress hit the backs of her knees. Greedily she pulled him down on top of her. Over and over they rolled, tongues, arms and legs tangling, and ended up with Emily secure between Eric and the bed at her back. His fingers found her hot and wet, hers found him hot and hard. She opened to meet him as he plunged inside.

They came almost immediately, their cries of release echoing in the apartment's stillness. Afterward, muscles still quivering, nerve endings still dancing, they lay in breathless silence, stunned by the force of their passion. Sweat glistened on their bodies, the slick moisture cooling their heated skin as the dark night air wrapped them in its embrace.

Emily smiled. The apartment was pitch black. Eric hadn't even let go of her long enough to flip on a light switch.

"I'm sorry," he said against her neck. I didn't mean to jump you like that."

She smoothed her palms against his damp, taut back. "I did."

He lifted his head. "You did?"

She unlocked her legs from around his waist. "Why do you think I wore a dress with no buttons?"

"But sweetheart, we didn't..."

"Use protection? Yes we did. I visited my gynecologist

191

yesterday."

Silence, then: "You mean all night, under that mouth-watering dress, you've been wearing a—"

Her fingers on his lips shushed him. "I mean all night, I've been looking forward to being with you, with nothing between us." Sliding her fingers into his hair, she drew him down to her for a long, leisurely kiss. "Now, Mr. Cameron, why don't you turn on the light and show me what you *did* have planned for tonight and we'll see whose fantasy we like best?"

****

Emily awoke just before dawn, alone. She heard Eric rustling in the kitchen, sat up and ran a hand through her hair, grimaced at the mess of stiff tangles, then scooted off to the bathroom.

At some point, Eric must have moved her overnight bag, which he'd dropped immediately upon entering the apartment, to the bathroom. He'd set her bag on the counter, beside clean towels and a washcloth. She smiled at his thoughtfulness, freshened up, then slipped on her sleep shirt, shivering against the cold morning air.

As she returned her brush to her bag, she spotted Eric's shaving kit, packed for travel. Sadness squeezed her heart. He was leaving for St. Louis today.

Hello? Was that a bottle of *White Linen* peeking out behind the shaving cream? It was. More than that, it was *her* bottle of White Linen. The bottle she'd given up looking for weeks ago.

What was Eric doing with it? Intending to ask, she left the bathroom. Eric was still rooting around in the kitchen, so she checked out his apartment. All she'd seen so far was the bed. Not that she minded. She loved the sight of Eric, bathed in candlelight, his eyes dark and depthless as they moved in a slow, sensual rhythm that gave a whole new meaning to the concept of delayed gratification.

But there was something to be said for hot and heavy, too. She grinned at the trail of discarded clothing from the front door to the bed, then shook her head and chuckled. All that money she'd spent and he'd tossed her dress and matching lingerie aside as if it were gift-wrapping on Christmas morning.

192

The apartment was smaller than she'd expected, with only three rooms, the largest a combination living, dining, and bedroom. The soft pink and gray light that filtered through the horizontal mini-blinds provided the only hint of color in the room; everything else appeared to be in basic beige.

So Eric wasn't a man to give a lot of thought to interior decorating. The nondescript dining room set and living room couch and chairs in front of the entertainment center gave the impression they'd been bought sight unseen. The walls were bare. The only clues about the man who lived here were the huge, state-of-the-art plasma television and stereo system, an extensive CD collection—surprisingly heavy on the classical side—and the brass music stand and cello propped in the corner by the window.

Emily blinked. *A cello?*

She padded over to investigate. The sheet music was well worn, with penciled notes written in the margins. The handwriting was dainty and feminine, not anything like the casual scrawl Emily knew to be Eric's. So who did the cello belong to?

"I'm sorry, Doctor, but you're not allowed to wear that pained expression until you've heard me play."

"This is yours?" She looked up to see Eric watching her, wearing nothing but a smile. Her confusion faded as she feasted her eyes on the sight, and knew she'd never tire of looking at him. Or of wanting to drag him off to bed. "Would you play for me?"

"Sometime. But not now. My neighbors and I have a deal. I don't play my music between the hours of ten and ten and they don't play theirs." His smile twisted into a grimace. "I'm afraid their tastes run along the lines of AC/DC and Twisted Sister played at top volume." He stepped closer. "What's that?"

She held out the perfume. "I believe this is mine."

"Wrong." He lifted it from her palm and grinned. "It used to be yours. Now it's mine."

She lifted an eyebrow. "You've taken to wearing White Linen on the ice?"

He grinned. "No, but it might be an idea worth looking into. Can you imagine how surprised the Blues

193

would be if we showed up smelling like a department store perfume counter? They wouldn't know whether to hit us or kiss us."

Emily's answering smile faded as the sun burst over the horizon and filled the room with soft, golden light. Eric stilled, realizing she was seeing his body for the first time without her vision clouded by need or lust. Dread filled him as her sharp doctor's gaze took in the bruises on his body not yet healed from Wednesday night's game. Silently he cursed his impatience and greed. He should have taken her home after the banquet, made love to her there, then slipped away before she awoke. During the regular season he sometimes went for weeks without sprouting more than a minor bruise or two here and there. But the playoff games were more physical than most. More was at stake.

And it showed.

Faced with his twenty-two year collection of battle scars, her eyes went dark with an emotion Eric couldn't define. It was all he could do not to pull her into his arms and make them darken with passion instead, make her forget what she saw.

But distracting her wouldn't solve anything. Afterward the scars would still be there, silent testimonials to the fact that her lover used his body as both weapon and shield in his work.

Emily was a healer. Pain was a given in Eric's profession. Would his lover be able to separate in her mind what she saw at the shelter and in the ER from what she saw on him? Would she be able to accept his willingness to subject his body to such abuse?

An eternity passed before she lifted troubled eyes to his. Terror gripped Eric's heart. If she rejected him now...

Her eyes softened as she stepped forward. With heartbreaking tenderness, she bent her head. Ever so gently, she blessed each of his physical imperfections with a healing kiss.

Eric closed his eyes and gave thanks to God for this woman he knew he would love for the rest of his life.

"Eric, am I missing something here?" Emily asked as they enjoyed the snack he'd made while she explored his apartment. She wore an old T-shirt of his and sat cross-legged in the middle of his bed while he sat propped up against pillows with the sheet pulled up to his waist, the plate of fruit and cheese between them.

He arched an eyebrow, treated her to one of his blood-warming head-to-toe looks. "I'd say you've got all the right parts in all the right places."

She blushed, going warm all over. "I'm serious."

He grinned. "So am I.

"I mean it. I'm curious. Why do you live here? In this apartment? With neighbors you have to negotiate quiet hours with?"

"Where would you prefer that I live?"

Loaded question, that. One she was nowhere near ready to answer. "Wherever you want to, of course, but—" She looked around the apartment, unsure how to put it. "I don't mean to offend you, but this isn't a home, Eric. It's a...a stopping point. From what I can see, the only piece of furniture that gets any regular use is the bed."

"A man's got to sleep somewhere."

"Yes, but he's also got to have someplace he can call his own. Someplace to come home to." He'd told her earlier when she'd asked if he'd personally picked out the furniture, the only pieces that belonged to him were the television, stereo system and the bed. The rest were rented. She found it strange that a man who made the kind of money he did had so few personal possessions, but short of baldly asking him what he did with his money...

"I have a home, Emily," he said quietly. "It just isn't here."

"Oh." Emily could have kicked herself. Why hadn't she left well enough alone?

"I have a house just outside of Barton—Minnesota. Where I grew up."

Her relief was almost palpable. At least it was in the same state. "And that's where you'll go when the season ends."

"That's the plan, yes."

Emily remembered how knowing he would be leaving in a few months had softened her initial resistance to Eric. How she'd thought what harm could it do to let him into her son's life for a little while. Now she regretted her shortsightedness.

Eric resumed eating and fell into his own thoughtful silence. It occurred to Emily that she knew almost nothing about Eric's life before he'd come to Minneapolis. Most of that, she knew, was her fault. She'd been so determined to keep her secrets she'd avoided asking him about his past. Her relationship with Ryan had been totally different, filled with all kinds of sharing—at least on her part. She hadn't been able to keep a single secret from him—and he hadn't wanted her to.

She'd fallen in love with Ryan because he was so different from anyone she'd ever known. Wealthy, sophisticated, charming. At his encouragement, she'd told him everything about her minefield of a childhood, naively assuming he wanted to know because he cared, because they were falling in love.

Instead he'd turned her trust against her, used her deepest hopes, fears and dreams to control her.

She hadn't made that mistake this time. She'd fallen in love with Eric not knowing or caring what had come before. If the look in his eyes when they made love was any indication, he cared for her, too. True, he'd told her he loved her, but only once, and in the heat of the moment at that.

With a pang of disappointment, Emily realized that deep down she'd hoped he would tell her again tonight.

But he hadn't. And now, looking around his pit stop of an apartment, she knew why.

Eric Cameron was just passing through.

Chapter Twenty-One

Despite the cheery late-morning sunshine that surrounded her, Emily sat alone in her kitchen, feeling lost and left behind. Eric had kissed her goodbye and left to catch his plane over an hour ago. Robbie had barreled into the house ten minutes later, given her a huge smacking kiss, then wheedled ten dollars out of her to go to a matinee movie at the mall with Glen and his mom.

With unexpected time on her hands, she'd wandered into the kitchen to pour herself a cup of coffee, then debated whether to read the Sunday paper in bed. But the idea of doing so alone suddenly held no appeal, so for the past twenty minutes she'd simply sat at the kitchen table, and wondered how long it would take for this listless, empty feeling inside her to pass.

Five days was her guess. Until Eric returned.

Lord, what a mess. How could she have been so foolish as to fall in love with the man, knowing he was leaving? True, he'd be back in the fall, but that didn't mean they'd still see each other. Then again, maybe he wouldn't return to play for the Saints. His contract was up at the end of the season. Come fall, he could be playing just about anywhere in North America—or Europe.

The telephone rang, saving her from wholesale misery. "Hello?"

"Hello, ma'am, this is Carmen Martinez with the *Star Tribune.* I'm trying to reach Dr. Emily Jordan."

Emily paused. They'd never met, but Carmen Martinez was a respected features writer for the Tribune. "This is she."

"Oh, good. I'm glad I caught you. Do you have a few minutes? I'd like to talk to you about an idea I have for an article on domestic violence."

Emily's fingers tightened on the phone. "Excuse me?"

"I understand you volunteer your medical services at Harmony House."

Her heartbeat slowly returned to normal. "Well, yes, but I'm not at liberty to discuss the details of my cases."

"That's not what I'm looking for. Have you by any chance read any of the articles in my five-part series about battered women this week?"

Emily looked at the newspaper on the kitchen table and saw today's article featured on the "Inside" banner across the top of the page. Chances were she wouldn't have read it. She tended to avoid journalists' reports on the subject, having decided that no one who hadn't been there could adequately describe the humiliation and degradation battered women suffered.

"I'm afraid I haven't."

"I'd like you to do me a favor and read the first three."

"And then?"

"I'd appreciate your perspective on the subject for a sixth article."

"Ms. Martinez. I'm not sure I feel qualified to—"

"Please, Dr. Jordan. Don't say anything until you've read the articles. I can have copies sent to your office first thing in the morning."

Emily realized she was letting her personal fears and prejudices cloud her thinking. Of course she was qualified to speak on the subject. Hadn't she spent hours doing that just the night before? "No, that won't be necessary. I can dig them out of the recycling bag."

"May I call you in the morning to discuss setting up an interview? I'm sorry to put you on the spot like this, but to add a sixth article to the series, we'll have to move fast. The fifth is scheduled to run Tuesday and my editor won't run a sixth if I can't have it ready for Wednesday's edition."

"Of course. Around eight. Call me at the hospital. Minneapolis General. The emergency room."

"Great. Until then."

"Wait. Where did you get my name and number?"

"I got your name from a woman you spoke with at last night's United Hope banquet. I called the hospital, and a Dr. Caldwell gave me your home number after I explained what I wanted to do."

"I see," Emily said, not sure she appreciated having her cover blown like that. She did what she did at the shelter for herself and the other women there, not for recognition of any kind.

She decided to sort things out with Augustus later and fished the newspaper sections with Carmen Martinez' articles out of the recycling bag. Back in the kitchen, she read the three articles twice over, impressed. The woman had presented her report on domestic violence in the metropolitan area with admirable insight and sensitivity, not the lurid sensationalism Emily had come to expect from such exposés.

Mulling over what she might be able to add to the subject that Ms. Martinez hadn't already covered, Emily leafed through the rest of the paper. She hit the society page and froze. Staring back at her in full color was a large photograph of herself, Eric, Ronald and Catherine Stump, and John and Patricia Montgomery.

The caption identified each of them by name and inanely stated they were congratulating Eric on receiving the United Hope Community Service award. Inanely because she was speaking, her hands in the air as if emphasizing a point, Catherine and Ronald Stump were giving her their undivided attention, Eric stood beside her looking at her as if she were the only woman in the room, Patricia wore a vacant but socially correct smile, and John stared with simmering hostility at the photographer.

Emily groaned. Of all the pictures of Eric they could have run. John and Patricia would be appalled by the reminder of how they'd had to endure listening to her views on battered women. Ryan would be livid, seeing her with his parents and fiancée.

Whoa. What was she thinking? Ryan Montgomery no longer controlled her life. No longer had any say in it at all. She could talk to anyone she wanted to. Go anywhere she wanted to. Do anything she wanted to.

She smiled grimly. Including an interview on battered women for the *Star Tribune*.

The interview with Carmen Martinez over lunch the following day went exceptionally well, with both women in agreement about the slant the article should take. In short order, they'd wrapped up the subject in a neat, if not pretty package. The end result would be an in-depth piece recognizing the psychological and emotional signs of abuse, followed by information on the avenues of support available to women seeking to escape an abusive relationship. It was a common misconception that the only recognized form of abuse was physical abuse. But there were all kinds of abuse that could be perpetuated without ever hitting a woman. Power and control, intimidation, coercion, verbal abuse, financial abuse, spiritual abuse, isolation, and sexual abuse to name a few. The article was designed to get readers to see physical abuse as only one piece of the entire picture. Emily was pleased with how much they were able to cover, considering the amount of space they had been allotted.

Pleasantly surprised by the instant rapport she'd shared with Carmen, Emily had agreed to give a follow-up interview in a few months. She didn't understand it, but there seemed to be a connection there—something that went beyond a professional relationship. When Eric called that night she was still riding high on the wings of her success. Eric was fired up as well; the Saints had skated circles around the Blues the night before and the team felt they had a strong chance to win the division finals without going the full seven games. Emily let Eric's enthusiasm carry the conversation, and decided to save her own news until he returned.

The article ran on Wednesday, the day before Eric was due back. Emily spent most of her day fielding compliments from her colleagues. Her patients, on the other hand, had no intention of letting her enjoy her flirtation with fame. Business was brisk, and kept her busy all morning.

After lunch, Augustus drew her aside. With an uncharacteristically sheepish expression, he explained that a friend in St. Louis had offered him a center ice ticket to tonight's game. Would she cover for him until seven?

Since they'd already agreed that as long as the Saints stayed in the playoffs any conflicting Wednesday night visits to Harmony House would be shifted to non-game nights, Emily sent him on his way with her blessings. Her generosity backfired, however, when she ended up working past seven-thirty. Game time was at eight. She finally escaped the ER at a quarter to, her thoughts centered on plotting the quickest route home that included a pizzeria. She'd promised Robbie they'd share a large double cheese, pepperoni and mushroom while they watched Eric play.

The night was unseasonably warm, so she didn't bother to put on her coat. She'd tossed both coat and briefcase into the Suburban and was halfway into the driver's seat before she noticed the large manila envelope with her name on it stuck to her windshield. She slid back out of the car and reached around to pluck the envelope from beneath the wiper blade.

Maybe it was something from Carmen, who'd mentioned she might stop by the hospital today. Emily took a moment to check. Instead she found several cozy close-ups of herself and Eric at the United Hope banquet. One showed them sharing a quiet kiss on the dance floor.

"Hello, Emily."

Her blood ran cold. Slowly, she turned. Her worst nightmare leaned against the driver's door of the dark blue van parked next to her car.

Ryan smiled chillingly, while Emily noted exactly what he wanted her to. One, it was dark. Two, the van blocked the view from the hospital and pedestrian traffic. Three, its proximity to the Suburban had left her no backward avenue of escape once she'd opened her door.

As always, he'd planned his ambush well.

"I think it's time we had a talk," he said.

Emily knew better than to bolt. When it suited him, Ryan could move faster than a rattler. And running made him angry. Very angry. So she stayed perfectly still—and prayed she looked perfectly calm.

His smile became mocking. "Cat got your tongue? Interesting, considering how chatty you were in this morning's paper."

Obviously he'd read the article, and recognized many of the references to methods of abuse that left no physical marks as those he'd inflicted on her. Emily swallowed. "What do you want, Ryan?"

"What I've always wanted. For you to know your place and stay in it." His pale blue eyes glittered with suppressed fury. "Who do you think you are, appointing yourself public expert on this kind of bullshit?"

Ruthlessly Emily quelled her fear, knowing he'd zero in on it like a vicious dog. Fingers flexing, he moved closer. She forced herself to hold her ground—a first between them. "You forget, I am an expert, thanks to you."

Ryan only smirked. "Cordell was right. You *have* changed."

"Cordell?"

"Peter Cordell. Catherine's cousin. You made quite an impression on him the other night. He couldn't wait to tell me all about it. Or about what you've been up to these days."

Emily's mind spun. Peter *Cordell* was behind this?

"I can't tell you how embarrassing it was to hear about this idiotic crusade of yours," Ryan said. "Then to open today's paper and read all that garbage about—"

"Letting women know how to escape from their abusers isn't garbage, Ryan."

"You never escaped, Emily. I let you go. If I still wanted you, we'd still be together."

"How can you say that?"

"Because I know you. And I also know what you're up to here, trying to point a public finger at me to gain support for your stupid little organization."

"This isn't about you, Ryan. I didn't mention names."

"You didn't have to. Anyone with half a brain can tell you're speaking from experience. It won't be long before they start putting the pieces together and make the connection between us."

"I'm a doctor, Ryan. I volunteer at a women's shelter. Anyone with half a brain will think that's the source of my experience."

"Wrong, Emily. I've already had a few eyebrows raised in my direction and I don't like it."

Whose? Catherine's? Her father's? Emily didn't dare show her pleasure at the idea, or ask. Instead she surreptitiously angled her body towards her car. The door was behind her, trapping her in the V between door and car. If she could just swing around and jump inside—

"Don't even think about it, Emily. We're nowhere near through, yet." Ryan smiled nastily. "Why do you think I rented a van?"

She stilled, the ugly possibilities racing through her head. She remembered how he'd enjoyed messing with her mind, threatening things she knew he was fully capable of, yet rarely followed through on. Back then the threats had been enough to keep her in line. She chose to let him think they still did. Slowly, she turned to face him.

"As I was saying," he continued, I'm getting some strange looks because of your interview and I don't like it."

"I only presented the facts," she said calmly, quietly. "I can't be held responsible for how others interpret them."

"The hell you can't! You're the one who stirred up this whole mess, spouting off at that banquet about your stupid shelter for whiney women. I'm warning you, Emily. You take this campaign to discredit me any further and I'll come down on you so hard what happened before was child's play."

"You call breaking my jaw, my arm and three ribs, then trying to run me over with your car *child's play?*"

"You're overreacting, Emily. Just like you always do. You shouldn't have run from me that night. I wouldn't have hurt you."

"If you believe that, or any of this business about me trying to personally discredit you, you need professional help, Ryan. What you attempted that night was murder. You should be in jail for it."

He tensed, then seemed to relax with a visible effort. No doubt keeping his dark side from Catherine had given him considerable practice at restraint. "Instead I'm in private practice," he said, apropos of nothing.

Emily blinked. "What are you talking about?"

"I'm a doctor, Emily. I've been in private practice for four years now. Plastic surgery."

He had to be kidding. When she'd left him he'd been flunking out of med school, content to let his father's connections get him through his courses. Now he was a plastic surgeon? The irony of it didn't escape her. Nor did the power and control aspects of it. As a plastic surgeon, he could physically change women into whatever he wanted them to be.

"How...nice for you," she said uneasily, realizing he was waiting for an answer.

He smiled. "I'm glad you approve. But I'm afraid I can't say the same for you."

"Your approval doesn't concern me any more, Ryan. I'm no longer your wife."

"No, now you're a hockey player's whore." Smoothly, he removed the photos and manila envelope from her hand, then tossed them into the open driver's window of the van. "It's obvious you're spreading your legs for him."

Emily said nothing, sure of Cordell's hand in this now. He must have paid someone to snap those pictures of her and Eric, knowing exactly the kind of trouble they would cause.

"What? No denials, Emily?"

"My social life is none of your business, Ryan."

"It is when you're corrupting my son's morals."

Emily froze. *Ryan knew about Robbie?*

"You thought I didn't know?" His chuckle was chiding. "Of course I did. This city isn't that large, Emily. If you'd wanted to keep our son a secret, you should have gone farther than across the bridge."

She lifted her chin and braced herself for a backhand. "He's not yours."

Instead, Ryan laughed and stepped forward, tracing a cold, lazy finger down her cheek. Emily fought back a flinch. "Of course he is. He was born nine months after our trip to Barbados."

She remembered the Barbados trip well. A true honeymoon period between them. She'd left him two weeks before, during mid-year exams. He'd spirited her off to the island between semesters to woo her back. He'd succeeded admirably, making a complete fool of her. Within days of their return, he'd beaten her again. Savagely.

"It was so good between us, Emmie. Do you remember how good?" He touched her hair, bound only by barrettes, and idly twisted some around his fingers. "I love it when you wear your hair down," he murmured, canting his head and looking at her, an unholy lust entering his eyes. "I've always loved running my fingers through your curls," he said as his free hand brushed between her legs.

She jerked back in revulsion. "Stop it!"

He fisted a hand in her hair, yanked her closer. Instinctively her hands came up to keep their bodies from touching. "Or you'll do what? Call for your award-winning lover to save you? Sorry to disappoint you, Emmie, but he's in St. Louis thinking about plays and pucks, not you." Ryan's sneer filled her field of vision. "I want you to stop seeing him, Emily."

She blinked, partly in pain, partly in confusion. "Eric? What's he got to do with—"

"Everything," Ryan snarled. "Cameron has *everything* to do with my having to run down here and set you straight tonight. Until *he* came along, you were content to live in your dull little house in the suburbs and bandage scraped knees for a living. Now, thanks to him, you've suddenly taken it in your head to become some sort of misguided advocate for complaining women."

"That's not true..."

His grip on her hair tightened. "Isn't it? If it hadn't been for that overrated puck chaser squiring you around like some social paragon Saturday night, you never would've attracted that reporter's attention."

Emily grimaced and fought to keep her knees from buckling. Ryan smiled at her pain. "She's using you, you know. Capitalizing on your disgusting affair with Cameron for her own benefit." His smile turned mean. "You always were too gullible for your own good, Emily. Don't you realize that in latching on to Cameron, you've only made a fool of yourself? Carmen Martinez is probably laughing her head off right now."

Emily's eyes began to tear. She gritted her teeth against the burning pain in her scalp.

Ryan only chuckled. "The irony of it amuses me. You, and Eric Cameron. The social mismatch of the year." His hand tightened again. "What were you thinking, Emily? Don't you know the man has a well-documented temper?"

"That doesn't make him abusive."

"Ah, Emmie. Your ignorance never fails to astound

205

Liana Laverentz

me. Catherine's father owns the Saints, remember? Stump keeps extensive files on his players. I know all there is to know about Cameron—which is obviously a hell of a lot more than you do. You're whoring with a man who's no better than a gutter rat." His voice hardened. "Stop seeing him, Emily. If you don't, I'll sue for custody of Robbie."

Emily felt the blood drain from her heart. Ryan laughed, knowing he'd scored a direct hit. "I'll win, you know. Especially when I tell the judge you deliberately kept knowledge of my son's existence from me for nine years."

"It...won't work. You've...admitted to knowing about him all along." Pain was stealing her voice.

"I'm prepared to swear under oath that I only recently learned I had a son, and when I tried to see him, you refused me."

"I'll...tell them you're lying."

"No one will believe you after I've proven you're an unfit mother. What else would you call a woman who leaves her only child with sitters at all hours of the day and night? Or a woman who places him in moral jeopardy by exposing him to a man who's spent time in jail for—"

"For God's sake, Ryan! Let go of my hair!"

Surprisingly, he did. For the longest time they stood there, facing each other in the streetlamp's halogen haze, both breathing hard. Emily's scalp burned, her legs felt like rubber. Slowly she lowered her arms and backed away a step. Ryan made no move to stop her.

"As I was saying," he continued coolly, "You're subjecting my son to a man who's spent time in jail for—"

"It was only for a few hours, and he wasn't even guilty," she said tightly, thinking of the night she and Eric had met.

"Try a few days, Emmie. Twenty, to be exact. It might have been twenty years if his wife hadn't dropped the charges."

Emily blinked. "His wife?"

"His wife. The woman he supposedly worshipped. He beat her so badly she had to be hospitalized. If she'd died, he could have been tried for murder."

Emily's mind reeled. Murder? Eric? Unthinkable.

206

"Eric wouldn't hit a woman," she said fiercely. "Any woman."

"Grow up, Emily. It was in all the papers. Call your new friend Martinez if you don't believe me. I'm sure she knows all about it. She'd have to be as stupid as you are not to."

She turned away in confusion, a fist pressed against the pain in her heart. "No. It's not possible. Eric isn't like that."

Ryan laughed again, the harsh sound all too familiar. He had the upper hand and knew it. "You sure can pick them, Emily. First your father, now Cameron. But what can you expect from poor white trash? If he'd stayed a no-name rink rat, I'd say you belong together."

Emily tried to think. Eric wouldn't have beaten his wife. Ryan was lying. He had to be.

"What's the matter, Emmie? The truth hurt?"

Enough was enough. She glared at Ryan, her voice low with hatred. "I'd rather be poor white trash than the scum of St. Paul society."

Ryan blinked, his expression incredulous. Emily gave him a hard backward shove, her only thought to get past him and put something large and solid like a car—any car—between them. She didn't make it. His fingers clamped onto her arm, biting into her flesh. Her scream was cut off as he swung her around and slammed her into the van, knocking the wind from her. Before she could recover, he backhanded her across the face. She stumbled and fell, landing on her hands and knees on the concrete. He grabbed a handful of hair and jerked her upward. She screamed again, but his fist hurtled into her stomach and silenced her. Doubling over with pain, she crumpled to the ground. The first kick caught her in the breast, the second in the hip. The third barely missed her head as she rolled to avoid it—and found herself trapped between the wheel of the van and Ryan's booted feet.

Instinctively she curled into herself, hands protecting her head. Her heart pounded, blood pumped and lungs burned as she choked back a sob and waited for the attack to continue. She knew better than to try to scoot away or even stand. Ryan liked seeing her down on the ground. He'd only knock her down again and again until she quit trying or was dead. For Robbie's sake, she had to stay alive. If Ryan knocked her out and put her in the van, there was no telling what would happen to her.

Suddenly she realized Ryan wasn't kicking her any more. She could hear the distant sounds of traffic and his heavy breathing as he stood over her. An eternity later, his low, satisfied laugh tainted the cooling night air. Slowly she lowered her hands, just as he squatted beside her, his smile malevolent.

"I'm afraid you left out a few details in your story, Emily. Now that your memory's been refreshed, let's just say I trust you'll think twice before you embarrass me like that again. Because next time, I won't stop like I did tonight. Tonight was just a warning. Got that?"

Not waiting for an answer, Ryan rose to his feet, dusted his hands—-and found himself looking into the barrel of a gun.

Chapter Twenty-Two

"I'd aim for your balls," Carmen Martinez said conversationally, "But it's obvious you don't have any."

Ryan paled, then flushed violently and started forward, clearly intent on snatching the gun. Carmen cocked the pistol, her coal black eyes narrowing into slits. "Try it and you'll be lucky to wake up wondering what hit you. One look at what you did to *her*, and they'll know I acted in self-defense."

The truth carried more than enough steel to contain him. That, and the fact that at that range, she couldn't miss. Sweat beaded on his forehead, but Ryan didn't move a muscle. Behind him, Emily slowly pulled herself to her feet.

"You okay, Emily?"

Emily wiped the back of her hand across her bloody mouth. "I will be."

"Then move out of the way before this asshole comes up with any more stupid ideas."

Emily eased past her car door, leaving it open to block Ryan's retreat, then moved around the Suburban to stand beside Carmen. Ryan glared at them in impotent fury.

"There's a red mustang parked three rows over," Carmen said. The keys are in my pocket. My cell phone is on the seat inside. Call the police while I make sure this sonofabitch stays put."

Emily looked at Ryan, felt singed by his virulent hatred, and knew he'd stop at nothing to get his revenge if she had him arrested. If she'd had only herself to think about, she'd have done it in a heartbeat. But the image of her innocent, trusting son rose in her mind and she knew she couldn't take the risk. Not yet. Robbie didn't even know his father was alive. To find out from the

209

newspapers, or worse, the kids in school, that his father was alive and had tried to kill his mother would be too much.

She couldn't do it. "No. Let him go."

"Are you fuckin' nuts, Emily? You've got the bastard dead to rights."

Emily knew the pattern, and knew it looked like she had fallen back into it. But there had to be a better way to deal with Ryan than jail. He was a Montgomery. The legal and financial backlash his family would inflict on her would be enormous. She didn't even want to *think* about the emotional, social or professional backlash. All of her family secrets, laid bare for everyone to see...

The stress of it was more than Emily could handle at the moment. She might well go to the police in a few days, but first, she needed to pull herself together. She also needed to talk to Robbie. He was her main concern in all of this.

"I know it seems that way, but I'm not. Let him go."

For a long, taut moment, it looked like Carmen would refuse. Finally she spoke, her voice low and gritty. "Get moving, creep, before she comes to her senses and changes her mind."

Ryan opened the door to the van and eased inside, his eyes not leaving Carmen's gun. The instant he revved the engine, Emily reacted. She yanked Carmen out of the way just in time to avoid being sideswiped as the van shot forward. Tires squealing, the van careened out of the parking lot.

Adrenaline flowing, hanging on to each other, Carmen and Emily watched the taillights vanish into the night.

"Thank you," Carmen said finally, not sounding nearly as confident as she had when she'd been speaking to Ryan. "I...had no idea he'd try something like that."

"He gets...fearless when he's angry."

"More like certifiable," Carmen muttered, stepping away from Emily. She gave Emily a startled look. "You know him?"

"He's my ex-husband."

"Holy shit, Emily. Do you know what you just did?"

Emily held up a bloody hand. "Please, Carmen. Not

now."

"Jesus. I'm sorry. I'm not thinking straight. C'mon. Let's get you off your feet." She reached for Emily's arm, but Emily held back. Carmen's eyes darkened with concern. "Hey, are you okay?"

"I hurt like hell and my knees won't stop shaking, but nothing's broken."

"I should have gotten here sooner. I heard your screams, but couldn't tell where they were coming from at first."

Emily didn't answer. She was staring at Carmen's gun. Slowly she lifted her gaze to Carmen's. Carmen shrugged. "A woman alone's got to protect herself somehow. There's a lot of crazies in this world. C'mon." She checked the safety, then put the gun in her coat pocket and nudged Emily toward the Suburban, handing her a wad of tissues to press against her split lip.

Emily slid across the front seat, giving Carmen room to join her. It would be a while before she felt strong enough to drive. The blinking yellow light at the entrance to the hospital underscored their thoughts as the two women fell into a deep silence.

Carmen spoke first. "I should have gotten here sooner," she repeated quietly. "Warned you there might be trouble."

"Trouble?" Emily's heart sank. Ryan was all the trouble she could handle right now. "From whom?"

"Disgruntled readers. Male readers. I got several harassing phone calls today. Seems we struck a few nerves with our article."

"Come on, Carmen. The information isn't new or confidential. Any woman who wants to know..."

"How many women in abusive relationships have the freedom to go to a library and look it up? Surf the net for some info? Attend a talk or seminar on the subject? How many of them even suspect that what is happening to them is wrong? After all, it's been ground into them they're only getting what they deserve." Carmen grinned. "So this morning we simply delivered the information to their doorstep. How to recognize your abuser for what he is and leave him in ten easy steps. Well, not quite, but the point is we didn't have to resort to subterfuge to do it."

Emily couldn't help but grin back. "You're right. We didn't, did we? We put it right out there for everyone to see."

Carmen reached over and squeezed Emily's hand. "Damn right we did. And now, girlfriend, what do you say we get you cleaned up, find some kind of take-out and—"

"I can't. I promised my son—" Emily froze. "I need to go home."

"Do you think he'll go after him?"

"I don't know. I just—oh, hell, this is such a mess."

"How old is he?"

"Robbie? Eight."

"Is someone with him? Someone you trust?"

"Of course."

"Then he should be all right for the time being. But you'd better call home and warn your sitter your ex is running loose." She looked Emily over. "Things were pretty quiet in the ER when I left ten minutes ago. Maybe we can slip you inside and get you cleaned up before—"

"Not a good idea," Emily interrupted, thinking of the furor her attack would cause among her co-workers, the questions she'd have to answer. They would insist on calling the police.

"You think going home looking like that is a better one? Try it and you'll scare your son into adulthood."

Emily looked down at her soiled clothes, torn and bloodied panty hose, and realized Carmen was right. Closing her eyes, she took a deep breath and leaned her head back for a moment. "Okay. Pull up to the rear ER entrance, go inside and ask for Sarah Ferguson. She'll know what to do."

Secreted in the staff lounge minutes later, Emily called home.

Robbie answered. 'Lo?"

He sounded so heartbreakingly young Emily wanted to cry. "Hi, honey," she said, aching with the need to hold him.

"Mom? Where *are* you? I'm *starving*."

"I know, honey. I'm at the hospital."

Disappointment colored his voice. "You gonna be late again?"

"I'm sorry, sweetheart. Something came up."

"Aw, Mom. You promised we'd watch Eric's game."

Her heart split in two. "You can still watch it with Nanna until I get there," she temporized, before inspiration hit. "In fact, if you ask her real nice, I bet she'd take you over to her house so you can watch it there."

"On the wide screen TV?"

Emily smiled in relief. "Mm hmmm. And I'll have a large Paisan's pizza delivered while you watch the game if you promise to save me a piece."

"Paisan's? All right! Nanna! Guess what? Mom's gonna—"

Emily winced at the crack of a dropped receiver. One of these days she was going to have to spring for a cordless phone.

"Emily? You still there?" Anna sounded harried.

"My eardrum may never be the same, but yes, I'm still here."

"I'll have to have a talk with that boy. I understand we're going across the street to watch the game?"

Clearly Robbie hadn't asked, but *told* Anna of the change in plans. She'd have to have a talk with him herself. "If you wouldn't mind."

"Of course not, but what's going on? Why aren't you coming home?"

Quickly Emily outlined the situation, telling Anna only that she'd seen Ryan and they'd argued about Robbie. Anna was aghast enough. She didn't need to know Ryan had attacked her. "And you think he's coming here? Tonight? Does he know where you live?"

"I don't know. But he was so angry when he left I don't want to take any chances."

"This doesn't sound good, Emily. From what you've told me about him..."

"We'll talk later, all right? Just remember, if a dark blue van—or any strange car—pulls into my driveway, call the police." If Ryan tried anything with Robbie, all bets were off.

"With pleasure," Anna vowed. "And Emily? When you get here, plan on staying the night."

Emily's heart melted. "I appreciate the offer, Anna, but—"

"But nothing. I don't want you staying in that house alone."

"I can't simply run away. I have to think of Robbie. I don't want him getting the idea he's not safe in his own home."

"Like you said. We'll talk about it later."

Emily sighed. "I ordered a pizza. I'm having it delivered."

"All right. I'll take care of it."

"Thanks. I'll be there as soon as I can."

Her son's safety and hunger seen to, Emily turned her attention to her cuts and bruises. A glance in the mirror above the sink as she filled it with soapy water took her back ten years. Her left cheek was swollen and purpling, her bottom lip split down the center. Five small, purplish bruises marred her left upper arm where Ryan had grabbed it. She didn't even want to think about her hip or ribs.

Her palms stung as she immersed them in the warm suds, her knees burned as she dabbed at them with a washcloth. Using tweezers Sarah had provided, she gingerly removed bits of debris embedded in her skin, then gritted her teeth and applied disinfectant to the raw cuts. To her relief, the bandages didn't show beneath her skirt hem when she stood. After washing what she could of the dirt and bloodstains from her clothes, she called Sarah at the front desk. "I'm ready to leave."

Sarah entered the lounge moments later, a pair of pantyhose in hand. "Here. I keep these in my purse for emergencies."

With a grateful smile, Emily sank back onto the sofa and slipped off her shoes. The hose eased past her bandaged knees, she looked up to see Sarah watching her, shaking her head in disbelief.

"Jesus. It creeps me out to think of some maniac loose in the parking lot. When I look at you and think of what could have happened—"

Emily stood and pulled the pantyhose to her waist, wincing as it encased her bruised hip and sore knees. "But it didn't. I'm okay."

Sarah shot her a look that said, *Yeah, right.* "What if he's still out there?"

Emily smoothed her skirt and slipped into her shoes. "After the scare Carmen put into him, I doubt it." She hadn't identified her attacker to Sarah, or told her about the van.

"I still think you should call the police."

"There's no point. He's gone. I saw him leave."

Sarah shook her head again. "Eric's going to have a fit when he sees your face and finds out the guy got off scoot free."

Emily paused. She hadn't thought of that. "Then he won't see it." She reached for her coat lying on the couch.

"He's coming home tonight, isn't he? After the game?"

"His plane won't get in until one or so. He'll probably go straight home and stop by the hospital tomorrow."

"That bruise isn't going to disappear overnight, Emily."

Emily agreed, but hoped an artful application of makeup would minimize its ugliness.

"I don't understand why you want to keep this from him," Sarah persisted. "If there's one thing I've learned about relationships, it's keeping secrets only causes more trouble than it's worth."

Emily raised an eyebrow. "Who said we were having a relationship?"

"I saw you the night of the ice storm, Emily. I saw the way he paced the halls, waiting for you, the way he bolted over from the coffee shop when I called to tell him you were off-duty. If you're not having a relationship with the man, then step aside so someone else can give it a shot."

"You?"

Sarah grinned. "In a New York minute."

Emily laughed, then sobered. "Oh, Sarah. What's the point in telling him? What could he do about it?" *Except make things worse?* An idea of what Eric might do to Ryan flashed across her mind. She shoved it aside, unwilling to even *think* about it.

Leaving a disgruntled Sarah behind, Emily returned to the Suburban to find Carmen waiting, still seated behind the wheel. She approached the driver's side and spoke through the window Carmen lowered. Inside, the Eagles sang about life in the fast lane.

"Carmen. You didn't have to stay."

She shrugged and scooted over. "It was a no-parking zone. I thought I should stick around and keep an eye on your car."

Emily smiled her thanks and slid behind the wheel. When they pulled up to Carmen's Mustang, Carmen said, "I've been thinking. You're probably going to need legal help to get your ex off your back. My cousin's a divorce lawyer, and I'm sure—"

"I already have a divorce, Carmen," Emily interrupted wearily. She knew Carmen meant well, but was getting tired of people telling her what she should do. Anna wanted her to move out of the house, Sarah wanted her to tell Eric and presumably let him take care of her problems, and now Carmen wanted to push her into legal action. All she wanted to do was go home, hug her son, and pull her thoughts together.

"I'm aware of that," Carmen said. "Apparently it isn't enough."

"Carmen—"

"Let me call my cousin. He won't mind us calling him at home. We can call from my condo. It's only a few blocks away. I think you'll be more comfortable there."

Reluctantly, Emily gave in. She didn't want to repay Carmen's kindnesses by being bull-headed. On the way to Carmen's condo, she called Anna on the cell phone to say she'd be delayed indefinitely.

When they got there Carmen led Emily into her home office, dialed her cousin, spoke with him in Spanish for a few moments, then put Emily on the phone and left the room. Miguel Sandoval greeted her warmly, not seeming the least bit put out by Carmen's call. Carmen was family, Emily realized. When family called, you did what you could to help. The thought made Emily homesick for her own family.

Miguel asked her a few innocuous questions about herself, then slipped into a no-nonsense question and answer mode so smoothly she didn't have time to get uncomfortable about telling her story to a stranger. Even so, she emerged from Carmen's office forty-five minutes later feeling as though she'd been run over by a steamroller. The man would be hell on wheels in a courtroom, Emily thought—if it came to that. She rubbed the back of her neck, and swung her head from side to side. She'd be stiff in the morning.

"How'd it go?"

Emily looked up to see Carmen curled up on the couch, an open book in her lap, empathy in her face. On the coffee table waited a pot of what smelled like peppermint tea, a plate of cheese and crackers, a digital camera, and a fresh ice pack for her bruised cheek.

She set her soggy ice pack down and picked up the new one. "We have an appointment Monday morning—unless we need one sooner."

Carmen smiled and closed her book. "Good. Trust me, Emily. Miguel knows his stuff."

Emily had to agree. He'd asked enough questions to fill a legal pad, then assured her Ryan didn't have a prayer of getting Robbie. For that alone she was grateful. If she'd had to find her own lawyer, she wouldn't have known where to begin, whom to trust. The one she'd used to divorce Ryan had been next to useless. She didn't doubt for a minute he'd been paid off by the Montgomery's to make sure she ended up with nothing but a huge legal bill. Just one of many bills she'd spent years paying off thanks to Ryan. Having learned her lesson, she no longer even owned a credit card.

"He wants pictures of me."

"He told me that, too." She indicated the camera on the coffee table. We'll take them before you leave."

Emily sank onto the sofa with a weary sigh, reached for a cheese-covered cracker and her tea. She ached to get home to Robbie, but knew he was safe with Anna and the girls. After all Carmen had done for her, Emily didn't want to leave without at least trying to explain about Ryan. Why she'd let him go.

But first she had her own curiosity to satisfy. "Why are you doing this, Carmen? Don't get me wrong, I'm extremely grateful, but why involve yourself in my problems?"

"I've been there."

The two women's eyes locked across the couch, and Emily finally understood why she and Carmen had clicked from the start.

"I also know what it's like when you think you're facing it alone. That's probably why you let him go. Because you don't think you can fight him alone. But you don't have to this time, Emily. Whatever came before, you have friends now."

Emily looked into her tea and let its soothing steam waft across her face. The idea of having a woman friend her own age felt strange—and yet curiously appealing. It was something she'd never had before. Growing up, she'd had her sisters—but she'd always held a part of herself back, knowing they counted on her to be the strong one. Then Ryan had come along and made sure she had no time for anyone but him. She hadn't let herself get close to anyone but Anna since.

"Do you really want to hear the whole story?"

"Only if you feel like telling it."

Emily wasn't sure. She wasn't used to confiding in anyone, and this was new ground for her. Carmen didn't try to sway her one way or the other, and Emily appreciated that. They munched on crackers and sipped their tea in companionable silence until Emily finally opened with, "Are you at all familiar with the name Dr. John Montgomery?"

"The head of cardiac surgery over at St. Paul Memorial?"

Emily nodded, staring forward. "That was his only son whose balls you threatened to shoot off tonight."

"Ryan Montgomery? And his mother is Patricia?"

"Yes, that's them."

Carmen stared, seemingly stupefied. "Holy shit," she finally muttered. "I mean...wow...I thought he looked familiar, but...*Ryan* Montgomery? Cripes. Isn't he supposed to marry Catherine Stump this summer?"

"That's what I hear."

"I wonder if she has any idea what he's really like?"

"I've wondered about that, too." The thought still troubled her. Emily knew she should warn the woman. But would Catherine appreciate a warning—or would it only enrage Ryan even further?

If she had only herself to think about, Emily knew she'd speak up and gladly. But she had Robbie to consider.

"I hadn't seen him in nine years," she said finally. Carmen said nothing. Emily shifted to face her across the couch. "He came after me because of the interview. He was one of those men you mentioned who saw themselves in your article and took exception to it."

"Interesting," Carmen murmured. "They don't usually admit to it. Oh, they'll cuss you out, but won't really say why. Or if they do, it's always something *you've* done wrong, not them."

"He blames my sudden notoriety on Eric."

"Eric? Oh...as in Cameron." She grinned. Emily recognized the grin as the same one Sarah had sent her. Envious, but without malice. "Is it serious?"

Emily hedged, uncertain in her own mind. "Ryan seems to think so."

"Ah," Carmen said knowingly. "So he's running scared."

"You're kidding. Ryan?"

"Why not? You've suddenly got the power to put the kibosh on his wedding plans and he knows it. Not to mention his standing in the community."

"I didn't do the interview to interfere with his wedding plans—or his standing in the community."

"I know. But there's a reason for everything. And what goes around comes around. He abused you, and now you have the power to make him pay for it."

"How?"

"Eric has access to Catherine."

"So?" Emily rubbed her right shoulder, which had hit the van when Ryan had slammed her against it. "I'm not following you."

"I assume you haven't told Eric about Ryan."

"Well, no. I meant to, but—"

"Spare me the excuses. Been there, done that, too. So let's say you *did* tell Eric. Dumped the whole story on him, including what happened tonight. What do you think Eric would do?"

"I don't even want to think about that, Carmen." It was true. Eric wouldn't waste two seconds on talking if he came face to face with Ryan Montgomery. Emily was sure of it.

"No, no, no, Emily. I'm not asking what he would

want to do—we both know what that would be—but what *would* he do?"

Was Carmen saying Eric would restrain himself around Ryan? "I don't know," she admitted honestly. "I guess he'd still confront him somehow. Maybe warn Catherine off the marriage? But why can't I do that? I've met her. She knows me. What's to stop me from giving her a call?"

"You tell me."

Emily said nothing, realizing Carmen was right. Remarkably enough, after all these years, she was in the driver's seat now and if Ryan wasn't running scared, he should be.

"The bastard deserves to be shown for what he is, Emily. You should have brought him up on charges nine years ago."

"I didn't know how. Even if I had known, I didn't have the money. I left with only the clothes on my back. I wouldn't have stood a chance against the Montgomery money and influence."

"It's not too late to do it now. Especially not with fresh evidence."

Emily was starting to feel cornered again. Instinctively, she lashed out. "What about you? What do you get out of all of this?"

Carmen frowned. "What do you mean?"

"The Montgomery's are big news in St. Paul. You're a reporter."

Carmen's puzzled look relaxed into a smile. "Okay. I see where you're headed with this, and while I'll admit an exposé on the Montgomery's would sell a ton of newspapers, that's not my goal here. For one, I'm a writer, not a reporter. I sell stories. And while a part of me would love to write this story, and expose Ryan Montgomery for what he is, believe me, Em, that's not what this is about."

She looked Emily in the eye. "I'm here for you as a friend, Emily. A friend who's walked in your shoes and knows what it's like to think you're facing it alone."

Again, Emily felt that compelling tug toward friendship. "Thank you."

"You're welcome. More tea?"

Emily handed over her cup. Accepting her refill, she took a long sip, then said, "So what's your story?"

"Three years ago I had a leech of a live-in boyfriend who decided I wasn't supporting him in the manner he wanted to be supported in. He eventually tried beating some incentive into me. I wised up and threw him out after a year, but it's taken me this long to get over it." She smiled wryly. "You might call this latest series of articles my catharsis."

Emily sighed heavily. "I guess we all need one."

"Exactly, and I have a feeling you're just coming in to yours. I'm not trying to start an argument, Emily, I just want you to face the question of whether you're going to let Montgomery put a muzzle on you again, not to mention let him get away with beating the hell out of you again. If you sweep his latest attack under the carpet, you'll be sending the message he can terrorize you any time he wants to. You know this Emily. You *know* it."

Emily said nothing. Carmen sighed in frustration and sat back. "Okay. I'll let it go for now. But what are you going to do about Eric? He's not the kind of man to let it go if someone disses his lady."

"Carmen, I never said we were—"

"Come off it, girl. Denial doesn't suit you. One look at that picture in Sunday's paper and you'd have to be blind not to be able to tell the man's crazy about you."

Emily leaned her head back and blew out a long, slow breath in exasperation. Suddenly Ryan's ugly words came back to haunt her.

Grow up, Emily. It made the papers. Call your new friend Martinez if you don't believe me. I'm sure she knows all about it. She'd have to be as stupid as you are not to.

Obviously neither she nor Carmen was stupid. It was equally obvious Carmen had a strong opinion about Eric's character. An opinion that differed somewhat from her own in reference to what he would or wouldn't do if he found out about Ryan. The difference was worth exploring. She sent Carmen a sideways glance.

"Tell me, Carmen. How much do you know about Eric Cameron?"

Chapter Twenty-Three

Carmen reached for her tea. "I've never met him, if that's what you're asking. I was scheduled to interview him and several of his teammates shortly after he joined the Saints. A social profile to introduce the players to the city for a special advertising supplement Catherine Stump paid the paper to put out to generate interest in the team." She grinned wryly, then sipped her tea. "That Catherine is one amazing woman."

"What happened?"

"With Eric? He didn't show. Car trouble, I think. I interviewed the rest of the guys and got my story anyway." She smiled, remembering. "Quite a rowdy bunch. A few of them too arrogant for their own good, but nobody's complaining now." She glanced toward the television. "Which reminds me, the game's on. They're probably into the second period by now. You want to check the score?" She reached for the remote.

"Er, no. I'd rather not." Emily couldn't bear the thought of seeing Eric just then.

Carmen frowned. "What's wrong, Emily?"

I'm about to make a complete ass of myself, that's what. "Have you ever heard anything about...Eric's ex-wife?"

Carmen's frown deepened, then slowly faded. "I see," she murmured, then set the remote aside. You're wondering about that business where she landed in the hospital. If it has any implications for you."

Emily said nothing, the idea of digging into Eric's past like this repulsive to her. Where was her faith and trust in him? She couldn't believe she was falling prey to Ryan's lies again, but damn it, she needed to *know*.

"What exactly is it you want to know?" Carmen asked, spookily echoing her own thoughts.

"Is it true that he...that he..." Emily looked into her tea. She couldn't do it. It wasn't right.

"Are you asking if he was responsible for what happened?"

"Forget it. I shouldn't have asked."

"No, you brought it up, you want to know. I'd say you have a right to know. Word is he beat her so badly she had to be hospitalized. I don't know if it's true. Seems the story made a sizeable splash in the papers some ten years ago. My gut feeling is he was set up, but I've never had a chance to ask him about it."

"Set up? By his own wife?"

"Stranger things have happened."

"I...understand she dropped the charges." Emily prayed it was because he wasn't guilty.

Carmen nodded. "When he agreed to the terms of the divorce. From the looks of it she made off with a bundle, considering he was only a minor league player at the time. He must have had some money of his own. As for Eric, right about that time he began developing his reputation as a fighter. Unfortunately, he didn't discriminate between his opponents and his teammates when he let loose. Shortly after the incident with his wife, he was traded to a farm team that prized that sort of behavior. Within a month he'd fought his way into a prime position with the New Jersey Devils.

"But that was years ago. Once he left the Devils he started settling down, and by the time he'd joined the Canadiens, he'd evolved into one of the best and most respected players in the league." Frowning, Carmen looked around the room. "I've got a couple of books around here somewhere written by former players. They mention Eric frequently—and in a positive light. I'll loan them to you if you like."

"No, that's all right," Emily murmured, feeling too confused just then to dig any deeper. She needed to get home, needed to sort through her feelings, needed to make sense of the evening's events and the information spinning through her mind before she opened this Pandora's Box any wider.

Carmen studied her openly. "Emily, if the man's past bothers you so much, why don't you ask him about it?"

Emily arrived at Anna's during the last minutes of the third period. Robbie, sprawled on the family room floor next to a large, empty pizza box, barely glanced away from the enormous wide screen. Anna took one look at Emily's swollen face and practically dragged her into the kitchen.

"What in God's name happened to you?"

"Ryan."

Anna stared, her lips tightening, but said nothing. She spun away, hit the microwave button, then proceeded to make a pot of tea.

"Please, no more tea," Emily protested. "I'll be running to the bathroom all night."

"Won't bother me," Anna returned implacably. "At least I'll know you're safe."

So Anna still expected her to stay the night. Emily sighed, knowing she had yet another battle on her hands before she could go home to bed. The thought of Anna keeping Robbie for the night was a good one, but Emily refused to do anything that might make Robbie feel he was unsafe in his own home. They couldn't run to Anna's every time Emily had a problem with Ryan.

"We can't stay, Anna." At Anna's impatient scowl, she said, "Don't you see? I can't let the possibility that Ryan *might* show up again force me from my own home. That would be giving him the power and control again. I can't base my choices on what he *might* do. I'll drive myself crazy if I start thinking that way."

Anna harrumphed and turned toward the beeping microwave. "It's a good thing the season's almost over," she muttered, setting two steaming slices of Paisan's pizza in front of Emily.

Emily glanced up in surprise. "Why is that?"

"Your young man will be around when you need him for a change."

"Anna, Eric isn't my 'young man'".

"If he isn't you didn't have any business staying out all night with him. If I'd known you were just playing with him—"

"I wasn't playing with him, I was—"

Falling hopelessly in love with him.

Emily drew a deep breath. "Listen to me, Anna,

because I'm only going to say this once. Eric Cameron is not and never will be responsible for either my or Robbie's safety or well-being."

"And why not? What's wrong with the man? Seems to me he's just what you need with your smarmy ex-husband sniffing around."

Emily tensed. "He came by tonight?"

"No, but that doesn't mean he won't. God knows what he'll take it in his mind to do to you the next time. Are you going to let him get away with this, Emily? And don't tell me I don't understand. I understand plenty. You're not making any sense right now and you know it."

She sat down and looked Emily in the eye, speaking gently. "I've got a bad feeling about this, Emily," she said, her plump, maternal face creased with concern. "We need to call the police."

"He doesn't want *me*." Emily explained about the interview and Ryan's reaction to it. "He blames Eric for putting me in the spotlight. He says if I stop seeing Eric and back off on giving interviews and campaigning for funds for Harmony House, he'll leave me alone."

"And you *believe* him? Girl, haven't you learned *anything*?"

"He says he'll sue for custody of Robbie if I don't do as he says."

"Hogwash. If he wanted the boy, he'd have done something about it before now. You think those Montgomerys would sit still knowing they had a legitimate grandchild living in the same city? The man's manipulating you, just like he used to. You let him get away with it this time and he'll be back again and again, every time he wants to see you jump, expecting you to say, 'How high?'"

"Mom! Mom! Come look! Eric's got the puck—and he scoorrres!" Robbie bellowed.

Emily smiled at Robbie's perfect imitation of the game's play-by-play announcer. She'd joined her son in that same victory cry many times while watching Eric's games, then pulled Robbie to her for a big hug. Her smile faded at the thought that she'd never again be able to watch Eric play without wondering about his early career days. Or his ex-wife.

She pushed the thought away, refusing to dwell on it any more than she already had tonight. Her next priority was to speak to Robbie about his father, but from the sound of her son's hooting and hollering, to snare his attention while the game was on would be impossible. Her suspicions were confirmed when he crowed the game would run into overtime. Eric's goal had apparently tied the score at two-two.

"Mom! You gonna come watch Eric play or not?"

Emily knew if she stayed in the kitchen with Anna, she'd invite more lecturing. "In a minute, sweetheart. I'm finishing my pizza." She ignored Anna's disgruntled stare and went to join her son.

Robbie sat cross-legged on the floor—his gaze glued to the screen. Emily spied Augustus' vacant and hideously ugly leather easy chair in a shadowed corner of the room and made her way toward it. As she sank into its shiny, well-worn cushions, she finally understood why he refused to let Anna replace it with something more in keeping with the room's French Country décor. Its smooth contours welcomed her like a hug from an old and dear friend.

She slid back and propped up her feet, then closed her eyes and sighed, ignoring the dull throbbing in her shoulder, breast and hip. Instead she focused on the room's quiet comfort, and settled in to watch Robbie root for his team.

And watch Robbie she did. Not once during the next sixteen minutes did her gaze stray from her son to the television screen. All she needed to know about the game was reflected in Robbie's squirming body and animated face. When the Saints scored, he leapt up and whooped for all he was worth. Spotting Emily, he launched himself into her arms for a victory hug. Emily winced as his bony knee dug into her bruised hip, buried her face in his baby-soft neck and held him tight. Silently she vowed to do whatever it took to keep her son safe until he grew to manhood.

Five minutes later a disapproving Anna saw a determined Emily and a jubilant Robbie to the door.

"Thanks, Nanna. It was great."

Anna wrapped an arm around Robbie and bussed

him on the head. "My pleasure, Scamp." To Emily, she said, "We'll talk again tomorrow."

Emily nodded, her emotions too close to the edge to talk any more tonight.

****

Emily awoke to the feel of Robbie shaking her from behind, babbling frantically about being late. She'd forgotten today was the day the budding rocket scientists were to present their projects to the class. He raced from the room, shouted he'd get his own breakfast (A heaping bowl of Captain Crunch), and begged her to *pleeeze* hurry, or Glen was gonna *kill* him for being late.

Fifteen minutes later Emily and her dark glasses met Robbie at the front door. Taking a deep breath, she braced herself for his reaction to her puffy face. Last night he'd been too excited about the game to notice. She'd also made an effort to stay in the shadows. By the time she'd stopped in to kiss him goodnight, he'd already fallen asleep from sheer exhaustion.

But this morning he was wide awake and...clearly too anxious to get going to worry about why she wore more make-up than usual.

"Come on, Mom! Class starts in half an hour!"

During the ride to school, he tinkered endlessly with the cardboard and aluminum foil launch pad and rocket, then explained in great detail what each piece was before erupting into a plethora of lift-off sound effects. Emily was grateful he still sat in the back seat.

A panicky Glen paced under the portico at St. Stephens. He yanked opened Robbie's door, assured himself their project had arrived intact, then swept the project from Robbie's hands. As Glen made a beeline for class, Robbie popped off his seatbelt and scrambled after him, slamming the car door shut behind him. Emily spotted Miranda Manzelrod holding the front door open for the two boys, forced a smile and sent her a "Gotta run" wave, then shifted into drive and headed for work. The last thing she needed was for Miranda to see what Robbie had missed and tell Eric.

Eric. What was she going to do about him? Her head told her she needed to stay away from him, but her heart told her no matter what he might have done before, he

227

would never hurt her or Robbie. Just as she'd changed and grown over the years, so had he. The Eric she knew was kind, gentle, considerate, affectionate, funny and generous to a fault.

She'd tossed and turned all night as she thought about what Carmen had told her and wondered what to say to Eric when she saw him again. She had to say something. She couldn't let her questions hang between them. If he had an explanation, she needed to hear it. Deserved to hear it. From the man involved.

But what would happen when he saw her face?

Eric's going to have a fit when he finds out the guy got off scot-free.

He's not the type of man to let someone dis his lady.

It's a good thing the season's almost over...your young man will be around when you need him for a change.

Seems to me he's just what you need with your smarmy ex-husband sniffing around.

Emily lifted her gaze to the rearview mirror, removed her dark glasses—and felt her heart sink to her lap. She'd lost her touch; artistry had given way to garishness. Beneath her too-liberal application of makeup, her left cheek was still swollen, her eyes bloodshot and ringed with dark circles. The split in her puffy lip was already showing through her unusually dark lipstick.

A horn honked from behind. The light had turned green. Emily swore in frustration and stepped on the gas. Who was she trying to kid? Eric would notice her bruised face, and so would everyone else. What was she going to tell them? She'd been mugged? She wanted to scream at the unfairness of it all.

Instead she drove into the nearest parking lot, pulled into a spot and cut the Suburban's engine. For ten solid minutes she sat there, staring out at nothing, as her thoughts swirled fruitlessly.

What was she going to do?

Chapter Twenty-Four

Eric stopped by the hospital just before noon. He hoped to coax Emily into slipping away for lunch. His need to see her had gnawed at him ever since he'd stepped off the plane, exhausted and in need of someone to hug. Someone he belonged to. Someone who belonged to him. He'd been disappointed at not finding Emily among the crowd of wives, girlfriends and fans waiting to welcome the team home, but could hardly expect her to hang out at the airport in the dead of night when she had to get up at dawn to go to work.

He spotted Sarah Ferguson flipping through a file cabinet behind the admissions counter. "Hi, Sarah. How's business?" With any luck he could get her to help him spirit Emily away with him.

"Eric. What are you doing here? Oh, no. Has something happened?"

He grinned. "Nope. I made it back in one piece. Think Emily might be free for lunch?"

"Emily? She's ah, out today."

"I thought tomorrow was her day off." They'd planned to spend the day together, going wherever their mood took them. "Is she at home?"

"I...really can't say." Looking flustered, she turned away and went back to her files. Eric frowned and pulled out his cell phone. An avid Saints fan, Sarah usually talked his ear off.

"Ah...not here, Eric? Remember?"

"Right. No cell phones in the hospital. Sorry." He went out to the parking lot.

He let the phone ring a dozen times. "Damn." Normally when she was out, Emily left her answering machine on. He tried her cell phone. No luck. He decided to go to Emily's anyway. He found the house empty, the

229

Subway gone. For several minutes he sat in the driveway, the Boxter's engine running, torn between disappointment and frustration. He could accept Emily's not meeting him at the airport, but she could have at least let him know where to find her today. She had to know he would come looking for her.

He swore in frustration, shoved the car into reverse and headed for the nearest bookstore. He'd finished his latest James Patterson in St. Louis and needed something else to read. When he returned an hour and twenty minutes later, the Subway was back. He glanced at his watch and smiled. Robbie wouldn't be home for at least two hours. He just hoped Emily had missed him as much as he'd missed her.

Reaching across the seat, he swept up the roses he'd picked up at the florist beside the bookstore. After three knocks and no answer, he opened the front door and stepped into Emily's foyer, then called her name. The hearty aroma of basil and oregano drew him into the kitchen.

Setting the roses on the kitchen table, he noted the pasta machine, two-pound bag of semolina flour, and a loaf of Italian bread on the counter. She must have been at the grocery store when he'd stopped by earlier. He picked up a wooden spoon, dipped it into the sauce gurgling on the stove. He inhaled deeply, then tasted the sauce. Closing his eyes, he prayed for an invitation to dinner.

Peering out the back door, he spied Emily planting a double row of purple and white flowers that looked like they might be impatiens beside the steps. He smiled and savored the sight of her, just as he'd savored the taste of her sauce. She was kneeling on the ground, a kitchen towel smudged with dirt at her side, her hair gleaming like burnished gold in the late afternoon sun.

Two purple, two white, two purple, two white; methodically she planted. He wondered if she'd deliberately chosen Saints colors to plant. Amused by the thought, he opened the door and stepped outside. "Hi, sweetheart."

She stilled, slanted him a sideways glance, then resumed planting her flowers. "Hello, Eric."

Hello, Eric? That was all she had to say? After five of the longest days of his life? He stared at her bent head, then out across her yard. Beside the shed he spotted the mower, spattered with fresh grass clippings. The smell of spring lay heavy in the warm afternoon air. "I stopped by the hospital, but Sarah said you'd taken the day off."

"I had some things to catch up on."

"The yard looks nice. If I'd known you were planning to mow it today, I'd have given you a hand."

"I didn't mind. It gave me time to think."

She hadn't stopped with her planting, or looked at him again. Unsettled by her less than warm welcome, he sat on the back stoop, braced his forearms on his thighs, and loosely clasped his hands between them. She only had four more flowers to go. Waiting for her to finish would give him time to collect his own thoughts.

"About anything in particular?" he asked as she mounded freshly turned dirt around the base of the last plant.

"You could say that."

Something was wrong. This dispassionate woman was not the same woman he'd kissed goodbye five days ago—or even the same woman he'd spoken with on the phone Monday night. Then again, he'd been so full of himself that night, he'd barely given her a chance to get a word in edgewise. "What's wrong, Emily?"

"I don't think we should see each other again."

His stomach bottomed out. "May I ask why?" he asked with a lot more calm than he felt.

"We're not compatible."

He stared at her and wondered if he'd heard right. She finished planting and started tugging at some weeds, lying them in a pile beside her. "Seems to me we were plenty compatible Saturday night," he said slowly.

"In bed, yes," she said, surprisingly matter-of-factly. "Outside of it..." She paused, ran the back of her hand across her forehead, and stared at her faded white aluminum siding. "We're moving in different directions."

He studied her profile as she resumed weeding. Was that what this was all about? His leaving when the season ended?

"I'll be back, Emily." He figured it would take him a

231

few days at most to check on things in Barton. Not that there was that much to check on. A closed-up cedar and glass house, a solitary grave overlooking the Rainy River. Five hundred acres of rolling farmland, woods and streams where he planned to build a hockey camp for kids when he retired. He spent his summers there because he didn't have anywhere else to go. Because by the end of May all he wanted was to stay in one place for a while, unwind, enjoy some peace and quiet before the grind of another eighty-four-game season started up again. When he got tired of his own company, he hopped on a plane and made the rounds of his restaurants. It wasn't much of a life, but it was what he had.

He needed to ask Emily about her plans for the summer. Maybe she and Robbie could come up to Barton and visit for a while if she could swing some time off from the hospital.

But Emily clearly wasn't in the mood to discuss vacation plans. She yanked at the weeds harder now, all but slammed them into the pile beside her. "And when fall comes you'll leave again," she said. "A day or two here, a week or two there—"

"I have to travel. Emily. It's part of my job." She kept weeding. "Are you suggesting we save ourselves the trouble of saying goodbye later when we can do it now, before anyone gets hurt?" She weeded even harder, if that were possible. "Well, it's too late for that, Emily. It already hurts. I hated getting on that plane Sunday, knowing I wouldn't see you again for five days. Hell, I missed you before I backed out of your driveway."

She broke her rhythm. "I missed you, too."

"Then why the cold shoulder?"

"I don't want to spend my time missing you. It's not healthy. It gets in the way of my work, my relationship with Robbie..."

Her words sliced him to the bone—but he knew she was right. It wasn't healthy to spend every waking moment missing someone so much you ached in the night with loneliness. He'd been alone for most of his life, but he'd never known true loneliness until he'd gone to bed without Emily beside him. A long-term relationship between them would involve more lonely nights than he cared to think about.

"What do you want me to do?" he asked quietly. "Give up hockey?"

"Of course not. I'd no sooner ask you to give up your career than you'd ask me to give up mine. All I'm saying is the two aren't compatible. You work nights and travel, I work days, nights and weekends. You could be traded at any time and sent to another city. I have a home, a secure job..."

Something glinted in the neighbor's yard and she looked up, away from him, toward the neighbor's house, where a mammoth marmalade cat lazed in the sun. "...A son who deserves to grow up in a safe, stable environment, surrounded by people who love him...people he can count on to be there for him."

Eric thought of Robbie's hockey games he'd had to miss. "As opposed to someone who comes and goes on an erratic schedule," he said flatly.

She cast him another quick, sideways glance. "At this point, Robbie still considers you a part-time friend, an infrequent visitor. But if we continue seeing each other, he could come to depend on you as much as—"

She stopped, closed her eyes and bit her lower lip.

"As much as what, Emily? As much as you do?"

She didn't answer, just resumed weeding. Furiously, if he stopped to think about it.

"I don't know, Emily. I'm getting some seriously mixed signals here. You say we're not compatible, but you miss me when I'm gone. You say your son needs stability, but you've raised him to accept your own erratic schedule—"

Her fist thumped the earth beside her. "That's different! I'm not gone for days at a time."

"Sales reps travel too, Emily. A hell of a lot more than I do. So do pilots, truckers and most corporate execs. Do you see them forgoing relationships and families just because they're on the road most of the week? Or weeks, even months at a time. Think of the military, Emily."

She didn't answer. He sighed wearily. "Will you look at me, please?" he asked quietly.

"I'd rather not."

She'd rather not? He wanted to shake her.

"I think you should leave, Eric. Robbie will be home soon."

Robbie wasn't due home for at least another hour and they both knew it. "Not unless you look at me, first."

"There's no point, Eric."

"Bullshit! If you're dumping me for no good reason the least you can do is look me in the eye while you do it."

She only stared forward. Something glinted in the neighbor's yard again, but Eric was too focused on Emily to give it any attention. "I'm waiting, Emily. You look me in the eye and tell me you don't think we have a prayer of making this work and I'll be out of here so fast you won't have time to blink."

He waited. She closed her eyes and breathed deeply.

"One look, Emily. That's all it'll take." He meant it. He'd had about all he could take of her tap dancing on his heart.

Slowly, she rose to her feet and turned to face him. Eric felt as if he'd been hit with a sledgehammer. "My God." He was on his feet and reaching for her automatically. Emily stepped back, shaking her head, her eyes dull and lifeless.

"Don't."

Rage roared inside him, rage that someone would dare lay a hand on her. "Who did this to you?"

She looked at her flowers, cutting off his view of her bruised cheek and split lip. "One of my patients got out of hand."

She was lying. He knew it as surely as he knew how many points he'd scored last night. If Emily had been hurt on the job, Sarah would have told him. Warned him. "Try again."

Her eyes jerked back to his, and when he saw her fear he knew. This wasn't about conflicting schedules and domestic stability. This was about something deeper. Something he didn't understand. But he damned well would before this nightmare was over. He scanned her body, saw the bruises on her upper left arm, the scrapes on her knees. With renewed horror, he realized someone hadn't just hit her—they'd attacked her.

What she'd been trying to tell him suddenly slammed home. She'd needed him and he'd been gone. She'd come to depend on him, but in the end she'd had to deal with the terror of a physical attack and its ugly emotional aftermath alone.

"Emily..." He reached for her again, but she shook her head, her eyes tormented. Helplessly, Eric curled his hands into fists, his rage at her attacker returning. Whoever it was, he would find the sonafabitch and make him pay. Dearly. Not only had the bastard hurt Emily, he'd violated her sense of safety, and made her lose faith in *him*. "Who did this to you?"

"It doesn't matter."

"The hell it doesn't. Sarah knows, doesn't she?"

Emily shook her head, but the fear in her eyes grew. Eric got a very uneasy feeling. "Does this have something to do with *me*? Sweet Jesus, did the bastard attack you because he has a grudge against—"

"Eric, please. Robbie will be home soon, and—"

"Forget Robbie. I want to know who attacked you and why."

"So you can do what?" she snapped.

"So I can hunt the sonofabitch down—"

"And do what? Smash his face in? Break his hands and knees?"

"It's a start."

She shook her head, her eyes dark with pain. "Violence isn't the answer, Eric."

"No, but it can be a pretty persuasive tactic at times."

"Do you really believe that?"

"Absolutely. Some people won't listen to anything less."

"Then we have nothing more to say to each other."

The finality in her words rang in his ears like a death knell. Faced with the conviction in her voice that had been missing before, Eric knew he'd made a mistake. A huge one. This was Emily, not one of the guys. Emily didn't subscribe to the law of the jungle, where respect generally boiled down to violence. An eye for an eye only meant more pain and suffering to her.

He reached up to touch her face in apology. "Emily—"

She stepped back, her eyes misty, yet undeniably determined. "Please go, Eric."

His every instinct screamed at him to stay, to fight

235

for her, but that would mean fighting Emily. That he could not do. Not when he raged inside and she looked as if she were about to shatter.

"All right," he said quietly. "I'll go. But this isn't over. Not by a long shot."

Emily watched him walk away and wanted to die. He'd reacted to seeing Ryan's brutal handiwork just as she'd prayed he wouldn't. With barely controlled fury. If she'd identified her attacker, Eric would have made mincemeat out of Ryan before the day was done. And then where would they be?

Eric would be pacing a jail cell and she'd be pacing the floor, waiting to be served with a custody suit. Miguel Sandoval had insisted otherwise, but Emily knew Ryan wasn't one to give up that easily. If she pulled Eric into this, Ryan wouldn't hesitate to use him against her. He'd swear up and down Eric had come after him to coerce him into staying away from Robbie, then launch a mudslinging campaign to rival that of a presidential race. Eric's past would be dredged up for public consumption, her own would be distorted and smeared across the papers, and her innocent son would be emotionally scarred for life.

She was still working in the yard when Robbie burst through the back door. "Mom! Mom!"

"Over here, sweetheart, I'm trimming the azaleas."

"What's going on?" he asked, coming up on her right side.

She glanced over at him and smiled. "Nothing. Why?"

"How come you're home?"

She sent him a dry look. "Use your eyes, big guy. I've been busy."

"You mean Eric's not coming for dinner?"

She stilled. "No. Why would you think that?"

"Then why'd you buy roses?"

"Roses?"

"The ones on the kitchen table."

"Oh, those." She faked a nonchalant shrug. "I don't know, I just...thought they were pretty."

"Are you sure no one's coming for dinner?"

Enough was enough. She sent him a stern sideways look. "Very sure, Robbie. Now may we drop the subject?"

236

"You mean *we're* making ravioli? Just us?"

She laughed, finally understanding. Robbie adored her homemade ravioli. "Yep, a whole pot full. Just the two of us. But you'll have to help me stuff them if you want some. They're not made yet."

"All right! Home made! Wow, Mom, this is the best surprise, ever."

"That's because you're the best son, ever," she said, and gave him a big hug.

He pulled back with a huge grin. "Wait 'till I tell Glen. His mom always gets the frozen kind."

"Blech," Emily said, knowing it was expected of her, and feeling more carefree than she had in almost twenty-four hours.

Robbie's grin vanished. "What happened to your face?"

Emily sobered. Her face. She'd been so upset about Eric, she'd forgotten to go inside and re-apply the make up she'd scrubbed off upon returning home that morning. "I, uh, had a little trouble with a patient," she said, borrowing the lie she'd told Eric.

"He knocked you down, too?"

Robbie stared at her scraped knees, eyes hurt and disbelieving, lips trembling. He looked as if he might cry, then began to quiver the way he did before he erupted in tears.

Emily put a firm hand on one skinny shoulder, tilted his chin up. "Yes. But a big policeman came and took him away, and I'm fine, so we won't worry about it any more, okay?"

He didn't look convinced. "Okay."

Feeling like a fraud, she smiled brightly. "Wash your hands while I put the shears away. We have some ravioli to make."

She entered the house a few minutes later to find Eric's roses lying neglected on the kitchen table. She swallowed hard and reached for them. With fingers that trembled she tore the tissue and pushed it apart.

They were exquisite. Tiny, gently blossoming sweetheart roses. A dozen of them. All perfect. All pale pink. She brought one to her nose, inhaled...and felt her heart break.

Dinner was a subdued affair, but not for the reasons Emily had expected. She'd intended to soften Robbie up with his favorite meal, then sit down and have a serious talk about his father. She hadn't expected it to go well. His reaction could be anything from deep disappointment to wide-eyed disbelief to outright fury that she'd lied to him all these years.

But that was irrelevant now that she'd given in to Ryan's demands. She tried not to think about how cowardly that made her feel as she concentrated on coaxing a smile from her dispirited son. She tried several times, in vain. He would look at her cheek, his sweet face tightening, then plug away at whatever task she'd assigned him. When she finally lowered the stuffed ravioli into the boiling water, she said silent prayer of thanks that the ordeal was almost over.

"Mom?"

"What, honey?" He was speaking to her again. A good sign.

"Are you gonna be a doctor forever?"

She paused in stirring the sauce. "Probably."

When he didn't say anything else, she looked over to where he stood at the counter playing with leftover pasta dough. "What else would you like me to be?"

He shrugged. "I don't know. Just something where you don't have to work all the time."

"Honey, I have to work."

"Glen's mom stays home."

She also serves her children frozen ravioli. "That's because Glen's dad goes to work to pay the bills."

"Why can't we have a dad to pay the bills? Then you could stay home like Glen's mom."

"Things aren't that simple, sweetheart."

"I bet Eric would be our dad if we asked him."

Emily went still, then turned around slowly. "Where did you get that idea?" she asked. She could strangle whoever planted it in his fertile little mind.

"He likes us."

So the idea was apparently his own. That made things even harder. "Yes, well he's not going to be around much longer. When the season ends, he's going home." Robbie looked crushed. Emily felt cruel and insensitive.

But she had to nip this dangerous line of thought in the bud.

The buzzer sounded behind her. Grateful for the distraction, Emily strained the pasta and prepared their plates, while Robbie pulled the salad from the refrigerator and poured them each a glass of milk.

The rest of the meal was uneventful, even pleasant, as Emily asked Robbie about his rocket ship presentation that morning. After dinner they left the dishes and played computer games until it was time for Robbie's bath. It wasn't until after she'd checked his ears to make sure they were thoroughly dry and tucked him in for the night that she discovered the true reason for his earlier line of questioning.

Lying between his Batman sheets—teeth brushed, face scrubbed, hair still damp—he looked up at her with sad, serious eyes and said, "Think about what I said, okay, Mom?"

"What was that? You've said plenty tonight, Tiger." She smiled and brushed back a lock of his hair.

"About asking Eric to be our dad so you can stay home."

Her hand stilled. "Robbie..."

"Please? I don't want you to get hurt anymore, Mom."

Chapter Twenty-Five

Emily did the dishes with tears in her eyes.

When the kitchen was spotless, she brewed a cup of chamomile tea, sat at the table, and stared into the steam.

The grandfather clock in the hall chimed eleven. Emily's heart contracted. Eleven was the time Eric usually called, game night or no. Her tears welled anew as she stared at his roses. If he called, she'd have to reject him again.

It might have been different if he were someone she was planning a future with, someone who would stand beside her and fight for Robbie if Ryan did indeed attempt to carry through with his threats. But Eric was leaving come summer, and she couldn't risk her son's safety and security for a man who was just passing through, no matter how much she loved him.

The telephone rang. She groaned in despair, knowing it was Eric. Where was she supposed to find the strength to convince him it was over? She let it ring twice more before she remembered Robbie was asleep upstairs and answered it before it woke him.

"You saw him again. I hope it was for the last time."

Emily's blood turned to ice. "How did you get this number?"

Ryan laughed. "Connections, baby. I know where you live, who your friends are, who Robbie's friends are, where he goes to school, where he plays—"

"*No!*" The word was torn from her before she could stop it, the image of Ryan approaching Robbie on a playground unbearable.

"There's no need to shout, Emily. I've no intention of stealing the boy out from under your nose." His chuckle was dry, amused, letting her know he was enjoying himself. "Not when I can have my lawyer do it for me, nice and legal."

"You won't make it to court, Ryan. You don't have a case."

"That's where you're wrong. I'm getting married soon. It won't take much to convince a judge Robbie will be far better off living with Catherine and myself than with his promiscuous absentee mother. With us he'll have a stable home environment, financial security, two loving parents..."

"Over my dead body."

"Suit yourself."

She shivered in the silence that followed. A put-upon sigh came across the line. "You know, Emily, there *is* a way to avoid all this unpleasantness. I believe I mentioned it the other night," he said, as if he'd bought her a drink instead of slammed her around the parking lot. "All you have to do is ditch Cameron."

"And if I don't?"

"You'll lose Robbie. Between Catherine's connections and mine, you won't be able to find a judge in this town who'll let you keep a dog, much less my son. Count on it."

Ryan apparently interpreted her silence as defeat. His voice came across the line, smug with victory. "So remember, Emmie, I'll be watching you. Just like today."

"You were *watching* me?"

"Of course. Well, not me personally, but you never know. Would you like to see the pictures? At least you had enough sense not to kiss him this time."

Emily couldn't speak. Oblivious to her stunned silence, Ryan rambled on. "I wanted to make sure you took my advice. But you didn't, and now I'm calling to remind you to get rid of your lover...or I'll make sure you end up having to make an appointment six months in advance to see your precious son."

"Damn it, Ryan. You've no right to spy on me, to tell me who I can and can't—"

"Think again, cunt. I'm the boy's father. It's my duty to protect him from your moral corruption. See Cameron again and I'll serve you with a custody suit before you can hit the sheets."

"Fine," Emily snapped. File a dozen lawsuits if you

want to. I'll file a dozen right back. Robbie's mine, you miserable bastard!"

She slammed the receiver down so hard it cracked the plastic casing. Not three seconds later the phone rang again. Emily glared at it, ready to rip it from the wall and throw it across the room. Instead she unplugged the answering machine, silenced the telephone's ringer, did the same to the phone in her bedroom, and headed for the shower.

She felt unclean just talking to Ryan Montgomery.

****

The house was pitch dark. Dressed in her robe and slippers, Emily drifted from the back door to the front, checking the locks, regretting her loss of control with Ryan. Challenging him had not been in her best interests, but the idea that he'd actually had someone take pictures of her today had been too much. She felt violated, furious and frightened all at once. Was that same someone out there, even now?

She needed to reassure herself that the house was locked tight. She wouldn't put it past Ryan to retaliate somehow for hanging up on him. But for that, she was sure he'd come himself.

She was checking the front door when she heard the low-pitched rumble of a car engine moving slowly down the street. She stilled, then cocked her head to listen.

The rumble drew closer, stopped. She peered through the front window and saw a dark, low-slung sports car parked in front of the house. Her heart filled with dread.

Ryan. Bold as brass, he'd come in his own car this time.

Fear and adrenaline coursed through her as she watched him step out of the car. She glanced up the steps to where Robbie slept and vowed Ryan Montgomery would have a hell of a fight on his hands if he tried to get past her.

It wasn't until she recognized the man's fluid stride that she realized her late night visitor wasn't Ryan. It was Eric.

Relief barely had a chance to put in an appearance before her fear took on a new shape. She had to get rid of him. What if someone was watching the house? Worse yet, what if Ryan drove by and saw Eric's car?

There was no telling what he might do. But if the two came face to face, by morning Eric might very well be in jail again.

She couldn't let that happen.

She flipped the deadbolt, stepped onto the porch, and shut the door behind her. Eric halted in surprise. His dark eyes scanned her damp, tousled hair, robe and slippered feet. He studied her a moment longer, then joined her on the porch. His clean, masculine scent tempted her to reach out to him, to hold him close for just a moment, to draw on his strength for the courage to handle whatever Ryan threw her way, but she didn't dare. Instead, she crossed her arms over her chest.

"What are you doing here?"

"We need to talk."

"This isn't a good time, Eric."

His gaze scanned her robe again, lingered on the bit of lace that peeked out from beneath her deep V-collar, before he looked over her shoulder at the unlit house. "Are you alone?"

She took umbrage. "Of course I am."

"Then mind if we go inside?"

"Robbie's sleeping. I don't want him waking up to find you paying another middle-of-the-night visit."

"That's not the problem, Emily, and we both know it."

"Why are you here, Eric? I thought I made it clear—"

"I'm here because you unplugged the damned phone again!" He mowed a hand through his hair and stared at her, his eyes dark with pain. "Why, Emily? What's going on? Is someone harassing you?"

"It's not your affair."

"The hell it isn't. Something happened to you while I was gone, something I'm being punished for—"

"Punished for...?"

"You wouldn't call ending our relationship a punishment?"

"Eric, our relationship was over before it began. You made it clear from the beginning—"

"That I was leaving? Are we back to that again? Well get this, Dr. Jordan. You weren't the only one who did some thinking about us while I was gone. In fact, I hardly

243

thought about anything else. I'm surprised I played as well as I did, because you were with me everywhere, Emily, and I mean *everywhere*. I knew then there was no way I could leave you and Robbie behind this summer. I'm staying here."

"But—"

"But nothing, Emily. You and Robbie mean too much to me."

"Oh, no," she moaned softly.

"Oh, no? For God's sake, woman! I thought you'd be happy about it. Wasn't that the problem? My being gone when you needed me?"

She re-crossed her arms and stared at her feet. The time had come for a few home truths. If Eric stayed in Minneapolis, she'd find it impossible to stay away from him, and until she found a way to get Ryan off her back she had to do just that. Too much was at stake—for both of them.

"No. That's not the problem."

"Then please tell me what the problem is, Emily. I'm going crazy, wondering how to make things right between us."

She looked up at him, her eyes and voice flat. "You can't."

"Why the hell not?"

His rising frustration gave her the weapon she needed. Hating herself, she used it like a knife. "Look at yourself and you'll have the answer. You're ready to explode."

"Oh, for the love of—how many times are we going to have to—"

She interrupted, holding up a hand. "You asked the question, Eric, I'm giving my answer. Do you remember what you said this afternoon when I told you violence wasn't the answer?"

"Emily, I was wrong to answer the way I did, but I was angry, and—"

"Anger's no excuse, Eric. I was married to a man who tried to convince me it was. He also tried to convince me his anger was my fault. He also agreed that violence can be a `pretty persuasive tactic' at times. He used it to persuade me to suppress my thoughts, feelings and

244

desires, to convince me I was no good as a wife or woman and never would be, to undermine my determination to become a doctor, to—"

"Your husband *hit* you?"

"Hit me, kicked me, beat me, slapped me around for fun, and tried to run over me with his car. During the course of three years, he broke my jaw twice, both of my arms, several ribs, dislocated my shoulder and in general left me perpetually bruised and sore, physically and emotionally.

"Somehow he convinced me all of this was no more than I deserved, and I put up with it until I found out I was pregnant. After that, I knew there was no way on God's green earth I would stand for his 'persuasive tactics' any longer."

Eric's expression was one of stunned horror. "Emily, I never meant I would use violence against *you*—"

"Are you saying you'd never hit a woman?"

"Of course not!"

She plunged the knife deeper. "What about your ex-wife?"

His face went ashen. "Monica?"

"Is that her name? The woman you beat so badly she had to be hospitalized?"

The silence between them was deafening. "It's not what you think, Emily," Eric finally said quietly. "I never hit Monica. Ever."

She knew he was telling the truth, and it broke her heart. But she had to think of Robbie. She had to think of Eric. Ryan's viciousness would no know bounds if she didn't end this *now*.

"Newspapers aren't in the business of publishing fiction, Eric. Are you telling me they lied about her condition?"

"No. Her injuries were real."

"And just what were they?"

"Multiple contusions, a broken wrist, a fractured jaw and four cracked ribs," he said flatly.

Emily spun away, knowing if she didn't, she'd reach out to him, Ryan be damned. She braced her hands on the porch railing and stared out into the yard, trembling.

His voice was soft and full of quiet dignity behind

her. "I didn't do it, Emily."

Oh, Eric, I know you didn't. But I have to protect my son. I have to protect you. She couldn't bear the thought of the media coming after him like vultures, picking apart this sweet and gentle man's past and condemning him anew for a crime he hadn't committed. She straightened and hugged herself tightly, blinking back her tears. "I understand she pressed charges."

"She dropped them three weeks later."

"After you bought her off with a substantial divorce settlement."

"Yes, I gave her money. Everything I had at the time. But not for the reasons you think."

"What I think doesn't matter. The fact is it happened."

"You don't understand—"

She whirled on him. "I understand plenty, Eric. I've been there."

Nothing she could have said could have hurt him more. Stricken, Eric felt tears burn the backs of his eyes. He looked away and struggled to get a grip on his emotions. When he spoke, it was with a quiet conviction that came from deep within.

"I'm truly sorry about your marriage, Emily. But it has nothing to do with me or mine. I'm not your ex-husband, and I'm not the bastard who...who..." He looked at her then, his eyes dark and intense. "Emily, by now you have to know I'd never lay a hand on you or Robbie in anger."

Slowly, she shook her head. "People change, Eric. I've...been burned before." She swallowed, clearly struggling for composure. "I can't take the chance of that happening again."

He knew then that he'd lost her. Her trust in him had been shattered, and the wet, wounded look in her eyes told him it hurt her as much as it hurt him. She bowed her head, and it took everything he had not to reach out to her, to comfort her—to comfort himself.

"I'm sorry, Eric."

Her whispered apology couldn't begin to ease his pain, to hold back the dark, vast emptiness seeping into his soul. He looked down at her bent head and ached to touch her one last time. To beg her to let him explain. To promise her anything if she'd give him just one more chance.

Instead he jammed his fists into his jacket pockets.

"So am I," he said quietly, and left.

Chapter Twenty-Six

Emily awoke exhausted and on edge. She'd spent the night listening for the sound of cars on the street. She hadn't been able to shake the thought that Ryan might pay her a visit after all. Or that Eric might return and, this time, she wouldn't have the strength to send him away again.

It had nearly killed her to watch him return to his car, knowing he was hurting as much as she. She'd gone inside, then stood with her forehead against the front door for what had felt like forever before she'd heard him start the engine and slowly pull away. The long delay, more than anything else, had told her just how badly she'd wounded him.

Over breakfast, she and Robbie fought. St. Stephen's was closed for Good Friday and Robbie wanted to go to the park with Glen. Emily refused. Until she could be sure Ryan was out of the picture, she was determined to keep Robbie in sight.

She'd called Miguel Sandoval that morning to tell him about Ryan's renewed threats. She was grateful when he understood about losing her temper the night before, but became unnerved when he told her to keep Robbie inside until he could send someone over to check out the neighborhood.

The mother-son battle raged for almost half an hour before Robbie stormed into his room and slammed the door behind him. Emily let him go, since it would be the safest place for him. When Robbie emerged an hour later, Emily was lying on the living room couch, trying to read. At the bottom of the steps, he spotted her and paused. Clearly he'd hoped to slip outside unseen.

"Going somewhere?"

"No," he answered with a trace of belligerence.

248

"Still mad at me?"

His belligerence vanished. He lowered his eyes and shook his head, scuffed the toe of his high-top on the carpet. "I'm sorry, Mom. I didn't mean to yell at you."

His dejection tore at her heart. Emily knew what she had to do. She sat up and set her book aside. "Come here, Tiger." She patted the seat beside her. "We need to talk."

He came, and nestled against her like the confused child in need of reassurance that he was. She brushed his dark brown hair from his forehead, steeled herself against the pain she was about to cause him and prayed for the right words to come to her. For Robbie's sake, she didn't want to paint Ryan as a monster, but she had to let her son know his father couldn't be trusted.

"I'm going to tell you something that will probably make you upset with me, but I want you to know the reason I didn't tell you sooner is because I love you very, very much." She paused, mentally took a deep breath. "Your father lives in St. Paul." Robbie simply looked at her in bewilderment. "I've kept you from him because he has a lot of money, and I was afraid he'd use that money to take you away from me if he knew about you."

"He doesn't know about me?"

"Unfortunately, he does. He's known all along. He knows where we live, where I work, and where you go to school." She paused to let that sink in.

"Why hasn't he come to see me?"

Pain laced his question, and lanced her heart. Emily kissed his crown. There was no easy way to tell him. "I don't know, sweetheart, but I'm glad he hasn't. He's not a nice man, Robbie. He has a bad temper, and likes to hit people."

His dark eyes rounded. "You?"

"When we were married, yes."

His gaze lifted to her cheek. Emily waited in dread as he put the pieces together.

"Is he the man who hit you and knocked you down?" Robbie asked in a tiny voice.

"Yes."

"Why?"

"Because he wanted something from me and I wouldn't give it to him. Kind of like a bully on the

249

playground. Now he's mad and threatening to take you away from me."

"You won't let him, will you?"

"Not in a million years. Don't even think it."

But he did, if only for a moment. She saw the uncertainty in his eyes and ached for him.

"I'm sorry about this morning..." he began unsteadily.

She shushed him with her fingers. "No, I am. I should have told you sooner why I wanted you to stay home from the mall. I'm worried he might try to see you."

"I don't talk to strangers."

She smiled and hugged him close. "I know you don't, but he's a tricky man. He could have you talking to him before you know it."

The grandfather clock in the hall chimed twelve. Emily heard Robbie's stomach rumble and remembered he'd stomped off before he'd finished breakfast. He was probably starved by now.

"What's he look like?" Robbie suddenly asked. "Me?"

"Not at all." Thank God. "He's tall, blonde, and very...friendly looking. He has pale blue eyes and he smiles a lot, especially when he tells people what he thinks they want to hear, so he can get them to do what he wants."

"You mean he lies?"

"That, too."

Robbie's brow furrowed in thought. He was taking the news rather well, considering. Much better than she'd expected. She decided to let him guide the rest of the conversation and waited. She'd covered the important points.

"Is his name Ryan?"

Emily pulled back and studied her son's face. "How did you know that?"

"I heard you yelling at him on the phone last night."

The doorbell rang. Emily glanced toward the foyer, and suddenly wished Robbie was still in his room. "Sit tight. I'll be back in a minute."

She opened the door to a pleasant-faced man in a dark suit.

"Dr. Jordan? Mike Sulkowski." He handed her a card that identified him as a private investigator. "Miguel

Sandoval asked me to stop by. I hope I'm not intruding."

She invited him in and cast a concerned glance at Robbie. He sat on the couch, fiddling with the fringe on a throw pillow he'd pulled into his lap. Sulkowski spotted him and sent Emily a look that told her not to worry. Within seconds he'd introduced himself to Robbie and engaged him in a friendly conversation only a man familiar with eight-year-olds could carry off.

Satisfied Robbie would be all right, Emily offered the investigator a glass of iced tea. When she returned with it, she found him seated alone on the couch.

"Robbie's gone upstairs to get his Matchbox collection. I figured that would give us a few minutes to talk."

She smiled, liking the man. "Thank you."

He took a long swallow of his tea, smiled in appreciation. "Thank *you*. After a morning of asking questions, this hits the spot. I've canvassed the area, asked your neighbors if they've seen any strange people or cars in the area. They'll assume I'm asking you the same questions. I told them I'm investigating a robbery a few blocks away."

"Have you come up with anything?"

"A man that fits your ex-husband's description was seen cruising the neighborhood in a late model black Porsche yesterday afternoon around two. Actually, there were two men."

The photographer, Emily assumed. So it hadn't been her imagination working overtime last night when she feared he might come by. Apparently he still favored black Porsches, as well.

"So he was here."

"Twice. Apparently he returned today, around mid-morning." Using his finger and thumb, Sulkowski withdrew from his inside jacket pocket a manila envelope bearing her name. "He left this on the front step. I picked it up on my way in."

Emily stared. "I've been home all morning. If he was here, why didn't he show himself?" What sort of game was Ryan playing?

"My guess is he just wants to make you nervous. If he'd really wanted to harm you or the boy, he'd have confronted you face to face."

Emily didn't mention that he already had. If Sulkowski knew how she'd gotten the bruise on her cheek, he was being discreet. She preferred to let Miguel do the talking for her at this point.

"Mind if I see what's inside?" he asked.

She took the envelope, handled it as gingerly as he had, and lifted the flap. Inside were copies of newspaper clippings, dated ten years before, all about Eric. She skimmed a few damning headlines, then handed them over. "Apparently my ex-husband wants to drive a point home. He seems to think he can use whatever's in those articles against me to win custody of my son. I've been seeing the man they're about."

Sulkowski nodded and returned the articles to the envelope. "Would you mind if I kept this for a while? I'd like to lift your ex's fingerprints from the envelope if possible. It might come in handy if he decides to file suit."

"Certainly."

"I'll get them back to you as soon as—"

"Thank you, but that won't be necessary. I won't be reading them." She wouldn't add insult to injury. Eric was innocent. That was all she needed to know.

"I'll give them to Miguel, then." He slipped the envelope back into his pocket just as Robbie bounded down the staircase carrying a bucket of Matchbox cars. Sulkowski admired the cars for several minutes before he thanked Emily for the tea and excused himself. At the door, he asked her to give him a call if she received any more messages from her ex-husband.

Emily slipped his card into her pocket then rejoined Robbie, engrossed in a fantasy race with his cars. He seemed to have forgotten their interrupted conversation.

"How about some lunch at Friday's, big guy? I don't know about you, but I could use some soup, a sandwich, and a hot fudge Sundae right about now."

****

Two months later Emily was trying her best to enjoy a rare lunch away from the hospital with Carmen when Carmen mentioned she had two tickets to the Saints' opening Stanley Cup Finals game against the Baltimore Bombers the following night. The Saints had won the division quarterfinals against the St. Louis Blues, then gone on to defeat the Colorado Avalanche in the division semi-finals, and sweep the Dallas Stars in a particularly sweet series for the conference championship. They were now entering the finals to determine the winner of Lord Stanley's Cup.

Emily hadn't watched a single game. It hurt too much.

"Wanna go?"

Emily looked up from her tasteless Cobb salad. "Not funny, Carmen."

"I know it isn't. Neither is seeing you look like death warmed over and watching you pick at your food as if you're allergic to everything in it. You must have dropped ten pounds since I last saw you."

Emily poked at her lettuce. Carmen was close. She'd lost eight pounds since breaking up with Eric. Pounds she could ill afford to lose. But everything tasted like sawdust these days.

Carmen's hand covered hers. "Call him, Emily."

"I can't."

"Because of Montgomery?"

Emily shook her head and reached for her water glass. Ryan hadn't bothered her again once she'd let Eric go, but Emily suspected that was due to the letter Miguel had sent him, outlining exactly what she'd do if he attempted any custody suit. Her biggest regret was she hadn't had her meeting with Miguel sooner. If she had, she never would have caved in to Ryan's demands.

"Because of the things I said to him." But it was more than that. She'd thought about it long and hard. To return to Eric would open her life to the whims of a force she couldn't control—the NHL. If he were traded, she'd have two choices. Go with him—and possibly end up dependent on him—or say goodbye. She'd already said goodbye. She didn't want to have to do it again.

"He came to see me, you know."

Emily paused, her glass halfway to her lips. "Eric came to see you? When?"

"Three nights after your chat with your ex in the parking lot."

Emily felt betrayed. "Why didn't you tell me?"

253

"I was hoping I wouldn't have to. Sarah sent him my way. Apparently he tried to pry out of her what happened the night Montgomery attacked you."

Emily's stomach clenched. "You didn't tell him?"

"No, but watching you waste away before my eyes, I wish I had. Have you at least been following the games?"

"Robbie refuses to miss them," Emily prevaricated. She didn't want to give Carmen any more reason to badger her.

"How are you two getting along these days?"

Emily offered her first genuine smile. "Couldn't be better. I wish I'd told him about Ryan sooner. It's brought us closer."

She and Robbie had talked several times about Ryan, always at Robbie's request. She'd answered his questions honestly, presented only the facts, and let him make up his own mind about the man who had ignored his existence until it had suited his needs to intrude on their lives. With Carmen's help, she'd found a picture of him in a back issue of the *Star-Tribune*—his engagement picture to Catherine Stump—and now Robbie had a clear idea of what his father looked like and was up to these days.

"I'm glad I don't look like him," Robbie had said. "I don't want to be anything like him."

Emily had laughed and hugged him, knowing he never would.

"Tell you what—I'll give you my ticket, too," Carmen said. "You can take Robbie to the game."

Emily's smile faded. "No. That would be like dangling a bag of candy in front of him and telling him he can't have any." Not to mention what it would do to her.

Carmen studied her in thoughtful silence. "Did you ever ask him about that business with his wife?"

Emily's response was swift and sure. "He didn't do it."

"Did he tell you who did?"

Abjectly, Emily pushed her salad away. "I didn't give him a chance to."

****

The sound of Poison screeching at top volume dragged Eric out of his dream. Make that his personal nightmare. The nightmare he'd had regularly in the two months since Emily had turned him inside out by asking about Monica, then refusing to let him explain.

Monica. He'd bet the inheritance money he'd paid her to get out of his life that wherever she was, she was still scheming to her black heart's content, tormenting some other gullible fool.

She'd seen him coming, all right. Nineteen years old and as green around women as they came. He'd taken one look at her and ached all over. Nothing like it had ever happened to him before, so he'd figured it had to be love.

He now knew it had been a bad case of hormones.

A social outcast who'd dropped out of school when he was sixteen, Eric had foregone dating in favor of his first love, hockey. He'd thought he'd have plenty of time to meet women later, when he made it big.

He was right. As soon as he started playing in the juniors things had started looking up. By the time he was drafted into the NHL, however, women were throwing themselves at him. Eric had gone back into his shell, the groupie scene damn near terrifying him. He hadn't been raised to consider sex as something you did with strangers. He also wasn't keen on catching any diseases.

But then Monica and her three-inch spiked heels had sashayed into his life. Within days he'd fallen head over heels for a woman five years his senior with long black hair, soulful brown eyes, a body so hot it sizzled, and the sexiest set of legs in the state.

Legs he'd never suspected had been wrapped around his coach's waist more times than a politician shook hands.

Until the day he'd come home and found them in bed.

He'd felt run down that day to start with. Since his mother's death, he hadn't played well, and Coach Granger had told him if he didn't shape up, he'd be riding the pines more than he already was.

Rather than give in to the flu he'd been fighting off, Eric had stayed behind after practice, as usual. He'd been so determined the extra hours would get him back in the game. Once he cracked the line-up again, he'd have a chance to get called up to the majors. Nothing like ice time to attract a scout's attention. But he'd felt so miserable that day he'd given up and slogged home to bed.

Only to find it already occupied.

Poison gave way to something more palatable as Eric lay in his bed, hands stacked beneath his head, and recalled how he'd stood at the foot of another bed ten years ago, a naïve twenty-year-old discovering his wife asleep in his coach's arms.

The bedside alarm had gone off, and Granger had silenced it without opening his eyes. He'd rolled over, wrapped an arm around Monica, burrowed his face in her neck. "Rise and shine, sweetcakes, time to make the bed."

She smiled and slid a hand down his body. "Sure you don't have time for a quickie before you go? I'm going to need something to sustain me until tomorrow."

"Try your husband. He'll be here in half an hour."

"Are you kidding? The three-minute man? I blink and it's over."

He chuckled. "That's what you get for marrying an amateur."

"That's what I get for trying to make *you* jealous." She opened her eyes, gasped and yanked the sheet over her breasts. "Eric! What are you doing here?" The question held more horror than guilt, as if *he'd* been the one caught in bed with a man who had a wife and three teenage kids who adored him.

"I live here," he said.

Numbly, he left the room and found the bottle of bourbon he'd bought for their six-month anniversary. The bottle they'd never opened, because of Monica's miscarriage that night. A miscarriage that had driven them apart emotionally these past two months.

Or so he'd thought.

As the bourbon seared his throat, Eric began to suspect Monica's miscarriage for what he later learned it had actually been—a botched abortion to keep her lover from losing interest in her young, sleek body.

Sightlessly Eric stared out the apartment window, feeling used and dirty. He'd heard the rumors about Monica and Coach Granger, long before he'd married Monica. But love had blinded him to the truth. Love, and the desperate need to have someone to call his own after his mother had died. He'd gone wild with grief when he'd heard the news. Nearly quit hockey altogether.

But then Monica had taken over his life, his emotions, his common sense. With her dark, soulful eyes and clever lips and hands, she'd convinced him the rumors about her and Coach Granger were just locker room talk from a bunch of horny hockey players with nothing better to occupy their pea-size brains. The truth was he'd only been a convenient smokescreen to allow them to continue their affair behind a façade of respectability. The coach was happily married, and suddenly Monica was too—to a man who openly adored her and had placed her on a pedestal beyond the reach of the telltale rumors.

Someone entered the room behind him. Eric continued staring out the window. Several long seconds later he heard the front door click shut behind the man he now knew kept him off the ice to keep his mistress within screwing distance. If Eric had been called up to the majors, his 'devoted' wife would have had to go with him.

When Monica emerged from the bedroom ten minutes later, Eric still sat at the dining room table, contemplating his bottle of bourbon. He wondered how long it would take him to polish it off. He heard the familiar rustle of silk against satin, and waited for her to tell him she wanted a divorce.

Instead, she slipped her arms around him from behind, bent to trace her tongue around the curve of his ear.

Eric lost it. He swore and reared back, toppling her from her stiletto heels. Whirling around in his chair, he found her half-lying, half-sitting on the floor, wearing the black silk camisole and shorts set she'd worn the night she'd told him over a candlelit dinner she was pregnant. The night she'd made him the happiest man on earth. All he'd ever wanted out of life was a family. A big one.

"Eric, don't do this. Please." She lifted a pale, perfectly manicured hand as if to ward him off.

"I'm sorry. You startled me," he lied, then swallowed his rising bile. Had she really thought she could fuck him into forgetting what he'd seen and heard? The thought of touching her now made his skin crawl.

She straightened into a sitting position, her wary eyes not leaving his. She looked obscene in her skimpy black silk, her long white legs nowhere near as sexy as he'd thought before. All he had to do was picture them locked around his coach's waist and he wanted to retch.

Gingerly, she massaged her right wrist. Despite his revulsion, his mother's teachings nudged his conscience. He'd been raised to respect and protect women, not maim them. "Did I hurt you?"

She shook her head and her long black hair rippled across her breasts. "I just fell on it a little hard."

Slowly, she stood. He wondered how long she planned to tiptoe around the topic of her affair as she went to the cupboard, got herself a glass, poured a shot of bourbon into it. She tossed it back and met his eyes, her own cool and direct.

"I think you should leave for a few days, until we've calmed down enough to discuss this rationally."

It was Monica at her ice princess best. From the first, she'd called the shots between them, the sophisticated older woman guiding her rough-around-the-edges lover through the dance of courtship, then marriage. Rather than argue, he nodded. He knew he wasn't coming back. The sudden flicker of fear in her eyes told him she knew it, too.

"I'll be at the Ramada in case anyone calls."

He left, the bottle of bourbon stashed in his suitcase. He'd be damned if he'd leave it for her to enjoy. The rest of their things she could have. He wanted no part of anything she'd touched.

He checked into the Ramada, broke open the bourbon, and drank himself into oblivion.

The next thing he knew he was being arrested for assaulting his wife in a fit of drunken rage.

Chapter Twenty-Seven

When Emily returned to the hospital from lunch with Carmen, Sarah flagged her down from across the crowded reception area.

"You've got a visitor. Said she was a friend of yours. Things were getting crazy out here, so I let her wait in your office."

Emily frowned and headed for her office. The only friend besides Carmen who might visit her at work was Miranda. Had something happened to the baby? Eric? Fear quickened her step. But when she crossed the threshold, it wasn't Miranda she found waiting for her but Patricia Montgomery.

In her lap was Emily's picture of Robbie, dressed in his hockey uniform, grinning like a monkey. Reverently her fingers traced Robbie's features. As she lifted her head, Emily saw Patricia's tears. For a long moment the two women stared at each other.

Patricia spoke first, her smile watery. "He looks like my father did at that age."

Emily recalled Anna's words about how the Montgomery's wouldn't sit still knowing they had a grandchild nearby. Dread filled her as she realized Ryan hadn't backed off on the custody suit; he'd simply regrouped and called in reinforcements.

Patricia gave the photograph a final loving look, returned it to its place on Emily's desk. "I didn't come to cause trouble."

Old hurts prevented Emily from accepting the admission at face value. "Why did you come?"

"To say something I should have said years ago." Patricia reached for her Gucci handbag. "You may find this hard to believe, but I honestly wasn't aware I had a grandson until a few minutes ago." She withdrew a

259

monogrammed handkerchief, dabbed at her eyes, and sent Emily an embarrassed smile. "You'll have to excuse me, I'm still a bit overwhelmed by the discovery."

"His name is Robbie. He's in third grade."

Patricia's smile became one of pure gratitude. Emily moved to sit behind her desk. She needed distance, detachment. She'd never seen the unflappable Patricia Montgomery in tears before.

"You said you had something to say to me?"

Patricia tucked her handkerchief back into her bag and straightened. "I never realized how bad it was between you and Ryan until I read your interview with Carmen."

Emily didn't confirm or deny Patricia's assumption.

"I've worked with Carmen on several occasions," Patricia explained, much to Emily's surprise. "Articles about charity functions and the like. It was I who suggested she contact you for an interview."

Emily stared. "You? And Carmen? She never said a word. Why?"

"After listening to you at the banquet—and I *was* listening, despite what it may have looked like—I took a hard look at myself and realized I'd done you a grave injustice by turning a blind eye to your suffering at my son's hands."

"Patricia..." Emily began, "This is all a little too much for me to—"

"Please, hear me out. It's taken me more than two months to work up the courage to come here, but what I'm about to say needs to be said. When I saw you at that banquet and realized how much you'd made of your life, despite the...obstacles my husband and I threw in your path, I felt very small and ashamed. I've known all along I should have stood up for you when you left my son, but I didn't have the courage.

"I'm a coward. I always have been. That's why I've stayed with John all these years. I've never been able to summon the strength to walk away from the prestige of being a Montgomery. But you did, and I admire you for that more than I can say.

"When I realized how dedicated you are to helping others in...situations similar to ours, I knew I had to try to do something to make amends. So I called Carmen and suggested she speak with you. I thought if between the two of you, you could help even one woman escape an abusive relationship, I'd have done something to be proud of for a change."

"Patricia, you've done plenty to be proud of."

Patricia continued as if she hadn't heard. "I couldn't do it myself, you see. I didn't have the courage. But after seeing you that night, I knew you did."

Emily realized Patricia had come to the end of her speech. She sank back into her chair to digest what she'd just learned. The irony of it almost amused her. Here Ryan thought Eric was responsible for her fifteen minutes of fame, when all along it was his own mother. She dragged a weary hand down her face.

"Oh, Lord. What a mess."

"I beg your pardon? Have I said something wrong?"

Emily looked up. "No...no, of course not. I'm deeply flattered that you think so highly of me, but..." The hell with it. Patricia had offered her honesty; the least she could do was the same. "I wish you hadn't contacted Carmen."

"Why not? The result was an excellent article. Insightful and informative. Hasn't the response been positive for Harmony House?"

Emily sighed, feeling guilty about letting her own problems diminish the interview's success. "Oh, it has. Overwhelmingly so. Donations have poured in. But I'm afraid things haven't fared so well for me. Your son took a strong exception to that insightful and informative article. He paid me a visit."

Patricia stared. "Ryan?"

As tactfully as possible, Emily told Patricia about her son's ambush in the parking lot. When she finished, Patricia's face was filled with abject apology. "Oh, Emily. I'm so sorry. I never meant to..."

"I know you didn't, and I don't blame you. I guess I assumed if Ryan read the article, he'd do so with a remarkably clear conscience. He's never accepted any responsibility for his actions before."

"A family trait," Patricia murmured bitterly.

Emily frowned, then saw her former mother-in-law in

a new light. "Patricia? May I speak frankly?"

With as little fanfare as possible, Emily explained that Ryan had admitted he knew about Robbie all along. When Patricia recovered from her astonishment, Emily said, "The point is, why didn't he confront me sooner?"

Patricia's response was caustic. "Because he's just like his father. A selfish, egotistic bastard who has no use for anyone unless they can be of benefit to him. Admitting he had a son would have placed Ryan in the position of acknowledging his responsibilities to the boy, and he's too self-centered and greedy to—" She halted abruptly, as if she'd been struck dumb.

Emily leaned forward in concern. "Patricia?"

The older woman sent Emily an enlightened look. "That's it. My mother's trust fund. Her will explicitly states that if Ryan has no children by age forty, the principal reverts to him. At present, he's only entitled to the interest proceeds."

"That doesn't make sense. Wouldn't she want Ryan to perpetuate the family name?"

"My mother was a bit of an eccentric, but a shrewd woman. I'd venture to say she fully expected Ryan to marry and have children, but worded her will that way to ensure that there would be something left for them to inherit when the time came." Patricia sighed. "Heaven knows Ryan's spendthrift ways have given his father and I more than one uneasy moment."

The Montgomery's were having money problems?

Emily was still trying to absorb that one when Patricia suddenly rose. "If you'll excuse me, Emily, I have some long overdue business to attend to." She met Emily's eyes, fire in her own. "The first time Ryan got into trouble, his father convinced me to let him be, saying the boy would grow out of his irresponsibility. I foolishly gave in, and kept on giving in as he grew into manhood, but no more. No son of mine will get away with ignoring his only child."

"Patricia—wait."

But Patricia was on a roll. "You were married to my son. You bore him a child. I intend to see that at the very least, Ryan honors his financial obligations to you and Robbie."

She was halfway out the door before Emily caught her arm. "Patricia, no," she said firmly, desperately, envisioning the mayhem this would create. "We don't need the money. We don't want it. We don't want *anything* from Ryan. Do you understand?"

"But Robbie's a Montgomery."

"No. He's a Jordan. He's been my son since the moment he was conceived. My son. Not Ryan's. Ryan's name appears on no document pertaining to his birth."

"Emily, as his grandmother, I owe it to him to—"

"You owe him nothing, Patricia. Nothing. You don't even exist as far as he's concerned." Somehow she had to get through to the woman.

Patricia stiffened, then wilted. "But he's my only grandchild..."

Emily's heart softened. "I understand that, and you're more than welcome to see him, but on *our* terms. No money."

"I can see him? When?"

"That depends on Robbie. It has to be his choice, his decision. He's confused enough as it is after what Ryan put us through. I won't see him hurt again."

"Ryan saw the boy?"

"No, but I was afraid he might try to, so I had to warn Robbie. Ryan threatened to take him away from me."

Patricia's jaw dropped. Emily gently escorted her back into her office. "I didn't mention it earlier because I thought it was over. Ryan made some demands, I met them, and he stopped harassing me."

"Harassing you?"

"He threatened to sue for custody of Robbie, on several occasions."

Patricia clearly found this incomprehensible. After what she'd just told Emily about Ryan and his grandmother's trust fund, Emily could understand why. Then again, maybe he'd found a loophole in the will and had thought if he had custody of Robbie, he'd be able to get his hands on his grandmother's money that much sooner. She'd have to have another talk with Miguel. Ryan might not be through with her, after all.

"But Ryan's going to marry Catherine..." Patricia

began.

"His argument, exactly. He insisted the two of them would make better parents than myself."

"Impossible. Catherine doesn't want children. She's made that very clear to him. Her career comes first."

"Are we talking about the same Ryan Montgomery here?" The one who had done his best to keep her from having a career so that she could stay home and cater to him?

"His relationship with Catherine is different than yours. Catherine treats him like a lap dog."

"And he lets her?"

"She's got the power he craves, the status..." Patricia lowered her eyes and flushed. "...the money. He wants this marriage so badly he's terrified of doing anything to jeopardize their relationship."

"He's told you that?"

"No, but I'm his mother and I'm not blind...or deaf. Several weeks ago she suggested she might want to postpone the wedding. He nearly fell apart after she left. Flew into an uncontrollable rage. I've never seen him like that before. Afterward, he courted her relentlessly, until she agreed to leave things as they were."

"Does Catherine know about his temper?"

"He's kept it well hidden from her, but I believe she suspects. Secretly, I was glad when she proposed pushing back the wedding date. I hope she'll come to her senses in time."

"And if she doesn't?"

"No offense, Emily, but I've already learned what happens when I try to interfere with my son's marital plans."

"None taken." She and Ryan had eloped after a bitter argument with his parents. They hadn't considered her good enough for him. Which was exactly why he'd married her. To spite them.

"Besides, John wants this marriage as much as Ryan does."

"And what John wants, John gets."

Patricia's bitter smile returned. "Exactly."

Emily couldn't stay silent. "Does he still—"

"Yes."

"Then why do you stay?" Emily asked softly.

Patricia looked away. "I'm not like you. I don't have a profession. I've never worked. All I know is being a doctor's daughter, a doctor's wife. I'd have nothing if I left John."

"You'd have yourself."

Patricia sent her a bewildered look.

"Think, Patricia. How many charity balls have you organized? How many boards have you sat on? How many fundraising drives have you led? You're a lot more talented than you think, and a hell of a lot more talented than your husband gives you credit for."

"Do you really think so?"

"I know so. I've seen you in action. Resented you, even." Patricia's eyebrows lifted. "Ryan was always telling me how I could never live up to your sterling example."

Patricia winced, and Emily waved a dismissive hand. "But that's the past. We're talking about the future now. Your future. If you stay with John, do it because you want to, not because you feel you have no choice."

The women's gazes locked over the desk. Emily wasn't sure how the conversation had gotten so sidetracked. Briefly she questioned the wisdom of counseling Patricia on such matters, but while they'd talked, she'd forgotten who Patricia was, and treated her as she would any other battered woman who had come to her for advice.

And felt damned good about doing so.

Patricia lowered her eyes first. "I couldn't face the shame."

Emily knew what she meant. The scandal, the social ostracism, the smears that would accompany the divorce of such a prominent couple. Her own divorce had been quiet, but she hadn't been spared the social ostracism. She'd lost her own family over it.

"I can't help you with that, Patricia. The best I can do is refer you to some excellent counselors I know."

"Harmony House?"

Patricia clearly hadn't considered the shelter as an option for a woman of her financial means. Emily smiled gently. "They make no class distinctions there, Patricia. They'll help anyone who wants to be helped."

****

Late that night, unable to sleep, Emily sat at her roll top desk, reconciling her bank statement for the Jordan Foundation, a mug of chamomile tea beside her. As she flipped through the canceled checks, she marked them off in her checkbook. She and Anna had agreed Anna would handle the foundation's day-to-day correspondence and paperwork, and Emily would make the deposits to the account and balance the books at the end of the month.

In the beginning Anna had tried to get Emily to read the letters of thanks she received in return for the checks, but Emily had refused, saying she didn't do it for the thanks. The truth was she couldn't stand the thought of being written to as if she were a stranger. So Anna had stopped asking, and to this day, Emily had no idea what she did with the letters.

Usually Emily was able to pretend she was simply helping some deserving students find a better life. But tonight—after her unexpected reunion with Patricia Montgomery and their discussion about family obligations—Emily was all too aware that the people she helped through the foundation were her own brothers and sisters. Brothers and sisters she hadn't seen in nine years.

She missed them so much. Missed their laughter, their love, their sharing. They hadn't had much, but what they'd had, they'd shared without reserve.

She took a sip of tea, and tried to imagine the adults they'd become. It was hard to picture them with homes and families of their own when the last time she'd seen them, they'd been a rag-tag bunch of adolescents with disappointment and disillusion dulling their eyes. She leaned her elbows on the desk and rubbed the heel of her hand across her brow in frustration.

She'd been their leader. Their big sister. The one they'd turned to for comfort, security, and solace. The one they'd depended on to help them escape the hell into which they'd been born. By earning a scholarship to a local college, she'd given them something to strive for. When she'd been accepted into medical school, they'd sent her off with proud tears in their eyes. When she'd written to say she'd met a wonderful man, they'd been thrilled for her. When she'd brought him home to meet them, they'd been charmed. When she'd told them she and Ryan had eloped, they'd understood.

Maybe it had been wrong to let them pin their hopes on her, but she'd wanted to show them it was possible to break the chains of poverty. To prove it was possible to overcome the handicap of a severely dysfunctional family. Their mother had loved them, but she hadn't stood a chance against their abusive, tyrannical father.

But then it had all gone sour. And when she'd realized she'd escaped one hell only to enter another, she'd been too ashamed to tell her family the truth. Instead, she'd come home one weekend and quietly told them she'd left her charming husband.

But by divorcing Ryan she had committed the unforgivable. Divorce was unacceptable in her Catholic family. As proof, one needed only to look as far as her parents. What else besides her faith would have enabled Catrina DeAngelo to endure over thirty years of marriage to an over the road trucker who spent five days a week on the road, then drank and ran roughshod over her during the two he was home?

Years later, once Emily had attained her goal of becoming a doctor, she'd considered trying to make peace with her parents. She'd even gone so far as to call them. But her father had answered the phone and told her she was dead to them all.

She might have pushed the issue if it hadn't been for Robbie. Might have tried to contact her siblings directly. If they'd rejected her and her alone, she might have borne the disappointment. But she'd refused to subject Robbie to the pain of knowing he had aunts, uncles and possibly cousins who would refuse to see him simply because she'd divorced his father.

But now they were adults, she mused, as she tamped the month's canceled checks into a neat pile. Educated adults, well beyond their father's reach, and capable of making their own decisions.

Should she try again? After all this time?

Her pride said no, you have enough on your plate as it is, but her reunion with Patricia Montgomery had planted a seed of hope in her heart. If she could make amends with a woman she'd been convinced hated her, why couldn't she do the same with her own flesh and blood?

As the night grew longer, Emily brewed more tea and thought about her family until she ached to hear her mother's voice. Did she still hoard her grocery money? Did she still buy cheap knick-knacks to brighten up the house, knowing the expensive ones broke just as easily? Did she still spend Friday afternoons cleaning until the house shone, Sunday mornings sweating over the one solid meat and potatoes dinner a week the family had always shared after church?

Did she still love her husband?

Her husband. Emily's father. Emily tried, but couldn't conjure up a picture of the embittered man who blamed his wife and children for the loss of his freedom and his inability to afford his own eighteen-wheeler. Duane Jordan had long since receded into the dim recesses of Emily's mind, his memory serving only to keep her from losing sight of her own goals. From losing sight of her vow to see that her younger siblings attained their goals...even if she had to honor her childhood promises to them through anonymity and deception.

But the time for deception and fear was over. She'd faced Ryan and won. She'd reconciled with Patricia. Surely she could face whatever Duane Jordan chose to throw her way.

In the morning she called home.

Chapter Twenty-Eight

Catrina Jordan answered on the third ring. For a moment Emily thought she'd dialed the wrong number. It was Saturday before noon. She'd called thinking her father would be asleep. Instead, loud rock music blatted in the background.

"Mama?"

"Just a minute, dear, I can't hear you. Annalise! Will you please turn that down? I'm on the phone with your sister." The noise level lowered several decibels. "Forgive your baby sister's rudeness. She seems to have forgotten her manners today."

"Hello, Mama, it's—"

"Merciful God in heaven."

Annalise's concern floated across the line. "Mama, what's wrong? Who is it?"

"It's...Emily."

Emily waited in dread, expecting to hear her father booming next, expecting to be cut off any second.

Annalise came on the line. "You'll have to hold on a minute, Emily. Mama's crying. Mama, come on," Annalise cajoled. "Emily called to talk, not to listen to you cry."

Emily heard a muffled, weepy response, and felt the guilt of a child. She'd never meant to make her mother cry.

"Another minute, Emily, she's getting her handkerchief. So where are you? In Detroit?"

"No...I'm in Minneapolis."

"Minneapolis! Mama, hurry up! She's calling long distance! Is that where you live?"

"Emily? Is it really you?" Her mother's voice was watery, but there was no mistaking the joy in it.

Emily's fears evaporated. "Yes, Mama. It's me."

****

Eric swore and flung the sports section aside in disgust, sending the mug of coffee perched on the arm of his sofa toppling toward his lap. Reflexively, he caught it before it scalded his naked vitals, and swore again when it sloshed onto his hands. He set the cup on the coffee table littered with empty pizza boxes and pop cans, snatched up a pile of napkins and mopped up the mess. Tossing the wet wad across the room, he grunted in satisfaction when it landed with a plop in the trash can.

He glared at the discarded newspaper, and itched to shove it down Robert Granger's throat. It wasn't enough the backstabbing bastard had gotten him to roll over ten years ago. The sonofabitch expected him to do it again. The Saints' weakest link, Granger had called him. Too volatile, too undisciplined to lead a team all the way, he'd said. On the front page of the sports section.

"Christ," Eric muttered, and ran a hand over his face as the old rage reared its ugly head. Where did Granger get off passing judgment on *him*? Granger was the one who'd slept with another man's wife. Granger was the one who'd let *him* take the fall for beating the tar out of her, let *him* rot in jail while Monica told anyone who would listen a pack of lies about how violent their marriage had been.

Eric had been so hurt and confused and torn up inside that anger was the only emotion that had kept him sane. But his lawyer had told him to keep his mouth shut if he wanted to play hockey again. If it had gotten out that he'd caught Monica in bed with another man that afternoon, a dozen fancy-suited lawyers wouldn't have been able to get him off. He'd have been convicted in no time flat. Crime of passion, there you go. It wasn't until years later that he'd found out what had really happened.

And Bob Granger had counted on that.

Just like he was counting on Eric to keep his mouth shut now, dissing him in print with no fear of retaliation. Granger knew Eric didn't give personal interviews. He also knew why. Eric could live with the stigma of having been publicly branded a batterer. But his pride prevented him from publicly admitting he'd been cuckolded, then blackmailed into handing over everything his mother had left him, by his poor, victimized wife.

He'd never seen or spoken to Monica again after that night. She'd convinced everyone she was too terrified to be in the same room with him. She'd even had *him* convinced when he'd seen the pictures. Then, he'd almost felt sorry for her.

Until he'd read her proposed divorce settlement.

He'd sweated it out, refused to let go of everything his mother had worked so hard for, until his lawyer had told him he had no choice. He'd been drinking that afternoon. The assault had taken place in his home. There wasn't a soul who could prove he'd been in that hotel room getting stinking drunk at the time of the assault.

In short, he'd had no alibi.

So he'd swallowed what was left of his pride, signed the settlement papers, and returned to work with a chip on his shoulder the size of Minnesota. For three weeks afterward, Granger sat back and watched him vent his fury on anyone who said good morning wrong. Then, satisfied his dirty little secret was safe, Granger arranged for his "too volatile" center to be traded, and sent him off with a smug smile.

Now he was back with that same smug smile, taking potshots at Eric in the paper and expecting to get away with it.

Eric eyed the stack of Bombers videotapes he'd invited his teammates over to watch the night before. Since he'd learned the Saints would face the Bombers in the championship finals, he'd done nothing but review tapes and plot strategy, anticipating the moment he'd meet Granger's eyes across the ice. Anticipating the moment he'd let the smug bastard know Eric Cameron wasn't the amateur Granger had called him while lying in Monica's greedy arms. The moment he let Granger know he *knew* who had sent Monica to the hospital ten years ago and let him take the fall.

It hadn't taken much to figure it out. Only a clear head and some quiet thinking. When she'd realized she'd lost her devoted husband, Monica had obviously called her lover back to the apartment. She'd probably given Granger some sort of ultimatum—but Granger hadn't knuckled under. She'd probably threatened to tell his wife about their affair. So Granger had beaten the shit out of

271

her.

Having lost both men in her life, and most likely her flawless looks, Monica had gone after Eric's inheritance from his mother. It hadn't been anything, compared to what he made now, but at the time it had meant the world to him. He'd refused to touch it, no matter how much Monica pouted. He'd planned to use it to honor his mother in some way when he retired and built his own hockey camp for kids. Instead, he'd opened several Amelia's in her memory.

But at the time, he couldn't conceive of owning several classy restaurants named after his mother. At the time, all he could see was everything she'd worked so hard for being snatched away by a lying, cheating, *murdering* Monica.

Was it any wonder he'd gone ballistic? He'd been too full of anger at the time to react with anything *but* his fists. Then, when he'd finally calmed down, he'd found himself with a reputation to uphold if he wanted to keep moving forward.

So he'd shut the door on the past. At times he'd convinced himself Granger had actually done him a favor. He'd shed his unfaithful wife, moved into the big leagues a lot faster than he would have if he'd stayed in the minors under Granger's thumb, and embarked on a career that had eventually taken him in the direction he'd wanted to go in all along.

But now Granger was back, saying Eric's success was just a matter of being in the right place at the right time. Hard work and the determination to overcome his reputation as a hothead didn't play into it at all. "Eric Cameron is still the same volatile, undisciplined player he was in the minors," Granger had said, making this whole thing personal. "And tonight, against the Bombers, he's going to prove it."

"Up yours, Granger," Eric said. He'd come out fighting all right. But not in the way Granger expected him to. Tonight Eric planned to hit the ice with a powerhouse team of talented men behind him, a team determined to win the Cup hands down. So far the Saints had defeated their opponents with teamwork and superior skill. They'd finessed their way into the finals by playing like the professionals they were. While Granger's goons exploited their reputation as the most vicious hockey club in the league. They hit hard, fought dirty, cheated as often as they breathed...

But couldn't skate for shit.

And the Saints knew it. Eric had seen to that. He and the guys—except for Cordell, who couldn't be bothered with such mundane details—had talked strategy until they were half hoarse. When they'd left at midnight Eric had never seen a more pumped up group of men.

With a satisfied smile, Eric pushed off the couch, poured another cup of coffee, and popped another tape into the VCR.

****

Robbie couldn't stay still. Emily couldn't blame him. If she hadn't been so excited herself, he would have worn her out. From the moment she'd told him he was going to fly in an airplane and meet his Grandma Jordan and a whole bunch of aunts, uncles and cousins, he'd been unstoppable. Wide-eyed and full of questions, he skipped along beside her as she juggled tickets and luggage, and coped with her own disbelief.

Her father was dead. She was going home.

She'd barely had time to absorb the former before her mother had issued a firm invitation for the latter. When she'd hesitated, mostly from shock, her mother had calmly insisted it was well past time she met her eldest grandson.

Unable to disagree, Emily had dialed the airport. A brief call to Augustus had netted her a long overdue week off with his heartfelt blessings, and Anna had promised to call Robbie's principal to inform her he would miss a week of school.

"All I know is your grandma's planning a family picnic for next Saturday," she said in answer to his latest question. "We'll see who shows up then, okay?"

Emily fastened his seatbelt and remembered how she'd begged her mother not to go to all the trouble, not to upset everyone's schedule, but Catrina had insisted. It wasn't every day her eldest child came home, and she deserved a full-fledged homecoming party.

But Emily knew not all of her family had returned to

273

Michigan after college. Many were scattered across the country, and it was anybody's guess who would be able to drop everything and come home on a week's notice. Still, she couldn't wait to find out.

Two hours later, the fasten seatbelts light dinged and the plane began its descent into Detroit. Amid the whir and hum of decelerating engines, Emily leaned over Robbie's shoulder as they burst through the clouds and approached the city below. Once they claimed their baggage, it would be less than an hour before she was home.

Home. Her stomach dipped and she was glad she'd insisted her mother wait for her at the house instead of corralling someone to drive her to the airport. Catrina Jordan didn't drive and never had. Suddenly Emily wondered if somehow her own traffic anxieties had anything to do with her mother's decision not to drive.

It was something to consider, but not today. Rental car or no, Emily was glad she'd have a little more time to pull her emotions together before she stared her past in the face. She just hoped they had a decent-size vehicle available. When she'd called for the reservation, they'd been unable to promise her anything.

"Ow! My ears just popped, Mom."

Prepared, she pasted on a confident smile and passed him a stick of bubble gum.

****

Eric drove toward Emily's, determined to tell her about Monica whether she wanted to hear it or not. With Granger nipping at his heels, Eric had no idea what would show up in the papers next, and he wanted Emily to know the truth. The rest of the world could think whatever they wanted about him, but Eric couldn't stand the thought of Emily believing Granger's lies.

Not after what she'd told him about her husband.

Eric wrapped his fingers around the steering wheel, and wished it were the cowardly bastard's neck. That was something else he would get to the bottom of. His visit with Carmen Martinez had led his thoughts down some pretty strange paths, all of them pointing in the same direction. The man who had attacked Emily and her ex-husband were one and the same.

Carmen hadn't come right out and said it—in fact, she hadn't said much at all other than a cool, neutral, "I'm sorry, I can't answer that," but the look in her eyes had been anything but cool and neutral. It told him she wished she *could* answer his questions, and she wouldn't have minded at all if he'd gone after the sorry SOB and torn him apart.

If Eric hadn't respected her loyalty to Emily so much he would've kept at Carmen until he found the right buttons to push. Because he'd also sensed she wanted something from him. Something related to that personal interview he'd blown off when he first came to town. She'd mentioned it as he was leaving, mentioned giving it another shot next season if he was still interested.

Not bloody likely, he'd thought. Not after reading her mind-boggling interview with Emily.

He'd read it at least ten times, and it still had the power to send him into a slow burn. Miranda had handed him the article, and when he'd read Emily's name in the opening paragraph, it had nearly blown his mind.

She hadn't said a word about having been a battered wife, not one, until that hellish night on her front porch. But the day before, while he'd pined away for her in some hotel room in St. Louis, she'd as good as announced it in the newspaper. Why?

Eric planned to find out.

He strode up to the house, pleased to see her Suburban in the garage. He wondered if she'd gotten new tires, then snorted in disgust. The woman considered *him* a threat to her safety, but didn't give a second thought to driving around on a set of tires that looked like they'd explode if they hit an acorn.

Five minutes later, Eric was ready to kick in the front door. Only the thought that doing so would reinforce Emily's bad opinion of him held him back. That and the fact that he couldn't afford another visit to jail right now. Granger would eat it up.

He peered in the front window and called her name, asking in as calm a voice as he could manage for her to please open up and let him in. No answer.

Feeling like a fool, he went to try his luck at the back door. At least the whole neighborhood wouldn't see him make an ass of himself that way. Minutes later, swamped by frustration, he swore and gave the doorknob a solid wrench.

"It works better if you have a key."

Eric spun around and met Anna's inscrutable eyes. "Anna." He struggled to control the heat rising in his cheeks. "How's it going?"

"A damn sight better than it's going for you from the looks of it. What are you trying to do? Break in?" She eyed him blandly. "Won't do you any good. They're not here. I dropped them off at the airport three hours ago."

"They've left town?"

"Went home to see Emily's family."

Eric swallowed his surprise. Emily had never mentioned her family. He knew she had one somewhere from the time she'd nosed through her canceled checks, but from the banks they'd been drawn on, she could be anywhere from Michigan to Pennsylvania.

"Did she say when she'd be back?"

"A week from Sunday."

By then the playoffs might be over. So she'd written him off, not caring to stick around and see how things turned out. His gaze fell on the purple and white impatiens she'd planted so determinedly. They didn't look so puny anymore. They looked happy and healthy. Two rows of strong survivors—like Emily.

An image of her as she'd looked that day rose in his mind's eye—face and arm bruised, lip split, knees scraped. It sliced him wide open all over again to think she considered him capable of hurting her or Robbie.

"How is she?" he asked softly.

"Confused."

"About?"

"A lot of things. Her family, her ex. You."

"I'd never hurt her, Anna. Or Robbie."

"I know that. She does, too. She told Augustus so almost three months ago."

"Then...?"

"You have to understand, Eric, she's been taking care of herself and Robbie for a long time now. I suspect it's hard for her to imagine living any other way."

He hesitated, knowing he was prying, yet knowing he

might never get another chance. "Would you tell me how you met?"

Anna studied him, then looked away, toward her house across the street. Eric waited, feeling a hard lump form in his throat. When it came to placing her trust in others, Emily Jordan chose carefully and well. Anna wouldn't betray her secrets any more than Carmen had.

"Come on," Anna said quietly. "I've got some muffins in the oven. They'll burn if I don't get back to them."

Chapter Twenty-Nine

"She came to me with nothing," Anna said, and set a tall glass of milk in front of him. She motioned for Eric to help himself to a basket of piping hot blueberry muffins. "Nothing but her pride. She'd heard I was renting a room and showed up on my doorstep, nothing but skin and bones, wearing a sling on her arm and a fading yellow bruise on her jaw."

Anna lowered her bulk into the chair across from him and broke open a muffin. "I took one look at her and thought 'Trouble, any way you look at it,' but I showed her the room anyway."

"She didn't say anything, just looked around like a hurt puppy needing someplace to hide. When I told her what the rent was, she stared at the floor for a minute, then lifted her head and looked me in the eye and said, 'I know you don't have any reason to trust me, Mrs. Hamilton, but I'm a fourth year medical student at Mercy. I've got one more semester before I graduate. I haven't got any money right now, but I will later. In the meantime, I can cook and clean and do yard work if you'll let me in exchange for the room. I'll eat at the hospital."

Anna's muffin turned to ashes in Eric's mouth.

"I just stared at her, like you're staring at me now, felt my heart go out to her, and wondered how the devil she thought she'd do any housework with a broken arm. I finally said as much." Anna's hands stilled as she stared past Eric's shoulder, remembering. "She didn't move a muscle, just stared back at me with those big, clear green eyes, then nodded and said in that quiet way of hers, 'Thank you for your time, Mrs. Hamilton.'"

Anna shook her head and wiped her fingers on her napkin. "I made up my mind right then and there I'd let her stay as long as she wanted to. She needed a place to stay more than I needed the money. I was only renting out the room to have some company after I retired. My first husband had died eight years earlier and the old house—it was this big old Victorian—got lonely with just me rattling around in it all day."

"Where was she staying when she came to you?"

"I never asked. From the looks of her, I'd have guessed one of the shelters around town. You want some more milk?"

"I'm good, thanks." He was afraid it would curdle in his stomach.

"How about some tea?"

He declined, waited while she made herself a cup. Surrounded by the cozy smell of blueberries and cinnamon, he thanked God she'd been there for Emily. He hated to think of what might have happened to her and Robbie if Anna hadn't taken her in, but deep down he knew she'd have found a way to survive. If there was one thing Emily wasn't short on, it was determination.

"She didn't say much those first weeks," Anna said, returning with her tea. "It was like I had a ghost living with me. She came and went, shut herself up in her room with her medical books. She took her meals at the hospital, just like she'd said she would, but she got skinnier by the day. No one came to see her, no one called her or wrote to her. She didn't leave the house except to go to class.

"I didn't find out she was pregnant until I heard her retching in the bathroom two months later. When I asked her about her family, she looked me in the eye again and said she didn't have one anymore. End of discussion.

"Things changed between us from that day on. I insisted she take her meals with me. By the time Robbie came along, she was a regular butterball and we were the happiest threesome around. I watched him while she put in her thirty-six hour shifts at the hospital, and held him on my lap when his mama got her diploma. They stayed with me until Robbie was old enough to go to school. She didn't want him to go to school in the city—the neighborhood was getting run down by then and she was worried about him walking back and forth by himself.

"I said I'd be glad to take him, but she said I'd done

enough for them already, it was time to stand on her own two feet. So she bought the house across the street and moved out here. I sold my house six months later and moved in with her—I'd been spending most of my time out here anyway, looking after Robbie while she worked. Then I met Augustus and moved in here."

"Did she ever talk about her husband?"

"Once." Anna's eyes grew distant again as she stirred her tea. "She probably wouldn't have done it if I hadn't bought her that vase." Quietly, Anna explained what had happened that day. That was the only time I ever saw her cry."

"So her husband's family was rich," Eric said, easing toward the subject of the man's identity.

"Richer than sin. And they'd tossed her out like she was yesterday's garbage. Just like her family."

"Why?"

"Because she divorced the man who made her life a living hell. Her parents were Catholic. Her father disowned her. Her mother didn't have any choice but to obey him. He was one of those men who don't go to church, but know enough about the Bible to quote it out of context and twist the message to suit himself. Personally, I think he disowned her because he was afraid she'd give her mother ideas."

Eric frowned and thought of the foundation. "What about her brothers and sisters?"

"They were too young to make a stand at the time, even if they'd wanted to. Emily's the oldest."

"And takes that responsibility seriously."

"Very."

Eric looked at the clock on the stove, saw it was past time for him to leave for the arena. He reached for one last muffin. "Tell me about the Jordan Foundation." Anna raised her eyebrows in surprise. "I gather she's putting her siblings through school?"

Anna nodded, then explained how Emily had been determined to see that her brothers and sisters had a chance for a better life. "She set up the foundation to get around her father's refusal to let them have anything to do with her. To preserve her anonymity, we rented a post office box and decided I'd handle the correspondence and sign the checks."

Eric stared. "They don't know *Emily* is paying for their educations?" Forty thousand dollars she'd shelled out last year and they didn't have a clue?

"She was afraid they'd refuse the money if they knew it was from her."

"But now she's gone home. Why?"

"She found out her father died."

Eric left Anna's knowing nothing short of a miracle would bring Emily back to him. There was nothing he could offer Emily and Robbie that Emily couldn't provide for them herself. She'd pulled herself up from nothing and put six siblings through college, to boot.

She didn't need him, and never had.

****

While Eric sat at Anna's kitchen table downing blueberry muffins and grappling with Emily's past, Emily sat at her mother's kitchen table eating ravioli, grappling with the same.

The changes were almost overwhelming. What she'd remembered as a cramped and dreary house was now cozy and cheery, filled with happy noise and sunshine. Annalise and Robbie were in Annalise's room (Emily and her sisters' old room) checking out her CD collection, while Emily and her mother shared maternal winces as their children screeched along with their favorite songs.

She wriggled her toes in the late afternoon breeze that whispered through the back door and studied her surroundings while her mother cleared the table and dished out homemade spumoni ice cream. She'd refused to let Emily lift a finger, and insisted she sit back and put up her feet, slightly swollen from the flight.

The tiny house teemed with the knick-knacks her mother so loved. Catrina had a collection of ceramic cats, another of dogs, oodles of figurines, and an assortment of crystal animals that rivaled Emily's. The tiny crystal rabbit Emily had picked up at the airport gift shop occupied a place of honor on the kitchen windowsill, and winked at her mother as she bustled about in domestic bliss.

The once dark and dank walls had been painted with warm, welcoming colors, and now boasted pretty pastels painted by her sister Sheila, the family's acknowledged artist. Bright throw pillows and hand-crocheted afghans decorated the living room couch and chairs. The second-hand throw rugs that had covered the warped wooden floors had been replaced with sturdy wall-to-wall carpeting. The kitchen's linoleum floor was new vinyl, but still squeaked familiarly in the center. The gleaming new refrigerator hummed quietly, whereas the one Emily remembered had rattled incessantly.

Her mother's handmade quilts graced every bed in the house, although there weren't nearly as many beds as there had been when Emily lived there. All that remained were two twins in Annalise's room, two sets of bunk beds in the boys' old room (for the grandchildren when they came to visit), and Catrina Jordan's ten-month-old waterbed. The dimly lit, severely water-damaged single bathroom Emily remembered now boasted a skylight and had been redone in soft pastels and a feminine floral print.

Nowhere was there any evidence of her father's reign of terror.

"Robbie! Annalise! Come and get dessert!"

Even that had changed, Emily thought wryly, as she removed her feet from Robbie's chair. She'd never heard her mother raise her voice. Her father had shouted enough for the both of them.

After dessert, Robbie and Annalise disappeared again, while Emily went to sit on the front porch swing and drink her decaf while her mother turned on the new dishwasher. Emily studied the pale blue vinyl siding, recalled the ugly ochre aluminum siding that had once covered the house, and thought she might do her own house in blue when the time came.

"So what do you think?" her mother asked, after she'd settled on the swing beside Emily.

Emily smiled. "That I've never seen you happier."

Her mother returned the smile with maternal affection. "That's because my baby's finally come home."

"I wanted to come sooner."

"I know you did."

They rocked in silence, listened to the crickets and cicadas vie with the distant rumble and hum of traffic on the nearby interstate. Emily wanted to ask about her father, but her mother hadn't mentioned him beyond telling her he was dead, and the night was so peaceful she didn't want to disturb it with unpleasant memories. She sighed, knowing the memories would be just as unpleasant in the morning.

"Ryan hit me, Mama."

"I suspected as much. I knew you wouldn't have left him without a very good reason. I didn't raise you that way."

"I'm sorry about the divorce, but I had to think of Robbie."

"I'd have done the same if I could have."

Emily stared at her mother in stunned surprise. "You'd have divorced daddy?"

"I wouldn't have divorced him, but I would have moved out."

"But I thought—"

"I believed a woman's place was with her husband? I do. As long as they treat each other with kindness and respect. If they don't...well...divorce wasn't for me, but I can't condemn others for taking that path. Certainly not my own children. Martin's divorced, Suzanna is, too. I'd sooner cut off my arms than turn my back on them the way your father turned his back on you. But they stayed in town, so it was easier for me to keep in touch with them. Duane wouldn't have liked it if he'd known about it, but I wasn't about to lose another child because of his selfish insecurities."

Catrina sipped her coffee, her expression sad. "What little love I still felt for him died the day he disowned you, and I vowed as soon as the children were gone, I would come looking for you." She stared out at the descending twilight. "I think he knew it, too."

Emily thought of her abortive telephone call after she'd gotten her job at Minneapolis General and silently agreed.

"But then he died, and I knew one day you'd call, and I wanted to be here when you did." She smiled and patted Emily's knee. "I figured sooner or later you'd want to find out if your foundation money had been well spent."

"You knew?"

Catrina smiled serenely. "I knew your father didn't have any rich relatives in Minnesota who'd suddenly decided to shower his children with educational grants."

"What did he say? About the money?"

"There wasn't much he could say. You made sure he couldn't touch it. But I'm sure he knew it came from you. Whatever else he was, Emily, he wasn't stupid." Catrina studied her eldest daughter. "I wrote several times, but you never answered. So did the others."

Emily recalled the letters she'd refused to read. She prayed Anna still had them. "I'm sorry, Mama, I..." Awkwardly, she explained about the letters.

"I understand, baby."

They swung in silence for a while before Emily quietly asked, "When did daddy die?"

"Almost a year ago. He plunged his truck into a ravine in Idaho."

"Had he been drinking?"

"He never drank on the job. He was happy on the road. It was only when he came home to us that he drank." She said it without bitterness, as if it were simply a fact of life.

"Then what happened?"

"I suspect that's between God and your father, sweetheart."

Emily pictured her father driving someone else's eighteen-wheeler along some long and lonely highway, thinking about his life and shattered dreams. Thinking about his wife, who no longer loved him, and privately disobeyed him, but publicly stood by him despite his tyranny, thinking about the children he'd never bothered to get to know, who were leaving one by one to fulfill dreams of their own. Dreams he knew nothing about and would never share with them.

Was it possible he'd finally realized his mistakes, realized it hadn't been his wife and children who held him back, but himself? Had guilt driven him over that ravine? Remorse?

The thought gave Emily no satisfaction. Instead, just as when she'd seen John and Patricia Montgomery at the United Hope banquet, pity stirred inside her. Pity, and sadness for what might have been. If Duane Jordan had only given them his love, his children might have helped him to achieve his dream of owning his own rig one day, might have even helped him to buy one.

Look at all they'd done for their mother in the past year. The new carpeting, new appliances, siding, furniture, plumbing, had all come as gifts from her children. Her father hadn't believed in insurance. Hadn't seen fit to provide for his family beyond the barest necessities, even in death.

"Have you forgiven him?" Emily asked.

Catrina Jordan smiled softly. "Would I be at peace if I hadn't?"

Tears welled in Emily's eyes. "Oh, Mama, I've missed you so much."

"Mom! The game's almost on." Robbie slammed through the back screen door, interrupting Emily and Catrina's hug. "Can we watch it?"

Catrina sent Emily a misty-eyed look. "The game?"

"Hockey," Emily explained, and surreptitiously brushed her tears aside. "The Stanley Cup finals. The Minneapolis Saints are in contention for the championship. Robbie's their number one fan." She ruffled her son's hair. "He's quite a skater."

Catrina beamed at her grandson. "Well, then by all means ask Annalise to turn it on."

"All right! Aunt Lise, Grandma says it's okay!"

As Emily watched him barrel back into the house, a part of her wished she had the courage to follow. Instead she turned to her mother and forced a smile.

"So tell me, what was everyone's reaction to the picnic?"

****

Damn, he hadn't felt this whupped since his fighting days, Eric thought in disgust as he lay in bed, his hands stacked behind his head, an ice pack pressed to his ribs. His body ached in places he'd forgotten existed, and not for the first time since he'd moved to Minneapolis he regretted not taking the time to find an apartment with a Jacuzzi.

The Bombers had beaten the devil out of the Saints— literally. Drilled them into the boards so hard and often it was a wonder they'd only lost one player to injuries. Even so, Cordell wouldn't be back any time soon. Not after hitting the ice head first. The man's brains would be scrambled for months.

Eric barely remembered skating off the ice when the debacle was over. He'd been too focused on not letting his pain and exhaustion show. The rest of the guys, judging by the sheer number of cuts, bruises and welts he'd seen in the dressing room afterward, had been doing pretty much the same.

He couldn't blame the team. They'd played their hearts out, played an excellent game by most standards. But finesse alone wasn't going to win the Cup, not at this rate. Eric still burned as he remembered the sly smile Granger had shot him as he'd skated past the Bombers' bench after the game.

If the Saints didn't make it up on Monday night, they'd have to re-evaluate. Opt for more physicality and less finesse. It galled him to think they might have to sink to their opponents' neanderthal level of playing, but he couldn't dismiss the option. Because when they played in Baltimore on Wednesday, the going would only get tougher. Baltimore's fans were almost as intimidating as their robo-cop players, and twice as bloodthirsty.

Eric's last thought as he slipped into sleep was how good it would have felt to come home to Emily's healing hands.

Chapter Thirty

Late Wednesday night, Emily sat alone on the back porch swing, restless. Not for the first time in four days, she thought of Eric. The Saints had lost—again. According to the papers, the Bombers were proving to be a more cunning opponent than anyone had given them credit for. In each of their three games, they'd come from behind to win. One more Bombers victory and it would be all over for Ronald Stump's All-Star Saints.

Sadly, Emily recalled how excited Eric had been about taking his team all the way. She still couldn't bring herself to watch his games, but with each loss, it became harder not to reach for the phone.

But what would she say?

What *could* she say?

****

"Are you sure there's nothing else I can do to help?" Emily asked as she sat at the kitchen table and snapped green beans for the three-bean salad Catrina was making for the picnic the following day. "What about rolls and condiments?" She hadn't seen either in the dozen grocery bags she'd carried in from her rented Explorer earlier. She'd taken the largest vehicle on the lot, and it seemed to be working out well for her, even if it did remind her of riding in Eric's Explorer.

Catrina gave a final shake to her vinaigrette marinade. "Martin's department. He'll bring them along tomorrow."

"What about—"

"Relax, Emily. Everything's under control. Sheila and Suzanna are coordinating the vegetables and casseroles, and we've got enough hamburger patties and hot dogs in the freezer to feed an army. All that's left is for you to enjoy yourself."

Emily looked at the twenty napkin-wrapped sets of eating utensils she'd rolled and tucked before she'd tackled the beans. "I still can't believe they're all coming."

Her mother sent her a surprised look. "Why wouldn't they?"

Emily could think of several reasons, all of them practical. But practical apparently wasn't on the agenda this week. Catrina called, and expected her family to come. The first out-of-town arrivals were due in tonight, sometime after ten.

"Where do you plan to put them all?"

"Between Suzanna's and Martin's houses and here, we'll have plenty of room. Sheila's also got a spare room we can use."

Laughter floated from the living room, where Robbie and Annalise sat cross-legged at the coffee table, doing Robbie's schoolwork. The moment it had arrived via Fed Ex, Annalise had appointed herself his tutor.

"She plans to be an elementary school teacher," Catrina had said with maternal pride as Emily turned to her with an arched eyebrow.

And a wonderful one she'd be if Robbie's sudden dedication to schoolwork was any indication. Annalise seemed to know all there was to know about keeping an eight-year-old in line. Then again, his utter adoration for "Aunt Lise" was also a powerful motivator.

Emily smiled. That, and their standing date with the Nintendo when his daily assignments were done.

"Where does Annalise want to go to school?" Emily asked, thinking of the foundation.

Catrina wiped her hands on her apron and reached for Emily's bowl of snapped beans. "Northwestern. But you're not to worry about that, either. You've done more than enough for this family. It's time you retired that foundation of yours and spent your money on yourself for a change."

"I have enough money..."

"When was the last time you took a vacation? Or bought something for the sheer pleasure of owning it, instead of settling for something else because it was on sale or more practical? Or making do with what you already have for another year?"

Emily looked at her mother and knew she faced a losing battle. "I didn't mind, Mama."

Her mother's features softened. "I know, sweetheart, but you've sacrificed more than any of us had a right to ask. It's past time to let your brothers and sisters carry the load." She rinsed Emily's beans in the sink, transferred them to the boiling water on the stove. "Martin, Sheila and Suzanna have already discussed it with me, but you'll have a family meeting when everyone else gets here before you make any final decisions."

Emily knew better than to argue with her mother when she used that tone of voice. She stood and stretched. "I think I'll take a walk."

Catrina smiled. "Dinner's at six. We'll make pies after."

Emily grinned. Her mother hadn't forgotten how much she enjoyed helping her bake pies. She checked on Robbie and Annalise, who were wrapping things up and challenging each other to their daily grudge match, then stepped into the afternoon sunshine.

Aimlessly she strolled, and enjoyed herself thoroughly. With no hospital to go to, no schedules to meet, and with Robbie being doted on by his grandma and aunts, for the first time in her life, Emily felt free of responsibility, free to come and go as she pleased.

Her mother had encouraged her shamelessly—spoiling her rotten to boot. She'd read spine-tingling bestsellers into the wee hours, slept late, and awoken to find a spatula-wielding Catrina prepared to whip up anything her heart desired.

Evenings she'd spent on the back porch swing with her mother and whichever siblings dropped by. Each night she'd gone to bed missing Eric, but secure in the knowledge she'd never be alone again.

She took a circuitous route around town this time, having decided it was time to visit her past. Until today, she'd preferred to explore the newer parts of town, the busy streets and stores that had sprung up with the advent of people moving out from Detroit. What she'd remembered as little more than a two-stoplight town in the middle of nowhere had, with the arrival of an interstate exit four years earlier, emerged as a thriving community of young urban professionals intent on escaping the city to capture their own slice of Michigan country.

She liked the changes. She liked knowing she'd helped contribute to them. Martin was hip-deep in land surveying projects, Suzanna was head of the town council, and Sheila's distinctive signs adorned businesses all over town.

Like her mother's house, the town seemed cheerier now, welcoming and prosperous. With Detroit less than an hour's drive away, Turnersville now provided the best of both worlds for commuters and natives alike. She thought of the sprawling new medical complex on the edge of town, and decided it wouldn't take much prodding to consider a move back to Turnersville. Her mother had hinted at the idea, but Emily had reserved comment until she had time to mull it over.

She doubted Robbie would oppose the move. Just this morning he'd asked her wouldn't it be neat if he could join Little League with Damien, Suzanna's oldest. But thoughts of how disappointed Anna and Augustus would be, how much she'd miss Sarah and Susan and the others kept her cautious. She worked with a team she could count on. The prospect of diving into the unknown daunted her.

Then again, maybe it was time for a change. A fresh start. In Turnersville she wouldn't have to worry about crossing paths with Ryan...and wouldn't be reminded so much of Eric.

Or would she? Bittersweet thoughts of him snuck up on her at the most unexpected times. Like when she'd driven past the local movie theatre and seen Harry Potter was playing. Or when she'd snitched a piece of lemon meringue pie while her mother took a nap. Or when she'd gone to the sports store to buy a volleyball for the picnic and passed the hockey sticks.

Or when the phone rang after eleven.

Hands stuffed in her denim skirt pockets, she walked until she found herself across the street from the health care clinic—now a computer store—her mother had worked at as a receptionist until her marriage. The present gave way to the past as she remembered the warm generosity with which the staff had treated her family. With nine children, they'd visited the clinic almost as often as they'd visited the supermarket. And with no insurance...

Turning away, Emily wondered what had happened to the doctors and nurses whose kindness and compassion had inspired her to study medicine. Had they moved on to the new hospital? Or, like Anna, had they retired, taken up other pursuits?

Half an hour later, perched on the bleachers at the community ballpark where she and her siblings had spent countless Saturdays, she felt the dry, dusty wind whip through her hair, closed her eyes and remembered the smell of hot dogs and the swell of cheers in the stands. Robbie would be in heaven here. She pictured him proudly stepping up to home plate, knowing he had his own cheering section behind him in the bleachers.

Shortly thereafter, she eased into the last pew of the empty church her mother and siblings and she had attended every Sunday. Emily hadn't been to church in years, but as the dust motes floated in the jewel-tinted air like blessings from above, she recalled the quiet coughs and rustles of the congregation, the deep baritone of the priest's voice, the peace she'd felt when the choir sang...

With a small smile, she also recalled the surreptitious signals her siblings and she had used to communicate amongst themselves during what had seemed like interminably long homilies.

She'd been remiss in bringing up her son, she realized now. Every child should experience the furtive enjoyment of passing secret messages back and forth in church.

Determinedly Emily refused to dwell on her darker memories. Like the reason her mother had had to rely on the goodwill of friends to keep her children healthy. Or the reasons she and her siblings had spent their Saturdays in the park—rain or shine. Or the shame she'd felt in church, wishing her father was there like other fathers, instead of sleeping off his Saturday drunk.

Focusing only on the good memories, Emily collected them with care, like a basket of colorful ribbons, and chose only the best and brightest to share with her siblings in the days to come.

She returned to her mother's doubly eager to see everyone again, her high spirits continuing through dinner. She was in the middle of cajoling from Catrina her secret recipe for elderberry jam when Robbie's shouted, "Mom, come quick. Eric's been hurt bad," stopped her cold.

Without a second thought, Emily ran into the living room. "What happened?"

Before Robbie could answer, the television offered a replay of the brutal hit. Eric had been rushing the net when he'd been cross-checked from behind. He'd sailed right into the goal, hit the crossbar—snapped his head back and sent the net flying off the moorings—before he tumbled over the goalie, who took a couple of vicious swipes at him as they went down. Eric had ended up on the bottom pinned under three hundred pounds of irate goalie.

He now lay face down on the ice, immobile.

Emily stood with a flour-dusted fist shoved against her mouth and barely breathed. The television cut to a commercial and she wanted to scream. Instead, hugging herself to stop shaking, her gaze glued to the screen, she slowly sat on the sofa.

An eternity later the game returned...and promptly resumed. The goal was awarded to Eric—he'd managed to slip the puck between the goalie's legs before he'd been slammed from behind. The cross-checker had been sent to the penalty box, another Bomber had joined him there to serve the goalie's roughing penalty, and Eric was nowhere to be seen.

The Saints scored again and tied the game. During the time-out, Emily learned Eric had been carried off the ice on a stretcher. The color commentators didn't know what his injuries were, but nearly drove her mad with their dispassionate speculations. She closed her eyes and replayed the hit in slow motion in her mind, the doctor in her coming up with several possibilities, none of them remotely reassuring.

For an agonizing hour she watched the game and waited. She barely noticed when either team scored, or when her mother settled on the opposite end of the sofa with her knitting. The scent of baking pies wafted through the house, but Emily didn't spare them a thought, even when Catrina went to check on their progress.

Instead she clutched a pillow to her churning insides and sat through the second intermission, hoping some news would break on Eric. When he stepped onto the ice with his team at the beginning of the third period, looking pale and haggard but undeniably determined, Emily didn't know whether to cry or kill him.

Chapter Thirty-One

The Saints won, 4-3.

Robbie crowed in ecstasy, Emily nearly wept in relief. Relief that the game was over and Eric was still in one piece.

"Didja see that, Mom? Didja?" He hopped around the room, fists raised in victory.

"I saw, sweetheart, I saw," she murmured. Her heart still raced from fear.

"I think this calls for a special celebration," Catrina said, hastily setting her knitting aside and pushing off the sofa when Robbie nearly knocked over a lamp in his exuberance. "What do you say, Robbie? How about some ice cream?"

"All right!"

Catrina ruffled his hair. "Chocolate, vanilla, strawberry or butter pecan?"

"Strawberry!"

"Emily?"

She shook her head as she tried to catch a last glimpse of Eric. "None for me, Mama. Thanks."

Catrina studied her daughter for a moment, then smiled at Robbie. "Strawberry it is, young man. But first, I think it's time you put your PJs on."

He leapt away, still hooting and punching the air. "Man, oh, man. Those Bombers never knew what hit 'em!"

Emily searched for Eric in the crowd and silently agreed. She'd known he wouldn't let his brutal treatment at the hands of the Bombers go unanswered. She suspected it had taken him longer than it would have if he'd been playing at full strength, but she had to admit his timing had been magnificent.

With less than thirty seconds to go and the Baltimore crowd threatening to bring down the house with their maniacal cheering, Eric had slammed a slap shot past the Bombers' goalie and tied the score, three-three. Twenty seconds later, while the Bombers and their fans were still recovering from their shock, he'd scored again—and put the Saints back in contention for the Cup.

She spotted him surrounded by backslapping teammates, his triumphant grin distorted by a swollen and darkly bruised jaw, and was torn between pride...and fury.

How *dare* he take such chances with his life? How *dare* he put her through such hell? She'd flinched every time he'd come into contact with a Bomber, knowing his body had to be screaming in pain. Knowing another hit to the face could send him to the hospital with a shattered jaw...or worse.

But was he worried? Of course not. He was laughing as if he'd had the time of his life. And she was shaking all over.

With a growl of frustration, she threw the pillow she'd been mangling aside. She had to get out. She needed fresh air. She needed time to pull herself together before the others arrived.

Catrina Jordan looked up from the ice cream she'd just dished out as her eldest daughter, still wearing her pie-baking apron, sailed past the kitchen window and into the night. She sighed and returned the ice cream to the freezer, then went into the living room to put away her hastily abandoned knitting.

She found the television still on. The man Emily had nearly destroyed her mother's favorite petit-point pillow over was being interviewed. His face was a mess, but Catrina could see the strength in it. His voice was deep, pleasant, educated. He smiled readily and sweated profusely as he offered the interviewer a wry, almost self-deprecating wit. He seemed happy enough about the win, but his eyes lacked the devil-may-care sparkle she would have expected from a man who'd risked life and limb to save his team from elimination. Instead they bespoke of pain, and not the kind one got from slamming his opponents into walls at breakneck speed.

"So that's the way the wind blows," she murmured, then picked up the remote and turned off the television.

Robbie emerged from the bathroom, dressed in his Batman pajamas. "Where's Mom?" he asked as he scooted into a chair at the kitchen table. "Isn't she gonna have ice cream with us?"

Catrina set their bowls on the table, thankful her grandson had been too wrapped up in his own excitement to notice his mother's heartache. She smiled softly, her own heart aching a little as she feathered his hair back with her fingers. It didn't look as if Emily and Robbie would move to Turnersville anytime soon. "She went for a little walk."

He rolled his eyes. "*Again?*"

Catrina laughed. "Again."

****

As the chartered jet banked over Baltimore, Eric stretched out his legs, settled deeper into his seat and tried to tune out the raucous victory party going on around him. If he'd thought he was a hurting pup after that first game against the Bombers, it was nothing compared to the agony he felt now. His jaw throbbed, his head pounded, his ribs ached, and his knees felt like hot rubber.

But if he hadn't given himself that final push, he would have let Granger beat him again. He closed his eyes, smiled, and savored the stunned look on Granger's face when he'd realized Eric had snatched the cup out of his greedy grasp at the last second. It had been worth every screaming muscle. Still was. Even if he did feel more dead than alive.

Doc Springer had ranted and raved when Eric told him he was going back out on the ice, but Eric had refused to listen. He wasn't about to concede defeat just because some goon decked him from behind. As long as he could skate, he could play. And it wasn't as if he had anyone other than himself to consider. No one sat at home waiting for him, worrying about him.

Which was why he'd ordered Doc not to release his condition to the media. "Keep 'em guessing," he'd said, not wanting the Bombers to think he was shark bait just because he'd taken a clip to the jaw. A whopper of a clip, he amended, pressing the ice pack to his chin. He winced, remembering the jabs he'd taken in the ribs as he went down. But he'd repaid that debt, as well.

Two goals for two bruised ribs. Not a bad deal.

He fell asleep wondering if Emily had seen the game.

****

"Would you like to talk about it?"

Emily knew better than to pretend she didn't know what her mother meant. Ever since she'd returned to the house, dry-eyed and drained, to find it teeming with the first arrivals for the weekend, Catrina had run interference for her. Emily had managed to greet Tom and Sharon and their two children, and Mark and Jill and their newborn with the appropriate amount of enthusiasm, but when it came to answering questions that required coherent thought, she'd found it too much of a strain. Her mother's tactful interruptions had saved her more than once.

"There's nothing to talk about. It's over."

Catrina entered the living room, where Emily had retreated with a novel after everyone left to bunk down at Suzanna's. "He ended it, then?" she asked as she joined Emily on the couch.

"No, I did." Her voice was dull and flat.

"May I ask why?"

Emily closed her book, studied the author's smiling picture on the back, and wished she could crawl into bed and lose herself in the pages. She didn't want to have this conversation. She'd made her decision. She didn't want to lay it open for questions. The answers hurt too much. Although it had little to do with the truth, she chose the most obvious response, and hoped it would be one her mother could relate to in light of her own experience.

"He's a hockey player, Mama."

"So?"

Emily sighed and forced the words out, feeling as if she were sticking a knife in Eric's back. "You saw him tonight. You saw what he—"

"All I saw was a man determined to do what he could to see that his team won."

Her head came up. "But the violence—"

"Is part of his work. I doubt it's part of the man."

"How can you say that? You don't even know him."

"But you and Robbie do. Quite well, I understand."

297

"You've talked with Robbie about Eric?"

"No, Robbie's talked about Eric with me. I've simply listened. I didn't consider it my place to offer opinions on a subject you clearly didn't intend to discuss with me."

Emily flushed as if she'd been caught lying. Catrina settled deeper into the sofa. I don't mean to embarrass or pressure you, Emily. In fact, I try to make it a point not to meddle in my children's lives. But you're hurting, sweetheart, and that tears me up inside.

"I've known since you arrived that you were troubled about something, and when you talked about everything but a certain man your son thinks the world of, it wasn't hard to put two and two together. I saw the way you reacted to the news he'd been hurt. The house could have burned down around you and you wouldn't have noticed."

Emily stared at the blank television screen and remembered the sight of Eric, bruised, battered...and laughing. "My reaction doesn't change anything, Mama."

"A woman who claims not to care doesn't flinch when a man wearing protective gear and padding collides with—"

"Of course I care, Mama. He could have ended his career, playing hurt like that!"

"I thought his career was the problem."

Caught, Emily groaned in defeat. "You don't understand."

Catrina's eyes remained steady and calm. "I'd like to." When Emily didn't respond, Catrina gave her daughter an assessing look. "Do you know your son thinks you should marry this man?"

Emily nodded sadly, recalling Robbie's simple solution to their problems, the solemn earnestness with which he'd asked her to "think about it."

"He wants me to marry Eric so he can have a father, so I can stay home and take care of him."

"I see. Has Eric asked you to marry him?"

"No."

"Does he love you?"

"Right now, he probably hates me."

Catrina thought of the pain and loneliness she'd seen in the man's eyes. The way he'd played as if he had nothing left to lose.

"I doubt that."

Emily smiled. "You're just biased."

Catrina returned the smile. "Only because I love you so much." She reached out and smoothed Emily's hair. "Now, why don't we start at the beginning? Where did you meet?"

Emily chuckled dryly. "Where else? In the ER."

"After a game?"

"After a barroom brawl." She explained about the brawl, described her first meeting with Eric. "Then he showed up at Robbie's school." She told her mother about Eric's lectures, the athletic equipment he'd donated to the school, his community service award, and before she knew it, she'd backtracked and told Catrina the story from beginning to end. Including the part about Ryan's attack and threatened custody suit.

When Emily finished, Catrina asked in her non-judgmental way, "Do you believe Eric beat his wife?"

"No."

"Do you believe he would intentionally harm you or Robbie?"

"Never."

"Then why do you refuse to see him again?"

"Mama, I said some awful things to him."

"You were frightened and upset. You were protecting your son from what you considered a very real, very imminent threat. You were also trying to protect Eric. I'm sure he would forgive you if you explained what happened that night."

"I'm sure he would, too."

"Then I don't understand. Are you still worried about Ryan?"

Emily shook her head. She'd talked with Miguel after her meeting with Patricia. Ryan was no longer an issue. He could file all the lawsuits he wanted, but his chances of being awarded custody of Robbie were nil with Patricia on their side.

"I know it doesn't make sense, but...I'm scared, Mama."

"Of what, sweetheart?"

"I'm not sure anymore. Of making another mistake, I suppose. Of making a commitment and having it go sour.

299

Of losing myself again." She met her mother's eyes. "If I married Eric, my life would never be my own again. I could end up in a strange city, totally dependent on him. And after Ryan...I don't want to lose my independence, Mama. I don't ever want to need or depend on a man again. It would be all to easy to depend on Eric." She looked into her lap. "All too easy," she whispered.

Catrina was silent for several minutes. Emily plucked at the petit-point pillow she'd nearly shredded earlier and blinked back her tears.

"May I offer a suggestion?" Catrina asked quietly.

Emily sniffed. "Go ahead. I sure don't know what to do anymore."

"Is it possible you're not comparing Eric to Ryan, but to your father?"

Emily frowned. The idea had never occurred to her. "What are you saying?"

"It seems to me, that since you haven't mentioned him since the night you arrived, you still have a lot of unresolved feelings about your father."

"I'm sorry. I thought...I...didn't want to upset you."

"I have no problem with talking about Duane. I'll admit it hasn't always been that way, but for my children's sake I felt I had to put our relationship in perspective. More than a few of your brothers and sisters felt the same way I suspect you do. I suppose I should have made that clear sooner, but I thought it best to let you make the first move, as I did with the others."

Emily said nothing, still processing the idea that she might be comparing Eric to her father.

"Do you think about him at all?"

In the face of her mother's honesty, Emily could offer no less. "I try not to."

Catrina smiled with gentle understanding. "Then your feelings for him are still buried deep inside you. Feelings of confusion, anger, perhaps disgust..."

"Mama..." Emily protested, embarrassed.

Catrina covered her daughter's hand, gave it a reassuring squeeze. "It's all right, sweetheart. I, better than anyone, know what your father was...and wasn't." Her eyes grew dark and solemn. "But I've made my peace with his memory. It's past time you made yours. If not for yourself, then for Eric." Her voice gentled. "You're making him pay for another man's sins, Emily."

The idea appalled Emily. She started to object, but Catrina held up a staying hand. "Think about it. On the surface the similarities between Eric and your father seem quite visible. Your father was a big man, known for his temper. Eric is a big man, and from what you've told me, also known for his temper. Your father was a drinker and barroom brawler. You met Eric after he'd been drinking and in a barroom brawl. Your father's profession kept him on the road more than at home. Eric's profession involves a lot of traveling...do you see where I'm heading?"

Emily nodded, too stunned to speak. Catrina gave her hand a final squeeze. "Good. Then pick up the thread and see where it leads you." She rose and dimmed the lights, preparing to leave.

Emily suddenly felt bereft. "Mama, don't go now..."

"I have to, sweetheart. This is something you have to do alone. You don't need me or anyone else to direct your thoughts or interfere with your memories." She kissed Emily's forehead. "When you're through, I'll be in my room if you need me."

For over an hour Emily sat in the shadows and contemplated her mother's quiet wisdom. She wondered how often Catrina had had similar conversations with her other children. Wondered how often her mother had sat alone in the darkness of the house she'd shared with her husband, surrounded by painful memories, until she'd finally summoned the strength to lay the past to rest.

Weak-willed? Hah. Catrina Jordan didn't have a weak bone in her body. Emily had certainly been wrong about that.

As she had been about Eric.

Determinedly Emily called up memories of her father, paged through them like an old scrapbook, and forced herself to lay them side by side with her memories of Eric.

Her mother was right. Surface similarities existed, but beyond those, the two men were as different as could be. Her father had spent most of his time and money on the road, and left his family to fend for themselves. Eric traveled often, but would never leave his family without support or security. Her father had ignored his children, while Eric had treated Robbie as his own from the start.

Her father had vented his frustration and bitterness on his wife, while Eric had channeled his into an acceptable outlet and forged himself a career in a profession he believed in. Her father had refused to give an inch, refused to apologize to anyone for his beliefs or actions, while Eric had been willing to try to work it out every time they disagreed.

Emily dug deeper and deeper and continued her comparisons. When she'd finished, she didn't know whether to laugh or cry. Her relationship with her father had colored her responses to Eric from the start, painted her involvement with him the same shade of black. As for Ryan...

She now saw her spoiled, selfish, insecure ex-husband for what he was. Young and naïve when she'd met him, she'd been drawn to his outward confidence, his seeming strength. By the time she'd realized his cocky attitude was a façade, it was too late. So she'd vowed never to be taken in like that again, and pushed Eric—another strong, self-confident man, away.

She'd used her memories of her marriage to obscure the fact that she'd subconsciously measured Eric against the same warped yardstick she'd used to measure and condemn her father. And while she loved Eric, there had always been that seed of doubt in the back of her mind that one day he might turn on her like her father had turned on her mother.

She didn't seek out her mother. She called Miranda.

"Emily!"

"I'm sorry for calling so late." It was well past two, but she wouldn't be able to sleep until she knew Eric was all right.

"Don't give it a second thought. I was up anyway, waiting for the guys. They'll roll in, in about an hour or so. What's up? I heard you were visiting your family. Something about a reunion?"

"Yes. That's right. A picnic up at Sutter's Lake."

Miranda groaned. "Don't talk about food. My mouth waters at the thought of it these days."

Emily laughed. "How's the baby?"

"Growing every day. I think we've got a hockey player from the feel of it, but Bill insists she's just a clumsy ballerina."

"She? You're having a girl?"

"What can I say? I couldn't stand the suspense."

Their small talk faded into silence. Emily wondered how to broach the subject of Eric without dampening Miranda's welcoming mood.

"Did you see the game tonight?" Miranda asked.

"Yes. How is he?" Emily's heart constricted at the memory.

"Holding up pretty well, considering. I'm going to be blunt here, Emily. The man's an emotional wreck without you. He's doing his macho best to hide it, of course—"

"Miranda, please. I feel badly enough already."

"That's a good sign, at least. But seriously, I got your number from the school, and if you hadn't called, I would have called you. Eric's hurting, bad, and I'm not talking the kind of hurt that comes from bumps and bruises, although Lord knows he's got plenty of those these days. Those Bombers are animals. I'm glad Bill's not playing any more, and just between you and me, I was half hoping the Saints would lose tonight, if only to put the guys out of their misery."

"Do you see him often?"

Miranda laughed. "I ought to charge him room and board. He's been staying here while he's in town. He's beginning to drive me up a wall, but neither Bill nor I have the heart to throw him out. Besides, it's only another week at most."

Emily didn't want to think about Eric leaving town. "Why doesn't he go to his apartment?"

"The one time I got irked enough to ask, he muttered something about ghosts. He needs your support, Emily. Especially with this Granger business eating at him."

"Granger?"

"The Bombers coach. He really has it in for Eric. I'm not sure why, though. I just know it's getting to him. When are you coming home?"

"Sunday."

"You can't make it any sooner?"

"The reunion's tomorrow."

"What time Sunday?"

"Around four."

"Great. I'll get you and Robbie tickets for the game. You can pick them up at the ticket office when you get there."

"Miranda—"

"Whatever else is going on between you, Emily, right now he needs to know you're in his corner. That's the best way to show him."

Emily hesitated, torn. She'd envisioned a more private reconciliation. Despite Miranda's enthusiasm, she wasn't sure what her reception would be.

"That is why you called, isn't it? You're coming back to work things out?"

Emily hesitated, but Miranda was right. Eric needed to know she was in his corner. Off the ice and on. "All right. We'll go to the game."

"Good girl. Come to think of it, if you keep him overnight, I'll name the baby after you."

"Miranda!"

"I'm not kidding, Emily. I'm a desperate woman. I need some time alone with my husband. I promise if you take Eric off my hands, I'll never push you into anything again."

Emily smiled, and looked forward to the idea of spending the night with Eric. But in the end it would have to be his choice.

"I'll give it some thought. See you at the game."

Chapter Thirty-Two

"I'm telling you, she called."

Eric sent Miranda an I-really-don't-need-this-right-now look and returned his attention to the steaming mountain of buttermilk pancakes she'd set in front of him just moments before she'd made her off-the-wall announcement. "Yeah, right."

"You don't believe me? I'm telling you, Eric, Emily called me last night around two—"

"Just like that? Out of the blue?"

"She was worried about you. She saw you get hit."

Eric ruthlessly squelched the hope that rose in him at the thought that Emily still cared. "I've been hit plenty of times lately, Miranda. You're telling me that after two months of silence the good doctor suddenly decided to see how I was feeling?"

"It was more than that, Eric, and you know it."

"Miranda..."

She thumped the syrup on the table, making both Eric and Bill, who was trying to move as gingerly as possible this morning, wince. Eric felt for his friend, but last night's win had been nothing short of a miracle. He'd even reluctantly joined the celebration. Between two lousy lukewarm beers, the seven pounds of sweat he'd lost during the game and the dehydrating effects of air travel, he'd felt no pain by the time they'd touched ground. But this morning his head hurt like hell.

"Fine," Miranda was saying, "You don't believe me, I won't suggest you might want to meet them at the airport and bring them to Sunday's game."

Eric nearly choked on his coffee. "Now I know you're spinning fairy tales. You know as well as I do Emily doesn't want anything to do with coming to a game."

Miranda looked at her husband, who was pilfering a

piece of sausage. "Tell him, Bill."

"Sorry, Hon. I wasn't here to take the call."

"You believed me last night!" She'd told him as they slipped into bed. He'd murmured that was wonderful, pulled her to him for a long kiss, then sighed and promptly fell asleep.

"Honey, last night I believed cows could fly." He kissed her cheek and shuffled off to get the morning paper.

Miranda watched him desert her and gritted her teeth in exasperation. It was true. Bill had tumbled out of the taxi so soused she could've told him she'd had the baby and he would have believed it. Assuming Eric was in the same sorry state, she'd decided to wait until morning to tell him the news. An incoherent Eric on the line was the last thing Emily would've needed at three in the morning.

She turned back to the griddle and whipped more batter. "Forget I said anything. I'll just call her and tell her not to bother coming home. Maybe she'll find someone in Turnersville who'll appreciate her concern."

Eric's head snapped up. "You've got her number?"

"She called me, didn't she?"

Something in Miranda's voice let Eric know she'd had enough. He studied her stiff back and jerky movements for a long moment before he figured out what it was. Clearly, she'd put up with him as long as she had because of his friendship with her husband. A friendship he'd abused by monopolizing Bill's time for the past few weeks, talking game strategy.

"I'm sorry, Miranda. I've been a bear. I'll leave as soon as I'm packed." He pushed away from the table.

She whirled on him then, looking near tears. "Don't be ridiculous."

Eric didn't get it. He'd agreed with her, hadn't he? Maybe her tears had something to do with being pregnant. But she did have a point. "I'm not. Ridiculous is hiding out here because I'm too damned lonely to face my apartment walls. You're not my keeper, and I've been a selfish SOB, hanging out here for as long as I have. If I were you, I'd have thrown me out weeks ago. I'm sorry, Miranda."

She smiled then, startling him. Apparently an apology was all she needed. He'd have to remember that. Women appreciated apologies. Or maybe they just appreciated being appreciated. She sniffed and pointed to his plate with her spatula. "Finish your breakfast before it gets cold. I'll get Emily's number for you as soon as this batch is done."

Eric smiled for the first time in weeks.

By seven-thirty that night he was no longer smiling. He'd tried the number Miranda had given him half a dozen times—with no luck. Nobody home, and apparently no answering machine, either.

Jeez, he thought, staring at his apartment ceiling as twilight fell, how long could a simple picnic take? And why the hell didn't he have her cell number? Just another mistake he'd made in a sea of them with Emily.

He rolled over, reached for the phone and dialed again. Somewhere around the sixteenth ring a breathless sounding young woman answered. "Hello?"

Eric's stomach dipped and clenched. "Hello. This is Eric Cameron. Is Emily in?"

"Emily? Sorry, she's not here. Last time I saw her she was on her way over to Martin's to play Texas Hold 'Em with the guys."

"I see." Eric hoped Martin was one of Emily's brothers, not an old schoolmate, or boyfriend. Beating back the urge to ask—and admit how little he knew about Emily's family—Eric asked instead, "Do you have any idea when she'll be back?"

The girl laughed, which unsettled him even more. "Hard to say with that crowd. I'd be surprised if she gets back before midnight, if at all."

"What about Robbie? Isn't he with her?"

"I think he went over to Suzanna's for the night."

Another unfamiliar name. "You think? You don't know?"

"You try keeping track of twenty people going in thirty directions. Listen, I just came home to change. I've got to get to work. Can I give Emily a message if I see her again? Maybe they'll stop by the DQ sometime tonight."

Oh sure. What was he supposed to say? If it's not too much trouble, Emily, could you stop having fun long enough to call the man you've ignored for the past two months? "No, no message."

He hung up and wondered if they'd been talking about the same woman. Poker with the guys and staying out until all hours of the night? That didn't sound like Emily at all.

****

Emily scooped up the pot, shrugged and grinned from ear to ear. "Sorry, guys. Beginner's luck."

Tom, Mark and Patrick grumbled good-naturedly as they watched their eldest sister rake in her winnings.

"I told you we had a shark on our hands." Patrick reached into the refrigerator. "Anyone need a refill?"

Emily laughed and tucked her winnings into her jeans pocket. "Tell you what. To show what a generous winner I am, I'll spring for the movie." She looked at the kitchen clock. It was nearly eight. "Shouldn't the others be here by now?"

As if on cue, the front door burst open. In bustled Emily's sisters, less Annalise, who'd left after supper to go work at the Dairy Queen. After a day of non-stop eating, volleyball, badminton, gossip, swimming, and more eating, the reunion had split into two groups. The guest of honor and her brothers had gone to Martin's, while Catrina and her remaining daughters and two daughters-in-law had shuttled the children to Suzanna's. Catrina would babysit at Suzanna's while the parents spent Saturday night on the town.

Their arms overflowing with snack foods and leftover desserts, the Jordan women spilled into the kitchen and told the poker players to get in gear. Within minutes everyone had piled into Martin's Jeep Cherokee and Sheila's Dodge Caravan like a bunch of rowdy teenagers and headed into Turnersville for a never-to-be-forgotten night of fun.

Well after midnight they returned to Martin's to eat and drink until dawn, reminisce, tease each other mercilessly...and discuss Emily's foundation. Amid pretzels and beer, brownies and macaroons, laughter and tears, the Jordan siblings renewed their commitment to helping one another, and agreed that Martin, Sheila, Tom and Mark would see to it that Mary Beth, Patrick and

308

Annalise completed their educations. Suzanna would pitch in what she could, but between keeping up her mortgage and raising two children on a public servant's salary, no one begrudged her her lack of funds.

As for Emily...the decision was unanimous. The only tuition she'd be paying from now on would be Robbie's.

Catrina called at nine in the morning to say the troops were mustering for round two. Amid moans and groans from lack of sleep and too much fun, the parents roused themselves to reclaim their progeny. After a hair-raising breakfast for the staff at the Pancake Pantry, they packed up the SUV's and mini-vans and pulled out for points east and south.

Clustered on Suzanna's sidewalk, Emily, Suzanna and Catrina waved as the others rolled out of sight. With matching smiles, the three women shared a "Ready, Ladies?" look and went inside to clean up after nine pairs of curious little hands. Robbie and Suzanna's two elementary-schoolers were in the back yard playing some form of good guys versus bad guys.

As she loaded the last of the leftovers into her rented Explorer to take back to her mother's, Emily called again for Robbie to say his goodbyes. They'd have to hurry to make it to the airport in time. He came racing around the corner of the house flushed and bright-eyed. Emily assumed it was from spending the last hour running around the yard yelling and screaming.

"I guess this is it," she said, and faced Suzanna as their mother instructed Robbie to keep a close eye on the casserole dishes she'd set beside him on the back seat.

"It was a great reunion, Emily. I'm glad you finally came home. We've missed you."

Emily hugged her sister. "Thank Mama. She organized this madness." She pulled back and smiled. "Next time we'll spend more time one-on-one." Somewhere during the night, Emily and Suzanna had discovered a special bond brought on by single parenthood.

Suzanna grinned. "Next time we'll do this at *your* house."

"Mom, can you hurry up? I don't feel so good."

Emily exchanged a knowing parental look with Suzanna, then turned to peer at Robbie, squirming in the back seat. "We're on our way, Tiger. Just sit tight."

It wasn't until after she'd helped her mother unload the food and picnic supplies from the Explorer, and re-loaded it with her and Robbie's luggage, that Emily realized her son hadn't been simply complaining with eight-year-old impatience. After calling him and receiving no answer, she found him sound asleep on Annalise's bed, his color high.

"Robbie?" She tested his temperature with a kiss to the forehead. He burned with fever, opened glassy eyes to her touch.

"Mom?" He winced and she scanned his slim body for signs of injury.

"Where does it hurt, sweetheart?"

"My head. My ear."

His ear. In all the excitement she'd forgotten about Robbie's susceptibility to ear infections if he didn't dry out his ears after bathing...or swimming. Almost every time she'd looked around yesterday, he'd been splashing with his cousins in the lake.

Emily glanced at her watch. They'd never make their flight now. Wouldn't make *any* flights as long as Robbie had an ear infection. She ignored the sinking feeling in her stomach at not seeing Eric again as soon as she'd hoped and scooped her son into her arms.

"Come on, sweetheart, we've got to get you to a doctor who can prescribe what you need. I'm not licensed in this state."

Catrina rounded the corner of the house just as Emily carried Robbie out to the car. "Emily? What's happened? I was looking for him in the back yard."

"It's all right, Mama. Robbie's got an ear infection. I have to get him to the hospital. He's running a fever and I'll need some antibiotics."

At the hospital they waited over two hours in the reception area. By the time they were ushered into an examining room, Robbie was cranky and whimpering with pain, and Emily was fit to be tied.

"This never would have happened at home," she muttered, pressing a cool compress to his forehead. Catrina had gone to call Annalise and tell her where they were. Emily had also asked her to call Anna, to let her

310

know they wouldn't need to be picked up at the airport. "Doctors work on Sundays in Minneapolis."

All her hopes and plans, shot down again. She hoped Miranda hadn't told Eric she was coming to the game. She hated to think of how disappointed he'd be when she didn't show.

"We work on Sundays in Turnersville, too," a pleasantly amused male voice said from the doorway. "Unfortunately, we're direly understaffed at present, since the hospital's only been open for a few months."

Emily looked up and met the warm brown eyes of a doctor she recognized from her past. Catrina's past. He noticed she'd helped herself to his supplies. "I'm Dr. Melrose. Are you by any chance in medicine? You look familiar."

"I'm a doctor. I work in the ER at Minneapolis General."

"Excellent hospital." He looked at Robbie, squirming on the examining table. "What do we have here, Doctor?"

"My son, Robbie. He's got a case of swimmer's ear. We were up at Sutter's Lake yesterday."

The doctor slipped his stethoscope into his ears. "What brings you to Turnersville?"

"We're visiting my mother. Catrina Jordan."

His eyes flickered in startled recognition before he broke into a broad smile. "So you're that determined young lady who used to ask me all those questions about being a doctor. Welcome home, Emily."

They were out of there in twenty minutes, prescriptions filled by the hospital pharmacy tucked into Emily's purse. As they left the hospital, Emily spotted Dr. Melrose getting into his own car in the parking lot. He saw her and waved, then came over and pressed a card into Emily's hand.

"If you're ever in the market for a job, Dr. Jordan, please give me a call. We could use someone with your background in ER medicine. We haven't had much luck at drawing established doctors from the city, and we're pretty picky about who we hire."

Emily smiled, honored. "I'll keep that in mind."

"In fact, if you're going to be in town a while, I'd like you to come back for a tour of the facilities."

"I may take you up on it, since we'll be here longer than we planned." They'd determined Robbie wouldn't be able to fly for at least two days.

Dr. Melrose looked over to where Catrina was helping her grandson into the Explorer. "Your mother's welcome to come along on the tour as well...if you think she'd be interested."

Emily didn't miss the double meaning in the doctor's invitation. She smiled as it confirmed her suspicions. She'd sensed a subtle change in his friendly demeanor when her mother had joined them in the treatment room. Her mother's answering smiles had seemed almost shy.

Emily smiled and nodded. "I think she'd be interested."

****

It was after three before they got Robbie settled into bed. Emily dropped into a kitchen chair, prepared to put up her feet and enjoy the tall glass of iced tea her mother had waiting when she remembered to call Miranda.

She heaved herself to her feet and dialed Miranda. No luck. After much internal debate, during which her pride took a well-deserved beating, she dialed Eric's apartment. No answer. Damn. His cell phone number was on her desk at home. On a long shot, she dialed Anna. Maybe she could run over to the house and get Eric's number for her.

Strike three.

She sighed and left Anna a message, then settled in to wait.

****

Eric felt like a kid on prom night as he paced the airport terminal. Despite his baseball hat and dark glasses, several people stopped to ask, "Aren't you Eric Cameron?" Each time, he cursed his purple jaw anew, but somehow managed to convince them he wasn't who they thought he was.

For the umpteenth time, he checked Emily's flight number against the monitor. They'd landed. His pulse picked up speed. He hoped he wasn't jumping the gun. But he couldn't wait to see them again. He'd even rented a limo to take them all to the arena. He'd wanted his hands free to hold onto any part of Emily he could. Then, after the game...

His heart dipped and squeezed. He could only hope she didn't have other plans. He reached the boarding area as the first arrivals streamed through the door that led to the jetway. With each unfamiliar face his nerves stretched tighter. Good grief. Weren't they supposed to let women and children off the plane first or something? Where were they? Around him families and lovers melted into hugs and kisses, and it made him ache with the need to hold his own loved ones close.

The arrivals slowed to a trickle, giving him a clear view of anyone crossing the threshold. Still no Robbie or Emily. Had she changed her mind again? Decided she couldn't stomach watching him play after all? His insides knotted all over again.

The flight crew emerged, joking amongst themselves. Eric was the only non-passenger that remained at the foot of the ramp. He started up the ramp when they locked the door to the jetway. No. It wasn't possible. They had to be on that plane. He needed them to be on that plane.

"Excuse me, sir. May I help you?"

He looked down at a pretty brunette in a navy blue uniform who blocked his path, a polite smile on her bright red lips. He had to give her credit for planting herself in front of him.

"I...was expecting someone. A woman and a boy. They didn't get off the plane."

"If they were on it, sir, they would have used this exit."

"You're sure?"

Her smile never faltered. She'd obviously had this conversation before. "Quite sure. Everyone on the flight has deplaned. If you'd like, we can check to see if they were on the flight."

Feeling completely off-balance, he followed her to the check-in counter in the boarding area. "Names?" she asked.

"Jordan. Emily and Robbie. Maybe Robin," he answered, with a last hopeful look at the door to the jetway.

"They did have reservations. If you'll hold on a minute, I'll call to see if they boarded in Detroit."

"Thank you," he said, but already knew the answer. She'd changed her mind.

****

Emily, seated on her mother's couch with Robbie's head in her lap, watched Eric play like a man possessed. A man possessed with an angry need to win, an angry need to prove he wasn't a loser. She didn't flinch when he rammed into his opponents this time, but her heart ached for him just the same. She'd wanted to be there. Wanted to cheer him on in person. Wanted to hold him in her arms and assure herself he was fit to play again after Friday's fiasco.

Fit or not, he was clearly determined to handle whatever the Bombers threw his way tonight, and then some. In time, they appeared to have picked up on his mood, and apparently decided to give him a wide berth and focus on disabling his teammates instead. For that, Emily was selfishly grateful.

She'd called Miranda several times before the game, to no avail. She'd even called the arena, but found the people there singularly uncooperative. Sure, she needed to get a message to Eric Cameron. They'd see what they could do. Miranda Manzelrod? Never heard of her. There would be no help from that quarter.

Anna hadn't called back, either. Heartsick, Emily had settled in to watch the game. Nothing she could do until it was over.

The Saints won again, this time by a landslide six-one. Emily felt as if she'd been given a reprieve. The next game, the sixth of the series, would be in Baltimore in two days. Assuming the Saints won, there would be a seventh game in Minneapolis, which meant Eric wouldn't leave for his home in Barton before she could get back to Minneapolis. Starting at eleven, she called his apartment again. And again, and again. When she'd received no answer by three, she collapsed on her bed in defeat. She dreamed of Eric smugly smiling at her across a crowded room as he celebrated his victory with a gorgeous woman on each arm. You left me, he said. Was I supposed to wait for you to come back?

After she tried Eric again in the morning, without success, a frazzled and frustrated Emily finally touched base with Miranda at work.

"Emily? Where were you last night?"

"I'm still in Turnersville, Miranda."

"What? Why? Good grief, Eric went to meet your plane!"

"He what? Oh, no. Oh, *no*. Tell me he didn't."

"Sorry. I told him you were coming home."

Emily didn't have the energy to debate the merits of *that* decision. "Listen, Miranda, Robbie has an ear infection. He can't fly until it clears up. I didn't find out until we were leaving for the airport. I tried to call you. I even tried to call Eric's apartment. Do you have his cell phone number?"

"He was so angry," Miranda murmured, almost to herself. "I've never seen him so upset. After the game, he asked me if I'd heard from you, and when I said no..."

Emily didn't want to hear it. "His cell phone number, Miranda. Do you have it?"

"Sure. It's saved in mine. Let me get it for you."

"If I can't reach him, and you happen to see him..."

"I'll tell him to call you right away. Do you have a cell number?"

"Of course." She gave Miranda the number.

Chapter Thirty-Three

Eric wasn't calling anybody. He was too busy hiding out at the Hilton, licking his wounds. It didn't matter anyway. He didn't have his cell phone with him. He didn't know what he'd done with it, but figured he must have left it in his apartment. No way was he going back there. Not anytime soon, anyway.

Feeling too raw inside to face the champagne and roses that waited in his apartment, he'd had the limo drop him off at the hotel instead. He didn't leave his suite until the following afternoon, when it was time to catch the flight for Baltimore.

He settled into a seat apart from the poker parties and bull sessions and immersed himself in his dog-eared notebook on the Bombers' hockey strategies. What had once been a source of friction between himself and his teammates—his pre-game aloofness, was now a respected tradition. All he had to do anymore was reach for his notebook and he became invisible.

Just as well. His emotional annihilation at Emily's hands had left him in no mood for socializing. All he wanted now was to find the key to beating Granger at his own game, then get the hell out of Dodge. With any luck, come fall, he'd step onto the ice somewhere far, far away. Even Europe was looking good these days.

A shadow fell across his notes. He glanced up and saw Bill watching him, a look in his eyes that made Eric want to deck him, best friend or no.

"You okay?"

The question set Eric's teeth on edge. He didn't want pity. He wanted to be left alone. He had a job to do. A score to settle. A woman to forget. "Sure. Why wouldn't I be?"

"You didn't show up at any of the victory parties last

night."

"I was busy."

Bill studied the coffee-stained pages covered with diagrams and cryptic notes strewn across Eric's seat back tray. "Looks to me like you've been obsessing."

"I'm entitled. The man tried to bury me ten years ago."

"Doesn't explain why you're so hyped on retaliation now. It isn't like you haven't had other chances over the years."

"You got a problem with the way I'm playing, Coach?"

Bill's smile dropped. "Don't start that player-manager shit with me. I'm asking you what the hell's going on with you as a friend. You want to play hardball, I'm in. But I'd rather find out what's been eating at you these past few weeks."

Eric said nothing, his glower warning Bill to back off. Bill stayed put. Wearily, Eric raked a hand through his hair. "Three guesses."

"So Miranda was right again. This is personal. She's said all along more than just a need to show up Granger was driving you. She's worried about you, you know. She feels awful about what happened at the airport."

Miranda was worried. Miranda felt awful. Not Emily. Eric had thought his shattered heart beyond pain. He was wrong. It hurt like hell. "Well, you can tell her I survived being stood up by our fickle doctor friend—again."

"Miranda said she called again. Something about—"

Eric held up his hand. "Don't even go there, man. I don't want to hear it. Not now." He indicated his notes. "All I want right now is to find a way to make sure the Saints whip Baltimore's ass tomorrow night."

His friend studied him for a long moment, seemed to come to some sort of decision, then nodded. "Need someone to bounce ass-whipping ideas off of?"

****

By Wednesday night Emily was at wit's end. Eric seemed to have fallen off the face of the earth, except to suit up for his games. Miranda, who called daily to check on Robbie's progress, insisted no one—Bill included—knew where Eric was staying. He kept to himself and simply vanished when the team parted company.

He didn't answer his cell phone, either. Again and again she called, and became more and more frustrated. When Suzanna stopped by on her lunch hour and caught Emily brooding on the porch swing, then gently suggested she might be better off without a man who could disappear so easily at whim, Emily actually agreed—then burst into tears.

By the time Suzanna left, Emily knew what she had to do. On a burst of inspiration, she called Sheila to ask her for a favor, then drove into town for supplies. On her way home she picked up the portfolio case holding the signs Sheila had made for her, then got Robbie in gear while Catrina packed a cooler. At dusk she waved goodbye to her misty-eyed mother and headed for the interstate in her rented Explorer, her driving phobias be damned.

Emily Jordan was going to a hockey game.

While Robbie counted license plates from the back seat, Emily prayed for good weather. Her luck held as far as Chicago, where a torrential downpour forced her to pull into a rest stop or risk being washed off the road. As the wind howled and rain hammered at the windows, beating a relentless tattoo against the Explorer's roof, Emily slid her seat back down, and closed her eyes. Her last thought before sleep claimed her was she'd lost her mind.

She awoke to the steady hum of traffic and a sparkling clear sky. They entered Minneapolis just after ten. As she pulled into the hospital parking lot to make a pit stop Robbie insisted couldn't wait another half hour, Emily exhaled in relief. She'd made it. Home turf at last.

While Robbie used the restroom, Emily used the phone, once again with no luck. She was listening to her voice mail messages when she heard a name and number combination she'd never expected to hear. Patricia Montgomery was staying at Harmony House?

She listened to her messages again, and counted three messages from Patricia, left Tuesday, Sunday, and Friday the week before.

"Something wrong, Emily?" Sarah asked from the doorway. "I stopped by to say hi, but...you look rattled."

"Um, no. I'm fine. Just dazed from sixteen hours on the road."

"Sixteen hours? Did you have car trouble?"

"No, but I spent most of the night stuck at a rest stop because of the weather. Otherwise we'd have been home hours ago." Between that and coming back to this..." She waved a hand at her overflowing desk.

"I know. Makes you want to turn right around and go back on vacation."

Or think about finding another job, Emily thought as Sarah left to answer a page. She recalled how impressed she'd been by the facility in Turnersville, how friendly the staff had been when Dr. Melrose had given her his promised tour. The man definitely wanted her on his staff. He also definitely wanted to spend some time with her mother.

But Emily didn't have time to think about Doctor Melrose and her mother. Not when her own romance was on the rocks. Where the hell was Eric? And why didn't he answer his phone? Grimly, she went to collect Robbie. She found him charming the ladies at the nurse's station with tales of his trip.

"Time to go, Tiger. Mom needs to catch up on some sleep." She winked at Susan and the others. "See you all Monday, bright and early."

At home she found Anna airing out the house, two tickets to tonight's game tucked in her dress pocket. "Miranda dropped them off. Said she didn't want to take any chances."

"Great." As she accepted Anna's bear hug of welcome and the tickets, Emily smiled her relief. "I'm amazed she could swing them at such short notice." She'd called both women before she'd left Turnersville to apprise them of her plans.

"Is everything still set for tonight?" she asked after she'd dispatched Robbie to start unloading the car. Anna would meet them after the game and take Robbie for the night if things worked out the way Emily hoped they would. Prayed they would.

Anna nodded and transferred the food from the cooler to the fridge. "Have you told him yet he's going to the game?"

"No. I want to make sure he takes a nap this afternoon. If I tell him about the game, he'll be too excited."

319

The three of them finished unloading the car, then Anna followed Emily to the car rental lot to return the Explorer. On the return trip home, Robbie chattered non-stop about their trip to Turnersville.

Robbie heard only the love and encouragement in Anna's voice, but Emily caught the sadness in Anna's smile as Robbie gushed about his grandma. Promising him a special treat if he took an extra long nap, Emily tucked Robbie into bed as soon as they got home. He was asleep almost before she left the room. She craved a nap herself, but instead went downstairs to where Anna waited to hear her version of the trip.

"It sounds like he had a wonderful time," Anna said, her smile firmly in place as Emily poured them each a cup of tea.

"You'll always be his Nanna," Emily said gently. "You know that, don't you?"

Anna's smile wobbled and her eyes misted. She tapped her head with her finger. "Up here, yes." Her hand moved to her heart. "Down here, I'm a little shaky."

"Oh, Anna..."

She waved Emily's protest aside. "Don't mind me. It'll just take some getting used to, that's all." She sighed and smiled again, this time more naturally. "So tell me about your family."

Emily obliged, but only because she didn't want Anna to feel any more left out than she already did. When she'd finished, Anna's eyes glistened. "I'm so happy for you, Emily. Will they be coming to visit?"

Emily laughed. "Hopefully not all at once, but they know my door is always open."

"And the foundation?"

"Is defunct as of Monday. I'm afraid you're out of a job."

They talked a while longer about the foundation, possibly re-vamping it into Robbie's college fund, then reconfirmed their plans for the evening before Anna rose to leave. As was their custom, she would meet Augustus downtown for dinner before they went to the arena. "We'll catch up with you outside the dressing rooms after the game, to pick up Robbie."

"Thanks again. For everything. I don't know what I'd

do without you."

Anna cupped her cheek. "You'd manage just fine, child. I've known that all along." Her eyes twinkled. "Besides, I've seen that determined glint in your eye before. It tells me you're not about to let anyone or anything get in your way. I look forward to seeing the fireworks tonight."

Emily laughed and hugged her, hard. "Tell Augustus I owe him a week of Sundays for giving me the rest of the week off."

Upstairs she peeled off her traveling clothes and automatically checked her pockets before she tossed her jeans into the hamper. She pulled out the phone number she'd written down at the hospital, stared at it for a long moment, undecided, then took a deep breath and sat down on her bed to call her ex-mother-in-law. A woman whose voice Emily recognized only vaguely answered, asked Emily to please hold, and went in search of Patricia. Several minutes later Emily heard a very frightened and alone sounding hello.

"Patricia. It's Emily. I'm sorry I didn't return your calls sooner. I've been out of town."

"Oh, Emily. I'm so glad it's you."

Emily closed her eyes. She didn't need this right now. "What happened?"

"I've left John. We...we had words."

Emily doubted words were all they'd had if Patricia had fled to Harmony House.

"Can we...meet?" Patricia asked hesitantly.

"Of course." Emily knew Patricia meant as soon as possible. She'd already been there for at least six days, stranded in an unfamiliar world.

"I...haven't got a car. I haven't got anything." Patricia's voice broke.

"I'll be there as soon as I can."

Emily's long, leisurely soak became a quick shower. Her plans to fuss with her makeup became a couple of strokes of mascara and a dab of lip gloss. A call to Anna's brought Melissa over on the double to keep an eye on Robbie until Emily could get back. She pulled up in front of Harmony House less than an hour later.

Patricia waited for her in the common room, her

elegant features pale and drawn, her eyes shadowed and uncertain. A large green-yellow bruise covered her left cheek. Emily took the older woman's hand and gently drew her toward a loveseat in a more private area of the room. "Tell me what happened."

"We argued. About you." Patricia sniffed. Emily lifted a tissue from one of several boxes strategically placed around the room and pressed it into Patricia's hand. "After I left you at the hospital, I went to confront Ryan. I was unable to reach him for three days—he and Catherine were spending the weekend with friends, but by the time he returned, I knew exactly what I was going to say to him."

"You didn't speak with John, first?"

"No. I wanted to handle this on my own."

Emily wondered if Ryan had been the one to hit Patricia.

"I confronted him at dinner Tuesday night. John wasn't home. I told Ryan I'd spoken with you and was appalled by his behavior and lack of responsibility toward his child."

"I see." Emily decided not to remind Patricia that she wanted nothing from Ryan. The woman's hold on control was too tenuous.

"He denied Robbie was his. He said if you made claims to the contrary, you were only trying to get your hands on the Montgomery money. I told him I knew he was lying. I've seen the boy's picture. I reminded him a majority of the Montgomery money was once St. Clair money, and as the only living former St. Clair, I had considerable say in how it was distributed. I told him if he refused to acknowledge his financial responsibilities toward his son, I'd see to it his grandmother's funds were frozen until such time as Robbie's share could be determined and—"

"Oh, Patricia, you didn't."

"It's Robbie's birthright! Ryan has no right to squander it!"

Emily ran a tired hand over her face. "He was livid, I suppose." She was glad she'd been out of town. There was no telling what Ryan might have done had he come looking for her.

"He threatened to have me declared incompetent. I...suffer from depression. I have for years. I have these attacks, and..."

She faltered. Emily gave Patricia's hands a reassuring squeeze. "I understand."

"We've kept it in the family, but it's been well documented. I've been hospitalized twice for treatment."

Treatment Emily suspected wouldn't have been necessary if Patricia hadn't been subjected to her husband's abuse for over thirty-five years, but she held her tongue. "Then I admire you all the more for taking the steps you have. When did you arrive at Harmony House?"

"Friday morning, while John was at work. I took a cab to your hospital, and your supervisor directed me here."

Augustus again. "When did John hit you?"

"Wednesday night. When Ryan refused to take me seriously, I told John what he had done. He called Ryan into his study and confronted him again. Ryan denied Robbie was his son and repeated his claims you were only after his money. He admitted he'd seen you, but claimed it was at your request.

"John believed him. I knew he would. He's as obsessive as Ryan about money. When Ryan left, John turned on me. He ordered me to never mention the subject again, and said if he ever found out I'd tried to see you or Robbie, he'd make sure I regretted it.

"I don't know what came over me. I snapped. I told him I'd see my grandson as often as you would let me and there wasn't a damned thing he could do about it. He threw me against the bookcase. When I tried to walk out of the room, he grabbed me again and backhanded me across the face."

Emily closed her eyes, picturing the scene all too well. She'd lived it often enough herself. "But you stayed another two nights. Why?"

"I had to decide if I could live with his edict." Her dark, wounded eyes lifted to Emily's. "I couldn't. Not this time."

"What will you do now?"

"I don't know. I left everything behind."

"Do you want to go back?"

"Never."

Emily considered her next words carefully. "Would you like the name of a good attorney?"

"I'd like any help you can give me. I know I don't deserve it after the way I treated you, but I have no one else to turn to."

Emily knew the feeling. No one in Ryan's circle of friends would have come forward to help her. "You've got friends here."

"I don't mean to sound like a snob, Emily. Truly I don't. But I find it difficult to talk to the people here. They treat me differently."

"The staff?"

"No. They've been wonderful. It's...the others."

Women who felt they had as little in common with Mrs. John Montgomery as she'd once felt she had. Again, Emily understood. "Give them time. They've each got their own set of circumstances to work through. Once they get to know you..."

"I was hoping you'd take me in. At least until I can get back on my feet."

Emily didn't know what to say. To refuse would be unconscionable. To agree...she hadn't told Robbie about Patricia yet. So much had happened in the last two weeks. She also had their safety to consider. By taking Patricia in, would she expose herself and Robbie to danger?

Instinct and experience told Emily no. Her ex-father-in-law was the type of man to cut his losses. Saving face, keeping up appearances was all-important to Dr. John Covington Montgomery. He wouldn't come after Patricia physically. He wouldn't risk his image that way.

"I shouldn't have asked."

Emily looked Patricia in the eye. "How soon can you be packed?"

Patricia's smile of gratitude cemented Emily's decision. Smiling, she stood and pulled Patricia to her feet. Before they could leave, they'd need to get the shelter's legal department to issue a protection from abuse order and set up a schedule of counseling sessions for Patricia. "We'd better get busy. I have an important date to keep tonight."

"A date?" Patricia asked as Emily pulled away from the shelter two hours later, the PFA order in the sheriff's hands and on its way to John Montgomery. For added insurance, Emily had had the legal department issue a PFA order for herself—to be delivered to Ryan. To violate it would constitute a felony, something neither father nor son could afford to commit.

Emily smiled. "And a rather public one, at that."

Patricia's eyes showed the first spark of life she'd probably exhibited in the past week. "Does it have something to do with the dashing Mr. Cameron?"

Emily arched an amused eyebrow. "Dashing?"

Patricia colored a bit. It looked good on her. "I must confess I found him quite charming and attractive that night at the banquet. And so utterly devoted to you. Is it serious?"

Emily glanced at her watch. Five-thirty. Her smile was grim. "I'll find out in about five hours."

"Mom! Where have you been? We're gonna miss the game!"

Emily stepped into the foyer with Patricia behind her and looked up in surprise as Robbie raced down the staircase. Behind him, Melissa poked her head out of Robbie's bedroom. "Sorry, Dr. Jordan. I had to tell him. When he woke up, he thought you'd gone to work and welched on his special treat."

Emily smiled and ruffled her son's hair. "Would I do that to you?"

"You mean we're really going? All right!" He took off for the kitchen.

"Robbie! Robbie, wait. I...have another surprise for you. There's someone I'd like you to meet." She stepped aside and drew Patricia forward. "This is Patricia. She's going to stay with us for a few weeks."

Robbie peered at Patricia with open curiosity. "Living with us? Like Nanna used to?"

Emily nodded. "Patricia, this is my son, Robbie Jordan."

"I'm very pleased to meet you, young man." They'd agreed in the car to wait a while before springing the news on Robbie he had yet another grandmother to love him.

"Did somebody hit you, too?"

Patricia faltered a moment, then: "Yes."

"Did you hit 'em back?"

"I'm afraid not."

"My dad hit my mom."

Emily cleared her throat in dismay. "Why don't we go into the kitchen and see what there is to eat? We'll have to leave soon if we want to get to the game on time."

"Mom told me to pull some stuff out of the freezer for you to microwave," Melissa offered from the top of the stairs.

Emily could have kissed her. For a sixteen-year-old, she had a remarkable sense of tact...and timing. "Thank you, Melissa. Patricia, why don't you oversee dinner? I need to change. And Robbie—mind your manners. No nosy questions or you're staying home tonight!"

She dashed upstairs, where she paid Melissa and sent the girl home with a hefty bonus. She stripped again and slipped into her new Victoria's Secret body shaping bra and panties, a sea green cashmere sweater and pair of designer jeans Annalise had insisted made her look as sexy as a movie star, then yanked on the pair of calf-length black leather boots Suzanna had pushed her into buying as well. She brushed her hair and let it fall loose and fluffy to her mid-back, touched up her makeup, and made it back to the kitchen in twelve minutes flat.

"Wow." Robbie stared, his eyes agog. "Is that you, Mom?"

"You'll take his breath away," Patricia declared.

"Hopefully not until after the game. He'll need it to play." Emily's eyebrows rose as she eyed the fully loaded table. "You two pulled out all the stops." There was roast beef, gravy, broccoli smothered with cheese sauce, baked potatoes and sour cream, and three slices of pecan pie.

"We just nuked what was in the bags," Patricia said airily, and flashed a smile at Robbie as he finished setting the table. Robbie grinned and sent his grandmother a thumbs-up sign.

Emily laughed. Everything was going to be just fine.

She didn't think so an hour later when the Subway had a flat two miles short of the arena. While traffic belched and honked all around her, Emily stared at the offending tire in frustration and wanted to weep.

"What are we gonna do now, Mom?"

She fished in her purse for her cell phone. "Call a tow truck. We're blocking traffic."

They were. Three lanes of filled-to-capacity arena traffic now tried to squeeze into two, several drivers not hesitating to let Emily know what they thought of her timing. But for the first time in her life, Emily wasn't afraid of their anger. She had more important things to worry about.

****

Eric knew he was chasing a pipe dream, but as the strains of the national anthem began, his gaze searched the wives' section. Miranda had sounded funny on the phone this afternoon when he'd called Bill to discuss some last-minute strategy. To his relief she hadn't mentioned Emily, but her self-satisfied tone of voice had made him wonder. Miranda wasn't by nature a smug woman.

He scanned the seats reserved for the team's guests and recognized several of his teammates' girlfriends and family members. Miranda was there, belting out the Star Spangled Banner along with about twenty thousand other people who had more enthusiasm than talent. He spotted the two empty seats beside her, and tried not to hope. Still, if Emily planned to put in an appearance, it would have to be tonight.

The Star Spangled Banner ended. Still no Emily. Eric shoved his disappointment down deep inside. Time to forget about the woman once and for all, and focus on the game. This was it. The seventh of seven. Tonight, the Saints and the Bombers would finally see who took home the Cup. Eric took a deep breath, met Granger's eyes across the ice, and offered up his most chilling your-ass-is mine smile.

****

The tow truck arrived just as the game got underway. Emily heard the national anthem on the man's radio and wanted to scream in frustration. It seemed to take him forever to get the Subway hooked up to his truck. She paid the man, then picked up the art portfolio bag she'd retrieved from the Suburban earlier and leaned against a signpost. Snatching up Robbie's hand, she started walking toward the arena.

"Hey, lady, you want a ride?"

Her feet already stating to chafe in her new boots, she accepted the offer gratefully, but it meant they had to go all the way back down the access road and turn around again, which took a good twenty minutes.

By the time they pulled up in front of the arena they'd missed the first period. The first intermission was coming to a close as she and Robbie pushed through the turnstiles.

She found their section without any trouble since most of the spectators had already returned to their seats, but Miranda looked ready to blow a gasket.

"What happened to you? Where have you been?"

"Flat tire. Eric was right. The damned things are bald. We hit a board in the road and the right front tire fell apart."

"Are you all right?"

Emily leaned her portfolio against the seat, shook out her arm and blew out a determined breath. "We're tired, cranky, sweaty, and my feet hurt, but we're here, and that's what counts." She checked the score. The Saints were winning, two-one.

Miranda waved at the only unclaimed seats in the house. "Sit. Sit. Both of you. I'll get you something cool to drink."

"They're coming back out! There he is, Mom!"

Emily sank into her seat with deep sigh of gratitude, looked toward the ice, and felt her pain, tension, and anxiety melt away. She drank in the sight of Eric and knew she'd never tire of looking at him, under any circumstances. Wearing jeans and sneakers, suit and tie, uniform and pads, or nothing but bruises and scars, she loved him completely. She'd come here tonight prepared to prove it.

Miranda nudged her arm. "Here. Drink this."

"Thanks." Emily took a swallow, her gaze still following Eric. She nearly choked as the cool liquid burned her throat, then realized she was holding a mixed drink.

"Rum and coke," Miranda said. "It'll settle your nerves."

Emily nodded and took another fortifying swallow, her eyes locked on Eric. When the teams skated to the benches, she turned to Robbie and checked his forehead. His cheeks were flushed, but his brow was cool. "You all right, Tiger?" He assured her he was. She smiled and smoothed his hair. "Remember what you're supposed to do?"

He grinned. "Just as soon as you give the signal."

She looked around to see Miranda passing out the fourteen placards she'd carried inside her portfolio. Several of the wives turned to Emily and waved, smiling broadly.

"All set?" she asked as a noticeably pregnant Miranda eased into the seat on the other side of Robbie.

Miranda's eyes sparkled. "You bet. The girls can't wait."

"I just hope this doesn't backfire. The way my luck's been lately..."

"Trust me. You'll knock his skates off."

"Either that, or I'll embarrass us both in front of twenty thousand people."

Miranda grinned. "Don't forget the television audience."

Chapter Thirty-Four

Eric hurt in places he'd forgotten existed. The game was wide open and the fans were going nuts. The Bombers were going down, but not without a fight. They were determined to beat the crap out of any Saint who happened to be carrying the puck.

And everyone knew Eric Cameron liked to carry the puck.

He spotted nobody home in the Bombers' zone and headed that way. The puck danced against his stick as he sailed up the ice. The crowd's roar of approval was sweet music as his two wingers joined him in rushing the lone Bombers defenseman. Adrenaline raced through him like wildfire as he faked a pass to his left winger, then rushed the net. A split second later he spotted two blue jerseys homing in on his left. He twisted away before they could take him down, caught his own rebound, and tipped the puck past the goalie's outstretched leg.

Beautiful. The fans exploded. The siren wailed, Granger's glare could have forged steel. The Bombers defenseman who'd been caught with his pants down promised to make Eric eat a prized portion of his anatomy. Eric told him to get in line and skated for the bench.

Thirty seconds later he was back on the ice again, anticipating retribution's arrival. It appeared in the form of Clarence "Killer" Clementi. The hulking giant nailed Eric into the boards right after he intercepted a pass between two Bombers. Prepared for the hit, Eric grunted and rolled with it.

But Clementi wasn't done with him. The next time they met, he hooked Eric's legs out from under him. Eric went down hard, slammed into the ice, the air whooshing out of his lungs. He lay still for a few stunned seconds, waiting for the whistle to blow, the penalty to be called.

It wasn't. The game continued without him, the sharp scrape of steel against ice ringing in his ears. He scrambled to his feet on legs that felt like rubber bands and decided it was time to trade finesse for force. The thought had barely jelled before he spotted Clementi coming back for round three.

The fight was a whopper, one of his longest, and most intense. Clementi left the ice needing medical attention. Eric skated to the penalty box to do his time, plunked down on the bench, worked the kinks out of his aching arms and shoulders, then rolled his neck. His head still hummed from Clementi's left hook, since his face was still recovering from a close encounter with a crossbar a week earlier. True, the crossbar and not Clementi had nailed him on the jaw that night, but the Baltimore defenseman had been the force behind Eric's flight into the net.

He checked the situation on the ice. The Bombers had called a time out. The score was four-two with ten minutes to go. Half a period.

Half a lifetime.

But the team's brainstorming session this morning was paying off. The Saints were controlling the face-offs, and with the exception of an occasional run-in with Clementi, controlling the boards.

Now Clementi was gone. Across the rink, Granger was going apeshit. Eric itched to smirk at him, but knew better than to tempt fate. Victory wouldn't be his until the final siren sounded. He rolled his shoulders again. If he lived that long. When this was over he planned to crawl into the closest thing he could find to a cave and lose himself in it. Possibly permanently.

"Yo, Cameron," the official in the penalty box with him said. "You know somebody named E-W-I-L-Y?"

Eric removed his helmet and mouthpiece, reached for the water bottle. He doused his face in an effort to revive himself, then shook the water from his hair. "No, why?"

"Well, she either knows you or wants to. Take a look." The man hiked his chin toward the wives section.

Eric's heart shuddered to a stop. Three rows deep—in bright, bold, Minneapolis Saints purple and gold, the words EWILY LOVES ERIC screamed out at him.

Holding high the two-foot-square placards that bore one letter each were a dozen grinning women and one beaming boy—all staring straight at him. As fans began to elbow each other and point, Eric swallowed. Hard.

She'd come.

"Strange name," the man beside him mused. "Wonder how it's pronounced."

In silence Eric drank in the sight of the flame-haired woman who looked like some kind of supermodel in her light green sweater and blue jeans holding up the first "E"—the only woman in the group who wasn't grinning. Instead, she looked terrified—and near tears.

Slowly, he felt his aching body return to life.

She loved him.

The knowledge arrowed straight into his heart. Emily loved him. "Emily." Chest expanding, throat constricting, Eric breathed her name, unaware of anything at that moment but the joy rising inside him.

Someone must have said something to her, because with an adorable expression of dismay, Emily looked at the sign Robbie proudly held upside down beside her. She righted the "M" amid rumbles of laughter, rowdy cheers, and a ripple of applause.

"I take it you know the lady."

Eric sent the penalty box official a slow grin. "Not nearly well enough."

A horn sounded. The group in the stands sat down as one and tucked their signs away while the game resumed as if nothing out of the ordinary had occurred. After all, signs expressing support for the Saints filled the stands. Eric's name graced at least half of them.

But none had touched him like Emily's. He'd never forget looking up from the ice to find her watching him, telling him and the rest of his world how she felt about him. He stored the memory in his heart and returned his attention to the game. As the final seconds of his penalty ran out, he met Granger's contemptuous black eyes across the rink, smiled slowly, and exploded onto the ice.

The Saints won, six-three. Pandemonium erupted in the stands, mayhem on the ice. The Saints let loose with flying leaps and bear hugs, screamed, shouted and hugged each other in sheer exhilaration. Eric's teammates flew over the boards to join in the fray. The fans, not to be outdone, roared and surged forward. Eric glanced into the stands and decided the police deserved commendations all around.

Frenzied minutes later, as he skated into line for the post-game handshake between teams, he spotted Granger leaving the ice—alone. With startling ease, Eric let the past go with him. It no longer mattered. He looked into the stands again, spotted Emily and Robbie hugging, and knew why.

The time had come to look to his future. The past was over and done with.

Thirty minutes passed before the on-ice festivities ended—the presentation, the proclamation, and the picture. While Miranda took Robbie to buy souvenirs of the 'greatest team in the world,' Emily watched with blurred vision as the Saints took turns skating around the rink with the Cup hoisted above their heads, then posed for the official photo, Cup in the forefront.

The photo taken, the traditions observed, the Saints left the ice to head for the locker room party, waving to their families to join them. Emily spotted Eric deep in conversation with one of his alternate captains. As the other man skated away, smiling and shaking his head, Eric looked up at her—and beamed. Emily had never seen him look so proud, or so happy.

Just then Miranda and Robbie returned. Eric motioned for them to meet him outside the locker room, but by the time Emily and Robbie reached the corridor, it was so clogged with celebrants it took her ten minutes to move fifty feet.

"Emily! Emily! Over here!"

She scanned the sea of bobbing heads and spied Anna waving from a spot against the wall not twenty feet from the dressing room. Keeping Robbie close—Miranda had gone to meet Bill in Stump's skybox—Emily inched her way through the jostling crowd until Augustus reached out and pulled them between himself and Anna.

She squeezed herself against the wall and smiled apologetically. "I'm sorry. When I asked you to meet me here, I had no idea it would be such a madhouse."

"No problem at all, my dear," Augustus assured her.

"I haven't had this much fun since the Twins beat the Braves in the World Series."

Anna sent her husband a look of amused indulgence. "I'm surprised he isn't hoarse by now after all that shouting."

"Didja see our signs, Nanna?"

"Yes, and I liked yours the best."

Robbie beamed. "Do you think Eric liked them?"

"I think he'd be crazy not to." She looked up as a wave of excitement rippled through the crowd. "Here he comes now."

Emily turned to see Eric signing autographs at the entrance to the dressing room. His hair was wet and tousled, and he wore a damp Stanley Cup Champion T-Shirt that clung to his broad chest and biceps. She watched as he glanced around the crowd between signatures and smiles—until he spotted her by the wall. Her heart leapt as he excused himself, returned pen and pad to its owner, and started toward her. Their eyes locked, and Emily's breath backed up in her lungs. Eric picked up speed, all but plowing through the crowd, his body language daring his fans to move aside or risk being run over.

Reaching Emily, he hauled her into his arms for a victory kiss packed with enough voltage to light up the arena. Strangers hooted, cameras flashed, Robbie crowed, Anna beamed, Augustus chortled—and for a full minute Emily and Eric were oblivious to it all.

Eric pulled back first, kept one arm around Emily, scooped up Robbie with the other, then hugged them both, hard.

"God, I've missed you guys."

Chapter Thirty-Five

Emily awoke mid-morning to find herself surrounded by Eric. His face was buried in her hair, his arm draped across her midriff, one cotton-covered thigh territorially pinned her to the bed. She smiled, feeling utterly content...and well loved. They'd spent the night in the company of Eric's exultant teammates and friends, sharing in a madness that Emily wouldn't have asked Eric to miss for the world. He'd hesitated at first, but she'd insisted, and in the end they'd attended—and thoroughly enjoyed themselves at—half a dozen victory parties, the last of which had seen half the team and Lord Stanley's Cup cavorting in Bill and Miranda's backyard pool.

They'd returned to Eric's apartment just before dawn. Their coming together had been sweet and gentle, a slow, exquisite rebirth of their love while the sun gave birth to a new day. Emily had fallen asleep secure in her love for Eric, and his for her.

She eased away from him now, and slipped out of bed, his Stanley Cup Champion T-shirt falling to well past her thighs. Eric rolled onto his stomach, buried his nose in her pillow, murmured her name, then shifted his head and smiled. Her heart overflowed with love and she couldn't help but smile back.

Her gentle warrior. His hair was mussed, his jaw bruised and stubble-covered. He had half a dozen bruises on his back, and even more on his chest, but she'd never thought him more beautiful.

Silently she padded into the living room to stare out the window at the busy street below, and think about the night. It amazed her how easily Eric had accepted her return. How openly he'd welcomed her back. How proudly he'd introduced her to his teammates and their friends

and families. She wondered how much time they had
before he left for Barton.

Would he still leave? If he did, would he return in the
fall to play for the Saints? If he didn't, if he signed on with
another team, or was traded, would he ask her to follow
him? To quit her job? Sell her house? Uproot Robbie? She
considered the possibilities. With thirty teams in the
NHL, they could end up anywhere, from Boston to
Vancouver, Calgary to Tampa.

She wasn't sure how long she stood there, but as the
sun rose over the city, Eric slipped his arms around her
from behind. She welcomed his company, and leaned back
into his solid, sleep-warmed chest. He aligned their bodies
more closely, crossed his arms over hers and rested his
chin on her head.

"You're looking pretty serious this morning, Doctor.
What's the matter? Doesn't the prognosis look good?"

She turned in his arms, saw the vulnerability behind
his smile, the uncertainty in his eyes. It hurt her to know
she'd put it there; to know that no matter how deeply he
loved her, he might never again completely trust her.
She'd hurt him, badly, yet he'd welcomed her back
without question. He'd accepted her return on faith, and
deserved nothing less than her complete faith in him in
return.

It didn't matter where they went. What mattered
was being together, making sure she never again gave
Eric cause to doubt her love. Gently, she traced the bruise
on his shadowed jaw, stepped on her tiptoes to feather a
kiss across his lips, then smiled.

"On the contrary. Things have never looked better."

She had wonderful hands. Hands that healed and
aroused at the same time, they were nothing short of
magical. But then he'd always known that. It had been
her hands, the innate gentleness of her touch, that had
seduced him from the start. Eric lay on his stomach while
Emily straddled his hips, her hands moving surely and
soothingly across his back, drawing away the tension that
had knotted his vitals at waking up to find her gone.

He had no idea what she'd meant by 'things have
never looked better' but when she'd kissed him again,
long and deep and slow, then led him back to bed, he'd

have stopped breathing before he'd ask. Wordlessly, she'd stripped him of his pajama pants, her dark, depthless eyes not leaving his, then motioned for him to lie on his stomach. He'd complied...and discovered nirvana. The reality of Emily's hands on his battered body far exceeded his post-game fantasies. Surpassed even his most secret dreams.

"Roll over."

He blinked, and realized he'd nearly fallen asleep. He definitely didn't want to sleep through this. Moving slowly, as if through molasses, he pushed himself onto his back—and looked into the amused green eyes of an angel.

"You're enjoying this, aren't you?" he rumbled contentedly.

"Having you at my mercy? Completely."

She straddled him again and resumed her sweet torture. He found the smooth friction of her silk panties between them erotic as they slid across his skin in subtle rhythm with her hands. When he felt her dampness against his abs, an electric shock buzzed through his blood. It was all he could do not to rear up, roll her over and bury himself inside her.

But he held back, eager to see what else she had in store for him.

Her long, silken curls tickled him mercilessly and sensitized his nerve endings. She brushed butterfly kisses across his shoulders and chest, and smoothed her hands down his arms, her fingers flexing on his biceps as she molded their shape and contours. She linked her hands with his, then lifted her hips and moved lower, until she knelt between his spread thighs. The cool air on his damp, exposed abdomen fanned a fire that seared him with its heat.

But Emily didn't seem to notice. With warm, loving lips she blessed his bruises and ignited tiny fires across his skin as she moved from breast to navel. She released his hands and fluttered her fingers along the insides of his thighs. He closed his eyes in primal pleasure, and prayed he wouldn't explode. When her hand closed around him, he groaned in relief. When she took him inside her mouth, he nearly rocketed from the bed.

His head came up, his eyes glazed and unfocused, his

breath rough as his hands found her hair. "Emily...Emily you don't have to..."

Her smile was infinitely gentle. "I want to."

With that, she dipped her head and returned to him. His hands clenched and unclenched in her hair as she loved him with a devotion more shattering than anything he'd experienced.

"Emily...Emily...you have to stop. I'm going to— *Emily!!*"

He went rigid as blood rushed like wildfire to his groin. He gasped for air and made one last attempt to pull her away, but she stayed with him, her determination stronger. Crying out her name again, he poured himself into her.

Trembling, spent, unable to lift so much as a dust mote, he lay there, his breath ragged, his mind and body rippling with the aftershocks of his release. If he died at that moment, Eric knew he would meet his maker with sheer joy in his soul.

Slowly he opened his eyes, to find her watching him. Her green eyes glistened as she reached out and touched his face.

"I've never seen anything so beautiful."

Somehow he found the energy to cover her hand with his. "I need you next to me."

With a smile so full of love he thought he'd die from it, she drew the oversize T-shirt he'd given her over her head. Then she kicked off her panties and came to him, melting against him as he fitted their bodies together like hand to glove.

Nothing had ever felt so good, so right, so natural.

On a serrated sigh of content, he kissed her crown, his body still tingling. She snuggled against him and echoed his sigh with a deeply contented murmur of her own.

"You...are incredible," he breathed against her hair.

She smiled, kissed his pectoral. "No, I'm in love."

Chapter Thirty-Six

Emily emerged from her shower to find Eric lounging on the sofa in his boxers, watching ESPN on his big plasma screen and eating a sandwich.

"That for me?" she asked as she toweled her hair dry. A thick ham and cheese on rye occupied a plate on the coffee table. A tall glass of milk stood next to it.

He looked up and grinned lasciviously. "Could be. Depends on what you're willing to trade for it."

She smiled, sank onto the sofa beside him, and helped herself. "Keep your shorts on, Cameron. Take it from a doctor. Too much of a good thing can be detrimental to your health."

He laughed and returned his attention to the screen. ESPN was loaded with stories and perspectives on the Saints' victory the night before. The camera cut to a site in downtown Minneapolis, where fans were already gathering for the celebration the city would host to honor the team that afternoon.

Emily washed down her sandwich with the milk. "What time do you have to be there?"

"Not 'til three-thirty. Want to come?"

Emily hesitated. "I can't. Robbie will be looking for me when he gets home from school. His first day back and all."

Eric hit the remote and shut off the television. "No problem."

"You're sure?"

He shot her a strange look. "Why wouldn't I be? I know you have other commitments. I always have. I'd never ask you to choose between me and Robbie. You're his mother. You know what he needs. If he expects you to be at home when he gets there, then that's where you need to be." He reached for her hand. "I have no intention

339

of making unfair demands on your time, Emily. And team promotional events like this come under the heading of unfair demands in my book. Sure, I'd love to have you with me today, but it's enough just to know you're thinking about me." He squeezed her hand, then reached for his own milk and took a long swallow. "Besides, it's going to be a madhouse down there. I'd spend all my time worrying about you getting trampled or something."

"You'll come by the house when you're done?"

He wiggled his brows. "I'll even bring my overnight bag if you want me to."

"Er...I don't know about that."

"You think Robbie would have a problem with me sleeping in the guest room?"

"No...but I think my houseguest would." At his look of surprise, Emily exhaled resignedly. "We need to talk, Eric. About the reason I told you I couldn't see you anymore."

Slowly, he returned his glass to the coffee table. "All right. What do you want to know?"

"Want to know?"

"About what happened with my ex-wife."

"Nothing."

Her lack of hesitation stunned him. "Nothing?"

"Unless you want to tell me, of course. But I don't have any questions. I know you didn't beat her."

Eric blinked. He'd waited an eternity for someone to accept his innocence on faith, and to have that person be Emily...

He swallowed past the lump in his throat. "How do you know that?"

"I spent twenty years living in fear of my father," she said quietly, stunning him anew. "I spent another three married to an abuser as well. Both of them were cowards. You may be many things, Eric, but you're no coward. You'd never hit a woman."

Touched beyond measure, Eric leaned back against the couch and opened his arms. "C'mere."

She set her empty plate aside, wrapped her arms around his neck and snuggled against his chest as if there were nowhere she'd rather be, no one she trusted more. Eric closed his eyes, felt the peace build inside him, pressed his lips to her hair and tightened his arms around her, holding fast to her love.

"Do you have any idea how much I love you?" he whispered, his voice catching.

She looked up at him and smiled demurely. "And here I thought it was only lust."

He grinned, his equilibrium restored. "I'll show you lust."

Half an hour later, sweated and sated, they lay tangled together on the sofa, Emily sprawled atop Eric, each unable to remember when they'd had so much fun.

"Lord, woman. Anyone ever tell you you're a wild one?"

Emily lifted her head from his chest, her hair in total disarray, her eyes sparkling like emeralds. "Me? You're the one who nearly bounced us onto the floor!"

Eric laughed, then winced as a muscle spasm shot through his lower back. "I guess I did get a little enthusiastic there, but...damn...I think we'd better move this to the bed."

Emily scrambled off of him. "Are you okay?"

He grimaced as his lumbar muscles spasmed again. "You're the doctor. You tell me."

She did. Before he knew it he was lying on his stomach in bed with an ice pack on his lower back, and Emily sitting cross-legged beside him, her back propped against two pillows and the headboard. Eric enjoyed the view of her thigh up close and personal while above him she combed the tangles from her still-damp hair. "So tell me about your houseguest," he said contentedly. It didn't get any better than this. The two of them alone, relaxed and happy and talking in bed. "Is it someone you brought back from home?"

"No. It's my ex-mother-in-law."

He frowned. "Your ex-mother in law?" That didn't make sense. Hadn't Anna told him...?

He noticed Emily had gone very still. He looked up and thought she seemed to be bracing herself for something. He started to rise. "Honey? What's wrong?"

She took a deep breath and blurted, "I really don't know how to explain this, Eric, but my ex-husband and his family live in St. Paul. You met then at the United

341

Hope banquet. John and Patricia Montgomery. They were sitting with Ronald and Catherine Stump."

Eric felt the shock all the way to his toes. Slowly he rolled over and sat up, causing the ice bag to fall off his back and on to the floor with a plop. "Those were your *in-laws?*"

Emily bit her lower lip and nodded uncertainly. "Unfortunately, yes."

He stared at her in confusion and disbelief. "Why didn't you tell me?" But before she could frame an answer, Eric had an untenable thought. "You mean you were married to—"

"Ryan Montgomery."

Eric continued to stare, his heart pounding. "The same Ryan Montgomery who is engaged to Catherine Stump?"

Her smile was brittle. "Small world, isn't it?"

Eric felt his control slipping fast. He looked away, took a deep breath and exhaled slowly, curbing his rage. "Eric?"

He reached out and took her hand, gave it a reassuring squeeze. "I'm okay, sweetheart. I'm okay."

She nodded, still looking uncertain, but accepting his words at face value. He squeezed her hand again, firmly, understanding that she was nervous about his reaction.

"One question. Is he the bastard who attacked you while I was in St. Louis?"

****

An hour after he dropped Emily off at her house, Eric parked his Boxter in front of an ivy-covered brownstone in one of the more exclusive sections of St. Paul and checked the address he'd looked up while Emily dressed for the trip home. One good thing about doctors, they were listed in the phone book.

He entered the foyer and checked the directory. Montgomery's offices were on the third floor. He hoped Montgomery was, too. His anger was ripe now. He didn't want to have to come back.

"Is the doctor in?" he asked the stunning blonde seated behind the receptionist's desk. Advertising at its best, he noted dryly. Sign on the dotted line and you, too can look this perfect was the subliminal message she'd no doubt been hired to project.

Her eyes widened in recognition or apprehension, he didn't care which. "Yes, but he's with—"

"Good." Eric strode past her, hearing only the yes.

"Wait a minute! You can't—"

Eric already had the inner office door thrown open. Montgomery was dead ahead. He looked disgustingly successful and trustworthy, standing behind his massive mahogany desk in his Armani suit, cordless phone in hand. His Florida tan faded a shade when he saw Eric.

Slowly Montgomery lowered the phone but continued to grip it, a nervous, watchful fear entering his eyes.

The slightly breathless receptionist spoke from behind Eric. "I'm sorry, Doctor, but—"

"Call the police, Ashley," he interrupted, his eyes not leaving Eric.

"Don't bother, Ashley," Eric said. "This won't take long. In fact, you're welcome to stay as a witness." He strode forward and braced his knuckles on Montgomery's big desk, then leaned forward until Montgomery stepped backward. "Sit," he barked.

Montgomery did—so fast Eric nearly blinked in surprise. Instead he leaned closer, his voice deliberately low with menace, his game face harder than any he'd used in the rink. "Now listen carefully, *Doctor*, because I'm not counting on any PFA order to take care of *my* business and I'm only going to say this once. If you call, or come within a hundred yards of Emily or Robbie again, you're going to need your own professional services. Is that clear?"

Montgomery flushed, made a futile effort to rally. "Now listen here, Cameron, you can't—"

"I can and I will. Make no mistake about it, Montgomery. There won't be a hole deep or dark enough for you to hide in if I have to come looking for you again."

He waited for that to sink in, straightened, and smiled coldly. "And for the record, it wasn't me who arranged that interview between Emily and Carmen Martinez, it was your mother."

Montgomery looked as if he'd been slapped in the face with a fish.

"Excuse me, Eric. But would you mind telling me

what this is all about?"

Catherine Stump sat on Montgomery's long leather couch, her legs elegantly crossed, a glossy magazine in her lap.

"Catherine."

She smiled enigmatically. "Quite a surprise, I'm sure." She set her magazine aside and rose gracefully. "You mentioned Ryan's ex-wife and, I believe, a protection from abuse order. Is there a problem?"

The lady had chutzpa, but Eric had always known that. He was glad she was there. It was time she discovered what sort of slime she planned to marry. "Only if you consider emotional blackmail, verbally abusive phone calls, terroristic threats and assault a problem."

Montgomery shot to his feet. "He's lying, Catherine! I never—"

She froze him with a look. "You threatened and assaulted Emily?"

"Almost nine weeks ago, in the Minneapolis General parking lot," Eric said, and turned to face Emily's attacker. "He waited for her after work. After dark." Lifting an eyebrow, he challenged Montgomery to make a move, any move.

Montgomery stayed put. "I swear to you, Catherine, he's—"

"He's got no reason to lie, Ryan."

"Of course he has!"

She arched her own elegant eyebrow. "Give me one."

"She put him up to it. She sent her...her goon lover in here to terrorize me into...into giving her alimony."

Eric was amazed Catherine didn't burst out laughing. He certainly wanted to. "After nine years, Ryan? I hardly think so. She moved past you a long time ago."

Montgomery flushed, but remained mute. Catherine calmly approached him, placed something small and chunky in the center of his immaculate burgundy desk blotter. As it sparkled in the afternoon sun, Eric realized it was her engagement ring.

She turned to face him and said, "I hate to trouble you, Eric, but I suddenly find myself in need of a ride into Minneapolis."

Chutzpa and class. Emily would love it when he told her—about twenty years from now. He smiled and turned toward the door. "My pleasure. I'm headed that way myself."

Without a backward glance, Catherine preceded him from the office and glided calmly past the shell-shocked receptionist. Unable to resist, Eric paused at the threshold and turned back to Montgomery. What he saw killed the parting shot he'd planned to deliver.

Ashen-faced as he gripped the edges of his mahogany desk, Montgomery looked like a man who'd just seen his life's ambition go up in smoke.

****

"You do realize you've just done me a huge favor, don't you?" Catherine asked as Eric drove to the celebration she'd planned to attend with Ryan. "I've been considering breaking off with the man for months."

Eric said nothing. He didn't consider it his business. Nor did he particularly care. But he was curious about one thing. "Would you mind if I asked what attracted you to Montgomery in the first place?"

Catherine laughed. "I've often wondered that myself. The best I can come up with is I'd recently been burned by a long-term relationship that I realized too late was going nowhere, was thirty-five and holding, and was convinced I was going to spend the rest of my life alone. Ryan appeared at a party I'd gone to in one of my more desperate moods, and seemed to be just what I thought I was looking for."

She laughed again. Softly. Eric wondered if it was so she wouldn't cry. "You'd never know it by his performance today, but he's usually articulate, witty, charming, and extremely good at sweeping a girl off her feet. He wined me, dined me, charmed me into bed, and before I knew it, I had a ring on my finger the size of the rock of Gibraltar. Pretty heady stuff for a woman who hadn't gotten a ring in ten years in her previous relationship.

"It was definitely a rebound thing. Ryan was educated, successful, a respected professional, reasonably well off, and I'd never met anyone who could hold a candle to him in social niceties. The perfect escort. Never a hair out of place, never a faux pas to be found." She cast Eric a

345

wry, almost self-deprecating glance, then gave him a glimpse of the woman behind her sophisticated façade. "Believe it or not, I learned a lot from him."

Her sudden shift toward informality intrigued Eric. "About?"

"The secret society of the elite. By dating Ryan, whose blood is considered blue by St. Paul's upper echelons, I had access to a world I've never quite managed to break into, despite daddy's millions. Did you know my birth name is Stumpinski? Daddy shortened it to Stump so it would sound like Trump. Pretty ridiculous, huh?"

Eric said nothing for a long moment, then: "Listen, Catherine. You're an intelligent, savvy, beautiful woman. You could put together a marketing strategy to sell ice cubes to Eskimos. You've got class, chutzpa, and a good amount of street smarts. You know when to jump in with both feet, and when to sit back and watch. I really don't think your name matters one way or the other, but if you didn't feel a little insecurity now and then—for whatever reason—you wouldn't be human."

He looked over to find her staring at him with something akin to astonishment—and regret. "Why didn't I look past that to-die-for body when I had the chance?"

Eric chuckled.

"I'm sorry. That was—"

"Very flattering. Thank you."

He pulled into the parking area reserved for the team and followed the attendant's sweeping directions, aware of Catherine watching and weighing his every move. He snagged a spot he hoped would give him a quick exit after the ceremonies, killed the Boxter's engine and looked at his unexpected passenger.

"It's been a pleasure, Catherine."

She studied his face, then nodded slowly. "Indeed it has. Emily's a very lucky woman."

"She's made me a very happy man."

"Really?" Catherine's smile of delight was genuine. "When's the date?"

"Date? Oh." Eric grinned sheepishly. "Don't know. I haven't asked her yet."

Catherine's sophistication vanished completely. "Well, for heaven's sake, boy, what are you waiting for?"

346

"The name of a good jeweler?"

****

When Eric returned to his car over two chaotic hours later, he found Catherine leaning against the Boxter's front fender. She looked slightly pale and ten times more troubled than she had when they'd parted company. Second thoughts about dumping Montgomery?

Cripes, he hoped not. "What's up, Catherine?"

"Drive me to Fanelli's and I'll tell you."

Since the jeweler she'd recommended had been his next stop anyway, he unlocked the passenger door and ushered her inside. As they cruised uptown in silence he bided his time. He didn't want to get any more involved in Catherine Stump's problems than he already had. Somehow he didn't think Emily would appreciate it if he took to consoling her ex-husband's ex-fiancé.

When she'd said nothing by the time they reached the jewelry store, he figured whatever she'd wanted to tell him, she'd changed her mind. Fine by him. He'd just pulled the keys from the ignition when she dropped her bomb.

"If I were you, I'd call my agent in the morning. My father's decided to sell the Saints. Come fall the team's headed for California. He just told me."

"But we just won the Cup." It was the only thing Eric could think of to say. He was too stunned to think.

"Which makes the team his hottest ticket right now." Her eyes grew uncharacteristically vulnerable. "He's hurting, Eric. Financially. It's no secret he overextended himself this year, trying to prove his point with the Saints. He poured so much into the new arena and team, his real estate interests—the resorts, hotels and shopping malls—are suffering."

He'd heard the rumors, but... "How bad is it?"

"He's going into Chapter 11 as soon as the hoopla over the Saints dies down. In the meantime he's going to milk it for all he can get. He has no emotional ties to the team. Not like...not like me."

Surprisingly, she looked embarrassed. "Why are you telling me this?"

"You did me a big favor today. I like to repay my debts. I also know your contract's up. And while I'm sure the front office will happily renew it unless you get all big-headed and demand a few more millions—which you well deserve after the miracle you pulled off this year—but you didn't hear that from me—I thought you might want a head start on finding a job closer to home."

Closer to home. Closer to Emily.

Eric closed his eyes and swore.

"My sentiments, exactly." Catherine opened her door. "Thanks for the ride. My condo's just up the street. The salon's open for another half hour. Ask for Henri. Tell him I sent you."

"Wait." She paused, hand on the door, eyebrows raised. "Will you be all right?"

Her smile was brilliant, but Eric saw the sadness beneath it. "Of course. I'm a Stumpinski. I thrive on challenges, live for corporate power plays. I'll be so deep in sharks I won't have time to notice I'm still single."

"But they will, Catherine. Trust me."

"It's not a shark I want, Eric. I want a partner."

In one fluid movement she slipped out of the Boxter and was gone.

Chapter Thirty-Seven

Eric pulled into Emily's driveway at seven-thirty, still wondering how to break the news to her. He had a week, two at most before any official announcements were made, but rumors could start any minute. He swore again, and almost wished Catherine hadn't told him. Then he would have been able to ask Emily to marry him with a clear conscience.

He couldn't ask her now, not without telling her about California.

Robbie answered the door and led him to Emily and Patricia, seated at a set kitchen table, their plates clean, unused. They'd waited for him. "Sorry I'm late."

Emily smiled in welcome. "No problem. Eric, this is Patricia. Patricia, Eric." Emily stood and gave Eric a quick kiss, as if she did so every night of the week when he came home for dinner. Happiness bubbled inside him at the thought. "Patricia and I were just discussing ideas for redecorating the house."

Redecorating the house. Strengthening her roots. Eric's bubble burst as he felt a stab of guilt and forced a smile. "Let me know if I can help. I'm handy enough with a toolbox and I'll be free most of the summer." At least they'd have that much.

Emily laughed. "We're talking accent pillows and wallpaper borders—not full scale remodeling." She smiled and patted his cheek affectionately. "But thank you. I might call you if I find a good sale on siding."

Home and hearth, Eric thought dully, taking a seat at Emily's insistence while she and Patricia put dinner on the table. Never had it felt so right. Never had it seemed so far out of reach.

"You're quiet tonight," Emily said later, as they sat on her front porch and watched the occasional car roll by.

The grandfather clock in the hall had chimed nine times just moments earlier. Through the windows, they could hear Robbie and Patricia talking as they watched the first Harry Potter movie. Patricia had never seen any of the Potter movies, and Robbie had found that inconceivable. He'd made it his personal mission to bring her up to speed on the storyline.

Eric stared at the stars and felt the ring burn a hole in his pocket. He couldn't propose to Emily under false pretenses. But he couldn't bring himself to tell her about the Saints being sold yet, either. Not after she and Patricia had spent most of dinner tossing color schemes and tile pattern ideas back and forth across the table. Even Robbie was excited at the prospect of changing his room from Batman to something more grown up.

"Pretty big project you and Patricia are planning." By dessert, it had somehow grown in scope to include several rooms, paint, new drapes, carpeting, and something called chair rails.

Emily smiled. "She's a very good decorator. I think this will be just what she needs to get back on her feet—restore her self-confidence."

Her compassion and generosity touched him in ways he couldn't describe. It also made him shake his head. The woman desperately needed a new car, reliable transportation, but was more concerned with turning her own home inside out to boost another woman's morale. A woman who had once stood against her in court and society. Eric liked Patricia well enough, but couldn't understand Emily's willingness to drown herself in debt just to make her former mother-in-law feel better.

"And what will it do for you," he asked quietly. "It's going to cost a bundle to do this place over the way Patricia sees it, Emily." He knew better than to offer to help with expenses. She'd veto that so fast his nose would spin.

Emily laughed, surprising him. "I can't believe you're worried about that."

"This from the woman who was waiting for her tax refund to get a tune-up for the Subway?"

"That was when I was putting four siblings through school."

350

He arched a skeptical eyebrow. "They're all graduating? At the same time?"

"No, silly. They found me out and forced me to close up shop."

She looked so pleased and proud he couldn't stay upset with her. "Sounds like you had quite a visit with your family."

"It was wonderful, Eric. I wish you could have been there."

He looked into her eyes and wanted to lose himself in the peace and love he saw there. He reached out and touched her cheek, and wished they were back in his apartment, alone and naked. "Take me there now. Tell me what it was like."

She did, painting such a warm picture of family togetherness it made his heart ache. In Turnersville, she had found what he had longed for all of his life. Emily Jordan was the answer to his prayers, but he, with his rootless, erratic lifestyle, would be the downfall of her dreams. Anyone with eyes could see Emily was the kind of woman who needed a home to call her own. Not a series of rented houses and spur of the moment moves.

How many times had he moved in the past ten years? Six? Seven? How many more times would he pull up stakes before he decided to retire? And what would be waiting for him then?

Damn it. He wanted it now. He wanted it all. Emily and Robbie, a house to come home to, a career that didn't tear him in two every time he turned around...

He exhaled heavily and decided to follow Catherine's advice. He'd call his agent in the morning. Once he knew what his options were, he'd be able to put things in perspective. He hoped.

Emily heard the weary resignation in Eric's sigh and felt a pang of guilt. But no regret. She'd deliberately chosen the best of her memories of her visit with her family in an effort to show Eric how much she wanted to share with him. How much she wanted him to stay a part of her life. She wanted him to know not only could he count on her, but the entire Jordan clan if need be.

Instead she'd made him withdraw.

"I'm sorry. I didn't mean to bring you down," she

said, hiding her disappointment.

"Bring me down? You didn't do anything to—"

"Ruin your mood, then."

"Honey, you didn't do anything to ruin my mood. It's just—" He caught himself. There was really no direction he could take that wouldn't hurt her. He settled for saying, "It's just that what you described...with your family and all...it's very different from the life I've known."

And not nearly as appealing as she'd hoped, Emily thought dismally. "You've never told me what it was like, growing up in Barton." She didn't want to discuss the life he led now. She wanted to make connections, not comparisons that might hurt her cause. "Do you still have family there?"

"No. There's no one since my mother died."

"Would you tell me about her? About your childhood?"

For the longest time, he said nothing. Emily was about to suggest they rejoin Robbie and Patricia when he said, "In the beginning, she was a lot like you. Soft and pretty, loving and caring, proud and determined." He sent her a quiet smile. "Very proud and determined. She was the only child of a banker in International Falls, about twenty-five miles east of Barton. She eloped with my father when she turned eighteen. Ten months later I came along.

"She was young, but she was the kind of mom every kid dreams of having. You might say we grew up together. She loved classical music, fairy tales, crossword puzzles, sunshine and spring. And her cello. It was the only thing she took with her when she eloped."

Emily was fascinated. "The cello was your mother's?"

"She hadn't played for years, but I couldn't bring myself to sell it after she died."

"Did she teach you to play?"

"No. I was too cool for that."

"I see. What made you change your mind?"

"Time. Maturity. Knee surgery. I was laid up for a year or so with nothing but time on my hands, so I decided to bring it down from Barton and give it a shot. This might sound strange, but when I play, I feel close to her, like maybe she's listening to me the way I listened to her play."

Emily smiled. She couldn't wait to hear Eric play. "And your father?"

The warmth in his eyes withered. "He owned a bar just outside of town. It wasn't much of a place, an old two-story farmhouse he'd picked up at an estate auction. Most of his customers came from a manufacturing plant a quarter of a mile down the road. They'd stop on their way home to unwind. Looking back, I think he must've seen my mother—the banker's daughter—as his ticket to easy street.

"Only it didn't work out that way. My grandfather disowned her when she ran off with my father, who was a good ten years older than she was. After I was born she tried to mend the rift between them, but her father was too proud to budge.

"Once, when I was six, she took me to see him." He looked at her then, his face stark and emotionless. "The first and last memory I have of my grandfather is him telling my mother, 'I have no daughter' and shutting this big oak door in our faces."

Eric pushed himself to his feet, walked to the shadowed end of the porch. "She cried all the way home. I'll never forget the sight of her, not saying a word, just looking straight ahead and driving and crying those silent tears. A few days later, my father took his own drive and never came back. Just like that, he disappeared. My mother didn't know he'd left her until she found out he'd cleaned out the bank accounts and the bar till. She'd thought he was on one of his monthly liquor-buying trips to International Falls. Turned out those were fake, too. The next delivery of liquor showed up right on time—and my mother had to figure out how to make it pay for itself, and us, if we wanted to eat.

"She talked the guy into giving her two weeks to pay, sold whatever she could to handle the booze bill, moved us into the three-room apartment over the bar, and took up barkeeping. Eighteen hours a day. The first shift from the plant would come in at eight, the third would leave around two the next morning. The only time I saw her between shifts, she was usually napping. Otherwise, she was working."

He turned and met Emily's eyes. "She worked like a dog, but she made that place support us. We always had enough food on the table, and she even managed to put some money away—which I didn't find out about until she died. The bar itself was never hers, so I couldn't inherit that, but somehow she managed to save up almost forty thousand dollars over the years."

He shook his head. "She never spent any money on herself. Everything she did was for me. Still, I grew up fast, living over that bar. By eight I'd discovered hockey and was a rink rat, just to get away from the endless smoke and noise. On the ice, I could build up my strength, work out my anger, vent my frustrations. Managed to turn myself into a hockey player—while my mother managed to turn herself into a lush."

He turned away again and shoved his hands into his pockets. "Leaving her was the hardest thing I ever had to do. But I knew if I stayed in Barton I'd end up washing beer glasses and busting up fights for the rest of my life. So at sixteen I left school and headed for the Junior Hockey League in Canada, promising her I'd get her out of that hellhole as soon as I was making some money.

"It never happened. She died three years later."

Emily didn't speak. She couldn't. Her throat was locked tight.

Eric looked at the sky, his voice breaking. "She was only thirty-seven."

Emily responded with her heart. She stood and slid her arms around Eric, pressed her face into his back and willed him to give her his pain. He remained rigid for several agonizing seconds, then slowly removed his hands from his pockets, turned, and wrapped his arms around her. A long moment later, he buried his face in her hair.

How long they stood there in the shadows of the porch, Emily didn't know. Nor did she care. She'd hold him forever if he needed her to. Finally he lifted his head, his eyes dark with grief and wet with tears. Gently she brushed them away, kissed his damp cheek. "Come on, let's go upstairs."

Eric looked down at Emily and wondered how he could leave her tonight, how he'd ever be able to leave her again. He needed her too damned much. She represented everything he'd lost, everything he longed to have again.

But he had nothing but upheaval to offer her in return.

Feeling raw inside, he scraped up the strength to release her. "No, I have to go."

"But it's still early."

He slid his hands into his pockets to keep from touching her again. "Yeah, but I'm not the best of company tonight."

"Which is exactly why you shouldn't be alone." She placed a palm against his cheek. "I want you to stay, Eric."

He eased away from her all-too-tempting touch. "I don't want your pity."

Her eyes flashed, but she spoke quietly. "I'm not offering pity. I'm offering a good night's sleep and a big breakfast. I'm offering a chance to be coddled by a woman who loves you to distraction. I'm offering the dubious honor of being pounced on at some unspeakably early hour by an eight-year-old boy who adores you. I'm offering—"

"Okay, okay, I get it." Eric smiled as he captured her hands against his heart to silence her.

"Then you'll stay?"

The words seemed to have a deeper meaning, but Eric was too tired to get into any more heavy stuff tonight. He brought her hands to his lips and kissed them. "I'll stay. But no coddling."

She grinned and bussed him on the mouth. "We'll just see about that."

Chapter Thirty-Eight

Eric awoke to the sound of Saturday morning cartoons, the aroma of hot bacon and coffee, and the soft, sweet comfort of Emily's peaches and cream bed. He thought he was dreaming, until he felt something light and sweet smelling tickle his nose. Slowly he opened his eyes, stared at the dainty white eyelet ruffle on the pillow beside him, and broke into a smile.

Closing his eyes again, he rolled onto his back, stretched, and felt Emily's scent wrap him in its warm embrace. Heaven on earth, he thought. There was no other way to describe it. And no other place he wanted to wake up again.

She'd coddled the hell out of him last night, rubbed the tension from his neck with her magical hands and fed him popcorn while they finished watching Harry Potter with Patricia and Robbie. By the time it was over, he'd made a decision.

He heard a rustle and lifted a lazy eyelid. Emily leaned against the doorframe watching him, dressed in flour-smudged jeans and an old sweatshirt. Her soft, welcoming smile sealed his fate.

"About time you woke up. I was beginning to think I'd have to send Robbie in here after all." She came to sit on the edge of the bed and brushed his hair from his forehead with fingers as gentle as dawn. Coddling again. He liked it too much to protest.

"What time is it?"

"Just past noon."

"You're kidding." He checked the nightstand clock. "Why didn't you wake me?"

"You obviously needed the sleep." Something uncertain flickered in her eyes, but before he could anchor the thought, she smiled and patted his chest. "But now

356

it's time to get to work." She leaned forward and gave him a peck on the lips. "Come on, lazybones, rise and shine."

He caught her wrist as she rose. "Not until I get a proper good morning kiss."

"Sorry, bud. You missed morning. You'll have to catch me some other time."

"Like fun." He tugged at her arm and she tumbled back onto the bed, where he brought her close for a long, deep, highly *im*proper kiss. She melted against him, and tasted of coffee, cinnamon, and sunshine.

"I missed you last night," he murmured against her lips.

Her eyes turned a dark, sultry green and her fingers curled into his chest hair as his palm caressed her backside. "I missed you, too."

"I still think you cheated," he said, nuzzling her nose, referring to the duly witnessed coin toss that had squelched his protests when she'd suggested their sleeping arrangements. She'd slept on the couch downstairs, and sent him to her much more comfortable room with a smug smile and a playful swat on the rear.

She kissed him again, a loud, wet smack. "You're right."

With a low rumble of laughter, he flipped them over so she lay beneath his chest, her legs draped over his hips. Capturing her hands on either side of her head, he proceeded to kiss her until they were both hot and breathless. When he lifted his head, her eyes were soft and dewy with love, and a surprising wistfulness.

"Emily?" Patricia called from downstairs, "Where do you keep the bread basket? Oh! Never mind. I found it!"

Eric glanced at the open doorway, startled by the reminder they weren't alone in the house. "Is that breakfast I smell?" he asked, corralling his hormones. Obviously the wistfulness in her eyes was because Emily *hadn't* forgotten her houseguest.

"Brunch. We've got ham, bacon, eggs, home fries, fresh fruit, cinnamon-apple muffins fresh from the oven—"

Eric's stomach gurgled. "Honey, you've got to stop spoiling me."

"We're not spoiling you. We're bribing you. You won't

feel spoiled after you've spent a few hours lugging furniture from one end of the house to the other." Her smile was lofty. "Because while *we* were on our second cup of coffee, and *you* were snoozing the day away, Patricia and I decided to start with Robbie's room. They picked out the paint and carpeting while I made the muffins. The carpet will be delivered on Tuesday."

Eric's stomach muscles tightened. He hadn't expected them to start so soon. "You're not wasting any time, are you?"

"Not when I've got a warm, breezy day, a whole weekend off and three extra pairs of hands at my disposal." She hesitated, suddenly looking uncertain. "Unless you have other plans?"

He smiled and told her with his eyes there was nowhere he'd rather be. "My hands are yours." He kissed her nose. "Just tell me where you want them first."

They consumed a huge brunch, then got down to business. Emily and Robbie sorted through Robbie's things for Goodwill, while Eric hauled boxes and furniture out of the room and replaced it with tarps, ladders and paint supplies. Rock tunes from CDs "Aunt Lise" had burned for Robbie blasted from his boom box as Patricia taped baseboards, window frames and light sockets, and Robbie peeled his posters and Saints hockey memorabilia from the walls.

Emily had them all painting, and directed Robbie's somewhat sloppy efforts with patience and an unshakable sense of humor that endeared her to Eric all the more. By dusk, they'd listened to Robbie's CDs until the beat echoed in their brains, their backs and shoulders ached, and their arms felt like they were ready to fall off...but the room was done.

Ravenous, they devoured two large, fully-loaded pizzas Emily had sent out for. After dinner, Robbie scooted off to watch TV, Eric cleared the table, and Emily and Patricia huddled over the wallpaper and paint samples like field-tested generals, plotting the transformation of their next target—the dining room.

As he ran hot water into the sink and added a squirt of detergent, Eric decided he had no complaints. Between the playoffs and painting, every muscle in his body ached, but spending the day with Emily, working side by side, had filled him with a sense of completeness he'd never thought he'd find.

His only regret was tonight he'd go back to his apartment alone. No way he'd let Emily sleep on the couch again after the day she'd put in, and with Robbie's bed stashed in Emily's room until his carpet came, the chances of joining her there tonight were nil.

He slid their dirty dishes into the soapy water, then glanced at the table to see if he'd missed anything—and found Emily watching him. Again. Several times during the afternoon he'd caught her doing the same, as if she were storing pictures of him in her memory. The feeling had unsettled him then, and it did now.

Patricia asked her a question and she turned to answer, leaving Eric feeling more on edge than he had all day. Now that the evening was winding down, he wanted to be alone with Emily. He wanted to sort out their future...before this redecorating business got out of hand. He didn't want her to spend a lot of time and money on the house if they weren't staying in Minneapolis. He thought of her soft, peaches and cream bed again, and felt a slow ache unfurl inside him.

Damn it. He didn't want to go back to his apartment. He wanted to start their life together now. Tonight.

He plunged his hands into the hot water and vented his frustration on the flatware. He had to be patient. Patricia needed Emily right now. Once Patricia was re-settled, there would be plenty of time for him and Emily.

Or would there? What if news of the sale of the Saints broke first?

Suddenly Emily slipped her arms around him from behind and pressed her slender body against his back. Eric looked over his shoulder in surprise and saw they were alone.

"Do you have any idea what watching you do dishes does to me?" She nipped at his paint-speckled T-shirt and ran her hands suggestively up his chest.

Eric grinned and reached for a towel to dry his hands, carrying her with him as he leaned forward. He turned to take her in his arms and braced his hips against the sink. "Not a clue. Why don't you tell me?"

She moved closer, into the welcoming cradle of his thighs. "I'd rather show you, but for now I'll just say it makes me want to drag you off to somewhere private and have my wicked way with you."

"I'll have to do dishes more often."

"As often as you like. So whaddaya say? Wanna go upstairs and indulge in a few fantasies? Maybe share a shower?"

He swallowed his surprise. "What about Robbie and Patricia?"

She traced a finger along the shell of his ear. "Robbie's asleep on the couch. Tucked in as snug as a bug in a rug." Her smile became satisfied as she felt his response swell against her belly. "And Patricia went up to bed five minutes ago, claiming complete exhaustion. So it's just you and me, cowboy. And suddenly I'm wide awake and lonely."

They showered by barely-there candlelight. Emily surprised again him by suggesting they make love in silence, communicating only with their bodies. The idea made sense, with Robbie and Patricia in the house, but Eric soon discovered sense had nothing to do with it. The experience of relying on touch alone to bring Emily pleasure was unbelievably erotic.

He immersed himself in the moment and reveled in the magic of her hands as she drew the day's tension from him with slow, sensual abandon. As they slid across his soap-slick skin, soothing, claiming and demanding, he discovered erogenous zones he'd never dreamed existed. Her touch nearly drove him wild, but he deliberately held back and honored their agreement, until Emily's kisses and caresses took on a strange edge of what almost felt like desperation.

"Honey?"

"Just kiss me, Eric. Please."

He recalled the disquiet he'd sensed in her earlier and reached for her, determined to make her forget anything but him. Steam filled the room as he tasted, tested, nipped and nuzzled. By the time he'd explored all there was to explore of her twice over, she was as soft as water beneath his hands and he was rock hard.

He wrapped his arms around her, brought her flush

against him and kissed her deeply, meeting her need with his own. Beneath the hot, pummeling spray he grasped her thighs and pulled her onto him. Swallowing her sharp cry of relief, he pressed her back against the tile and drove into her, feeding on her now almost desperate hunger.

Her legs locked around his waist like a vise, binding him to her in a way both primal and eternal. He felt her muscles convulse around him and with a low growl of possession gave a final thrust and exploded into her.

Afterward, she clung to him in silence, her face buried in his neck. He reached behind him to kill the steamy spray. The air was so thick with humidity he could barely breathe. For a long moment he held her, his heart thudding hard. When he had his pulse rate and breathing under control again, he slid the shower door open and lifted her into his arms.

She remained silent as he gently toweled her dry, then dried himself. Wrapping another towel around her to protect her from the blast of cold air that would hit them when they opened the bathroom door, he decided she was simply too wrung out from her day to speak. His own legs felt as weak as a baby's.

Her peaches and cream bed was a cinch to find in the moonlight that streamed through the bedroom window. Within seconds he had them settled in, an arm curved around Emily's shoulders while she lay with her cheek against his chest. He kissed her temple, closed his eyes and smiled against her still damp hair. She wasn't wide-awake or lonely any more.

He was just about to drift off when the first hot tear hit his cooling skin. He stilled and hoped he'd imagined it. Then the second tear scalded him, followed by a third.

"Emily?" She stiffened beside him, and he realized she must have thought he'd fallen asleep. "Honey, what's wrong?" On the heels of his question came a terrifying thought. "Did I hurt you?"

"No. Not at all." She sniffed and pulled back a little. He rose on one elbow to study her tearstained face, completely at a loss. He thought of the odd desperation he'd sensed in her earlier. The way she'd clung to him after they'd climaxed. Her unusual silence as he'd dried her off.

With fingers that suddenly felt big and clumsy, he touched her face. "Then what's the matter?"

"I read in the paper this morning that the Saints might move to California."

He said nothing, but remembered how she'd claimed the neighbor's dog must have made off with the morning paper. How they'd listened to Robbie's music all afternoon instead of the radio. How she'd distracted him from the evening news after dinner by taking him to bed.

He now realized she'd waited all day for him to tell her about it himself. Looking into her wet, wounded eyes, he didn't have the heart to ask why she hadn't asked him about it. He was equally guilty for not having told her as soon as he knew.

"I'm sorry, sweetheart. I should have said something sooner. It's more than a possibility. Stump's selling the team. I found out yesterday."

"I see." She looked away then, apparently unwilling to meet his eyes. "You've been so quiet. Last night I felt like you were pulling away from me. This morning, when I saw the paper, I thought I knew why. Maybe it was selfish of me, but I wanted to postpone reality a little longer. I wanted a chance to convince you what a good team we'd make."

"Oh, Emily, I've never doubted that. I knew that the day we met."

She turned back then, her eyes full of pain and confusion. "But..."

Finally, Eric understood what she needed. What they both needed.

The words came as easily as breathing. "Marry me, Emily."

****

They were married on Friday at five. The bride wore a cream silk suit and hat with a demi-veil, the groom and his eight-year-old best man matching charcoal suits. Peach rose boutonnieres matched the bride's simple peaches and cream bouquet. On hand to congratulate the beaming threesome after the civil ceremony in the magistrate's chambers were Anna and Augustus Caldwell, Bill and Miranda Saunders, Sarah Ferguson,

Carmen Martinez, Patricia Montgomery and Catrina and Annalise Jordan. Eric had insisted on chartering a jet to fly out and meet Emily's mom, and tell her the news in person. He'd been more than happy to have her mother and sister accompany them home. Patricia had offered to leave Emily's when they arrived, but Catrina and Annalise had insisted on staying at a nearby hotel.

After the ceremony, Eric ushered the wedding party into rented limos and treated them all to dinner and champagne at *Maison Rouge*. He then invited them back to the house for dessert and coffee, where, unbeknownst to his bride, he'd conspired with Melissa Caldwell and the catering staff at *Maison Rouge* to organize an intimate reception for twelve, complete with peaches and cream roses, balloons and silk-covered wedding bells.

That way the entire wedding party was on hand to witness Emily's wide-eyed disbelief as a smiling Eric presented her with the keys to the brand new white Explorer that waited in her driveway.

"Eric, it's...it's...it's *perfect!*" she exclaimed, and turned to him with a You-are-so-special-and-I-love-you-more-than-life look.

He smiled, knowing what she meant. She'd talked, and he'd listened. During one of their many heart of the night talks that week, she'd told him about her traffic anxieties and how she wasn't sure, but she thought she'd overcome them on the trip from Detroit.

"I know," he said, then took her into his arms and kissed her thoroughly. "And I love *you*, too."

Chapter Thirty-Nine

Three weeks later, after endless speculation, the media confirmed it. Ronald Stump had sold the Saints, and the team was on its way to San Bernardino. Emily was leaning against the kitchen counter, reading the article, when Eric came through the front door calling her name.

"In the kitchen," she called back, still reading, munching on a pre-dinner apple.

"Where do you want these?" He held his boxed up stereo equipment in his hands.

"Our room," she said without hesitation. She wasn't about to let Robbie get his mitts on *that*. He'd already claimed the plasma TV for the living room. Darned thing was bigger than Anna's piano. Somehow Emily saw a new family room in their future.

"Gotcha." Eric winked and sent her a slow, smoldering smile, then disappeared up the steps, whistling *Clair de Lune*.

Clever, clever man, she thought, and went soft inside at the memory of them sneaking off to his apartment on her lunch hour and making love to Debussy. Maybe she could talk him into keeping the apartment. Or renting one even closer to her work. Wouldn't that be handy?

She grinned at the thought of it, knowing Eric would, too. Their adjustment to married life was proving to be much easier than either of them had expected. Even with Patricia—who had talked her way into a part-time interior decorating job downtown and would move into her own apartment the first of July—and Robbie to contend with.

Robbie now knew Patricia was his grandmother and the two were the best of buddies. Anna and Patricia still had their moments of friction, but were working on it.

Emily was just grateful that between Eric, Anna and Patricia, Robbie had someone to watch over him at all times. School was out, and, as usual, her workload at the hospital was rising in tandem with the June temperature.

So was her curiosity. The team was on its way to California, but Eric hadn't mentioned moving. Come to think of it, they hadn't discussed the Saints at all since the night he'd proposed.

She found him sitting cross-legged on the bedroom floor, hooking up speaker wires. "We'll have to leave this stuff on the floor for tonight," he said. "The Subway's big, but not that big."

While Patricia used his Explorer to get her affairs in order, Eric had been using Emily's Suburban to move his things into the house—not to mention the boatload of paint and remodeling supplies he'd bought. Surprising her, he'd thrown himself into the house renovations, working on them all day while she was at the hospital. He'd already started re-siding the house in baby blue, and was making noises about getting bids to build a master suite over the garage. Hmmm. Maybe the plasma screen TV would go in there.

"I'll have to figure out a way to get the entertainment center over here tomorrow," Eric was saying.

"Fine," she said, bringing her mind back to the present. "But we need to talk."

He glanced up, frowned. "Sure. What's up?"

She sat at the foot of their bed, newspaper still in hand. "This."

He scanned the headline. "What about it?"

"It's confirmed. The Saints are moving to California."

He shrugged, returned to his wires. "I told you that a month ago."

"And you haven't mentioned it since."

"Didn't see any need to."

"September's not that far away, Eric. Don't you think we need to discuss our plans?"

He looked up at her, his eyes unreadable. "We don't have any plans. We're staying here."

"I don't understand."

"I'm retiring."

Emily felt as if she'd been poleaxed. "Retiring? *You?*"

"It's time."

If she hadn't been so stunned, she might have caught the edge in his voice. "But you love playing."

His eyes flickered, but he said nothing. Suddenly worried he'd sustained some sort of injury during the playoffs he hadn't told her about, she asked, "Eric, what's going on?"

"My contract with the Saints is up. I decided not to renew it."

"Why on earth not?" What about the hardware gleaming in the middle of their dining room table? Two nights earlier, at the NHL banquet in Toronto, Eric had won the Hart trophy for being the league's most valuable player. He'd hired a jet to fly the two of them up and back for the night. She'd never forget the quiet pride in his eyes as he looked at her and gave his acceptance speech.

As they had then, his dark eyes fixed on her now. "I've found something more important than hockey."

Emily was aghast. "You're kidding. You're quitting because of *me*?"

"Not quitting. Retiring."

She dropped her face into her hands. "Tell me this isn't happening. Tell me my husband hasn't lost his mind."

Eric rose from the floor and came to sit beside her on the edge of the bed. Gently he touched her hair. Emily lowered her hands and stared across the room. Instead of Eric's mother's cello in the corner and their new Laura Ashley wallpaper, she saw her marriage crumbling as surely as if she'd given Eric an ultimatum.

Hockey or me.

"I haven't lost my mind," he said quietly. "California made a respectable offer, a more than respectable offer, actually, but it's only for a season, and I can't see uprooting you and Robbie for that, especially after all the work we've put into this place."

A hard lump formed in Emily's throat. Eric had taken her goals for fixing up the house and made them his own, thinking it was what *she* wanted.

He took her chin in his hand, his voice low and solemn. "And I certainly have no interest in a commuter marriage."

Paralyzed by guilt, Emily stared into his eyes, and saw the pain in them behind his resolve to make her happy. Her astonishment that he'd chosen to leave hockey vanished at the knowledge he'd reached that decision alone. He hadn't even bothered to ask her if she would move. Within seconds, her guilt gave way to anger.

She pulled away and sent him a look of disbelief. "I thought we were partners."

He frowned at her attempt to place distance between them. "We are."

"Then how could you make a decision to abandon your career without talking to me about it?"

"It's not as if we'll go broke, Emily. I've still got the restaurants and—"

She popped off the bed in frustration. "I don't care if you own a hundred restaurants, Eric. You're a hockey player, and a damned good one. It's who you are."

"Emily—"

"Let me finish, Eric. Please."

He sat back, then, and focused on her the way he always did when he sensed something was important to her. "All right. Shoot."

She looked at him, sitting at the foot of their bed, arms braced behind him, his attention completely on her, and loved his easy willingness to listen, but refused to let it distract her from what she had to say. When she spoke, it was with clear conviction. "I'm your wife, Eric. I married you fully prepared to do whatever it takes to make this marriage work—and that includes moving to California or Florida or even Italy and back six times a year if I have to."

"Honey, I'd only planned to play for a couple more years anyway. It's not like—"

"Then *play*, Eric. I don't care where, but play. Please."

He studied her adamant expression, then plowed a hand through his hair and exhaled heavily before standing to face her. Holding her gently at arm's length, he looked into her eyes and said quietly, "I'm sorry. I thought you'd be happy if I left hockey."

"How could I possibly be happy knowing you gave up the biggest part of yourself for me?"

He looked away and flushed, dropping his arms and the connection between them, and she knew she'd hit the heart of the matter. "How could I live with *my*self, knowing I yanked you from a job you love and a house you've poured your heart and soul into to drag you halfway across the country, dump you in some strange city, then leave you to fend for yourself for eight solid months while I go jetting all over the damned continent?"

"I'm not helpless, Eric. I can get another job. Buy a new house. Find Robbie a new school. I've done it before, I can do it again."

"But you shouldn't have to!" Eric closed his eyes and drew a calming breath. "You deserve better, Emily. You deserve a real home, not some rootless existence with a man who won't be there when you need him."

At the raw note in his voice, Emily's anger evaporated. She moved toward him, caught his face in her hands. "I have a real home. With you. Wherever you are. The city doesn't matter. Neither does the country. It's being together that matters. Don't you know that by now?"

"I'll be gone more than I'm home, Emily."

"Then the time we spend apart will make the time we have together that much more precious."

His eyes betrayed how much he wanted to believe her, but he shook his head. "No, I won't ask you to give up your—"

She shushed him with her fingers. "I'm not married to my job, Eric. I'm married to you. And as for the house, I know we've put more work into it than we originally planned, but I only went along with it because I thought that was what *you* wanted. I'd never have taken things this far if you hadn't been here, no matter what Patricia thinks." She smiled wryly. "In fact, if it hadn't been for you, I probably would have..."

She stopped, thinking.

"What?" Eric asked. "What are you thinking?"

"Turnersville." She looked at him, her eyes wide with self-revelation. "If it hadn't been for you," she repeated slowly, "I probably would have sold the house and moved back to Turnersville."

They stood in their bedroom and stared at each other,

their minds spinning, excitement building between them like a couple of kids on Christmas morning.

He smiled.

She smiled.

A compromise was born.

"Detroit?" he suggested hopefully.

Emily laughed in pure delight, then kissed him soundly. "How would you feel about being a Red Wing?"

Eric grinned down at her, all traces of his former tension gone. "For you, I'd let them have me for free."

Epilogue

Eric knew something was up the minute he rounded the last bend in the driveway and saw the huge sign in the middle of the front lawn proclaiming *Lordy, Lordy, Daddy's Forty*. His birthday wasn't until tomorrow, but he'd learned over the years that Emily loved surprises, and he'd never met a family better at keeping them secret. One year he'd come home to a dark house full of Jordans wearing hockey jerseys shouting, "He scores!" when he flipped on the light. Another, he'd looked up from the ice in Vancouver to see, "Happy Birthday, Dad, Give 'em Hell" blinking at him from the score-recap board.

Then there was the time she'd rented the Turnersville bowling alley and with Suzanna-the-mayor's help, secretly invited half the town to the "Eric 'Can't Bowl Worth Beans' Cameron Open." Last year, she'd kidnapped him from the camp and whisked him away for a thoroughly wicked 'ski weekend' at Lake Placid. They'd never made it to the slopes.

He entered the house silently. For once he'd get the drop on the two-year-old twins who usually tackled his knees the minute he got home. He cocked an ear to try to figure out his youngest daughters' whereabouts, and heard instead the strains of classical guitar music filtering out from the great room, the muted clank of pots and pans in the kitchen. He caught the aroma of basil and oregano and smiled. Ravioli. The family favorite.

But where was the family? He removed his shoes and padded toward the kitchen, then paused in the archway to savor the sight of Emily, humming to Gabrielli as she prepared a tray of garlic bread, popped it in the oven and set the timer. Almost ten years of marriage hadn't diminished his desire for her a bit. All he had to do was look at her and he wanted to drag her off to the nearest flat surface.

Unfortunately, that was easier said than done with a savvy teenager, an inquisitive eight-year-old, a precocious six-year-old and two rambunctious toddlers underfoot most of the time.

Her hair was loose and fluffy, and she wore a soft, sexy pair of green silk lounging pajamas that, along with the growing suspicion they were alone, reminded him of Lake Placid. He grinned, thrilled at the prospect of a night at home alone with his wife. He watched her reach into the refrigerator and pull out a bottle of champagne, and decided this was one surprise he would enjoy thoroughly. "Hey."

She looked up in surprise, her green eyes immediately softening with the love he never failed to see in them whenever they came together after having been apart, whether it was for a few hours or a few days. Even though he'd been coming home at six-thirty for almost five years now, she still met him with the same 'welcome home' smile he'd come to cherish during his Red Wings days.

"Hey, yourself. I didn't hear you come in."

"I came in the front door. I was trying to get the drop on the twins for a change. Where is everyone?"

She slipped into his arms and gave him a kiss that raised his temperature several degrees, along with another part of his anatomy. "Robbie's on his way to the game in Detroit with his cousins, Billy's on a sleepover, Alicia's at Suzanna's making party favors, and I suspect Patty and Trina are up to their ears in ice cream at Gramma and Grandpa's right about now."

"Then what's the story with the sign?"

"That's for tomorrow."

"Tomorrow?"

She smiled. "Patience, my love. You wouldn't want to disappoint your children, would you?" Her eyes twinkled with mischief. "I will tell you this much. We've decided to go with a "Recapture Your Youth" theme this year, so be prepared."

"What's your part in the plan?"

"To make sure you get a good night's sleep, of course."

He laughed, then kissed her again, long and deep and

slow. They forgot about dinner and birthdays and children until the stovetop buzzer went off beside them. She pulled back, her eyes bright and cheeks flushed, then removed the garlic toast from the oven, while Eric poured the wine and rummaged in the overhead cabinet for matches to light the candles she'd set out.

Over dinner they linked their fingers and shared their day, a simple pleasure usually reserved for the quiet moments they spent in each other's arms at night. Emily worked six hours on weekdays in the Turnersville hospital ER, leaving the twins—the little surprises, as she and Eric called them privately—in the hospital's employee day care center, run by the firm but loving hand of Catrina Melrose.

Emily's schedule supposedly gave her time to beat Billy and Alicia's school bus home, but as yet she hadn't quite mastered the art of punctuality. She teasingly blamed it on the twins when she could, but everyone knew Mom was hopeless at being on time. Robbie had told them so.

Robbie, who according to his younger siblings knew *everything*, was a senior at Turnersville High, captain of their hockey team, and headed for Michigan State to study computer software design and play more hockey. Three afternoons a week, he helped Eric at the junior hockey school he'd built just outside of town upon retiring from the NHL.

They cleared the table, then settled on the family room sectional sofa. Champagne glasses in hand, they turned on the Red Wings game Robbie was attending with his cousins. Much to Eric's delight, Emily had become a huge fan of the sport he loved almost as much as he loved his wife.

His arm on the sofa behind her, he studied her profile as she sipped her champagne and watched the wide-screen TV. To this day he had no idea what he'd done to deserve her.

With Emily's full support, he'd played three more seasons, seasons he'd enjoyed the hell out of and seasons he was convinced were his best. And not because the Red Wings had won any championship titles, although a couple of times they'd come mighty close. His enjoyment had come from the fact that whenever he'd looked up from the ice in the Joe Louis Arena he'd seen Emily smiling at him from the stands, surrounded by so many relatives his teammates had nicknamed him "Papa Bear."

He closed his eyes, leaned his head back, and savored the quiet joy that flowed through him every time he thought of his extended family. He'd never met a more open and friendly bunch, and he'd felt blessed beyond measure by their easy acceptance of him, their willingness to love him simply because Emily did.

They'd watched over her for him when he'd been on the road, been there to welcome him home when he returned. Martin had found him the land for his camp, and Suzanna had talked him into opening a sixth Amelia's in Turnersville, instead of Detroit.

Finally, Eric had the home and family he'd always wanted. And he owed it all to his wife, who took special pride in making sure he knew how much she and the rest of his family loved him.

Feeling a strong need to return that love the best way he knew, he reached for the remote and clicked off the game. Emily looked over at him in surprise, then grinned in delight as she recognized the look in his eyes.

"Hubba hubba. Got something besides hockey on your mind, cowboy?"

He offered a slow smile, then just as slowly removed the champagne glass from her hand, before easing her back against the soft, wide leather cushions. "Any objections, Doctor Cameron?"

She linked her hands behind his neck, and pulled him down to her for a kiss that made him feel twenty again.

"Not a one."

About the author...

Liana Laverentz got hooked on reading in the second grade, when the exchange gift she received was a Nancy Drew mystery. Her love of writing followed shortly thereafter. She's best known for the thousands of letters she has written to family and friends over the years, but Thin Ice is her second published novel. Her hobbies are reading, writing, mixed martial arts, soup making, and road trips. She lives in Pennsylvania with her son and three cats.

You can write to her at P.O. Box 196 Harborcreek, PA 16421, or email her at lianalaverentz@yahoo.com.

Printed in the United States
74586LV00001BA/79-498